FIONA McCALLUM

Sunrise Over Mercy Court

FICTION

SUNRISE OVER MERCY COURT
© 2023 by Fiona McCallum
ISBN 9781867299431

First published on Gadigal Country in Australia in 2023
by HQ Fiction
an imprint of HQBooks (ABN 47 001 180 918), a subsidiary of HarperCollins Publishers
Australia Pty Limited (ABN 36 009 913 517).
This edition published 2024.

HarperCollins acknowledges the Traditional Custodians of the lands upon which we live
and work, and pays respect to Elders past and present.

The right of Fiona McCallum to be identified as the author of this work has been asserted
by her in accordance with the *Copyright Amendment (Moral Rights) Act 2000*.

A catalogue record for this book is available from the National Library of Australia
www.librariesaustralia.nla.gov.au

Printed and bound in Australia by McPherson's Printing Group

MIX
Paper | Supporting
responsible forestry
FSC® C001695

'A heart-warming book that deals sensitively with issues of loss, financial uncertainty and emotional repair.'

—*Canberra Weekly* on *Trick of the Light*

'A deeply moving story about loss and the unexpected benefits of having to find your feet when the whole world seems to be conspiring to knock you off them.'

—*Australian Country* on *Trick of the Light*

'*The Long Road Home* is a lovely read that transported me away for the day … this story was as comforting as it is entertaining.'

—*Better Reading*

'It's an inspiring tale about finding hope.'

—*Daily Telegraph* on *The Long Road Home*

'Fiona McCallum is one of Australia's most popular authors and *The Long Road Home* is another inspiring tale about rebuilding your life and taking chances … a heart-warming and timely book.'

—*Canberra Weekly*

'This is a story for readers on a quest to find their wings and fly.'

—*Townsville Bulletin* on *A Life of Her Own*

'Her central character is usually a woman to whom the reader immediately warms … you stay loyal to her despite everything.'

—*Country Style* on *A Life of Her Own*

'McCallum has a keen eye for fine detail and writes about raw emotion better than any other contemporary writer.'

—*WarCry Magazine* on *Making Peace*

'This truly is a divine book about very close friendships, finding new friends and dealing with loss.'

—*Beauty&Lace* on *Making Peace*

'Fiona McCallum writes *Finding Hannah* with tenderness and insight ... will leave no reader with a dry eye.'

—*The Weekly Times*

'I am not ashamed to say I cried in places for the heartbreak was real and the everyday situations easy to relate to ... This is a wonderful story of recovery.'

—*Books at 60* on *Finding Hannah*

'McCallum writes to inspire her readers to find their true meaning in life and *Standing Strong* is certain to do this.'

—*The Weekly Times*

'*Standing Strong* considers duty, how to do what you know is right even when it's emotionally challenging. With its relatable characters, dialogue and issues, this is a novel that will ring true for many readers.'

—*Better Reading*

'This is a very fine story, well-handled, and does not avoid the hard issues.'

—*Weekly Times* on *Wattle Creek*

'If ever there was a farm-lit book designed for competitive horse riders, this has to be it.'

—*Newcastle Herald* on
Leap of Faith

'Fiona McCallum wears her literary heart on her dustcovers and with her stories swirling through towns we know and live in, she turns next-door-neighbours into larger-than-life characters – plus a little horse with a big heart.'

—*Riverine Herald* on *Leap of Faith*

'A beautiful novel filled with romance, inner strength and above all, friendship.'

—*That Book You Like* on *Time Will Tell*

'*Saving Grace* is a must-read.'

—*Woman's Day*

'McCallum captures the nuances of a country town and the personalities of the characters that live there.'

—*The Big Book Club* on *Saving Grace*

'A moving melodrama.'

—*Courier-Mail* on *Nowhere Else*

'A truly great read, I loved it from beginning to end.'

—*Aussie Book Reviews* on *Nowhere Else*

'This is one story on track for success.'

—*Woman's Day* on *Paycheque*

Fiona McCallum was raised on a cereal and wool farm near Cleve on South Australia's Eyre Peninsula and remained in the area until her mid-twenties, during which time she married and separated. She then moved to Melbourne and on to Sydney a few years later.

Fiona's first novel, *Paycheque*, was published in 2011 and became a bestseller. In the twelve years since, she has written another thirteen bestselling novels. *Sunrise Over Mercy Court* is Fiona's fifteenth book.

Currently residing in Adelaide, Fiona is a full-time novelist who writes heart-warming stories that draw on her rich and contrasting life experiences, love of animals and fascination with human nature.

For more information about Fiona and her books, visit her website at fionamccallum.com. She can also be found on Facebook at facebook.com/fionamccallum.author

For CW

Part One

Chapter One

Elsie was in the pantry tidying up the jars and tins and checking that all was neat and in order and everything was correctly labelled. A lack of labelling wasn't a problem for them – well, so far – with both of them knowing, for instance, that the icing sugar and not the cornflour occupied the bulbous shaped old coffee jar and the cornflour the taller, squarer and more slender glass jar, despite their contents appearing identical through the clear glass. But they didn't want to cause more of a kerfuffle for daughters Janine and Corinne after their demise – on their own terms, if all went to plan – than was inevitable. Thus, they were in an organising and sorting frenzy, performing whatever was the opposite of nesting. Purging, Elsie thought it might be termed. That probably wasn't quite right either, was it? Hmm. She frowned before letting it go. Anyway, this was one of the items on her and Howard's to-do list, that they were gradually making their way through. They both loved being orderly and getting things done and out of the way. And there wasn't a whole lot else to do at their age of seventy-eight, in between the medical appointments – just general maintenance;

they had no health issues – and attending the funerals of their peers, which was happening far too regularly.

Elsie was enjoying being deep in the pantry: it meant less of the disconcerting occurrences where she thought the movements out of the corner of her eye grabbing her attention were their dear old dog Maisie, who had succumbed to age a month ago. Maisie had never been into the pantry – the space was a bit too tight for a human and a large German shepherd and the dog had remained cautious to the end.

Elsie still felt guilty for not being there with her and Howard at the final moment and also at the thought that she was glad she hadn't been. The best thing about Maisie's passing – though, god, she missed her more than she could probably put into words – was that they hadn't had to make the decision to have her put to sleep after all. They'd spent ages fretting over it, questioning each other over and over about how they'd know when the time was right. The dear old dog had kept them on their toes and on tenterhooks for the last few months of her life. One day she'd seem to be reasonably energetic and bright, the next she'd be spread out on the floor looking like her demise was imminent. They'd had a great vet, a kind, gentle, patient and reassuring woman. But she wasn't living with the dog and didn't do house calls. Lucky that, Elsie had often thought, otherwise they probably would have spent a sizeable chunk of their remaining superannuation having her popping in to check on the dog. As it was, several times they had rushed poor Maisie in to see her – thankfully the dear old dog didn't mind the vet surgery and loved being in the car – only to have the dog brighten up completely and be sent home again after a quick check-over. That roller-coaster had been hard and a strain on their nerves. But the last time, Howard had been at home alone with her, Elsie having, finally, after all the Covid palaver, felt safe enough from the dreadful disease to meet a friend, Judith, for coffee and to go to a movie.

She'd had her phone switched off, and had forgotten to turn it back on once she was on the bus heading for home. She was so out of practice with catching the bus – it was her first time in around three years – that she'd been caught up in remembering to tap her card and put it away again, and checking her phone had completely slipped her mind. She'd never been as keen on the thing as Howard – useful, yes, but also a bit hard on the eyes, she found.

She'd entered the house, humming to herself, and wandered down the hall only to come out into the open-plan kitchen, dining and living area to find Howard at the kitchen table, head in hands, sobbing. Slowly he'd revealed that soon after Elsie had left, Maisie had collapsed on the floor – actually flopped from standing, this time – and he'd not been able to find a pulse. He'd rushed her to the vet – only a few minutes away by car – and urged them to revive her so Elsie could have the chance to say goodbye.

As Elsie stood there with her arms around Howard, head on his shoulder, sobbing herself now, the pain, relief, guilt had started. The relief at not being there and having to help make any decisions and the guilt of not being there to support Howard and also not holding Maisie's paw – never leaving her; being there for her right to the end, like she'd promised her so many times. How he'd even had the strength to lift the large dog into the car and then into the vet from the car park – and hadn't done his back in – was beyond both of their comprehension.

Her grief had begun in a split second, as grief always did. She'd walked into the house, keen to discuss the movie, cheerful, buoyant, feeling finally fear-free about being out in public properly after the Covid years and look what she'd come home to. In an instant there was a big hole in their lives and souls, and the maelstrom of emotions attached to it all.

In the first minutes, all she could do was apologise over and over for her inattention regarding the phone. Howard, of course, her darling Howard – best friend of seventy-four years, husband of fifty-nine – was his usual beautiful self; sad of course, but not at all upset with Elsie. He was more concerned about her not having the chance to say goodbye. That was the reason for the eight missed calls on her phone, he'd explained later. They'd revived dear old Maisie and he'd wanted her to say goodbye. When she'd died soon after, they'd gently said this was it. She'd gone. Gradually he'd pulled himself together enough to ask for her to be cremated and to let him know when to collect her ashes, paid and driven home.

Elsie ranged from being bereft and sick with guilt to glad and relieved that her last goodbye had been that morning as Maisie had followed her to the front door. She'd said, 'I'll see you later, darling girl. Remember, you are loved,' as she had every time she'd left the house. They had both told the dog they loved her many times throughout the day, because the precious thing had arrived from the RSPCA after an apparently horrendous former life, which had left her timid and malnourished, and they'd taken it upon themselves to reassure her as often as they could.

Elsie sighed, let her reminiscing slide into the background, and returned to her task in the pantry.

She blinked and stared at the two tins of chickpeas she'd just found buried right at the back of the cupboard. When had they bought these? Though 'why' was the more pertinent question. She racked her brain for a recipe they might have needed them for once – a salad, perhaps? – but came up empty. They hadn't entertained in ages – their first time having people other than their daughters around since the pandemic was next Thursday.

She left the tiny room, carrying the tins, frowning, and crossed the space to where Howard was in the study working through the many photos. His current task, also on their to-do list, was to sort the digital photos and scan all those in the many albums and save them so Corinne and Janine would have a copy each of everything in digital form. They could fight over the physical albums at a later date.

'Howard?' she called from the doorway, holding up the cans of chickpeas.

'Hmm,' he said, eyes still on the screen in front of him. *Damn stock market, when are you going to start going up again?* he thought with a sigh and shook his head. He'd checked it while taking a break from sorting the photos and wished he hadn't.

'Any idea why we have two tins of chickpeas in the pantry?'

Howard backed his chair back and turned fully around to face Elsie. 'Um, let me just think for a moment.' He took his glasses off and rubbed his face. 'Oh, I know. I remember now,' he said a few moments later. 'We got those that last big shop we did just as the supermarket went completely mad with the people hoarding toilet paper and everything. They were the last thing on the shelves, so I grabbed them.' He shuddered in response to the flood of memories. How traumatic those last days in the supermarket just before lockdowns had been. All that jostling and fear and panic. He'd got caught up in it and was a little embarrassed to admit he'd been influenced. Hence the damned chickpeas, which he knew nothing about – other than the fact they apparently came in tins.

'What? Because they were lonely?' Elsie said.

He grinned at his darling wife and rolled his eyes. *Trust you, cheeky minx.* How wonderful – and incredible, really – to still have a wife you adored, loved and regularly found hilarious after nearly six decades. 'Very funny. No, because I thought they'd be useful – you know, if the worst happened. Nutritionally, I think was where my mind was going. Remember back then, the chaos? We didn't know what would happen with the supply chain, or if we'd be able to buy food in lockdown, et cetera. Remember?'

'Oh god, yes, that's right.' Elsie shuddered as the memories flooded back. It was quite incredible how quickly she seemed to forget the details of major parts in her life. She shuddered again. 'Okay, so what are we going to do with them?' she said.

'Eat them, I suppose,' Howard said. 'We're not throwing them out, if that's what you're suggesting.' He frowned. *Do we even like chickpeas? I sure hope so.*

'No. Now come on, Howard, when would I ever advocate for wasting food?'

'Sorry, no, of course. I'm being a bit tetchy. I'm trying to sort through a stack of images that are almost identical, within hundreds. Damn this digital photography that's made it so easy to end up with thousands of photos with the mere press of a button. Oh well.' He sighed and gave his face another rub.

Elsie stood there with the cans, and waggled them. She really wanted to deal with them, despite being aware she was being slightly obsessive about them. Though they both were, about all sorts of things. It seemed to have come with retirement fifteen years ago. And more recently had stepped up a notch in their determined effort to get their affairs in order and move on to the last item on their list.

'Let me see,' Howard said, wheeling himself back to the desk. Now facing the computer screen, he tapped on the keyboard. 'Ah, we could make hummus. We like that, don't we?'

'Yes. Oh, yum.'

'Okay, here's a recipe with plenty of five-star reviews. We'll also need tahini. What's that when it's at home?'

'Sesame seed paste, isn't it?' Elsie said.

'Ah, yes, you're quite right. Well, why don't they just say that, then? They're fine with peanut paste – don't need to give that a fancy name.' *Why does everything have to be so damned complicated?*

'Who's they, dear?' Elsie said, just for fun. She loved when he muttered about the strangeness of the world. They enjoyed great long conversations about how screwed-up everything was – another major reason for this final plan of theirs. But Howard ignored her, simply waved his hand and kept on peering at the screen and tapping on the keyboard.

'And how the hell did I get to this age without knowing that?' he muttered, shaking his head. 'Right,' he continued a moment later, making a note on the back of an old envelope on the top of the stack beside him, 'tahini. Garlic, salt, olive oil and lemon juice we have plenty of. Might get some fresh ones. Hmm. Cumin. Do we have any cumin, dear? It's a spice, by the looks.'

'Yes, that's in the cupboard. I saw it yesterday when I invento-ried the spices. You know – it's the one we use in stews and curries.'

'Great, well, I'll just print this recipe out and we're good to go.' He carefully tore off the portion of the envelope containing his list and, after a final tap on the keyboard, turned to the printer as it roared to life.

He tucked the scrap of paper into his pocket, collected the page from the printer and got up. 'I'll see you in a bit,' he said as he handed Elsie the recipe on his way past. 'You can bone up on this, if you like, while I'm gone.'

'Are you going now?'

'I thought I might. Good to have a mission. I need to clear my head for a bit – this is doing me in,' he added.

Elsie sympathised. He'd been doing this for months, on and off right through last year. Before that it was research on the family tree. He'd loved that. But this task was dragging on and he often complained that it was driving him spare. Why did old people use that term? What did it even mean? she wondered, before letting it go. She blinked it away just before Howard kissed her on the forehead.

'Anything else?' he said, moving past her.

'No, I don't think so.' It didn't matter, anyway, Elsie thought, Howard trekked to the supermarket at least once a day, sometimes twice. She knew it was partly because of how much he missed Maisie – their gentle walks together and also her presence. She'd noticed his patience with the photos had shortened considerably since he'd lost his companion, whom he used to mutter to almost constantly as she snoozed in her bed or sprawled out on the floor. She too understood the impact of this large missing piece from their lives and the accompanying constant haze of grief, so she didn't rib him about how often he traipsed back and forth to the shops. It was very convenient for her, too. As part of their planning, it also made sense to keep less fresh fruit, veg and meat on hand than previously. Also, because Howard preferred to walk to the shop and there was only so much he could carry. At their age they had to pace themselves – in all areas. It was a vicious cycle, really – not much food in the house because he didn't want to carry much food from the supermarket. Or rather, a friendly cycle, she decided, because it kept her darling husband occupied.

'Okay, back soon. Call if you remember anything,' he said, holding up his phone. Elsie nodded as she made her way to the table to read the recipe in preparation for Howard's return.

★

'Here we are,' Howard said, reappearing in near-record time. He put a jar of tahini paste and three lemons on the bench. He'd rushed and was slightly out of breath. It hadn't been an altogether fun trip to the supermarket.

'Great. Do you realise we only need half a cup of tahini for each tin of chickpeas?' she said, looking at the large jar, turning it over to see how much it contained.

'Oh. Well, it was the only one they had. Damn. Regardless, I should have checked. It was in the spreads section.'

'So perhaps we could use the rest of it on our toast in the morning, or something, just as it is.'

'It must be what people do, on account of it being where it was. The lad I asked knew straight away, was on the verge of sighing at me in that exasperated way so common with the young ones. We love sesame seeds and sesame oil, so it might be nice for a change,' he said with a shrug as he opened the third drawer full of assorted kitchen utensils and took out the strap wrench.

Elsie watched as he undid the lid, marvelling, as she did every time either of them used the device, how effortless opening jars was again. For years they'd had to resort to belting them with the back of a heavy knife to break the air seal, but that was fraught with issues.

Once they'd never needed to give such an activity a second thought. They'd laughed off struggling with the odd tricky lid, which they'd always somehow manage to conquer after passing the offending item back and forth between them a couple of times. But about a decade ago, they'd both ceased to be able to get any jar open at all.

More than being simply frustrating, it had served as a stark indication of the ebbing away of their independence. But worse than that was the additional reminder of their increasing isolation and lack of belonging to a community. They were the last of the long-term residents in the cul-de-sac and everyone moving in these days seemed keen to keep to themselves. So, while the natty contraption Howard was currently using with ease couldn't cure their invisibility, at least they could easily open their own jars again!

Elsie was so grateful for whomever in one of their Facebook groups had raved about this device. They'd been so desperate to try it that they'd even stumped up for the full delivery fee, ridiculous for a single item, to have the thing delivered the other year during Covid from the hardware store's plumbing tools section. Now she told everyone she could of its existence. It was a godsend, for want of a better term. Howard and Elsie were not religious, by any stretch. Quite the opposite – thought it was all a con and the Bible a work of fiction. Every time they used this wrench, they extolled its virtue and then thanked it before popping it back in the drawer. Elsie thought it deserved to be mounted on the wall, or something more befitting of its value, rather than tossed into the third drawer along with various other utensils – all useful now; they'd finished sorting the kitchen drawers.

'Oh, that's hideous. Bitter,' Howard said, screwing his face up, having just dipped a teaspoon into the freshly opened jar of tahini. He was cringing with distaste, making a good imitation of one of Rowan Atkinson's Mr Bean expressions. He opened the top drawer again, retrieved another teaspoon, and handed it to Elsie. 'It's definitely not off, I made sure – I always do.' He stood looking at her with his eyebrows raised, waiting to see if she felt the same way. They had similar views about most things.

'God, you're right. That's awful. I don't like it one bit,' she said. 'People spread this, just as it is, you reckon?' she said, staring at him, sticking her tongue out.

'Apparently. Well, I certainly hope it tastes better once turned into hummus along with the chickpeas and other ingredients. And I sure hope we like hummus still, after all this.'

'Um, you do realise that we'll have to buy more chickpeas to use up the tahini now? We don't want to waste it,' Elsie said.

'No. Oh, god, this is a right can of worms we've just opened, isn't it?'

Elsie giggled. 'It's turning into a saga! No, no, I can see it becoming a hilarious skit,' she said, beginning to laugh loudly.

'I see what you mean,' Howard said, also beginning to chuckle. 'We could have an endless cycle of buying chickpeas and tahini until both run out at the same time on our hands. That could go on until we die.'

'Exactly,' Elsie spluttered and began to laugh hysterically.

Howard joined in and soon they were doubled-over, laughing uproariously. They fed off each other for several minutes, a new bout of laughter starting up every time they stood up, holding their stomachs, and looked at each other. Eventually they gave a final splutter, and then wiped their eyes.

'Oh, I needed that,' Howard said after clearing his throat.

'Yes, me too. Bless the chickpeas,' Elsie said, causing them both to giggle again.

'Let's make sure we like homemade hummus before I go back for the next lot of chickpeas, shall we?' Howard said.

'Good idea, dear,' Elsie said, grinning at him.

They worked together side by side, as they often did, and after around half an hour – twenty minutes or so of it spent standing waiting for the legumes to cook, key, according to the recipe's author – stood back from the bench with a half cracker each slathered in their fresh hummus.

'Ready?' Howard said.

'Yep. My fingers are crossed,' Elsie said.

Looking into each other's eyes, they popped their samples into their mouths.

Elsie closed her eyes to get the full experience and knew Howard was doing the same, when he spoke. She could always tell, by the way his voice sounded.

'Hmm. Well, that's an improvement on the tahini paste, I must say,' he said.

'Yes, it's actually rather good.'

'I agree,' Howard said. 'Right, so that's one problem solved. Next is, there's rather a lot of it. The hummus, that is. Shall we freeze some? Can we, do you think?'

'I don't see why not. And then of course the next big question is, just how many lots do we have to make to get to a point of having zero tahini and zero chickpeas? Because we're really not going to do anything with either ingredient again. Are we?'

'No, definitely not.'

'I'll tackle that question a little later.'

Chapter Two

Howard hummed as he set the outdoor table ready for their lunch guests. How good to be doing this again – a meeting of the grumpy old buggers' club. Not officially titled, of course, but these events always became a good old whinge-fest. Their age group had lots to complain about and the therapy to be gained from airing their grievances with like-minded people was a necessity for trudging through each day of this old age business. He and Elsie regularly bemoaned how it was a young person's world they were trapped in. They were clearly not welcome, in fact barely tolerated, if most of his interactions were an accurate indication.

'Howard, that's the door,' he heard Elsie call. She'd get there first because she was in the kitchen. He cast a quick final glance at the table and headed inside. Having placed the tray he'd used for taking everything out in one hit on the end of the bench, he slowly made his way out to join Elsie in greeting their guests.

Elsie wiped her hands on the tea towel and hurried down the hall to answer the front door. She tried to ignore the absence of dear old Maisie, who would usually be beside her, eager to approve or check over and escort visitors into the home, politely inclining her head to see if a snuffle would be appreciated before proceeding to do so. To keep from sinking into her grief, Elsie reminded herself of how high maintenance the dog had been at the end and that she wasn't missing some of what caring for an elderly dog entailed. But the absence of the pad of paws on carpet and the click click and scrape of claws on the tiles left a constant ache. Elsie still looked around her feet before moving lest she bumped the dog and continued to always check which side of the door Maisie was on before closing it behind her. These little pauses in her movements were like sighs leaking out of both her and Howard's hearts. It didn't help that they were both generally disappointed with the current state of most things. Today was a good day, though. They were looking forward to having friends for lunch after a long hiatus. Once they'd had people every month or so – upwards of two dozen, comprising neighbours, former neighbours and those they'd met playing tennis or cards eons ago, or on holidays overseas on the same tour or travelling around in their caravan. Today, though, there would only be six around the table.

The heaviness weighing Elsie down lifted a little as she opened the door to beaming Sandy, one of their former neighbours, who had lived three houses down along the opposite side of the cul-de-sac. They'd met the night they'd had to be evacuated due to a burst water main.

Sandy and her husband Jasper had split up soon after retiring, Sandy realising she couldn't stand his presence in her space after being at home for her working life, first raising their four kids and then running an online business selling her handmade candles and soaps.

Elsie hadn't really warmed to Jasper – he'd made too many quips putting Sandy down, though she'd always seemed to either barely notice or not mind. Perhaps she was a good actress or simply very well mannered – all their era of women had been raised to adore their husbands or at least be subdued and deferential in their presence. Some adhered, some pushed back, some had simply left.

Elsie often still sighed with gratitude at her fortune in meeting Howard; he was as good a good egg as you could get. Neither needed to submit or compromise much, though, as they were usually on the same page with everything and always had been.

They'd met at kindergarten over the drink fountain, both nervously navigating their first day. Their bond had been instant. Firm friends by the end of that first day, galvanised by learning they not only shared a birthday, but were both only children in their respective families. As they'd said goodbye at the gate, Elsie knew she'd want him to be in her life forever.

Their friendship had grown and then altered. When had romance roared to life? There had never been fireworks from raging teenage hormones; more a gentle warmth of love and trust building as they'd matured. Somewhere along the way they'd started looking into each other's eyes with a different gaze. And then they'd wasted no time in getting married – what would have been the point?

Elsie often suspected she'd have not come through the heartbreak of losing both her parents within four months without Howard by her side every step of the way. It was coming up to thirty years ago that they'd lost all four of their parents, all within the span of just two years, but still Elsie regularly thought about how grateful she was to have had Howard, rock-solid beside her, during their demise and afterwards. Not just to ease the emotional pain, but to help deal with the practical aspects of the funerals, sorting of effects and selling of houses. And to this day Howard often said the same.

They hadn't always been grumpy old farts. Age did that to people, they agreed heartily, as did many of their friends. And they weren't really grumpy, as such, they just liked to get things off their chests – mainly whinging about the general indignity that was ageing and the appalling state of the world and its inhabitants that were to blame. Often. Though Covid had destroyed their wonderfully cathartic whinge-fests. One-on-one discussions over the phone just didn't provide the same level of therapy and they didn't like to complain too much to Corinne and Janine lest they cause them to worry.

Once full of excited tales about where they'd been and what they'd done, their catch-ups with friends these days were more often than not an exercise in listing off all their current ailments and comparing treatments and medical personnel. The first time that had happened, someone – Elsie couldn't remember who it was – had cried, 'Listen to us. We've reached that age where all we talk about is our health! I thought this was a myth. My auntie warned me about this and I didn't believe her.'

Someone had then pointed out, with little humour, 'Oh, yes, we're like children playing snap now – we've come full circle. Everything does, you know. And history always repeats.'

Hearing a clatter come from the kitchen brought Elsie's mind back from her meandering. How long had she been off with the pixies and left Sandy standing there like that? Thankfully her friend showed no signs of having an issue.

'Sandy, oh, it's so good to see you! Welcome back to Mercy Court!' Elsie cried, throwing her arms up towards the woman who was a head taller than herself.

'Hello. It's wonderful to see you. But, sorry, I don't hug anymore,' Sandy said, holding up a hand.

'No, we don't either, I just almost forgot myself there for a moment,' Elsie said.

'Thank Christ we're allowed to forgo the masks nowadays, though,' Sandy said. 'My skin was really protesting. Chocolates for you.'

'Oh, they're lovely, Sandy. Thank you,' Elsie said, accepting the box with a clear acetate lid, her mouth instantly beginning to water. 'They look too pretty to eat. Is this your new line?'

'Yes. When everyone was saying my soaps look good enough to eat, I thought I'd branch out. Covid made me so restless. I pivoted – Christ, I hate that word now. But it is what it is,' she added with a shrug.

'How is business?'

'Great, thanks.'

Howard now stood by with his arm draped around Elsie's shoulders. As always, she leant into him. They fitted together perfectly still, like the indentations in their respective leather recliners in the lounge.

'Hasn't it been an absolute shitshow?' Howard said. 'Though we can't complain too much, can we, Elsie?'

'No, and … Anyway, no politics.'

'Yes. We'll leave that for a full stomach, eh?' Howard said with a laugh. Elsie couldn't see his face, but knew he'd just given one of his trademark winks. She'd felt his shoulder move slightly. She smiled to herself. She loved all his little mannerisms. Loved everything about him, really.

Over time she'd stopped defending them – both her appreciation of Howard's quirks and their status as a happy couple – when some of the less content couples and singles had generally sniped and also got stuck into the habits of their significant others. It seemed unhappy people who'd chosen to stay together, for whatever reason, didn't at all like being around happy couples. Elsie figured they must see it as having their faces rubbed in their decision, or something. People really were odd creatures. She'd often said that to Maisie, after a phone call or gathering. The wise dog had always looked up at her with a serious expression on her face, her tail wagging back and forth behind her, which Elsie took as complete understanding. She'd been like a small human adult trapped in fur and with four legs. She and Howard had often said that in their first days of having her, though Howard also said sadly that perhaps she was just so grateful to have landed on those beautiful four feet with them after being rescued from an atrocious puppy farm situation by the RSPCA.

Elsie still shuddered when she let her mind wander back to the day they'd first met her. So skinny, it had been hard to believe she'd already gained quite a bit of weight.

She shook the memories off before the lump gathering in her throat became too large.

'Come through, let's not stand in the hall all day,' Howard said with a laugh and gently ushered them through to the open-plan kitchen, dining and living area.

'Yes, I'm still so used to not having anyone come inside, it takes me a minute to realise we're allowed now,' Elsie said.

'I'm a bit the same,' Sandy said. 'What a weird time all round. And I think we'll never be truly like we were before it all began.'

'No. Sad but true,' Howard said.

The doorbell chimed again. 'I'll get it. I'm closer,' Elsie said. 'You look after Sandy, Howard.'

'We're eating outside – it's such a lovely day ...' Howard's voice ebbed away as Elsie opened the door.

'Hello. There's a whole gang of us at once,' Trevor said, beaming, his face flushed. His timid wife, Diana, stood beside him.

'You're all very punctual,' Elsie said, beaming back, making an extra effort to ease their anxiety. She'd known Trevor and Diana for over a decade but they still always seemed very nervous upon arrival. Elsie appreciated what it must take for them to come at all. If she had such social anxiety, she probably would never leave the house. They'd never been huggers. Both had explained on the cruise they'd met on that they were germ phobic. Elsie had wondered at the time, if that was the case, how they had managed to go on a cruise at all – and this was before the pandemic and the super-spreader venues that cruise ships were revealed to be early on. Elsie had thought a cruise a veritable floating petri dish of germs and bacteria even before all that. She'd not been as keen as Howard to go, but had gone and had a great time, including seeing the northern lights. They'd tried to do most things once. Even if recovery from the pandemic went well, they wouldn't go on another one, though. Their travelling days were over.

Elsie raised her hand and smiled and stood back to let everyone in. What ensued was a loud rumble of voices and footsteps and clattering of bottles.

'Welcome, welcome,' she cried, stepping aside in the hall to let them pass like a procession greeting the King.

'Marvellous to see you, finally,' Gerald said, pecking her on the cheek as he moved past.

'God, yes, what a time,' Maureen said. 'I feel reborn, finally getting out of the house and not having to worry about Covid-bloody-19! Actually seeing people socially – we were very cautious for ages, even after the all clear.'

'Yes, a huge relief,' Elsie said. 'Go on through – we're sitting outside. Please be sure to say if you're too cold. We can always migrate inside or get out the blankets,' she said.

'How good is it to be alive and on the other side of all that,' Trevor said. 'Though we think there's a lot of dust still to settle, don't we, Di?'

'Yes,' Diana said.

Elsie closed the door behind them and followed the throng out to the table where Howard was taking and fulfilling everyone's drink orders.

'Okay. A toast,' Howard said, raising his glass. 'To seeing the back of that ugly beast. And to absent friends.' Words were exchanged and glasses clinked.

'We made it,' Sandy said, raising her glass higher and then taking a long slug. 'God, that goes down well,' she said, putting her glass down and sitting back into her chair slowly.

'Have you become a full-blown alcoholic like us?' Maureen said jovially.

'Only thing to do, really, when the world is going to shit,' Gerald said.

'We couldn't afford to imbibe too much, what with the appalling interest rates,' Trevor said.

'Yes, quite,' Howard said.

'Great hummus,' Sandy said. 'Is this homemade?'

'It is, as it happens,' Howard said. He and Elsie looked at each other, and then giggled.

'What's that look for, is there something wrong with it?' Sandy said, her biscuit raised halfway to her mouth, now looking undecided about if she wanted to continue eating it or not.

'No. It's perfectly fine. It's just there's a funny story attached,' Elsie said.

'Oh, do tell, I could do with a laugh,' Gerald said.

'Yes, me too,' Maureen said.

Elsie nodded her encouragement to Howard.

Howard grinned. Laughter bubbled within him as he recalled his and Elsie's previous bout of hilarity stemming from this very topic. And he did so love telling a story – he just hoped everyone else would get it.

'Well, it might be a case of you had to be there, but here goes ...' he began.

Elsie sat back. She loved the way Howard told stories.

The table erupted into laughter and it was a full few minutes before everyone could speak again and the tears were being dried from faces.

'Oh, that is priceless,' Sandy said. 'I'd like the recipe. It's actually one of the best hummuses – god, that's a mouthful – I've ever had.'

'Well, just bear in mind, if you want to run out of chickpeas and tahini at the same time, you'll have to do three tins of chickpeas and one jar of tahini, but that's only if you use a three-hundred-and seventy-five-gram jar,' Howard said. 'If you get a different size, you could be in all sorts of trouble.' He chuckled and rolled his eyes.

'God, yes. All very confusing,' Diana said. 'When you print or email the recipe – whichever works is fine with me – please note which brand tahini you used, or just make sure the size is written there. My maths skills are atrocious.'

'Yes, well, we're a bit over the whole chickpea-slash-tahini wrangling at the moment,' Elsie said, feeling the need to say something.

'It really is too funny,' Sandy said.

'Good to find something to laugh about these days,' Gerald said.

'Yes, though sometimes I think we're losing our minds,' Elsie said. 'The most inconsequential things can crack us right up.'

'You're lucky – the couple that laughs together stays together,' Sandy said knowingly.

Howard squeezed Elsie's knee under the table and she patted his hand.

'I suppose you guys weren't feeling as stifled as the rest of us, Howard and Elsie, given you've said you've stopped travelling?' Diana said after a lull in conversation amidst the crunching of mouthfuls.

'Yes, we have, haven't we, my love?' Howard said.

'But surely there's other places you want to go?' Sandy said, incredulous.

'Nope,' Elsie said. 'And that's not because of Covid. We'd already finished our travelling.'

'So, you're just sitting around now waiting to die?' Trevor said. 'Sorry, I didn't mean to say that out loud,' he added, his face flushing.

Um, yes and no – not exactly just sitting around waiting ... Howard thought.

'Isn't that what we're all doing, really?' Gerald said. 'I don't know about you guys, but what is there? I'm just about able to afford to do a bit of travel, but now it's hard enough being on my feet just to do the essentials, like the groceries. I'm too decrepit to tramp around, let alone enjoying doing so. The muscles and joints aching, and what-have-you – sucks all the joy right out of everything these days.'

I hear you, Howard thought.

'Yes,' Maureen agreed.

'But we're all that bit older than you two, aren't we?' Sandy said. 'You guys are only seventy-eight, aren't you?'

'Yes. But ...' Howard said and gave up.

'Sorry. I've clearly forgotten how to interact socially. You do you. We're all doing us,' Sandy said and waved a hand dismissively.

'To me it feels like a new phase. I know we should be excited about the future. Glad and relieved to have got through Covid, but I just feel tired – not the sort of tired a good few nights' sleep will fix, either,' Trevor said.

'Yep, I know what you mean,' Gerald said.

'It doesn't help that society has us on the scrap heap at our age, or at least invisible,' Maureen said. 'Well, that's how I feel, actually. I'm ready to go. I'm bored, sick of it all. Sick of budgeting. Sick of scrimping. Sick of cooking, sanitising my bloody hands. We want to be taken care of, don't we, Gerald? But there's no way we're going into a home, before any of you suggest it,' she said, holding up her hand.

'Exactly,' Gerald said. 'That Royal Commission was a joke and aged care is still a disaster, unless you can buy into one of the fancy resort-style ones.'

'Well, there's that,' Sandy said.

'Only option, really, is to commit a crime and get locked up – three square meals a day and all that,' Gerald said with a grin before picking up his glass, his eyebrows raised.

'Yes, but it would have to be murder. And then you'd be in with murderers – pretty much anything less than that is a monitoring bracelet and home detention these days. You'd still have to bloody cook and clean and all the rest,' Trevor said.

'You've clearly been thinking about it. A lot,' Sandy said with a laugh.

'Oh yes, as I said, I'm tired,' Trevor said.

'You sound depressed to me,' Sandy said.

'I probably am, but not as though I'd top myself. Seriously, I'm fine, just venting. Isn't that what we're here for?'

There was a collective sigh of relief.

'Oh,' Sandy said, looking around.

'What?' Howard and Elsie said at the same time. 'What's wrong?' Howard frowned as he tried to see what Sandy was looking at.

'I've just realised what's wrong – what's different, I mean. Where's your darling Maisie?' Sandy said, looking around again.

'Rainbow bridge. A month or so ago,' Howard said. He rubbed Elsie's leg under the table. He didn't want to think about the gaping hole in their lives right now, let alone talk about it. He'd successfully shoved the topic down that morning and put a lid on it – *sorry, darling Maisie* – and was desperate to change the subject. But he now found himself rendered speechless.

'God, I'm so sorry. You must be heartbroken,' Diana said.

Howard and Elsie nodded.

'Bloody hell. I'm sorry. Trust me to bring the mood down,' Sandy said.

Howard, with some effort, managed to clear his throat and then speak. 'No need to apologise, Sandy, you weren't to know.'

'No,' Elsie said, having swallowed her own rising lump of grief down.

'Let me swiftly change the subject to a silly thing I saw online the other day,' Maureen said. 'Could be the whole situation getting to me, but this made me nearly wet myself – though it didn't take much, doesn't take much these days. Bloody bladder leakage. Anyway, it read: *I got a chicken to make sandwiches, it didn't. It just shits on the floor.* Ha! How do you like that?'

Most of the table laughed. *That's actually pretty funny*, Howard thought, joining in.

'Get it – shits on the floor?'

The remainder of the table erupted into hearty laughter.

'Something I saw the other day made me chuckle, but was a little too close to the truth,' Trevor said. 'It was along the lines of:

All my friends are exercising, but here I am watching a show I don't even like because I dropped the remote.'

'That is both funny and a bit too close to the truth,' Gerald said.

'Yes, that was me the other day, actually,' Maureen said.

'You need a little pocket thingy to hang over your recliners, like we have. Game changer,' Howard said, turning a little in his chair and waving towards their reasonably new recliners, positioned near each end of the two large leather couches which were at right-angles to each other, all visible through the glass doors.

'Oh, yes, I see. Lovely. Are they new – the recliners, that is?' Diana said.

'Our gift to ourselves,' Howard said, nodding.

'They look comfy,' Trevor said.

'Yes, perfect for contemplating our demise,' Howard said deadpan.

'Yeah, right. That'll never happen. They'll wear out before you guys do. You're the fittest and healthiest of all of us. You haven't had a divorce or any major health issues to navigate, yet, have you?' Sandy said.

'No. We've been very lucky,' Howard said.

'Good for you. Wouldn't wish it upon anyone. Navigating the chemo journey, so many times I wondered what was the point,' Maureen said.

'I wonder that every day. Still, even though I'm fit as a fiddle. And I don't think I can even blame Covid. It's just this old age business. I don't like it one bit,' Trevor said.

'No, but I will tell you, these sorts of get-togethers are a highlight in an otherwise dull and invisible existence. Thank Christ we can do it again,' Gerald said.

'I didn't like that zoom videoing much at all,' Diana said.

'Oh. We refused to do it, didn't we, Howard?' Elsie said. 'We stuck to the phone. Why does everyone suddenly need to *see* one another? It's quite ridiculous.'

'Good for you. We did it for the grandkids. Really, it was lovely to see them. Though I worry about my little Tilly. We used to have great long personal chats over the phone, but with the video system it wasn't nearly as private, given their computer was on the dining room table and anyone could walk by at any moment. They've decided to keep doing things that way and we have to pick our battles. The poor kid gets bullied at school – that was the one great thing about all the lockdowns interstate, though the pressure on the parents to work from home *and* be teachers was too much. What's that saying doing the rounds of the internet? Um, something about the future being a disaster because the next generation of business owners and those running the place were raised by daytime drinkers. Funny but, again, far too close to the bone,' Gerald said.

'Yes,' Diana said, 'it doesn't bear thinking about, really.'

'No. I'm so glad we don't have grandkids, to be honest,' Elsie said. 'Though, of course, it could be we don't know what we're missing. Most likely, that's the case,' she added, realising she might have gone too far. She concentrated on taking a sip from her glass while reminding herself not to lose track; these people needed to be fed more substantially in a bit.

'Ours are little shits. Precocious spoilt brats,' Trevor declared. 'Well, that's probably a bit strong, but still … Hopefully they'll come good when they're a bit older.'

'Yes,' Diana said. 'Meanwhile, there's not a thing we can do about it. We clearly failed with our own kids.'

Mouths dropped open around the table.

'Seriously,' Trevor added in response. 'And since I'm being really honest, I am so grateful to the pandemic for ending the ridiculous two days a week of us having them. Raise your own damn kids, I say!'

'Don't hold back, dear,' Diana said, with eyebrows slightly raised.

Elsie was stunned. Where were the meek and mild Trevor and Diana they knew and loved?

'Sorry, I too seem to have forgotten my manners. I do miss them a tiny bit,' Diana said. 'Though I can't say I missed the expectation that I will give up two full days a week to save them on child care fees. And whatever else. I'm immune compromised, so shouldn't have been anywhere near coughing, snotty people, full stop. But you try telling that to my daughter-in-law. Often she'd pretend she told me and I'd forgotten I was meant to be having them. So, cheers to Covid and the rules. Though we didn't have nearly enough lockdowns here for my liking!' Diana said, raising her glass, followed by Trevor.

Good for you, Diana and Trevor, Elsie thought.

Everyone else raised their glasses and clinked, though to Howard's mind rather than hearty, the little group seemed a bit awkward or bewildered now. Oh well, each to their own, he thought, and longed to debrief with Elsie.

'Doesn't help family relations, but we can't have everything,' Diana added. 'I feel I've done my dues and ought to be able to spend my retirement how I like. And if that means sitting all day watching TV, well, so be it.'

'We sound like terrible humans, don't we?' Trevor said.

'Oh well, too bad, so sad,' Diana added, and took a sip from her glass.

For the first time, Elsie realised Diana was drinking wine, not cola, as she always had. *Ah, the great social lubricator*, she thought.

'I think it's refreshing – your honesty,' Howard said. *There should definitely be more of it!*

'Yes, it's wonderful,' Elsie said, grinning broadly. 'We're silent too often, especially as women. Let it all out, I say! On that note, though, I'm going to get us some food.' She got up and, leaning on the table, said, 'I've gone retro – apricot chicken, Magarey beef, plain rice, garden salad and garlic bread. Magarey beef is a sweetish red-wine stew, for those who don't remember it. I'm not sure if it was ever widely known.'

There was a chorus of appreciation.

'I was going to say something smells good,' Sandy said.

'Well, I hope you're all hungry. We got a little overzealous with the catering,' Elsie said. 'Though Harold and Judith Smith were meant to be here.'

'Oh, are they okay?' Sandy said.

'No, didn't you hear? Sorry. I should have checked whether you knew. Judith died on Monday two weeks ago, I think it was – time is a bit of a mystery these days – and Harold soon afterwards. Their son rang us after he found our lunch listed in their diary. We weren't close, close, but I had actually only just met up with Judith for coffee and a movie in the city a few weeks before, and she'd seemed fine.' Elsie gave a sad and helpless shrug. Though the others didn't know that her mannerism was about so much more than her friend and she certainly didn't want to get into that. She really wished it hadn't come up – that she'd remembered to phone or email and let them all know before today, but she thought she'd have seen everyone at the funeral and had forgotten she hadn't.

'Yes, bit depressing to have got out the other side of Covid and into freedom and then that,' Howard said, much to Elsie's relief, and stood up.

'So, what happened?' Maureen asked.

'Heart attacks. Both of them. Her first and then he when he was sitting by her hospital bed saying his goodbyes. I know it's in really bad taste, but I can't help being a bit envious of them – going together like that,' Howard said.

'Yes. And by god, we're dropping like flies,' Gerald said.

There was a collective mumbling of agreement.

'We'll be back in a second,' Elsie said.

'Do you need any help?' Sandy asked, followed by the same question from the others.

'No, all good, we've got it, thanks,' Howard said.

'Actually, yes, another pair of hands is needed, thanks, Sandy.'

Elsie and Howard made their way inside where they exchanged raised eyebrows just before Sandy arrived. They did an inventory of the dishes on the bench out loud – they'd been known to find garlic bread still in the oven three days after one of these lunches – before all heading back outside, arms laden.

'Here we are,' Elsie said. 'And we're going retro with the helping ourselves too. I'm not sure we'll ever see a buffet again, so better make the most of it, I figure.'

'I think you're right. It's very disappointing – I used to love a buffet,' Trevor said wistfully as he picked up a serving spoon. 'I won't miss all the handshaking, though. I think that's largely gone by the wayside now too. Hopefully it will stay that way.'

'I've really missed hugging,' Maureen said. 'I'm a hugger and it's been torture not to. Not that I've really seen anyone, though I did yearn to spontaneously hug my doctors and specialists during the thick of it – they've been the only people I've seen recently. Even now.'

'Are you okay – not unwell again, I hope?' Elsie said.

'Oh yes. All good, thanks, it's just my surly disposition and poor attitude that's the problem now, but there isn't a specialist for that. Well, I suppose there is – psychiatry,' she added with a chuckle.

'Cheers to all of us grumps,' Gerald said, raising his glass again.

Everyone stopped what they were doing and raised their glasses, and said: 'To the grumpy old farts.' They all knew it was bad luck to not clink glass in a toast and at their age they needed all the luck they could get.

Chapter Three

Just as the plates from main course had been stacked in the dishwasher and Elsie was about to return to sit for a while before offering dessert – a suitably retro trifle – she heard a strange scratching noise coming from down the hall. She frowned and concentrated, trying to figure out what it could be.

'What's up?' Howard said, striding across carrying the water jug he'd brought in to be refilled.

'Shhh. Can you hear that noise?' Elsie said.

'I can hear something. Some sort of scratching at the front door. I'll go and check it out.'

Elsie listened as the front door opened.

'Hello there, can I help you?' she heard Howard say, and then what she thought was a female voice. But it was too quiet to be sure. She made her way to the end of the hall to listen. At that moment Howard let out a sound – a cross between 'Oh' and a strangled sort of utterance of surprise. Elsie peered around the corner in time to see a woman, of around their age, dressed in a floral frock, carrying a black patent leather handbag tucked under her arm, shove past Howard. She strode purposefully down the hall towards Elsie.

'Excuse me!' Howard said, still standing with one hand on the open door and looking bewildered. *What do you think you're doing? How dare you?*

Elsie stepped into the hall and said, arms folded across her chest, 'Who are you and why are you barging into our home?'

The woman ignored her question, instead saying, 'Haven't you finished yet? You should have been gone. Where's Andrew? Is he here?'

Elsie tried to block the woman's path, but was roughly shoved aside. The woman was of a similar size, but seemed to be on some sort of mission, giving her additional strength. Elsie and Howard shared raised eyebrows and shrugged. Howard closed the door and they followed the woman out to the back garden.

Sandy exclaimed, 'Doris! What are you doing here? I didn't know you knew Howard and Elsie.' And then she must have seen the expressions on Howard's and Elsie's faces because she simply said, 'Oh.'

'What?' Gerald and Maureen turned in their seats.

'Do you know this lady?' Elsie said, standing at the end of the table. The newcomer settled herself into her vacated chair, causing Elsie to raise her eyebrows again. *The nerve! What is she up to?*

'Yes,' Sandy said.

'Good. Because we don't!' Howard said. He was really feeling quite miffed at the intrusion but also didn't want to be too rude.

'This is Doris Trenwith, Howard, Elsie.'

Elsie crinkled her forehead. The name rang a bell, but from where? She'd been a part of so many groups over the years – the woman could be from anything.

Howard frowned. *I know that name from somewhere.* He scratched his forehead, but before anything came forth, Sandy spoke again.

'She had this house before you. Doris and Andrew,' Sandy said.

'Okay ...' said Elsie. 'Right.'

'Yes. But what's she doing here? What are you doing here, Doris?' Howard asked.

'Oh,' Howard and Elsie said at the same time, realisation dawning. *She must be having some sort of episode*, Elsie thought. She and Howard both looked at the woman who moments ago had bustled in full of purpose. Now she appeared as buoyant as a half-deflated balloon. Sandy was beside her, rubbing Doris's shoulder.

'I ...' said Doris quietly. 'I don't know where I am. I'm not supposed to be here, am I? Where's Andrew?' She looked around the table with the demeanour of a small and frightened lost child.

Oh god, Elsie thought, putting her hand to her mouth. Her heart seemed to stretch, as if trying to reach out to the woman.

Howard felt his face sag as the blood drained from it. 'We've never met. Only know the name from the paperwork,' he offered, dragging his mind back to the present issue.

To Elsie, Howard seemed as lost as Doris in that moment. Elsie wasn't doing much better, but it helped to keep her hand on Howard's arm. Dementia was their worst nightmare. They'd talked about it lots of times – what they would do if either saw any first signs in the other. They hadn't come up with a plan of what to do when they did; thankfully so far they hadn't needed to. Elsie's chest suddenly felt really tight. She knew she should be doing something, but she was stuck here standing, staring just like their other guests. At least she had Howard beside her.

'Should we call the police or an ambulance, do you think?' Trevor said.

Howard was grateful for Trevor speaking up, which served to drag him back from the slight shock he'd gone into due to Doris's abrupt appearance and confusion. The D word, as he preferred to refer to it, was one of his and Elsie's greatest fears. He shuddered involuntarily and gently chided himself to get a grip. *Me losing the plot won't help anyone*, he thought, and took another deeper breath.

Doris was now sobbing very quietly, barely able to be heard. Elsie couldn't see her face, but she could see her shoulders shuddering as she hunched over. And the movement in her arms suggested she was dabbing at her face with something in her hand. Sandy looked up and caught Elsie's eye.

'Do you think you could get Doris a glass of water?' Sandy said.

'Oh. Yes, of course.'

'I'll go,' Howard said, touching Elsie's elbow before moving away. Elsie couldn't make her feet move and her brain was struggling to connect.

'Any thoughts, Sandy?' Maureen said.

'It would be better if we contacted her husband, wouldn't it?' Gerald said. 'Rather than getting all official, I mean.'

'Yes, but she's clearly in distress,' Diana said. 'I say call the police. Look, she's calmer now. They can escort her to wherever she lives. Do you know, Sandy, if her husband is still alive?'

'And compos mentis, that's the thing,' Maureen said.

'Did she drive here, do you know? Or has she wandered in from having been visiting with someone nearby?' Gerald asked.

'Good point,' Howard said, reappearing. 'Here we are, Doris,' he said, placing the glass on the table in front of Doris, and then a box of tissues. 'I'll just go and check if there's a car outside.'

'I'll join you,' Gerald said.

Trevor got up as Gerald did.

Elsie watched the movement around her as the men vacated the table, still stuck in her vague state. 'I think I'll make some tea!' she finally said, as if it was the most brilliant idea since the dawn of time. 'Anyone?'

'Thanks. Good idea,' Sandy said. 'Lots of sugar and perhaps not too hot, right?'

Diana caught Elsie's eye and nodded, mouthing, 'Yes, please.'

Elsie's new sense of purpose seemed to propel her back to the kitchen to make the tea. 'This I can do,' she muttered to herself as she got mugs out while she waited for the kettle to boil.

'Yes, there's a car out the front. A lovely silver Mercedes,' Howard announced, appearing beside Elsie, startling her slightly from the reverie she'd slipped into while she listened to the familiar and comforting hum of the kettle.

Gerald and Trevor stood back a little, having trailed in behind Howard. 'You know,' Trevor said, 'Howard, if we can get hold of the keys, there will probably be a GPS unit that might tell us where home is.'

'I must say, that's a stroke of genius,' Gerald said with clear approval.

'Yes, good thinking,' said Elsie. 'I've made you all a cup of tea, too. Just in case. Perhaps sit back down so Doris doesn't get panicked. Sandy had her calmed down. She might be able to tell us something now.'

'I'll carry that, shall I?' Howard said, nodding towards the tray of mugs beside Elsie on the bench.

'Thanks,' she said. 'Perhaps wait until she's calmer – after a cup of tea – before trying to go through her handbag, dear,' Elsie added quietly.

Howard nodded and mirrored his dear wife's gentle smile. *Saved by my darling Elsie, yet again.* He was still rattled and probably would have blundered in thoughtlessly and caused all sorts of further upset. *Bless you for always having my back*, he thought, sighing to himself. He put his hand on her shoulder briefly before removing it and picking up the tray. 'After you. You take my seat and I'll get out a folding one and squeeze in beside you,' he added.

When they were all seated again and mugs distributed, Howard opened one of the fold-up wooden chairs, sat down beside Elsie and placed his hand upon her thigh. She reached down and cupped it.

'Do you remember I'm Sandy?' Sandy asked Doris, who clutched her mug in both hands, having taken a couple of tentative sips.

'Ah, that's lovely,' Doris said, ignoring Sandy. They all sat in silence drinking their tea. Elsie thought the way everyone was studying their beverages – as intently as someone thinking they could get answers from tea-leaves – they were all, like her, trying not to stare while most likely picturing themselves in the same situation and being similarly horrified and terrified.

'Thank you,' Doris said, sitting up straight, now with no hint of her recent distressed state. 'Golly,' she went on calmly. 'You good people must think me quite mad. Or at least very rude.' She let out a taut, nervous laugh.

Elsie thought it was a laugh; she might have been wrong. Doris might have been about to choke or something else.

'I'm terribly sorry for the intrusion. I seem to have become quite confused along the way somewhere,' Doris said.

'Where are you meant to be, Doris?' Sandy asked, her hand on Doris's arm.

Doris seemed to search her mind. First she stared up at the roof of the verandah above them. Then she closed her eyes. Finally, she said, 'You know, I have no idea. Um.' She pursed her lips and scrunched her forehead, including her eyes, which, again, made her seem quite childlike in Elsie's view. 'Nope, not a clue, sorry.'

'Do you have a mobile phone in your handbag, or perhaps a personal alarm around your neck by any chance?' Gerald chimed in.

Doris shrugged. She seemed to Elsie now to have lost all concern for the strange situation she found herself in.

'Oh, good point,' Sandy said, peering at Doris's neck. 'I don't see one. Can I perhaps … Would you mind if I looked in your handbag?' She tapped the object Doris was still clutching to her like a life preserver with both hands again now she'd finished her tea. Doris looked down at the black handbag with an expression that suggested she'd never seen it before, and then back up at Sandy, frowning. She tightened her arms around the object.

'How about a distraction? Food?' Elsie whispered to Sandy. 'Are you hungry, Doris?' she asked at her normal volume.

'I am a bit, actually. I don't want to be more of a bother, though. You've all been so kind.' She looked around the table. 'Thank you.'

'We've just had the loveliest apricot chicken and Magarey beef made by my dear wife here,' Howard said. 'Would you like some?'

'Oh yes, please.'

Elsie couldn't help smiling at the innocent wonder and enthusiasm. *Oh, to be that blissful and worry-free.*

'You sit tight and I'll get it,' Howard said, getting up and patting Elsie's arm again as he did.

'Thanks, darling,' Elsie said.

'Yes. Thanks. Good thinking,' Sandy said, beaming up at Howard.

Fingers crossed she's not allergic to anything, Elsie thought, searching through the ingredients of each dish in her mind. Though, strangely, very few people their age seemed to be allergic to anything – that seemed to be an affliction in the younger generations. Thank goodness Corinne and Janine's school hadn't banned peanuts – the girls had lived on peanut paste sandwiches for school and peanut paste slathered on celery or on crispbread most days afterwards while doing their homework. She thought of this every time she saw something on Facebook or the news about allergies and people having to work their way around them for catering or gift-giving of the edible variety. It was a bloody minefield. She'd never had a vegan or a vegetarian to accommodate either.

Glad to be away from the group, but still rattled, Howard's hands shook as he removed the covers from each casserole dish, carefully spooned out a little of everything onto a dinner plate, replaced the lids and returned the leftovers to the fridge. He concentrated intently on the meal going around in the microwave as it warmed so his thoughts wouldn't stray to the confused woman outside awaiting his return.

'Oh, here we are! Yummy!' Doris said a couple of minutes later when Howard returned with the plate of food, which he deposited in front of her and she responded by clapping her hands joyfully before accepting the knife and fork he was holding out to her.

'Ooh, it's lovely. Thank you so much,' she said, tucking in with gusto. After cleaning the plate with the speed and accuracy of a vacuum cleaner, Doris took a sip of water and then sat back in her chair as she uttered a long, confident, 'Ahhh.'

'Many thanks. I really was quite hungry. I feel much better now, so I'd better be going.' Doris pushed back her chair to get up, readjusting her handbag as she did. 'Thank you,' she said, smiling up at Howard. And then, as if thinking she was handing him her plate, or making an offering in return for the meal, or thinking he was her butler or manservant, or something, Doris picked up her handbag from her lap and held it out to him. Elsie watched as the woman then seemed to retreat back into her earlier state of being in a bit of a trance – appearing to not really focus on anything; a slightly glazed or blank look in her eye.

'Thank you,' Howard said reverently, only just managing to reel in his surprise in time.

If she wasn't so tense about the unusual and unsettling goings-on around her, Elsie would have laughed and ribbed him about the little bow he gave as he accepted the object in both hands, flat, like a ring-bearer's pillow.

'Thanks, Doris. Um,' he said, looking at Elsie a little helplessly before Sandy took it from him, which brought out clear relief in his features.

'Sorry about this, Doris,' Sandy said.

Doris, thankfully, ignored her, apparently off in another world and seemingly unaware she'd just given over her personal effects she'd been guarding so carefully.

'God, I hate the idea of going through someone's handbag,' Sandy said, cringing as she opened it.

'Oh yes, better you than me,' Trevor said.

'Yes, rule number one – for one's safety and longevity – never so much as peer into a woman's handbag without express permission, and even then proceed with great trepidation, right?' Gerald said.

'Here's a mobile,' Sandy said, bringing out a handset. She prodded it and pushed the buttons on the side. 'Damn. I think it's flat.' She put it on the table and returned her attention to the handbag. 'Here we are. What's this?' She held a piece of green ribbon. Slowly she pulled it out. At the end of it was a laminated card. 'Oh, jackpot. "Hi, my name is Doris Trenwith,"' Sandy read out. "'I think I'm lost. I live at Norwood Mews. Six five four Ormond Road, Norwood,'" Sandy finished. 'And here's a phone number. Do you think we should call there or drive her home?'

'I'll drive the Merc,' Gerald said.

Elsie smiled at the cheeky glint in his eye.

'I don't think it wise to drive someone's car – she can't really give us her permission. It could void her insurance or something,' Trevor said.

'Ah. Good point. Yes, I sure as hell don't want to be up for replacing it if something happens. Even a scratch on those things might cost a king's ransom,' Gerald said.

'True. You know, it might not be even her car out there. Is there a car key in there, Sandy?' Maureen said.

'Hang on. No. I can't see one for a car – just these, which look to be for a house or apartment, or whatever,' Sandy said, holding up a small, round cut crystal bauble with chain and three keys attached.

'I think follow the instructions and just call the number,' Diana said.

Doris looked past her, as if unaware and not a part of things.

At least she was calm again, Elsie thought, watching her and feeling very sad. *Getting old sucks big time.*

They all listened while Sandy phoned the first number listed. 'Hello, my name is Sandy Bolton. I have with me Doris Trenwith and ...'

The gasp and exclamation of relief was so loud on the other end of the call it was audible to Elsie.

Then the person on the other end said something that Elsie couldn't hear, to which Sandy said, 'She actually turned up at the house she and Andrew lived at fifteen years or so ago. I was a neighbour back then. Oh, I'm sorry to hear that. The poor thing. Okay. Yes, she's perfectly safe. We've given her a cup of tea and some lunch. She was a bit distressed before, but seems okay now. Right you are, then. No rush, it's fine. Thank you. We'll see you soon. Good news, Doris,' Sandy continued, having ended the call and put the mobile aside, 'your daughter, Tiffany, will be here soon to pick you up.'

'Oh, thank you,' Doris said, nodding enthusiastically. 'I hope she's not too annoyed.'

'No, not annoyed. She was very worried though. You were meant to be at lunch at her home,' Sandy said.

It seemed they'd all relaxed, sensing the crisis was over, when Doris spoke again, her words immediately putting Elsie on edge. 'Where am I?' she asked, looking about, worry taking over her features.

Uh-oh, Elsie thought, tensing. *Here we go. Is she going to get upset when we try to keep her here? Are we going to have to physically restrain her somehow? God, no, please.* Thankfully, Sandy was all over it.

Howard got ready to get up, to do what exactly, he wasn't sure, but relaxed when Sandy spoke again, indicating she had the situation well in hand.

'Doris,' Sandy said, placing a hand on the woman's arm, 'Tiffany, your daughter, is on her way to pick you up. She'll be here in a few minutes. She's asked us to keep you here. Would you like another cup of tea while you wait? Or perhaps to use the bathroom or something?' Sandy looked at Elsie with raised eyebrows. Elsie nodded and got up.

'No more tea, thank you, I'm awash. But I wouldn't mind powdering my nose,' Doris said, standing up. 'Oh, you have a lovely garden,' she said, looking up and out to the garden as if seeing it for the first time. 'It looks very similar to one I started many years ago,' she added before turning away from it.

'Come this way, Doris,' Elsie said.

'I'll help,' Sandy said.

Noticing Doris seemed to have shrunken back into herself again, Elsie found herself feeling quite bereft. *The poor woman must be exhausted.*

Doris had just washed her hands and come out of Elsie and Howard's powder room when the doorbell rang. 'That sounds like your ride, Doris,' Elsie said, relief flowing through her.

'Finally! I don't know what took her so long. I've been waiting here for hours!' Doris said.

Elsie caught Sandy's eye and had to bite her lip to stop from grinning. And then just as she had arrived, Doris pushed past them and strode down the hall and opened the door. As she went, Elsie was stunned to see the woman now brandishing a car key fob. Where had that come from? Did she have pockets in her dress? It was the only logical explanation.

'I didn't think for a second to ask if her dress had pockets!' Sandy whispered.

'No, me neither,' Elsie whispered back.

'Mum. Thank goodness you're okay. We were so worried!' said a woman who appeared to have a similar figure to Doris's, but with tired, drawn features, which included red-rimmed eyes.

She raised her arms, then let them drop as her offer of a hug was rejected and instead Doris pushed past her. She then held the car key fob up, pointed it towards the driveway and pressed a button, before thrusting the device at her daughter and carrying on, calling as she did, 'I'll wait in the car!'

'I'll be there in a sec,' Tiffany called as she grappled with the car key for a moment, almost dropping it. But her mother had disappeared. 'I'm so sorry about all this,' Tiffany said now to Sandy and Elsie, blushing slightly.

Elsie wasn't sure if it was from exertion, stress or embarrassment. Most likely a bit of everything. 'It's quite okay,' Elsie said. 'No harm done. She was really no trouble. Thankfully Sandy here recognised her,' she added, feeling the need to say something else.

'Oh. I almost forgot. Tiffany, this is Elsie Manning – she and her husband Howard live here now.'

Elsie nodded, but kept her hands in her pockets.

'Hello. What a way to meet – again, I'm so sorry about all this.'

'It's sorted out now, that's really all that matters,' Elsie said, offering the frazzled woman a gentle smile.

'The card in her handbag was what did the trick,' Sandy said. 'Genius, Tiffany.'

'Thanks. Oh, Sandy, it's so lovely to see you again.' Tiffany leant forward and lifted her hands and then dropped them again in a gesture that Elsie recognised to be the thought to hug someone being quickly abandoned a moment later.

'God, what a day,' Tiffany said, running her hands through her hair. 'She took the car. Doesn't have a licence. We've had the police out looking for her.'

'Oh dear. I'm so sorry. How's Andrew? She mentioned him,' Sandy said.

'He died six months ago.'

'I'm so sorry,' Sandy said again.

Elsie thought she should also say something, but didn't want to disrupt the reunion going on in front of her.

'Thanks, it's been hard,' said Tiffany.

'I'm sorry we've lost touch,' Sandy said, a little helplessly in Elsie's view.

'Don't be,' Tiffany said. 'Covid stuffed up everything and Mum and Dad haven't been well and up for much socialising anyway for a while.'

They lapsed into weary silence and Elsie took the chance to speak. 'Do you want my number in case you ever need to call and see if Doris is here again? If she goes missing again, that is?'

'Oh, yes, please,' Tiffany said suddenly, as if finally coming to her senses fully again. 'Yes. Yes, please,' she repeated. 'If you wouldn't mind.' She got out her phone and she and Elsie swapped numbers.

'And I'll give you my husband's details too – Howard. Howard and Elsie Manning. Just in case.'

They had just finished when the blast of a car horn was heard. They all turned around to look. Then Tiffany sighed and said wearily, 'Well, that's my cue. I'd better go. Again, please accept my sincere apologies. And thanks. For everything, Elsie, Sandy,' Tiffany said, gripping Elsie's arm and then Sandy's hand in hers before hurrying down the driveway, at the end of which sat a bright shiny silver Mercedes sedan. Elsie and Sandy waved as they watched Tiffany drive off, and remained standing until the car had left the cul-de-sac.

'Well. There we are,' Sandy said before taking a deep breath and letting a rush of air out noisily.

'Yes. Quite. That was significantly more excitement than I'd anticipated for today,' Elsie said. 'The poor things.'

They turned and silently made their way back inside where Elsie pushed the door closed behind them and stood leaning against it for a few moments, collecting herself, while Sandy disappeared into the house.

By the time she got back to the others, Sandy looked to have already finished filling them in on any missing pieces regarding

Doris, and they were all holding up their glasses for a refill from Howard who was standing by with wine bottle in hand.

'Okay, who's for trifle?' Elsie said, back at the table beside Howard, with her finger hooked into one of his belt loops and her chin against his shoulder blade. She longed to be alone with him to curl up together on the couch, nestled close like a pair of spoons.

There was a chorus of enthusiastic utterances of 'Yes, please' followed by exclamations of how long it was since their guests had had the particular dessert – decades, apparently, for those who had. Elsie figured it was that long since she'd had it, too. She was surprised to hear Diana and Trevor say they'd never had it before. For the first time ever, Elsie had done the dessert in individual bowls for ease of serving.

'How gorgeous does this look?' Sandy said, turning the bowl around in front of her to admire the various layers and colours.

'Yes, almost too beautiful to dig into,' Diana said. 'But I'm going to, because I need fortifying after that rather distressing interruption. Poor Doris's behaviour was a little too close to home. Cruel diseases, the cluster of dementias.'

'Yes, horrible,' Trevor said.

They fell into silence as they tucked their spoons into their dessert in unison. No doubt they were all, like she was, thinking of the people they'd known who had succumbed to dementia, Elsie thought. They all knew someone who had suffered from it.

'Oh, yum, this is the bee's knees, my love,' Howard said, his face the picture of serenity. His eyes were closed and his spoon hovered above his bowl.

'I'm glad. Thanks, darling,' Elsie said, patting his leg. She let out a little contented sigh before attacking her own dessert.

'Yes, absolutely. The duck's nuts,' Gerald said.

Elsie beamed bright inside. Being praised for her cooking never got tired. She hadn't been concerned today's efforts would be sub-par, but she had been preoccupied. And sad, this time around, without having Maisie by her side. Everyone knew the secret to good food – an absolutely vital ingredient in every dish – was love. And patience came a closely related second.

So many times she'd seen laments in the community Facebook group she was in from someone who'd followed a recipe to the letter, but found it didn't taste the same as when they'd had the dish at someone else's home, or even the last time they'd made it themselves. And always, the posts had plenty of comments from those who disbelieved in the magic emotional ingredient – or technique, Elsie supposed was a more accurate description. Didn't matter. This trifle – in miniature – was a triumph and her concern over the ratios of the layers being out of kilter due to individual bowls was unfounded. Yay for that!

'Do you know what really shits me off?' said Sandy suddenly, causing the group to pause and lift their heads to look towards her.

'Oh, so many things,' Maureen said sagely.

'Yes. Me too,' Diana said, and they all chuckled.

'Go on. Which particular nugget, Sandy?' Gerald asked. 'I have several of my own to share.'

'Okay. Let's declare the meeting of grumpy old farts who are sick of all this shit reopened, then, shall we?' Howard said jovially, and slapped the table.

'Oh yes, please,' Diana said.

'These new euthanasia laws that were passed not so long ago. It's great that we're finally going to be able to escape a horrible diagnosis, don't get me wrong, I appreciate that. But, Christ, there are so many hoops to jump through. Take Doris from just before and all those we've known in the same terrible situation – they don't have a hope of being put out of their misery if that's what they'd like,' Sandy said.

'Yes, and there are plenty of conditions that are inconsistent with a satisfactorily quality of life that wouldn't qualify, I think,' Maureen said.

'That's rather the point. It's not a good look, I suppose, having people check out just because,' Diana said.

'I don't see why not,' said Howard. 'Look at the money and angst saved by governments, if we could book in to be put to sleep when we feel like it.' *If only*, he thought, sighing to himself. It was how he and Elsie would do it if they were in charge of things.

'Apparently all life is sacred and you're meant to wring out every last drop of it before throwing in the towel,' Maureen said. 'I mean, we're here today, doing pretty well, for the moment, but a few years ago I would have happily put my hand up for a swift exit. Chemo was horrible, but of course I did it. Because, well, who doesn't? Now I'm not so sure why I did, given recovery means living with a constant underlying anxiety over whether the cancer will return sometime and if I'll be right back where I started.'

'So why did you do it?' Elsie asked.

'Peer pressure. And not wanting to let the little grandies down, I suppose. We're meant to be wise and self-assured and all that by this age. But no.'

'The thing that bothers me about old age the most, I think – though there's nothing I really am enjoying about it at all – is some of the things we put ourselves through and put our loved ones through. If they were a pet, we'd be up on charges of neglect and abuse. Sorry, I know that's terribly insensitive of me to say when you've just had to say goodbye to your darling Maisie,' Sandy said.

'What a horrible time it must be,' Diana said.

Elsie nodded, not trusting herself to speak.

'Not that it's any consolation, but we know what you're going through, and there's no way I would put myself through it again. We decided after our gorgeous Mr Darcy that he was the last pet we'd own. The thought of something happening to us and the kids putting our treasured pet up for adoption, was just too much to bear. Still is. Though we miss the presence of a pet terribly,' Maureen said.

'We've decided Maisie's the last for us. But, would they, though, your kids?' Howard said, aghast.

'No. Surely they wouldn't put your pet dog or cat, or whatever, up for adoption. They're family members,' Elsie said, mirroring Howard's look of horror.

'Oh, I can see it happening,' Gerald chimed in. 'They could be allergic or already have too many mouths to feed, et cetera. Or simply too selfish. I hate to say it, but I'm seeing a lot of that all over the place.'

'Why are humans so bloody ...? Oh, I don't know,' Diana said, waving a hand.

'Disappointing?' Howard offered.

'Yes, that's the one. Disappointing about covers it,' Diana said.

'Ah, that's a subject that needs a clear head,' said Howard. 'But back to the current topic of euthanasia for a moment, have any of you thought of suicide? I mean, not as part of being depressed ...'

'Simply because you're tired of all this shit, you mean? The lack of mobility, being patronised by the youngsters, being invisible, et cetera?' Gerald said. 'Oh yes, but I'm too gutless. I don't like pain. And if it went wrong, it could create quite a mess.'

'Are you suggesting we kill each other?' Trevor said with a chuckle. 'Sorry, you'll have to count me out. I'm no good with firearms and I'm not really switched-on enough to put in place anything else that is clever enough to work. Not that you can get hold of a firearm easily these days, anyway. Though I have heard you can hire a hit man for less than thirty grand, if that helps,' he added.

'Where did you hear that?' Maureen said and put a hand over her mouth.

Elsie couldn't tell if she was trying not to show her shock or a hint of laughter.

'I can't recall now. See what I mean about having lost my sharps. Completely useless up here these days, I am,' he said, tapping his head before returning to his dessert.

'Seriously, Elsie, I have to say, no word of a lie, this meal today, I would go on living this miserable existence to enjoy again,' Gerald said.

'Geez, thanks very much for the appreciation for all the meals I cook day in, day out,' Maureen said, glaring at her husband.

'Sorry, my love. You are appreciated,' Gerald said, cringing.

'I agree, today was fabulous. It was, but honestly, I enjoy anything I haven't had to rustle up myself. I'm so tired of it all. I was tired of coming up with ideas and putting food on the table when the kids were little and that's around fifty years ago,' Diana said. 'But we go through the motions, don't we? On and on and on and on.' She finished with a loud sigh.

'We wouldn't mind, or it wouldn't matter quite so much, if the next generation shared their appreciation a bit, right, Di?'

'Exactly,' Diana said, nodding.

'Yup. No guarantees they'll take care of you when you're older or infirm. Thankfully, I didn't have kids with that in mind. I'm still disappointed, though. Why did we have kids, again? Anyone have any idea?' Sandy said.

'Because contraception was unreliable and we enjoyed sex? Because what else was there to do back when you had to quit work when you got married?' Maureen said.

'And as a woman, we couldn't get a home loan without a man, remember?' Diana said.

'See, it always comes around to being our fault,' Trevor said cheerfully.

'Sorry, lovely ladies and gents. Speaking of *tired*, folks, it's been really lovely, but I'm going to have to head off,' Sandy said, stifling a yawn as she got up.

'Yes. Me too. Remember when we could have drinks and even dinner before heading out to the movies or a show? Now I'm lucky to make it through to when the murders in quaint English villages start,' Diana said.

'I'm the same,' Maureen said with a laugh. 'I always have to rewatch those programs via a recording or catch-up – I've always nodded off in my chair or taken myself to bed before the final reveal,' she said, getting up.

'No nocturnal shenanigans for me, either, I'm afraid, unless wandering around the house due to insomnia counts,' Gerald said.

There was a rumble of voices of agreement and gradually everyone was pushing back their chairs and standing up.

Chapter Four

'You'll never guess what,' Howard said, coming out of the office into the main living area where Elsie was working on a sudoku puzzle in her recliner. She looked up at him with her brows raised in question. 'I've just finished the photos.' Despite his exhaustion, he had a spring in his step thanks to the huge relief he felt in finishing the massive task. He could scarcely believe it – to the extent he'd just spent the last half an hour searching the computer in case he'd missed a folder or two.

'Wow. Well done. I honestly didn't think you'd get there – not because you couldn't, but because there were so many.'

'You and me both. I can't believe I've done it,' he said, slumping onto his leather recliner with a heavy but cushiony thwump. He took his glasses off and rubbed his face with his hands. 'Wow. Can you believe I've just finished sorting through a lifetime's worth of images – scanned all the albums, deleted the duplicates of all the digitals photos, saved them in a logical order, et cetera, et cetera? It's a little disappointing to think it all fits on one of these,' he said, holding up a USB stick. 'Kind of diminishes one's efforts, really.'

He looked at it and pouted. 'All those months toiling away and only this to show for it – well, three of these; one for each of the girls and a spare.'

'Well, I know what a mammoth effort you've put in, dear. I think it's been an incredible undertaking.' Elsie didn't think she'd have had the patience to see it through. A few times they'd both expressed concerns Howard wouldn't get there, either. Covid-19 lockdowns and them afterwards continuing to take precautions to stay safe had helped. There hadn't been much else to fill their time.

'So, is that really the last *actual* thing to do on the list? Are we done with that phase?' Elsie said.

'I believe so. Wow. I can scarcely believe it.'

'No.'

'Sorry, I know I'm harping on, but still …' Howard said. He remained really quite astounded.

They'd donated bags of clothes, keeping only a small selection to carry them through the seasons and any bouts of unseasonable Adelaide weather. Post-Covid they were a lot less sociable, anyway.

The Tupperware was tidied and all containers had lids. They'd kept most of the household items because they hadn't ruled out throwing themselves a final combined birthday and anniversary bash and also didn't know if the girls would want to use the house or rent it out fully furnished later.

They'd agreed to keep Maisie's things because it was still too soon. Her bedding, brushes, bowls and toys were now residing on the top shelf of the walk-in robe. They hadn't dealt with her ashes as yet, either; they sat on the built-in cupboards in the lounge area, high up above the TV.

All cupboards and shelves in the house and garage had been sorted, tidied and everything labelled.

Surplus books from their considerable library had been donated.

They'd taken the family tree and genealogy research as far as they were willing to, documented everything and put it on the USB sticks.

All paintings and photographs hanging on the wall and any heirlooms had been labelled on the back or underneath with as much detail as possible, including provenance, as well as having been documented in a separate folder.

Their important papers were collated, all service providers and banking details and online usernames and passwords and the like laid out in print, with everything in a large envelope, clearly marked on the outside, in the desk drawer.

They'd read about too many people on the various Facebook groups they were in lamenting about the emotional pain and effort involved sorting through the effects of recently departed relatives or elderly friends or loved ones they'd taken on the task for. Howard and Elsie only had fifteen years' worth of serious clutter, as they'd only been in this house that long, having downsized after their large family home that had also served as their office premises.

And they'd never been hoarders by any stretch, though they did, to some extent, subscribe to the *that might be useful again one day* philosophy that seemed prevalent amongst many of their contemporaries who had grown up without much and who had worked hard over the years to end up reasonably affluent. Careful, conservative, committed were Howard and Elsie Manning, through and through.

They'd achieved their goal of being completely self-funded retirees and not needing any involvement with Centrelink – independent and determined to stay that way until the very end. And, financially speaking, the end was coming up quickly – a major reason for them needing to hurry up with their plans. Upon death they probably wouldn't be leaving much by way of financial wealth for their daughters – just the house, really. They were determined to at least not be a burden. Though, of course, there was a limit to what they could actually do prior to their departure. The key was minimising the load they left behind.

'Do you think we should send some things over to the girls or ask them to come and go through anything?' Howard asked.

'No. We don't want to worry them.'

'True. I'll just get the actual list and double-check,' Howard said, getting up. He grunted and groaned as he eased himself back out of his recliner. They were relatively new pieces of furniture – gifts to themselves as they'd settled in to ride out the first wave of Covid – that were a great idea and very comfortable, but took an extraordinary amount of effort to extricate oneself from. They were clearly designed for those to stay put for the entire day or complete evening, not for the likes of Howard, who had a tendency to want to get up and down, or in and out, around every ten minutes.

He went to the cupboard in the little nook by the pantry, where their mobile phones and chargers resided and the landline phone used to sit before NBN came along and they'd decided to do away with a house phone altogether, and opened it. He took out the A4 lined pad with the latest version of their handwritten list, which covered two pages, and took it over to the lounge area, perusing it as he went. 'Oh,' he said.

'What is it? What haven't we done?' Elsie asked.

'Funeral plans, including writing our eulogies – there's a question mark alongside them.'

'No, we have the note in the Wills that we don't see the point in wasting that money, but that it's up to them, remember?' Elsie said.

'Ah, yes, that's right. Because it's not about the departed but those left behind, isn't it?'

'Exactly.'

'And we've never really prescribed to our kids on anything much, have we? No need to start now,' he muttered, wandering back towards Elsie.

'No.'

'I wonder why we haven't already scrubbed those items out. Oh well,' he said.

Elsie, noticing Howard looking underneath the newspaper on the coffee table, handed him her pencil.

'Thanks, dear,' he said, accepting it with a smile. 'Done!' he said jovially after drawing several lines through the items. He flicked over the page, checking for anything else they might have missed, thinking as he did, *I can't believe it. We've done it. Fantastic.* 'Yep, that's us all done. Well, except for the, you know, the final *final* thing – which is really two things: strategy and actual exit.'

Elsie nodded. 'And before September 12, our next birthday.'

'Exactly. God, seventy-nine, can you believe it?'

'It's a pity we can't now choose to be shot out of a cannon and into outer space.'

'Yes, that sure would save a lot of angst and palaver.' A moment later Howard said, 'Oh, I'm really disappointed now you've planted that idea in my mind!' He pouted again.

'Sorry about that. On that note, I'll make us a cup of tea, then, shall I?' Elsie said, getting up.

'Yes, please. I'm just going to spend a moment luxuriating in thoughts of an out-of-this-world demise.'

'Good-o then,' Elsie said, getting up. She levered herself out of her recliner and kissed him on the forehead on the way past.

Chapter Five

'Howard, it's time to turn and flip the mattress, okay?' Elsie said. 'It's in the diary, remember?' For as long as either of them could remember, each Monday Howard and Elsie sat at the kitchen table and checked their weekly schedule of commitments and items of note. Once, when running their accountancy business, it had been them and up to five employees; now it was just the two of them and their A5 week-to-an-opening diary. Often, recently, they'd been needing to check the diary on a daily basis. But they'd still kept up with their Monday meeting – their ageing brains usually managed to retain something, or enough to remind them to check the book again.

'Right. But now? I'm a little weary from wrestling with the underlay on the clothesline,' Howard said.

'As am I – from beating the damned underlay. But if we get this done, then that's it for another six months. We probably should even be doing it quarterly. Come on.' Elsie led the way down the hall to their bedroom.

'It'll be the last time, actually,' Howard muttered, as he followed.

'Oh. Yes. That's right.'

'So, should we bother at all, then?' Howard now stood with his hands on his hips staring down at the king-size ensemble, the top mattress of which needed to be lifted and turned, all without hitting the low hanging pendant light and ceiling fan, and without either of them doing their backs in, or any other part of their less than robust bodies. He didn't fancy tackling it at all, though had to admit the bed had been feeling a little saggy lately.

'Come on. Five minutes, and then we're done. Forever. And maybe we might even sleep better tonight,' Elsie urged.

'Darling, since when have you slept well during the last couple of decades?' Howard said.

'True. Good point.'

'And I might do better in the sleep department, too, if you didn't toss and turn and squidge around and mess with the covers.'

'Well, you try being an old woman, and all that entails. We really should have got the two single mattresses instead the other year. But here we are.'

Elsie's stance mirrored Howard's. They both looked down at the mattress as if it was a patch or puddle of something they didn't fancy stepping in.

'No bloody handles,' Howard said.

'You say that every time.'

'I know. And it astounds me every time. The stupidity of it.'

'All about warranties, I expect – too easily broken, or maybe it's to discourage turning, and thus alleviate them from being sued when someone injures themselves turning the bloody thing.'

'All of the above. Quite likely. So why the bloody hell have it in the instructions that it must be rotated and flipped, or whatnot?'

'Another of life's conundrums, my darling,' Elsie said with a sigh.

'Well, it's stupid,' Howard said.

'I agree. It most certainly is. As is so much of life and the world these days. Changing the subject slightly, at least now there's no chance of Maisie darling getting in the way and causing a ruckus,' Elsie said sadly.

'Dear old thing,' Howard said. 'Remember last time, she was moving around and trying to encourage us?'

'Actually, I think she was worried we were having some kind of medical episode and might miss out on her dinner as a result.'

'One thing for sure, she did love her food. I can't say I miss preparing her meals, nor having to constantly remind her that it wasn't dinner time, or that she'd already just eaten.'

'Yes. Right, come on, let's drag the top end so it's at the bottom and then we'll flip it, okay?'

'Fine. If you insist,' Howard said.

'Well, it's not really me. Blame the manufacturer. The warranty was very clear – turn and flip every six months. Otherwise, it's probably null and void.' Elsie didn't know why Howard was quibbling like this – they'd always followed every instruction issued by anything remotely resembling an authority, including carefully reading user and safety manuals and adhering to the details therein. It was in both their natures – instilled from an early age.

'Fair enough. For the record, this would be the only thing I hate about autumn and spring.'

'You're forgetting your allergies, dear,' Elsie said.

'Oh, yes. God, my nose is running just thinking about it.'

'Well, blow it – I don't want you dripping all over the place,' Elsie said.

Howard blew his nose noisily.

'Ready now?' Elsie said.

'As much as I ever will be, I guess. Come on, let's get this show on the road.'

'Stop the whingeing. It's not helping.'

'Well, I am a self-confessed grumpy old bugger. And, actually, it *is* helping.'

'Fair enough.' Elsie couldn't help smiling at his exaggerated pout.

'All right, then. Easy bit first. You go around to that corner and pull, Elsie, and I'll push this one.'

'Yes, I know. Come on, let's just get it over with.'

Howard dragged and Elsie pulled. Both huffed and puffed. They moved around the room, following the corners of the mattress, like a very bad rendition of a slow waltz, and finally with the bottom end now at the top, against the bedhead, they sat back wiping the droplets of sweat from their brows with tissues dragged out of their sleeves or pockets. Both flopped onto the bed across the mattress on their backs.

'Just a moment's rest,' Howard said breathlessly.

'Yes,' Elsie said, equally as short of breath. 'I really hope we're not sweating all over the damned thing,' she added.

'Right at this moment, I don't have the energy to care. I don't remember it being this exhausting last time,' Howard said.

'No, it probably wasn't. That's the problem with ageing, remember? It's like dog years but twice as bad, I reckon. Six months is probably like seven years ago, when we were practically spring chickens compared to now.'

'Well, all I can say is I'm glad this will be the last time with this and we'll be gone soon.'

'Yes. But enough grumbling. Now you need to get your second wind so we can flip the blasted thing.'

'Must we? Really?'

'Yes, we must because –'

'I know, I know – the bloody warranty. I still don't think it'll matter in the long run,' Howard said.

'I know you don't, Howard. But do it for me.'

'Okay, dear. I hope we'll notice a difference in comfort level.'

'I'm sure we will.' Elsie stared at the mattress, frowning. 'How do we do this bit again? I forget.'

'Lift it by the edge until it's standing on the other edge, then lever it across, I think. Just do as I tell you. I know what I'm doing,' Howard said.

'Of course, Captain. Yes, Captain.' Elsie stood to attention and saluted.

'Don't make me laugh. I might manage this, but not with the added exertion of laughter,' Howard said.

'True. Me too.'

'Right, ready?'

'As I'll ever be.'

'And, lift.'

Elsie lifted.

'Good, hold it there.'

Elsie's whole being protested at the weight, which wasn't helped by the flex and sagginess of the mattress.

'A little higher.'

Oh god. Unable to speak, Elsie summoned all her might and lifted. The mattress wobbled a little but she managed to hold it firm.

'That's it. Hold it there. I'll go around to the other side,' Howard said.

'Can you make sure you smooth the valance straight as you go – it's near on impossible once the mattress is back down,' Elsie said.

'I'll do my best,' huffed Howard, moving away.

'How do single people do this?' Elsie said as she waited, supporting the upright mattress.

'No idea,' Howard muttered from the other side of the bedroom.

'Designed by men, most likely,' Elsie mused, bending her head down to wipe it on her sleeve. The mattress wobbled slightly. *Shit.* She stopped. The more she wanted to wipe the droplets of sweat away, the more their presence irritated her. She was close to just dragging her forehead across the mattress instead, but resisted. 'A stupid way to do things. There must be a better option. After spending the value of a small car on it, it should come with a turning service,' she chatted on.

'What's that you're saying?' Howard called, barely audible from his crouched position adjusting the edge of the valance — well, Elsie assumed that's what he was doing.

'Just thinking to myself while I wait.'

'Right. Now I'll hold it stable while we swap sides, okay?'

'Yep. Got you. Just watch the light and fan. And make sure you keep the valance smooth as you go.'

'That bloody thing! Honestly, why can't that be better designed too? Stupid thing,' Howard muttered as they eased past each other.

'Careful,' Elsie said as the mattress teetered on its edge.

'Got it. It's okay,' Howard puffed. 'Right, now I'll take the weight if you tug that side out from underneath.'

'Easier said than done,' Elsie murmured.

'Okay, ready?'

'Yes, just watch the —'

'Yes, I bloody well know — the light, the fan, and straighten the bloody valance,' Howard mumbled.

'Don't get annoyed with me.'

'I'm not, it's my general poor disposition and attitude. Don't take it personally.'

'Oh!' Elsie exclaimed.

'What?'

'I'm losing my grip. Watch out. Oh, shit!'

There was a clunk as the mattress hit the light shade and then the fan before landing with a loud flop onto the base.

'Argh,' came from underneath.

'Howard? Are you okay?' Elsie hurried around to the other side where the mattress bulged over Howard's frame. His legs and one hand stuck out from the side. Elsie smoothed the rumpled valance as she went.

Howard wriggled his hand and feet to try to attract Elsie's attention.

'Howard, get out from under there and stop being silly,' Elsie scolded.

Well, that's what Howard thought he heard – it was rather difficult to hear anything with six inches or so of plush top-of-the range springs, foam, fabric and what-have-you lying on top of you. He was having difficulty breathing, too. *Don't panic*, he told himself, which served to do the opposite.

'I can't,' Howard said with as much gusto as he could muster. 'I'm stuck.'

But Elsie didn't seem to have heard him, or she had and he hadn't heard her reply. *Oh god.*

'Did you say something?' Elsie called. 'I can't hear you.' *What is he up to?*

'Get help. I'm stuck. And I can't breathe.' More panic rose in him at the word 'breathe'. He tried to slap and kick the side of the bed for attention.

'Come on. You're worrying me, now. Howard, get up,' Elsie said. She tried to lift the mattress on her own, but couldn't. 'I can't budge it on my own!'

Howard felt the weight of the mattress raise a bit but then sink back on to him painfully. *Urgh, don't do that*, he thought, unable to utter the words.

'I can't lift it!' Elsie cried.

Howard again tried to move, but couldn't. No doubt he looked like, from Elsie's view, a flailing seal flapping its flippers, or something. He felt a panicked giggle rising up. *I must look pretty funny. Oh, stop, I really can't breathe.*

'Get help.' He was saying the words, though there wasn't much point. Elsie clearly couldn't hear him. But he had to do something. 'Don't just stand there,' he urged, despite knowing there'd be no point; he was barely audible. Was she even still there?

'Just don't move,' Elsie said. She was becoming really worried at hearing no responses from Howard. Could he speak and her just not hear him? Or was he suffocating – had already died? Oh god.

As Howard lay spread-eagled across the bed, squashed by the mattress, trying to ignore the weight and rising panic, he wondered if this might be how he died – from suffocation, not actually being squashed. He wanted to tell Elsie if he did – god, he hoped not, he'd never in all their years together broken a promise to her and didn't want to now – that she was to sue the manufacturer of this bloody mattress.

Stop fighting it, Howard, he thought. Just relax. *Conserve your oxygen. Take a little nap.* He closed his eyes and focussed on relaxing. He was in no pain, even the aching muscles from the morning heaving the bedding onto the line and taking turns with Elsie spanking it with the wire beater and having got the mattress this far seemed to have disappeared. *Lovely rest*, he thought. *No point fighting it.*

He longed to feel the comforting wet nose and tongue of Maisie snuffling about at his bare ankles, urging him to get up or at least flopping down nearby with a loud groan and settling in to keep him company.

Elsie raced out of the house as quickly as she could, her feet shuffling as she struggled to keep her slippers on. *Damn, should have changed them*, she thought. She paused to get her keys from the hook – heaven forbid she allowed herself to get locked out and Howard locked in and trapped in a second manner. *Bloody mattress. It's my fault. I insisted. Oh damn. Oh damn.*

At the end of the driveway, she looked around the cul-de-sac. She didn't really know many of the inhabitants these days. And it was the middle of a weekday. Who was around? And, of those who were, who wasn't old and as useless in the physical stakes as she and Howard? *Oh dear, oh dear.* She rubbed her face and ran her hands through her hair. At that moment she spotted a burly young man leaving the house across the road. He seemed to be dressed in a dark blue or black uniform. She waved.

'Yoo-hoo,' she called. But her voice wasn't more than a hoarse squeak. She swallowed and tried again. She hurried across the road looking both ways, her hand raised. Her feet shuffled. *Stupid slow elderly feet.* The uniformed man had his head down looking at his phone, paused in the driveway.

No, no, no, no, no! She shouted in her head as he tucked his phone in his pocket and opened the driver's side door and got in.

'Help!' she cried with all the energy she could find. She managed to get behind his car and bang on the hatch as she, bent double, tried to catch her breath while hoping he had reversing cameras or an alarm, and/or was a careful driver, so she wouldn't get skittled. After a few huffs and puffs she detected a presence and looked up.

'Are you okay?'

She couldn't speak. She shook her head. After taking a great gulp of breath in, she let it out along with the words, 'Heeelp. We need your help, over there.' She pointed behind her back to the house, but remained leaning against the car panting.

'Oh. Right. Hang on.' Elsie watched as he opened the house door again, seeming to take an age to find the right key, and go inside. 'Joseph,' she heard him shout, 'We need your help.'

A few moments later another burly lad came out looking dishevelled, hair mussed, dressed in what looked like boxer shorts and pulling a t-shirt over his head.

'What's wrong?' he asked, looking from Elsie to the other guy. The other guy looked at Elsie, who could only encourage them to follow her, by waving her hand, as she headed back across the road.

'My husband is stuck under the mattress,' she finally managed along the way. 'Please help him,' she urged. 'Bedroom at the end of the hall.' She waved a hand and bent over double at the start of their driveway. 'I'm okay. I'll catch up.'

By the time Elsie had caught her breath, talked herself out of crumpling into a heap on the ground, and made her way into the bedroom, Howard was sitting in the chair and the mattress was flat again on the bed.

'Can you please just straighten that valance thing there, thanks – the fabric hanging down,' Howard said to the young guys, pointing.

'Oh, don't worry about that,' Elsie said.

'Now you tell me. That bloody thing is what got me in this mess in the first place!'

'There, that's all straight,' the guy in the boxer shorts said.

'Thank you so much,' Elsie said.

'No problem.'

'Yes, thank you. How bloody embarrassing,' Howard muttered.

'Ah, don't worry about it. You're not the first and you won't be the last. Stupid idea making you turn mattresses, anyway.'

'Thank you!' Elsie said triumphantly, throwing up her hands. 'I was telling Howard that earlier.'

'Well, it was you who insisted on following the instructions,' he said. 'It's not my fault.'

'Are you a paramedic?' Elsie said, noticing for the first time the detail on the first young man's uniform, aided by the fact he was looking carefully at Howard and holding her husband's hand. Checking his pulse was more likely than romantic inclination, she thought. Elsie had to bite her lip to stop a sudden burst of hysterical giggling from bubbling up.

'Yes.'

'Oh, Howard,' she said. 'You did look a sight.'

'I'm glad to have amused you, my dear.'

'You should have seen you flapping your legs and waving your hand. You were like … like the squashed Wile E. Coyote character from the Road Runner cartoon. Ha!' A laugh escaped before she could stop it. 'Sorry, but it was a little bit funny. Now you're clearly okay, that is.' She stood with her hands on her hips, taking in the people in the now crowded bedroom.

'Do you want me to call an ambulance, just in case?' the uniformed guy said. 'You seem fine. Any pain at all?'

'Everything hurts when you're this age,' Howard said.

'Dear, he means as a result of your … um … squashing.'

'Oh, yes. Of course. No, nothing untoward, as far as I can tell.'

'Well, take it easy and don't hesitate to call for one if you feel differently later. And, next time? Don't do this,' he said, waving his finger at the bed. 'We can help – we're right across the road.'

'Well, we know that now. Thanks,' Elsie said.

'Oh, there won't be a next time,' Howard said. He and Elsie shared a conspiratorial look. 'Anyway, we're Howard and Elsie Manning. I'm sure you can figure out which is which,' Howard added cheerfully. 'I'd shake your hand, but we don't these days, still – after the whole Covid fiasco.'

'No. Good idea. Well, I'm Joseph and this is Philip,' the guy in the uniform said. 'Philip is a police officer.'

'Oh. Great. Wonderful to have first responders in the street — how lucky are we?' Elsie said.

'Though we're moving out soon. We're currently renting but looking to buy. But while we're here, please feel free to knock on the door if you need any help with anything.'

'But don't you do shift work? We wouldn't want to wake you,' Elsie said.

'We always put a do-not-disturb sign on the door. But if it's an emergency, like this morning, knock anyway.'

'Careful what you offer,' Elsie said.

'Yes, quite,' Howard muttered. 'I assure you we were once very capable people. Now, thanks to this ageing business, not so much.'

'You're all right,' Joseph said. 'Look, I've got to get to work. If you're sure you're okay now?'

'Perfectly fine. Thank you so much.'

'I can stay for a bit, if you want,' Philip said.

'Thank you. But we really are fine now, aren't we, Howard?'

'Yes. Just significantly bruised in the pride department,' he said a bit sheepishly.

'Don't be embarrassed. Between us, with our jobs, there's not much we haven't seen.'

'Still, not very reassuring. But oh well,' Howard said, getting up.

'No, it probably isn't,' Philip said, smiling kindly. 'Well, you both take good care of yourselves. Take it especially easy today.'

'No other way to do it when you're our age, really. Sorry, I'm being a grumpy old bugger. Ignore me. Thanks again.'

Howard and Elsie walked them to the door and waited until they got to the end of the driveway.

'Well,' Howard said, looking at Elsie as they leant against the closed door, having returned inside.

'Yep. That about sums it up I suppose,' Elsie said. 'Oh, Howard, I was so worried,' she said, leaning into his chest and wrapping her arms around him.

'As long as you weren't packed up on the floor laughing.'

'Well, maybe just a little bit,' she said, smiling up at him. 'Just kidding. It was only funny when I knew you are okay. I hope the valance is not skew-whiff on the other side after all that. I can't bring myself to look.'

'I have a mind to rip it out and leave the bottom bare. Stupid thing. Come on. That's enough excitement for the day. I'm putting the kettle on.'

'Oh yes. I need some fortification before tackling making the damned thing. Goodness me,' Elsie said.

Howard pecked her on the forehead, clasped her hand in his and led her down the hall and out into the kitchen.

'I suppose you'll want me to get rid of the strap wrench now, so you can call on the hunky young chaps to come and open our jars for us?' Howard enquired, eyebrows raised, arms folded, leaning against the bench.

'Ooh, now there's a thought,' Elsie said, tapping her lip. 'Nice bit of eye candy. Perhaps I'll pretend to take up painting and they'll come in and be life models for me.'

'I think you've left starting new hobbies a bit late, dear,' Howard said.

Chapter Six

Elsie sat on the floor in front of the oven and huffed and puffed as she scrubbed the grime off all the surfaces, pausing and sitting back every few strokes to relax her arms and catch her breath away from the caustic fumes. Her eyes watered behind her glasses, her nose ran, and her hands sweated inside her rubber gloves from the exertion. It was such a stretch to reach to the back of the appliance that she practically had to climb inside the damn thing. *Whomever had designed this bloody thing clearly was not the same person who had to clean it! Probably related to the person who designed luxury mattresses. Well, this is the last time,* she thought, stretching in and struggling to get the tips of her fingers in and upside down in order to get the last suds from under the top element. It was meant to be self-cleaning, but that function had ceased to exist years ago.

Howard had just popped to the shops to get hot pies for their lunch. He said he'd do the oven after spraying on the cleaner earlier, but he was taller than her so it was even harder on his joints. She did also subscribe to the notion that it was best to just get on with most things and get them over with. Standing about wasn't going to help matters. And it wasn't something they could ask the boys from across the way to help with.

Five minutes into the task, however, and she'd had enough. Thankfully she also subscribed to never leaving something half-done.

So, there she was moaning angrily to herself, cursing the appliance; telling it in no uncertain terms what she thought of it. All while huffing and puffing.

Finally finished, with the inside of the appliance sparkling clean, Elsie tried to stand up. But she was stuck. Her knees were locked painfully. She leant forward and rested her head on the inside glass of the open door. Hopefully Howard would arrive at any moment and help her out …

Howard arrived in the kitchen to find Elsie sitting on the floor with her head in the oven. He immediately forgot his frustrating and humiliating last half hour or so. *What is she up to?* She looked a sight and he wanted to laugh, but the fact she seemed motionless stopped him. *Is she okay? Shit. Has something happened?*

'Elsie!' boomed Howard's voice, all echoey.

'What?' Elsie asked, slightly dazed. *Shit, did I just fall asleep, have a stroke or something?* she wondered, lifting her head, which she promptly banged on the top edge of the inside of the oven. Suddenly Howard was kneeling down beside her.

Relief swept through Howard at seeing her move and hearing her voice, which seemed to be okay. 'Are you all right?' he asked. 'I said I'd do that later.'

'Yes, I know, but … I couldn't get up. I'm stuck.'

'Is that all? Are you hurt?'

'No, but I just banged my head.'

'Yes. I heard that. Sorry I startled you.'

Elsie managed to shuffle back a bit. 'My legs are stuck under me.'

'Oh shit. I think mine are too now, actually,' Howard said. 'Dammit. I really probably should have stayed on my feet.'

Howard and Elsie twisted and pushed their legs out. *Sploosh.* There was a soft, squelching thudding sound as she flopped onto her stomach onto the tiles. Despite the exercise sessions they did on YouTube in front of the television, neither could squat down and get back up smoothly again these days.

Damn this old age business, Howard thought. He hated how useless he not just felt, but in this situation, actually was. And to think they both used to run around a tennis court only a few years ago. *Grrr.*

'Oh god, that's better,' Elsie said. She turned her head from her position, face down on the floor, to see Howard had moved to straighten his legs out and was leaning against the nearest cupboard behind him. They were facing each other across the galley-style kitchen, red-faced and slightly breathless from the exertion.

'I'm not sure I can get up, Else,' he said.

'No, me neither. Let's just rest here for a bit.'

'Do you know, when I came in, I thought you had your head in the oven trying to do yourself in?'

'That's not a bad plan right about now.'

Howard wanted to laugh now he knew Elsie was all right. But given they were both still stuck on the floor it probably wasn't wise to use up additional energy with a bout of hysterics. 'Except, of course, it's electric, dear. Best you'd do is burn your face off, and that would be a horrible way to go,' he pointed out and bit his lip to stop the laughter bubbling up.

'Yes, quite. How was the excursion?'

'A successful mission,' Howard said proudly. 'Two steak, mushroom and onion pies are awaiting our devouring. Except they'll be cold by the time we get to them. Oh well, we can heat them up in the sparkling clean oven.'

'No. We're not ever using it again! Well, I'm not cleaning it again! Can you, by any chance, reach them from there?'

Howard looked up at the bench and twisted his head around. 'No. Can you see a brown bag from your position?'

Elsie stretched her neck. 'Nope. Sorry, we'll have to get up and retrieve them. I still can't move. I'll have mine cold, when and if I ever get up. Hang on. Hold that thought, I'm feeling a burst of energy coming on. I'm going to attempt to sit upright.' Elsie squidged around and turned, and somehow managed to get herself from her stomach onto her bottom.

'I wish I could provide some assistance,' Howard said, lifting his hands in his lap and letting them drop again. 'And the pies actually might —'

'It's okay. I've got it,' Elsie puffed as she eased herself around until she was leaning against the cupboards and had her legs stretched out, mirroring Howard across the way. 'There we are. Much better.'

'Well done.'

'Sorry, I interrupted you. The pies – carry on.'

'Oh. Just that they might be okay – heat-wise. Apparently, they're the world's hottest pies,' Howard said.

'What are you talking about?'

'Well, the twelve-year-old child who served me went to great pains to warn me, several times, I might add, that they were hot.'

'Did you tell her you'd been dealing with hot food probably since before her mother was born?'

'No, but I did exclaim, "Ouch" as I picked them up, just to mess with her. Completely went over her head of course. But all wasn't lost – there was a couple of oldies behind me who got the joke. We shared a look – you know the one.'

'All too well. It's as common and familiar amongst us as the secret Masonic handshake would be known within the Masons' ranks.'

'The bloke laughed out loud, which of course caused the kid behind the counter to roll her eyes, with great exaggeration, and shake her head slowly. No doubt thought we all had Alzheimer's or we're just too stupid or something. The usual sort of encounter,' he added with a shrug.

'You might need to find another bakery.'

'Darling, if we only shopped where we weren't spoken down to, we'd never go anywhere or have anything to eat at all. And don't forget that treatment is preferable to being ignored altogether. I mustn't have had my invisibility cloak on today, because I was at least served quickly and in the right order. No youngsters even pushed past. Other than being patronised by said twelve-year-old, it was a most satisfactory trip. Oh,' he added, looking downcast.

'What? What aren't you telling me?' Elsie asked.

Howard's face began to burn with embarrassment. He didn't really want to admit to this but he also didn't keep secrets from Elsie. 'Um. I drove. And I might have lost the car for a bit – forgot that I had driven over. It's wet out. And then I almost backed into someone – a youngster, though everyone's young these days, so you can imagine the reaction. There was shouting, much shouting, and gesticulating. I could even see his red face from where I was. Thought about getting out and going over to gently warn him to get his blood pressure checked lest he have a heart attack. Only a matter of time, in my opinion.'

'Oh, Howard, dear. Are you okay?'

'Well, I can't get up.'

'Yes, dear, but okay after the car incident. You obviously got back all right.'

'Yes. Your skills of observation haven't deserted you just yet, that's something at least, Elsie.'

She rolled her eyes. 'Oh, ha ha. Imagine I'm throwing something at you.'

'Okay. Imagine me ducking, but not being quite quick enough and it hitting me in the head. Ow, that was hard. Steady on.'

They erupted into laughter as Howard rubbed his head theatrically. Elsie was mighty relieved she was sitting down and thus wouldn't also have a bladder leak to deal with. She wiped her eyes and then her nose with a sleeve. At least they had each other and at least they still laughed together.

They gazed across the space and then Howard let out a sad heavy sigh before saying, 'You're thinking the same as me, aren't you?'

'Probably. That Maisie should be here looking at us, licking and nuzzling and urging us to get up. Helping?' Elsie said sadly.

'Yes, exactly.'

Elsie's heart tumbled as Howard wiped at his eyes. She could see the glistening of fresh tears. And not tears from laughter.

'It's probably time we considered giving up driving. Both of us,' Howard said, abruptly changing the subject. 'You did nearly hit that chap the other week, remember?'

'How can I forget? I remain mortified.'

'So, is that settled, do you think?'

'I think so. But let's keep the car, though, just in case.'

'Yes, of course. The girls will need it when they visit. And selling a car opens one up for all sorts of trials and tribulations, and possible danger these days, by all accounts,' Howard said.

They sat in silence for a few moments before Howard said, 'I think I've recovered my breath. I'm going to try standing up again.'

'Pull out one of the drawers. Would that help?'

'Good plan, my love.'

Elsie watched as Howard slowly hoisted himself onto his knees and then onto one foot and then the other. Finally, he was standing up in front of her with his hands outstretched.

As she reached up, she had a flash of déjà vu to a time when they were much younger.

'Ah, that's better. Thank you,' she said, finally back on her feet. 'That had better be rule number one – remain on both feet always.'

'Yes. I'm not sure what you were thinking, my love.'

'But the oven needed finishing. Well, yes, okay, I do admit I did bite off more than I could chew. I don't recall not being able to get up last time, do you?' She leant against Howard's chest as he stroked her hair.

'I can't remember when we last did it. Last year when the girls were here, was it? I can't recall. Perhaps they did it. Oh, I don't know.' He shrugged.

'Could be. Doesn't matter. It's done now. Come on, I hear a pie calling. Quietly, because they're cold, most likely. But I'm starving now, so I don't care,' she said, giving his chest a gentle thump as she moved away.

'Yes. Quite. I'll get the plates, you get the cutlery and sauce bottle. Oh shit,' Howard said.

'What?'

'I completely forgot I got us both an ice cream for a treat. I meant to put them in the freezer, but seeing you on the floor like that completely discombobulated me. I feel they'll be quite melted.'

'Toss them in now and we'll see after.'

'I really was worried you were having an issue,' Howard said, putting his arm around Elsie's shoulder as they made their way over to the table.

'I was a bit worried myself.'

Howard squeezed her to him and kissed her on the forehead before releasing her. He placed the things on the table and pulled out her chair.

'Thank you, my love,' she said, gazing up at him.

'Always,' Howard said, thumping down onto his chair heavily. 'Shall I?' He held up one of the pie bags.

'Yes, please.'

Howard proceeded to tip each pie gently from its bag onto their plates, taking a deep whiff of warm savoury pastry goodness as he did. 'Should have heated the plates at least,' he muttered, as he handed Elsie hers. 'Sorry about that.'

'Don't be. All is fine.'

They silently added sauce to their plates and each proceeded to cut a piece from their pie, dip it into the sauce and then eat it; their mannerisms mirroring each other.

'I say, that's the business!' Howard said after his first mouthful. He did so love a meat pie – stuff what the health practitioners or whoever said about them being bad nutritionally!

'Yes. Almost worth cleaning that damn oven for.'

'Oh. I forgot to get us a drink. What would you like?' He put his hands down to hoist himself off the chair, but Elsie put her hand on his arm.

'I'll get it, you stay put,' she said. 'I need to stretch my legs and you did the hunting and gathering of the pies. My turn. Only fair.'

'If you're sure …'

'Perfectly.'

'Water for me, in that case, thank you.'

'Coming right up.'

'We nearly need a list on the bench for what we need to bring across to the table for each meal,' Elsie said when she returned and placed two glasses of water down in front of them.

'Yes, that's actually not such a silly idea,' Howard said.

'No, I didn't think it was, that's why I mentioned it.'

They shared a chuckle and returned to their pies.

'Howard?' Elsie said a few moments later.

'Yes, my dear?'

'I've been thinking.'

'Careful doing too much of that,' he said and then guffawed at his own tired old joke.

'I'm being serious now, Howard. This is serious.'

'Right, got it. Are you okay? What is it?'

Elsie sat with her fingers linked and looked intently at Howard. 'I think it's time we found a plan for the last phase. Are we still on the same page with that? Or have you changed your mind?'

'Of course not. I took our wedding vows very seriously –'

'As did I.'

'– And I clearly remember promising to never leave you. Which I stand by. I will do everything in my power to never leave you.'

'Me too,' Elsie said. Howard and Elsie had lost all four of their parents before the age of seventy-eight, which was the same age they currently were. Thus, they considered themselves to be already living on borrowed time.

'But it's not going to be easy.'

'I know.'

'Any suggestions on how to go about it, by chance?'

'No. You?'

'Give me half a chance,' Howard said with a laugh.

'And at what stage do we tell the girls, do you think?'

'I'm not sure about that either. Or if we even should.'

'How about we take our ice creams and go and have a nice soak in the tub. That should help.'

'Yes, the best plans always turn up underwater.'

Chapter Seven

Howard and Elsie, holding their ice creams aloft above the water line, carefully settled themselves at each end of the bath, closed their eyes and let out several loud sighs and moans of content-ment as the water began to warm them through. *Is there anything better than a long soak in a warm tub with the love of your life and a creamy delight?* Howard thought. As he licked at the defrosted cream running down the cone, his mind began to roam idly in the silence. 'Dear, do you think we should give ourselves a bit of a send-off?' Howard said, voicing the thought that had just suddenly come to him.

'Like a party, you mean?' Elsie said.

'Yes. We could call it wedding anniversary and birthdays combined.'

'It would be hardly appropriate to call it our last hurrah or grand farewell,' Elsie said.

'No, quite right.'

'But who would we invite? There's practically no one left. And it's not like the old days when networking or at least pandering or schmoozing with clients was a good idea.'

'Yes, that was a necessary slog.'

'Exactly. There's no need to waste money now on interacting with those who really aren't our nearest and dearest.'

'Hmm. So, who do we have left – who might be up for coming along? Just those from lunch the other day, really, but we've just seen them. Does not really a decent shindig make …' Howard mused.

'And do we really want to be taking on organising anything at all? Aren't we always saying how tired we are? We've finally finished the list – we still have to formulate a plan and put it into action.'

'Yes, no, you're probably right.'

'Tired and sick of it all is why we're considering A Plan or The Plan at all now, right?'

'Yes. I find it hard these days to believe everything we used to do. Do you remember all the parties we used to attend? There was practically one every other weekend. And we did all that even when the children were small. All the fundraisers, but even the private dos. Oh, and the dressing up. Remember that time when we went as Fred and Ginger and took dancing lessons to brush up and really play our parts?'

'Yes, what fun. That was Sylvia and Alistair's silver screen New Year's Eve party, I think it was, wasn't it?'

'I think you might be right.'

'Early eighties, I reckon, because didn't we leave the girls in charge of each other?'

'Yes, that's right. It was their first time without a sitter, because we were right next door. Oh, they were the days. Do you think the young ones do such things? Corinne and Janine never mention parties and dressing up and having fun,' Howard said.

'People do dress up still, because, remember, every year on Facebook there's all that panic over what to dress the kids up in for book week,' Elsie said.

'The week that seems to go on for a whole term , you mean?'

Elsie chuckled. 'Quite. I don't recall book week in our girls' day. Anyway, I'm glad we're well out of all that.'

'Yes. There seems to be a lot of pressure to do something better or at least different to the previous year. I'd be inclined to roll out the same thing and be done with it.'

'No, you wouldn't, Elsie, you used to go all in. Don't you remember? You loved creating costumes. You'd be tucked away for hours on the sewing machine of an evening – for weeks on end, right from when the girls came home from school and announced what part in which play they were doing. And then doing finishing touches in front of the telly of an evening in the final days. I seem to remember you sewing on lots of sequins and bits and bobs.'

'Oh, yes and you having to get down on your hands and knees and look for those that I dropped.'

'God, I couldn't do that now – get on my hands and knees, that is,' Howard said.

'No. When did life get so serious for them, do you think? It all seems so fraught, even the talk on Facebook about the dress ups – there seems to be competition about everything.'

'I don't know, but I remember you being pretty determined to have Corinne and Janine dressed perfectly,' Howard pointed out.

'Yes, but that was more about me being a perfectionist than trying to one-up or compete with anyone. And you can't talk! I remember you spending hours out in the shed making the most intricate box kite.'

'I remember that. Corinne got in a huff because I took over. Whoops.' Howard cringed, grinning. 'God, I miss those days.

They all talk about work-life balance but, you know, we had it down pat before it was even a thing.'

'Well, to be fair, it was probably always a thing, and aspiration.'

'Yes, you're right.'

'But I know what you mean; before everyone was going on about it. Shouting it from their social media posts.'

'It's not a thing unless it's making the rounds of the internet,' Howard said, rolling his eyes.

'Oh, don't get me started,' Elsie said. 'They act like they're the ones who invented everything.'

'Yes. Like sex.'

'Sorry? How did we get here? And before you go getting your hopes up, I'm quite sure I'm not up for anything tonight, Howard.'

'Oh no, I'm not up for anything either. Um, so to speak. I was just using sex as an example – how all the young ones go on about it like they invented the thing. That's all.'

'Well, you know what they say about sex?' Elsie said.

'What? And who's they?'

'Oh, you know – the royal they; the young ones; not one person as such.' Elsie waved a hand in the air.

'You're losing me, my love,' Howard said.

'Sorry. I'm losing myself. I've lost where I was going with that …'

'Oh well. I've loved our sex life from the beginning. For the record,' Howard said wistfully.

'Yes, me too. At least we have our memories now our bits don't fancy working much anymore.'

'Yes. Quite. Sorry, why was I talking about sex?'

'To depress us further by reminding us of yet another something that's disappearing by the wayside. Stuff this bloody ageing business.' Elsie finished her ice cream and rinsed her hands.

'Yes. Oh, I remember now – work-life balance.'

'Oh, that was ages ago,' Elsie said, leaning back into the bath and closing her eyes.

'Sorry, dear. I'm struggling a bit to keep up, I must admit. I'm just going to close my eyes here for a moment.' He ate the last bit of his ice cream cone and then busied himself with washing his hands in the bathwater in front of him.

'Oh,' Elsie said a few minutes later, suddenly remembering her previous train of thought.

'What's that, dear?' Howard muttered.

'Work-life balance and sex. I remember now. What I was getting at is you can tell no one is having any because they're all talking about it. It seemed more profound, funny and clearer in my head.'

'Still a valid point, dear,' Howard said. 'And I think you're right. Yes, why does everyone have to go on about everything publicly? Why can't people keep things to themselves?'

'Exactly. Why do they think anyone cares if they're going here or there and with whom? And what they're eating or reading or listening to? But I guess there must be enough demand – so many are doing it.'

'Well, it is the information age, isn't it? I think I heard that somewhere,' Howard said.

'Still, it's like constant diarrhoea. It's exhausting. Though, as I say, everyone's doing it, so it must be us who are the odd ones out.'

'I liked the early days of the internet and World Wide Web, before all this noise and clutter. When it was mainly for business and gathering information,' Howard said.

'There is a lot of information on there – the trouble is sifting through it all.'

'Yes. And knowing what to actually ask.'

'And I think the young ones would probably argue it *is* for business, particularly the Influencers, with a capital I.'

'Oh my god. Don't get me started on that,' Howard said. 'I can't fathom how someone with zero actual skills or education or experience in the particular field can make all that money and have all that apparent sway over other people through simply sharing something on a video – something we were most likely doing in the seventies, for that matter.'

'Yes. That's true.'

'See, prime example about the young ones thinking they know it all – and/or that they invented whatever it is they're currently going on about full tilt.'

'I agree, it's quite ridiculous.'

'Though, you know, I reckon our parents would have said the same about us once upon a time. I remember coming home in jeans and matching denim jacket and being called out for showing myself to be a hoodlum,' Howard said.

Elsie chuckled. 'I remember that. We'd been shopping – so it was my fault.'

'These days, heaven forbid one wears double denim. I saw something online about that the other day.'

'I think you'll find that's old news now – the double denim is back in,' Elsie said.

'Oh god, I can't keep up. Shoot me now.'

'No guns, remember, changing the subject to the task at hand.'

'Yes. There must be a way. It surely can't be that hard to do away with ourselves together without leaving a mess and without involving anyone else.'

'You'd think, wouldn't you?'

Elsie looked around and spied the hair dryer. She'd forgotten to pack it away earlier, instead it was sitting on the edge of the vanity. Instant death via electrocution – check. No mess – check. Elsie sat up straighter in the bath, becoming excited.

'What?' Howard asked.

Elsie tilted her head to indicate the hair dryer.

'Have you had an idea or developed a twitch or an itch you need me to scratch?' *Nope, I'm none the wiser, dear.*

'The hair dryer.' She pointed.

He frowned, looking around. 'What about it?' *What am I missing?*

Elsie thought that the fact it was sitting, plugged in, on the edge of the nearby vanity, cord hanging down just a stretch and tug away, was a promising sign. Ordinarily, she would have wrapped it up and put it away in the drawer right after use.

'The hair dryer,' she repeated. 'Well, okay, electrocution, to be precise.'

'Um.' Howard laughed. 'You silly-billy,' he said. 'Remember the safety switch that clicks in and shuts everything off quicker than the drop of a hat, when something short circuits, to prevent electrocution?'

'Oh. That's right. Damn. Could we turn it off somehow?'

'No idea. Probably tamperproof, though.'

'And we can't exactly ask anyone or get an electrician in to check, because that would open them up for issues,' Elsie said.

'Exactly.'

'Damn,' she said again. 'So that rules out the toaster and everything else involving electricity, doesn't it?'

'I'm afraid so. You'd better put your thinking cap back on, my love.'

'I know. You could drown me or even smother me with a pillow,' Elsie said.

'And then what about me? I believe it's quite difficult to drown or suffocate yourself – the body puts up a remarkably strong fight.

I read that somewhere. Anyway, there's no way I would have the mettle to harm you, even if you wanted me to. More hot water?' he added, his hand on the tap.

'Yes, please,' Elsie said, lifting her bum and holding the plug up to let some water out. 'Ah, that's better, thanks,' she said, settling back again.

'Hmm. What about poisons – household, garden plants, pharmaceutical drugs? Though, I'm not keen at all on a painful or icky death – nothing inducing vomiting; you know how I get.'

'Yes, but that rather narrows an already limited list of options.'

'Maybe I'm going to have to toughen up. But we can't do pharmaceuticals, which are the most logical option, because I don't think it wise to rope anyone into our scheme. And I don't have the energy or mind to doctor shop – I think that's what it's called. I can imagine someone from Medicare turning up asking us what we're about.'

'Expensive, too, probably. Aren't apple seeds poisonous – don't they contain cyanide?' Elsie said.

'I think you're right. I'll look it up online later.'

'Just use searches for suicide, don't use the M word – we don't want the authorities turning up.'

'What's the M word?' Howard said, furrowing his brow.

'Murder,' Elsie whispered.

'Darling, we've talked about the Covid vaccinations not *actually* having trackers or listening devices in them. And I don't think law enforcement employees sit monitoring everyone's internet searching, even if our 5G is exceptional now we have our implant,' he said, laughing. *You're so damned cute, my Elsie love!* he thought, grinning at her.

Elsie rolled her eyes and splashed Howard playfully.

'Though they do manage to find the online paedophiles, so they must somehow monitor things. So, yes, I'll be careful,' he added thoughtfully.

'Stabbing and blunt-force trauma, and that kind of thing, are out – too messy, too unpredictable. I don't want to leave a mess, especially a smelly one. Bleurgh. We don't know how long it will be before we're found.'

'And it's a no from me, from a pain point of view, without some form of anaesthetic – and Scotch won't do the trick. I'm a wimp. And a proper solution to that would mean involving someone else.'

'We'd better get a wriggle on and do it so the guys across the road find us – they said between them they'd seen everything. They won't turn a hair or be too traumatised,' Elsie said. 'We could leave the light on and I bet after a while they'd come looking.'

'That's a good idea. Now you're thinking.'

'Thanks. I still haven't come up with a decent solution, though. It's a lot harder than I imagined,' Elsie said.

'Why didn't we get the gas put on?'

'Because it was going to cost a fortune and wasn't worth it just for cooking, especially the small amount we do, relatively speaking. And, ironically, there's the reports of gas heating being a silent killer … Hmm, quite the missed opportunity that was.'

'Yes. Oh dear, I remember that now. If only we'd thought ahead.'

'Though we might have inadvertently taken out the whole neighbourhood with us. Kaboom!'

'Not that we'd have known anything about it if we did the job right.'

'True. God, there was the answer staring us right in the face. I'm really kicking myself now.'

'Let it go, love, it wasn't meant to be.'

'Hmm. It's getting cold in here – are we topping up the hot again or getting out?' Howard said.

'Getting out. I'm not feeling inspired,' Elsie said.

'It's not far off from being time to watch the early news, anyway. Come on then.'

They sat for a few moments while the water gurgled down the plughole. *Now to get back onto one's feet without anything untoward occurring*, Howard thought.

'Are you okay, Howard?'

'Yes. Just gathering my strength and psyching myself up. It's a process.'

'It sure is.'

'Another thing I miss is being able to get out of the bath with ease,' Howard said, reaching up and grabbing one of the shiny steel handles on the wall. 'Doing anything with ease, really,' he said, hauling himself up.

'Just don't step on me.'

'Yes. Bloody hell.' After much exertion, Howard was standing on the bathroom tiles and Elsie was gripping the rail and hoisting herself out of the bath with all the grace of an ungainly baby elephant. 'Do you need a hand?' he asked.

'No. I've got it.' After a few more grunts and groans and careful manoeuvring, Elsie was also safely standing on two feet on the bathroom floor.

'Here, dear,' Howard said, towel wrapped around his waist and holding another stretched out wide.

'Thank you,' Elsie said as she walked into the towel Howard held out for her. He wrapped her up and gave her a hug and then kissed her on the lips.

'At least our love for each other hasn't diminished,' he said.

'Yes, nor our desire to be together,' Elsie said.

'We really are very lucky.'

'Yes, we are.' They clung to each other for a moment, wrapped in their towels.

'It's been a good life. Thank you, Howard.'

'Thank *you*, my love. The pleasure's been all mine. And it's been better than good – it's been great, really. Come on. Sorry, but it's beans on toast for dinner.'

'I love beans on toast,' Elsie said. 'But no rush – after the news.'

'It's almost certainly going to all be bad, Else,' he said.

'True.'

Chapter Eight

Having dressed in their flannelette pyjamas, robes and slippers, Howard and Elsie shuffled out into the living room and slumped into their leather recliners, which welcomed them with audible harumphs and sucked them down into their plush surrounds.

'I'm disappointed we didn't come up with anything before turning into prunes,' Howard said.

'Hmm. But, ah, it's the simple things – I did enjoy my bath with you.'

'Yes. I did too – with you, that is.'

'And you are going to look into the possibility of apple seeds, remember? Oh, I've just had a thought,' Elsie said. 'Do you think we need a suicide note – we'd better explain things, hadn't we?'

'That's a point. We'd better add it to the to-do list.' Howard went and retrieved the pad of paper and made a note. 'It's never-ending, isn't it, the plans one needs to make?'

'You're right about that. Do you think we need to be fancy or just a simple see you later, we did this because life sucks … oh, and no one else helped us – just for clarity?'

'I suppose. But what do you mean by fancy?' Howard said. 'Rhyming couplet or something? I'm not sure ... Though, it would give us something else to do ...'

Elsie giggled. 'Howard, you really are too funny. I was actually meaning fancy as in typed rather than handwritten. But now you mention it ...'

'I haven't written poetry since we were at school, though I don't see why we can't give it a shot. Except, really, wouldn't we be best to actually find a method – keep focussed on the big picture, not get bogged down in details?'

'Yes, quite right. Park that idea,' Elsie said. They fell silent and Elsie picked up her book of crosswords, a thought having just struck her regarding the last clue of a puzzle that had been eluding her for several days. Moments later she was basking in her success. She looked up, ready to tell Howard, when she noticed he was engrossed with something or other on the ceiling. She followed his gaze and adopted his thoughtful expression. But she couldn't see whatever had his attention and after several minutes watching him gave into her curiosity.

'What are you doing, dear? Is there a spider's web or something? Or are you constipated or trying to construct a clever rhyme, perhaps?'

'No, none of the above,' he said.

'Well, what is it? You've been sitting there looking up for ages. And I can practically hear your cogs turning.'

'Yes, I admit I'm deep in thought,' he said, still looking up.

'What about?'

'I'm wondering if there's a way we could string ourselves up from the ceiling somehow.'

'Oh. Well, not without an exposed beam, I shouldn't think.' Elsie now studied the ceiling. 'And I doubt any of those hooks you can screw in would do the trick, even if we could get them in place,' she said.

'No. I suppose we could get someone in to put in some exposed beams,' Howard said.

'No way. I'm not having us getting scammed by some fly-by-night roaming tradesperson – they're everywhere now.'

'Very good point.'

'And remember the mess last time we renovated? Oh, the dust. It took months to get rid of. Kept appearing, despite all the vacuuming.'

'Do I ever! It was as bad as the confetti after our wedding – that stuff appeared as little reminders for years, popping up in the unlikeliest of places and when one was least expecting or had finally thought it was gone.'

'I loved that, actually. Such cute little reminders of a wonderful day,' Elsie said.

'That went on for years.'

'Yes, it came out of the car vents, was under the car mats, and in all the nooks and crannies in our suitcases until they gave up the ghost and we had to replace them – I'm sure we were still finding them a decade on.'

'It was even in your knickers' drawer! It was quite annoying at the time, if I remember.'

'Yes.'

'And I'm the one who does all the vacuuming, remember?' Howard said. 'Bloody annoying in those early days. Especially the little clumps of the damned things that warranted dragging out the cumbersome old cleaner.'

'Isn't it marvellous how small everything is now? That's one thing I like about technology,' Elsie mused.

'Oh, vacuum cleaners. How about now Maisie's gone we look at getting one of those robotic machines that wander around?' Howard asked.

'Bit of an unnecessary expense given we're not planning on being here, don't you think?' Elsie said. 'But, of course, the cleaning is your domain – so it's really up to you.'

'By all accounts they are quite good now. And there's no chance of dear old sleeping Maisie getting startled or having her tail caught up in it. We did always say we'd look into it when she was gone.'

'You did. I don't really have an opinion on the matter, now there's not Maisie to consider,' Elsie said.

'You're right, though, we're not going to be here. Except one of the girls might like to take it on when we're gone.'

'*Except* we've always been very careful to do things equally with them,' Elsie pointed out. 'Unless you want to get two.'

'Absolutely not.'

'Anyway, that's a moot point if we can't find a way to exit gracefully.'

'Yes, quite right. That's the current problem. So it's a no to beams, then, isn't it?' Howard said.

'I think so. And, anyway, what then?' Elsie asked.

'What do you mean?'

'Well, say we've gone to the trouble of having a couple of beams put in that will hold our weight. How the hell do we then get up there to do the deed? It's not like we could say to an installer, "Oh, and while you're here, you don't think we could trouble you to hang a couple of nooses up to save us the bother, do you?".'

'Oh. Yes, quite right.'

'And I don't want to fall off a ladder trying to get organised. I can just see us writhing around on the floor with a broken hip each or something similar and dying slowly from internal bleeding. No thank you very much!' Elsie said.

'We could put the mattress underneath, in case.'

'True. But that brings us back to, underneath what? Haven't we just established that hanging isn't a workable option?' Elsie said.

'Oh dear. Yes. Yes, you're quite right. Pity we replaced the original steel Hills Hoist clothes-line with the modern one that folds down against the fence – it's not nearly as robust as the old version.'

'Doesn't matter, anyway – goodness knows who has cameras that might catch us mid-act out there.'

'True. And knowing the current state of our luck with this confounded project, a drone comes past or the police helicopter. No, it has to be inside and out of sight,' Howard said with a decisive nod.

'Pity we didn't do that attic conversion in the end. We could have tied ourselves to the beam in the attic floor and jumped through the ceiling.'

'That's clever, Else. That might have worked. Are you sure you're totally against a bit of renovating?'

'Yes, absolutely. I couldn't face it. Remember how hard it is getting decent tradies. A local handyman to do a beam is one thing, though hard enough to find. But imagine all the hassle to do with a conversion. I'm about to have a panic attack just thinking about it. The time and budget blowing out, people not turning up ... Remember last time we declared we're too old for this shit? Well, that was, what, ten, fifteen, years ago? I'm way past being too old for this shit now!'

'Scrap that idea, then. Damn it.' Howard looked up again at the ceiling before removing his gaze.

'Anyway, it would involve a ladder. And remember how wobbly we are on just the stepladder?' Elsie pointed out.

'Do I ever. Yes, I'm quite forgetting myself. Too dicey just being a step or two off the ground. Why is it so hard?'

'Perhaps it's not. Maybe we're just being very particular. Do you think we need to stop being so?'

'Maybe,' Howard said. 'But I do think we need to be prudent in our approach – it's worked for us our whole lives, as has not being an undue burden on anyone else.'

'That's true. Cup of tea before dinner? All this thinking is making me thirsty,' Howard said, scrambling to get out of his chair. 'Why oh why didn't we get gas put on?' he muttered as he shuffled across to the kitchen.

'Because it was going to cost a fortune and, I've just remembered the other main reason, the roses would have had to be dug up, all mainly for the convenience of a gas cooktop,' Elsie pointed out. 'And when the induction was becoming all the rage,' she added.

'Ah, yes. That's right. Did you say you wanted tea?' Howard said, looking over from the bench, the kettle poised in one hand and his other on the tap ready to turn it on. They only ever put enough in for what they needed at the time. No point heating and reheating the same water over and over. Complete waste of energy.

'Milo for me, if you wouldn't mind.'

'Coming right up. Speaking of money. How long have we got, do you recall? We've checked the budget recently, haven't we?'

'Of course. We discussed it the other day. Or didn't we?' Elsie said, furrowing her brow.

'Are you losing it? Am I?' Howard felt a moment of panic.

'No. Sorry. My fault. We did. You said, I think eight months, tops, at the current rate, without any intervention,' Elsie said.

'Yes. That's right, certainly nothing in the kitty for a splurge on anything major at this point.'

'No. And it's going to be very sticky if we're still hanging around come Christmas.'

'I don't know how people just go along without knowing how much they have and how long it will last, et cetera.' That was an understatement – it fairly boggled Howard's mind that there were people out there who didn't do a budget.

'But people do, by all accounts.'

'We know they do, dear. Remember, we made quite a good living as accountants,' Howard said.

'I appreciated all our clients and some of them I genuinely liked very much. But the number of people who couldn't grasp simple concepts was pretty disappointing, wasn't it? I don't care what anyone says – there is such a thing as a stupid question!' Elsie said.

'I quite agree. Now there's Google and random strangers on the internet to ask. Here's a thought: imagine if there was a human in the background instead processing all the requests – well, millions of minions, actually.' Howard very much liked this idea and despite it not being a thing still regularly spoke to the computer – sometimes cursing it but also often thanking it for its assistance or praising its cleverness.

'Yes! And instead of issuing the list of results, they put up a note saying they refuse to waste their time on such a ridiculous question. That would shake things up a bit!'

'Now *that's* something I would like to see,' Howard said, handing Elsie her mug. 'Speaking of Google, I'm just going to do a quick spot of research.'

Chapter Nine

Howard returned to the lounge a few minutes later and sat down, bringing his iPad from the study with him. It had been both an enlightening and disappointing venture.

Elsie looked up at him. 'That was quick. How did you go?'

'The good news is that ingesting apple seeds can be deadly. However, one would need to consume a veritable shitload of the damned things – obviously that's not a technical term.'

'Right. Noted.'

'Apparently, we would need to crush and eat around forty apples worth each to be successful – though one article said double that figure. So, it's not an exact science, and, thus, not at all guaranteed to be a trouble-free.'

'Okay. But it's an option to keep in mind and start working towards in the absence of anything else right now. I guess we'd better up our sporadic consumption of apples, then.'

'Quite. And remember to keep the seeds. We'll need to dry them, too, so they don't go mouldy,' he said as he picked up the remote and turned on the TV. Highlights of the upcoming news bulletin were showing on the screen.

'Still a couple of minutes until the news,' he said. 'I'm hungry. Shall I get the beans now?'

'If you wish. I can eat. And don't forget to add apples to your shopping list.'

'Righteo.' He wriggled his bum back and forth, shuffled to the edge of his seat and eased himself out, trying his best to do so quietly. *I really need to think these things through – not get settled and then decide to get up every ten minutes.*

He'd just retrieved the toast from toaster and was buttering it when Elsie called to him: 'Howard …'

He turned around to see what was up.

'… look,' she said. Before he could ask, Elsie continued, 'Warnings about death cap mushrooms.' She was wriggling a finger at the TV, causing her whole arm to shudder, right to the shoulder. 'I fancy a deadly mushroom risotto,' she said with a grin and a wink.

'Ooh. Good idea. And a much quicker prospect, practically speaking, than the apple seed idea.'

'Do you think we should go tonight and look?'

'Sweetie, I can't. I'm too weary. And my eyes are terrible in the dark these days. I think there'll be plenty still there tomorrow. It won't be like that time, the other year, when someone mentioned on Facebook about there being magic mushrooms. Somehow I don't think there will be a stampede for death caps,' Howard said.

'But maybe if there are others of our ilk out there …' Elsie said.

'True. Though I do think we might be a rare breed.'

'Hmm, perhaps you're right.'

'Goodie, that gives us something to do tomorrow. What date is that?' Howard said. Something was ringing a bell up there in his tired brain. *Come on, old fellow, what is it?*

'I'm not entirely sure. Is something clicking in the old memory cogs?' Elsie asked.

'I'll check. Oh,' Howard said upon opening the diary on the bench to the current weekly spread, marked by a ribbon. 'It's Sylvia Pilkington's funeral.'

'Oh. I can't believe we nearly forgot.'

'We didn't nearly forget; we'd have seen it tomorrow when we looked over breakfast, as we tend to do most days now.'

'True. I'm tired of funerals. Well, more so the losing of friends,' Elsie said wearily.

'Would you rather not go?'

'No, better not. That might raise questions.'

'Good point. Business as usual until it's not, I say,' Howard said.

'Exactly. We could make a detour for mushrooms on our way back.'

'It's quite a detour, but I don't see why not.'

'Let's consider it a plan. Put parmesan and brown and white normal mushrooms on the list there, will you, dear?' Elsie said.

'We'll bother to go the whole hog, then, will we?'

'Of course. I'm not cooking or serving you up an inferior meal. You know how particular I am,' Elsie said.

'Fair enough. I just meant –'

'I know what you meant. And I appreciate the concern, but it's fine. Just make a note for the morning to get out the dried porcini mushrooms, will you, there's a dear. There's a packet in the pantry.'

'Done. I'll just get them out ready. Though I rather fancy your wonderful mushroom risotto now. Sorry to only be serving up beans.'

He looked down at the unexciting meal on the plates in front of him. *Oh well.* 'It's ready – do you want it in front of the telly or at the table?'

'Here's good with me,' Elsie said.

Howard shuffled over and placed his plate on the coffee table and handed Elsie's to her. 'Anything to drink before I sit down?'

'I'd love a glass of milk, if it's on offer.'

'Your wish is my command.' Howard gave a little bow.

'You're the best,' Elsie said, smiling up at her husband as she wrapped her hand around the glass he now held out to her.

'As are you. Cheers,' Howard said when he'd got himself settled into his chair, plate on his lap, glass of milk in hand, which he raised.

'Bon appetite. To death cap mushrooms being the solution.'

'Yes, to your wonderful mushroom risotto.'

'Oh. And here's cheers to Sylvia, poor dear.'

'Yes, but at least she's no longer suffering.'

'Promise me you won't let that happen to me, Howard.'

'I promise – to the best of my ability, that is.'

'Thank you. As do I for you.'

'Thank you.' They both let out long contented sighs before picking up their cutlery and digging into their baked beans on toast.

Later they were back in their recliners after having tidied the kitchen. Elsie worked on a sudoku puzzle while Howard prodded away at his iPad, the TV acting as a backdrop.

'Dear?' Howard said suddenly. 'I think the mushroom idea is a bit dicey.'

'How's that?' Elsie asked, her pencil raised above the book in her lap.

'I've been doing some research.'

'And what have you found?'

'Death is not a sure thing and, if it does happen, is, by all accounts, quite slow. Ultimately, it's down to liver failure. Sounds really quite ghastly – that's what I'm thinking. Most people get better, but suffer ongoing effects after a pretty horrid, touch-and-go time, in hospital.' He shuddered at the thought.

'If there's someone to take them there or call an ambulance, that is,' Elsie pointed out. 'And we are not in that camp, though, are we?'

'No, that's true. But it's the lingering that bothers me. It can take up to several days to actually do the trick. Honestly, love, I couldn't watch you writhe around in pain and not call someone to treat you, if it came down to it.' *There's no way I have the stomach for that.*

'No, same goes for me about you. I see what you mean. Though, we could take the SIM cards out of the phones and destroy them so we couldn't call and deadlock the doors and hide the keys so we couldn't leave if we lost our nerve,' she suggested.

'All good ideas, I grant you. But if it causes diarrhoea and vomiting, think of the potential mess we'd be leaving behind. That's one of our main criteria, remember?'

'Damn it. Yes. Scrap that idea then?'

'I think so. Sorry.'

'It's not your fault. It has got me thinking, though. Do you think we should still go and get some anyway, in the interests of trying to secure several options?'

'Hmm. Let's leave the mushrooms for now. Anyway, the news report was rather vague about location – and it's the same situation online,' Howard mused.

'I wonder if we're maybe overthinking things a bit.'

'You're right. Because, really, so what, if we leave a bit of a mess?' Howard said.

'I was referring to generally, actually. Meaning, if we think it through too much, we'll never do it.' Elsie said.

'Ah, I see what you mean. Yes, you could be right there,' Howard said.

'Do you maybe think we're struggling because deep down we're reticent?' Elsie asked.

'No. Well, I can't speak for you, but I'm keen to go. Honestly, if you've changed your mind just say. I respect that we're in this together. Or not.'

'I haven't. I just want it to work. And without too much kerfuffle.'

'It's a pity we can't just go to the vet's like we thought we might have had to with dear old Maisie. Though I rather liked your idea about being shot out of a cannon,' Howard said.

'Hmm. At least it's giving us something interesting to ponder,' Elsie said.

'Yes. I haven't had such an interesting project in ages. I think I'd still like your lovely mushroom risotto tomorrow night, though, regardless. I can make it if you're not up for it.'

'We'll see. Play it by ear.'

'Roger that.'

'Do you think you could turn the electric blanket on next time you get up? I'm thinking of having an early night,' Elsie said.

'I'll do it now, before I forget. I'm going to sit up and watch the end of that movie about the conniving family of rogues I started the other day. Though I'm feeling a bit restless. Damn those bloody mushrooms,' he muttered, hoisting himself up.

Well, that's what Elsie thought he said. The squeak and squawk of shifting leather as he went about trying to get out of his chair was loud, as was the accompanying soundtrack of groans and audible struggle.

She looked across at him and smiled. How lucky after all this time that they not only still liked each other but they didn't get too bothered by their idiosyncrasies.

Several of their friends over the years had confided the desire to commit murder over snoring partners and the tiniest of annoying habits.

Howard had adopted plenty of little habits along the way, and no doubt she had too, but she just thought they added to his character. She found herself wondering if she'd miss him when she was dead. Was there anything afterwards? Even though they weren't remotely religious, they half-heartedly entertained the idea of reincarnation. Elsie had no idea why, but she liked the thought that some parts of them might keep on going.

She remembered how dear old Maisie had the tilt of her head that reminded her of Howard's mother. She didn't think she'd ever thought to mention it to Howard. Or perhaps she had. Ah, who would know? No, probably not, because they'd always walked from their bedroom to the loo naked, when getting ready for the day or bed, and there's no way Howard would have been comfortable doing that if there was an inkling their dog was actually the reincarnation or spirit, or whatever, of his long-lost mother.

Elsie thought she wouldn't mind coming back as a politician, now that she thought about it. Get those euthanasia laws loosened. Insert a clever loophole or two, ripe for exploration. First things first though ...

Chapter Ten

Elsie and Howard were in the car, engine running, waiting for the vehicles in front to leave the cemetery's car park.

'I don't suppose I ought to be grateful to attend a funeral or enjoy it,' Elsie said.

'No.'

'But that was fun, to see everyone.'

'And a nice change of scenery,' Howard said.

'Yes.'

'I'm going to miss Sylvia,' Elsie said.

'Are you, though? We haven't really seen her or Donald for eons. Definitely not since before Covid hit.'

'That's true. Oh well. You're probably right. It seems like yesterday, or maybe more like last week, we saw them.'

'I must say, those bikkies were very good. Did you have one?' Howard said.

'Which ones?'

'The shortbread with icing in between. What are they called again?'

'Melting moments, you mean?'

'Perhaps I do? Whatever they were, they were damned good.'

'I used to make them all the time. Don't you remember? Around the same time I used to do the huge batches of custard slice.'

'Custard slice, oh, yes, now I remember.'

'That's another loss of becoming old and retreating from the world – no more dessert baking for functions.'

'We could bake them for something to do. Couldn't we? Just because.'

'You mean now? Sure. If you want to get diabetes, or some such other health ailment,' Elsie said. Though she was starting to salivate.

'I'm not sure if I much care at this stage in proceedings.'

'Good point. Maybe we also stopped because of the cost of ingredients – that's why we stopped buying Tim Tams.'

'Oh, yes. True. Bugger.'

'Also, custard slice didn't freeze, so you'd be eating it for weeks.'

'I'm not seeing a problem there,' Howard said with a laugh. 'Why should we be so sensible at our age?'

'We've always been sensible, Howard – we can't blame that on our age. Might I remind you our profession was the height of sensible, dear?'

'True, I guess you don't get more sensible than a pair of law-abiding accountants. It was crowded there today,' Howard said as the traffic in front started to crawl forward.

'Yes. All that extended family. We wouldn't drum up much of a turnout, would we, given we're both only children? And so few friends left these days. And there goes another one, dear old Sylvia,' Elsie mused.

'Yes. I wonder if Donald will actually be glad to be alone now.'

'Howard! What a thing to say!'

'I know. But Sylvia did always tend to rub me up the wrong way.'

'You never said.'

'Well, I'm saying now.'

'We had them around for all those years until they moved to the nursing home.'

'Yes, and hasn't it been quite nice not having them pop in all the time?'

'Oh, Howard, you are being awful.'

'I think Donald always had a secret crush on you.'

'Not so secret, actually.'

'Oh, do tell.'

'He cornered me in the kitchen at their place. Must have been the seventies when talk of wife and husband swapping was rife.'

'Jesus. Why didn't you tell me?' *I'd have given him what-for, the bastard!*

'I didn't need you knocking his block off. I was quite capable of doing that myself. I whacked him across the side of the head with my handbag – the small but hard black patent leather one, if I recall correctly.'

'Oh, good for you. Gosh, I'm quite shaken to hear that, I must admit. So why did you keep inviting them over and insisting we go to their place so often?'

'Because they were generally rather good fun. Well, I thought so. And I don't recall you objecting. I actually really liked them both, especially listening to them regaling us with tales about their lives as diplomats. Fascinating, that was.'

'That's right. That's no doubt why there was such a big turnout today, too. I'd quite forgotten that.'

'Oh, Howard. You just sat through the eulogy saying exactly that very thing. For goodness' sake. You were right there.'

'I might have nodded off for a moment, or faded out. I became a bit mesmerised counting the panels in the lovely stained-glass window. Weren't they beautiful with the light catching them?'

'They were that.'

'It's lucky I didn't know Donald had made a pass at you. I might have said something to somebody back there.'

'And I bet no one would have so much as turned a hair. Most likely half the women there, or more, had had him make a pass or two or three at them over the years. I don't particularly feel flattered, given his form. He had player written all over him.'

'Gosh, today's proving quite the eye-opener. Consider my mind blown, as the young ones say. I must admit, it is a little perturbing that you've kept it such a secret. I thought we told each other everything.'

'Oh, Howard. You're very cute. You didn't tell me Brenda Elderton made a pass at you at the Kerrs' New Year's Eve do in 1979.'

'Did she?'

'Yes.'

'And if I didn't tell you, how do you know? And why haven't you said anything until now, or have you and *I've* forgotten? Am I losing my mind?' *Oh god. Please no*, Howard thought.

'I saw it with my own eyes. I think, though, you might have missed what she was up to, which is why I didn't say anything to you. Otherwise, I might have knocked your block off. Or left you. Why do you think I never left you alone with her after that night before they moved? And why we never kept in touch.'

'Gosh, I am unobservant, aren't I? I didn't notice you keeping me from being alone with her. And I've never really noticed or been bothered that we didn't keep in touch. What's wrong with my powers of observation?'

'You're a man, dear. It goes with the territory. And I don't suppose you noticed I was careful to never be alone with Donald, either? Including today.'

'Nope. But I sure am glad you were. So, you weren't tempted to run off with him and become part of one of his stories?'

'Exactly.'

'What's that supposed to mean?'

'That's all I would have been – a part. And a small one at that, I'd be betting. I've never wanted anyone but you, Howie.'

'Me too, Else. And that's not because I wouldn't know what to do. We're doing all right for ourselves, aren't we?' *Other than the obvious ravages of time, from which no area of life was exempt, damn it.*

'Yep, we sure are. Though these days – eyes back on the road, dear – I'd still choose you.'

'As would I. Oh, shit. Where did he come from?' Howard gasped as a cyclist sped around them from the left and a motor-cyclist darted in from the right before going left again and disappearing between the two lanes of traffic, which had suddenly stopped. His heart started to race and his mind clouded. Then everything began to slow around him, as if he was in a bubble or cloud or something.

'Brake, Howard! Stop!' Elsie shouted.

'Oh! Ah. Shit.' Howard braked, so close to the car in front that Elsie could practically see the expressions on the faces of the stick-figure family depicted on the decal in its rear window. If it hadn't been a hatch, they probably would have connected already. Elsie glanced into the side mirror. The grille of a truck filled her view. She could almost read the small print on its number plate. A loud blast sounded from its horn.

Christ! What the hell?! Howard looked around. He began to sweat.

Elsie gasped and then held her breath. *Oh god.* She clutched at the seatbelt stretched across her chest, pushed herself back into her seat and tensed up with her eyes closed in readiness of them being hit from behind and the airbags exploding out towards them in all directions. A screech of tyres was heard.

After what seemed an age of holding herself taut, waiting, her head and heart pounding, Elsie realised there had been no impact. She opened her eyes and looked around. The cyclist was off his bike and on the footpath, to her left, gesticulating and shrieking obscenities. She looked across at Howard. Fear, not anger, was written all over his face. The knuckles of both his hands were white on the steering wheel and sweat was beading on his forehead, despite the car's temperature set to eighteen degrees.

Howard couldn't think beyond the fact they were stopped and unharmed. He was staring ahead but not really seeing. His hands tightly clutching the steering wheel hurt but he couldn't seem to get his brain to move them.

'Dear, you'd better pull over,' Elsie finally managed to say.

Howard thought he heard Elsie speak. He turned and looked at her.

'Turn into that side street there,' she said pointing. But Howard was now slightly hunched over the wheel, still staring ahead, busy taking several gulping breaths. She noticed his arms were quivering. Elsie nudged him and he seemed to come out of his slight stupor. He turned his wide-eyed bewildered-looking face towards her slowly. She pointed again. 'Pull into that street there.'

'Oh. Yes. Good idea,' he stammered. 'Oh shit, I've stalled it.' *Damn it! Pull yourself together, Howard, and move the damned car off the main road before you do get hit.*

There was another blast from the truck behind them. Elsie looked up. The road ahead was clear, the previous cars they'd been close up behind now far off. Vehicles of all shapes and sizes rushed past them to their right, honking in varying tones like a haphazard and off-key orchestra.

Howard flapped his hand. 'Shut up, everyone. I'm trying to think.'

'Breathe, Howard,' Elsie said, placing her hand on his thigh.

Howard nodded and finally managed to get the car started and then carefully manoeuvre it into the next side street, though only just managing to stop in time to let another cyclist past before he did.

'Christ. What happened?' he asked, letting out several deep breaths as all the traffic on the main road they'd just left began to move again, though not before another few final angry honks. *So there! Take that! Yes, get off the road!* they seemed to Elsie to say.

'Perhaps keep your window up in case the cyclist comes over,' Elsie suggested. 'He's still just there,' she said, nodding. He was drinking from his water bottle, staring up the street.

'I didn't even see him,' Howard said. He was shaking, clammy all over and close to bursting into tears he was so befuddled.

Elsie didn't think it wise to point out right then that the cyclist couldn't have been more visible in his fluoro pink lycra if he'd tried. And she couldn't exactly cast aspersions – the circumstances were far too similar to her own frightening experience the other week. She'd been left very shaken and happy never to get behind the wheel again, which she hadn't as yet.

'Should I get out, do you think, and go and see if he's okay?' Howard asked, his face now red. 'He's not shouting, but I'm a little scared, to be honest.'

'Well, we didn't hit him. I think he's just trying to find his wits, like we are. Look, now he seems to be trying to get his feet clicked back into his pedals,' Elsie said.

'I feel I should apologise,' Howard said, 'for giving him a fright, at least.' He was torn between good manners and his fear and all the physical reactions he was experiencing. He doubted he'd be able to stand up if he did get out of the car.

'We didn't hit anyone. And we weren't the cause of the kerfuffle – it was him cutting in from the left and the motorbike darting about, in and out, and between the lanes like a demon, both of which I'm sure are against the rules,' Elsie pointed out.

'True. I guess. I'm shaking.'

'Do you want me to drive the rest of the way?' Elsie offered, though she held her breath in the hope he'd decline.

'Would you? Could you?' Howard was careful to restrain his relief.

'Okay. But just wait a few more minutes,' she said.

'No rush,' Howard said. 'Gosh, my reaction time is a worry,' he added.

'Probably lucky it wasn't quicker, else you might have collected the car in front,' Elsie said.

'Yes, that's a point. That makes me feel a little better. Thanks. Phew. Well, I say, that's rather got the heart pumping.' He took several more deep breaths. 'Good. Look, he's going now.' They both watched as the cyclist performed a U-turn on the side street and then re-entered the main road and carried on his way. 'Are you sure you're okay to drive?'

'Yes. Come on then.' Elsie wanted to escape to the comfort and safety of home as quickly as possible. She undid her seatbelt.

Elsie was glad Howard went behind the car to change sides and she around the front. If they'd hugged, she might have dissolved and not been any further use to anyone that day. Her legs were shaking as it was and her head was swimming.

As she adjusted her seat and the mirrors, she took several deep breaths. Out of the corner of her eye she could see Howard rubbing his hands over his face, which was still very red. She really hoped he wasn't going to have a heart attack or some other medical episode. She'd had quite enough excitement for one day.

Carefully she navigated the last few kilometres and only when the roller door came down behind the car did she really fully let out her breath. Part of each one she'd kept in the whole way.

'I don't think I've ever been so pleased to arrive home,' Howard announced. 'That was harrowing. Sorry, dear, I'm sure you got quite a fright too.'

'I'm okay. Are you, that's the question?'

'A little better, yes, thanks.'

'Good to hear.' She smiled at him.

As they went inside, Elsie sighed with relief at them both managing not to fall apart at the same time, though it had been a close call. They hugged.

'Thank you for stepping up when I needed you,' Howard said into her hair.

'Always,' Elsie said, breathing in his wonderful familiar scent, which never ceased to make her feel safe and secure.

They broke apart and leant against the kitchen bench, side by side. 'I think I'm going to not renew my driver's licence when it comes due next month,' Howard said a few minutes later. 'That'll save some palaver. And money.'

'Don't make rash decisions when you're in a state,' Elsie said. 'Though I do tend to agree. I'm still a bit jittery after my little encounter the other week.'

'You know, once either of those incidents would have been the tiniest of blips on the radar.'

'I know what you mean.'

'God, I hate being old and useless,' Howard said.

'You're not useless.'

'I feel it. One's driver's licence is such an ... oh, I don't know ... part of one's identity, I suppose. It's been in my wallet for over sixty years.'

'Mine too.'

'I'm in need of a rather large sherry for contemplation. How about you?' Howard said, pushing back from the cupboards and heading over to the wall unit in the lounge area.

'Yes, please.'

Chapter Eleven

'Come on, Howard, the girls are calling,' Elsie shouted to Howard in the study from her position at the kitchen table where she was seated with both her phone and Howard's in front of her ready for when their daughters called to speak to them both.

Corinne and Janine phoned each of their parents at random times, but still often, depending on how long since they'd spoken, called on a Sunday evening and always at around six, though it was a random selection as to which mobile they called. As they had done with their kids regarding dinners together on a Sunday and then when they had moved out of home or were off travelling – a phone call home on a Sunday. It had started because phone calls were cheaper on a Sunday. Somewhere along the way it had become Sunday after six pm, because phone calls were cheaper after six. Elsie couldn't recall if the after six bit was relevant to a Sunday or not.

But, anyway, here they were. Well, *she* was. Howard was still off fluffing about, doing goodness knows what. She glanced at the two phones waiting, face up. It was six.

Her mind drifted again. She smiled at remembering how the girls had ribbed them every time they — Howard and Elsie, that was — went on a trip, about how life had turned arse about, with the girls staying home and their parents off travelling. Their last words were always 'call to let us know you're okay'. Just as they had been Howard and Elsie's last words to Corinne and Janine as they went through the gate of the airport or got into the car or taxi at home. *Arse about*, Elsie thought. *You don't know the half of it. We're practically un-growing — gradually disappearing back into childhood. Bloody ageing.*

'Sorry about that. What have I missed?' Howard said, settling into the chair beside Elsie. He peered at the phones. 'Oh,' he said, realising the devices were blank, with just the home screen black and time and date visible in white. At that moment Elsie's handset began to ring. 'Good timing,' Howard said.

'Yes, perfect,' Elsie said, dragging her finger across the green spot to answer it. She poked and stabbed at the device. Damned thing; it always seemed to take several prods for her to get the call connected, or whatever it was called these days. She had no idea why she had so much bother with it. Howard never seemed to have any trouble with his and they were the same phones, the only difference being the covers on them: his plain black, hers bright pink.

'Hello, here we are,' she said, leaning over the table to speak over top of the device.

'And me,' Howard said, also hunching over.

'Hi, Mum, hi, Dad, we're both here,' Corinne and Janine said at the same time.

'Where exactly?' Howard said.

'Janine's place,' Corinne said.

Elsie smiled to herself. She loved that the girls had continued their tradition of eating as a family together at least once on Sundays. Sometimes it was lunch, other times dinner.

As both were only children, Howard and Elsie had been quite desperate in their early days to instil close family values in their girls. Not that they really had much to go by. And, of course, as they knew through observation of friends and other families over the years, there was only so much you could do. Hope was what it really came down to in the end.

'So, what's news?' Corinne said, clearly the leader on this call, despite their location. It was, after all, her phone they had called from. Though she often took charge, being the older, which made sense to Elsie. She was also the most confident – a trait of being the elder, or perhaps her star sign. Elsie didn't ever give it much thought. People were individuals and had their own personalities. Neither she nor Howard had ever tried to steer them towards being anything other than themselves. Janine was quite quiet and introspective. Corinne outgoing and brusque at times. Howard and Elsie had only really ever corrected either around kindness. They could be whoever they were, whatever job they wanted, go wherever and do whatever. But if either girl ever displayed rudeness or a lack of kindness, they stepped in. So far, at forty-eight and fifty-one, the girls were still friends with each other and their parents. They knew lots of families who had become fractured along the way, so Elsie and Howard were grateful for what they had. 'We've just eaten a magnificent roast lamb – late lunch, early dinner – with all the trimmings, prepared by the wonderful Sonia,' said Corinne.

'Fantastic. Hi, Sonia,' Howard and Elsie called to Janine's partner of five years. 'Is Stephen there too?'

'Yes, but they've headed out – Sonia went to get ice cream for dessert and Stephen's on a call,' Corinne said.

'They might be back in time to say hi, but if not … hi from them,' Janine said.

'So what's new with you guys?' Corinne asked.

'Nothing much, really, dears,' Elsie said.

'No. At our age it really is just a whole lot of sitting around waiting to die,' Howard said jovially. *Or, to be more accurate, looking for inspiration on how to.*

'So, still grumpy old buggers then?'

'Yep.'

'As I said, nothing has changed,' Elsie said.

'We're thinking of getting t-shirts made up stating this fact, and with advance warning for people to steer clear,' Howard said cheerfully.

Both Corinne and Janine laughed. 'Good idea. I'll have one, too, while you're at it,' Corinne said.

'And me,' Janine said. 'Honestly, perimenopause is a bastard.'

'As is postmenopause,' Corinne and Elsie said at the same time, before laughing at their synchronicity.

'Sadly, it never really ends. Well, hasn't for me,' Elsie said. 'So, remain buckled, lovelies.'

'God,' Corinne said.

'Yes, that's just bloody brilliant – not,' Janine said.

'But on the upside, our annual heating bill has gone down,' Howard chipped in, 'on account of your mother always being hot in the temperature department.'

'Are you heading into too-much-information territory, Dad?' Corinne asked.

'Probably,' Howard said, chuckling. 'Oh. But then there's the added electricity needed to run all the fans. Lose–lose.'

'Yes, dear, thank you. Is it pick on Elsie day today?' Elsie asked.

'Sorry, dear. See, I did warn you all that I'm being a grumpy old bugger.' Howard's heart sank at noticing the slight pique to Elsie's tone. *Too far, mate, you're being an arse*, he silently chided.

'What else have you been up to?' Corinne asked.

'Funerals, groceries, doctor's appointments. I think that's about it,' Elsie said.

'Who's died now?' Corinne said.

'Yes. Anyone we know?'

'Sylvia Pilkington,' Howard and Elsie said at the same time.

'Oh. That's sad,' Janine said. 'Are you guys okay? You were friends forever.'

'Yes and no. We're getting rather used to losing friends and learning not to dwell too much, aren't we, Howard?' Elsie said.

'Exactly. As we've said, our age is all about sitting waiting to die. We're resigned,' Howard said.

'God. How depressing,' Janine said.

'Yes,' Corinne agreed. 'Are you okay? I mean, are you depressed? You sound it.'

'No. Sad, a bit lonely, maybe, but accepting of the reality,' Howard said.

'That's about it,' Elsie said.

'Are you still involved with the tennis club at all?'

'No. We never really went back after Covid,' Elsie said.

'And, anyway, our former teams have been decimated,' Howard added.

'Cards?' Janine said.

'Again same thing, pretty much,' Howard said.

'Oh, I'm so sorry,' Corinne said.

'Yes, it doesn't sound good,' Janine said.

'It's fine. Plenty to do here, what with the mountains of spam emails I get to wade through,' Howard said. He often wondered if they were all scammers or if some were actually legitimate companies. Though he couldn't see why a genuine well-run organisation would bombard people with information and offers if they'd never contacted said business.

'What do you mean?' Corinne said.

'I hope you haven't clicked on any of them or any links,' Janine said.

'We're old and boring and invisible, dears, but we're not stupid.'

Howard nodded. He had been tempted a few times to check some out online but so far had refrained. The last thing he needed was to inadvertently set off a technological avalanche of catastrophic proportions one couldn't recover from.

'So why are you spending time on spam?' Corinne said.

'He's teaching the email by marking them, isn't that right, Howard?' Elsie said.

'Yes, some bastard must have sold our email address to a million different people. I'm getting around three hundred a day.'

'Christ,' Janine said.

'Change your address,' Corinne suggested.

'But we've both had our addresses forever.'

'Which is exactly why every man and his dog knows them, most likely,' Janine said.

'But everyone we know has them, too,' Howard said.

'Didn't you say everyone you know has pretty much died, anyway? God, sorry, that sounded so insensitive,' Corinne said.

'It's true though,' Elsie said thoughtfully. 'Howard, maybe we should.'

'But there's the banks and all the official type places. It would be a pain in the arse to do, not to mention remembering who needs to be advised,' Howard said. 'Bloody email.'

'Yes. Fair enough,' Janine said.

'Can we help you with anything?' Corinne asked.

'No, we're fine,' Elsie said.

'We're okay, thanks – just grumpy,' Howard said. *Even more so now you've got me thinking about the bloody email!*

'Did you say you've been to doctor's appointments?' Corinne asked. 'Are you okay? Is something wrong?'

'No, not recently. Figure of speech, really – just the usual monitoring. Wait till you get to our age. There's a lot of maintaining: teeth, eyes – optometrist and ophthalmologist – prostate and breasts, bowels, and all the bits and pieces.'

'Yes,' Elsie said. 'I've no idea how we used to have time to do all the things we did. Anyway, please, enough about us and our boring life and old people grumbling. Tell us what you've been up to.'

'Well, my life probably isn't any more exciting than yours,' Corinne said with a laugh.

'Same,' Janine said. 'Work, gym or walk or run. Cook meals, watch TV, read books. That's about it.'

'Yep, that's all,' Corinne said.

'Any plans to travel?' Howard asked.

'Not really, still dreaming,' Corinne said.

'Me too,' Janine said.

'Where will you go, do you think?' Elsie asked.

'Italy, maybe,' Corinne said.

'I'm not so sure,' Janine said. 'I've been too busy to think about it and I'm concerned still about travel insurance changes. It's risky.'

'Remember, it was like that after the terrorist attacks?' Howard said.

'I do. The travel companies all added terms to their PDSs about not covering anything to do with terrorism. That put us off a bit didn't it, Howard?'

'Yes, but then we accepted that if your time is up your time is up. And of course there's plenty to see here at home.'

'Also true.'

'Though I think every second man and his dog is still roaming around here for the same reason,' Howard said. 'You'll figure it out. Or not. Doesn't matter.'

'And you're sure you guys are okay?' Corinne asked again.

'Oh, yes, aren't we, dear?' Howard said, placing a hand on one of Elsie's.

'We're as good as can be expected at our age, I think. Nothing to complain about really.'

'You do realise you're not actually old?' Janine said.

'Yes, seventy-eight isn't, really, in the scheme of things these days,' Corinne said.

'So they say. We beg to differ,' Howard said jovially. 'You wait until you become invisible and slow with people rushing by you, bumping you or bustling past in their hurry.' *Hopefully things will be different when your time comes. But right now, best you don't get me started!*

'It's a metaphor for the life leaving us,' Elsie said.

'Oh, come on, you two. Stop it,' Corinne said.

'You're too funny,' Janine said. 'Go jump out of a plane or something fun.'

'Now that's a good idea,' Elsie said, looking at Howard with raised eyebrows.

He shook his head. 'No, thanks. Remember that balloon ride we took?' Howard's spine tingled in response to remembering how terrified he'd been.

'Oh god. Yes. I thought we were all going to die,' Elsie said.

'Exactly. It landed far too abruptly for my liking. And that was in a basket. I shudder to think how it would be trying to land on our feet strapped to someone, without the basket. Anyway, I've always said I don't see the point of jumping out of a perfectly working plane.'

'I remain of that view,' Elsie said.

'Anyway, I don't think my heart would take it,' Howard said.

'Oh. Is there something wrong in that department? Something you haven't told us?' Corinne said.

'No, we're both as fit as fiddles, as we've already said,' Howard said. 'Stop taking everything we say so literally, or pessimistically.'

'But we worry about you,' Corinne said.

'Yes,' Janine said.

'And we appreciate it,' Howard said.

'We really do,' Elsie reiterated. 'But other than not enjoying this ageing business one bit, we're fine.'

'Just have to hang in there, as they say,' Howard said.

'Well, if you need anything –' Corinne said.

'Yes, anything at all,' Janine chimed in.

'– you are to tell us. Is that clear?' Corinne said.

'Yes, perfectly,' Elsie said.

'Got it.'

'I've got to go – that's the doorbell,' Janine said.

'Thanks for the call. Love you both,' Howard said.

'Yes. Love from me,' Elsie said. 'Have fun until we speak again.'

'You too. See ya,' Janine and Corinne said at the same time.

Elsie and Howard sat staring at the phone after the call had been disconnected. Elsie felt hollow, a little cast adrift or something. She couldn't really put a finger on it. She loved talking to the girls, but there was so little to discuss these days, especially nothing much to laugh about. It was all so dull.

'They sounded tired and overworked,' Howard said.

'Yes. I got that impression, too. Though it didn't help we had nothing of interest to share.'

'Well, we can't really, can we. If we own up to our plans …'

'Yes, can you imagine the uproar? And the incident with the mattress was funny, but I think would cause them to worry.'

'I agree.'

'I don't like being old.'

'No. This we have established.'

'I need a sherry. Want one?' Elsie said, getting up.

'Oh. Go on then.'

'What's the hesitation?'

'The last couple of nights it's given me a spot of indigestion.'

'Well, that's no good. Port wouldn't be any better, would it?' Elsie said, now at the bar area by the built-in bookshelves.

'No. Probably not. Not to worry – give me a sherry, anyway. I'll have a Milo afterwards, that might help.'

'Okey-dokey.'

'Actually, scrap that. I'll just have a hot Milo.'

'Make up your mind, dear,' Elsie said, putting the stopper back in the decanter.

'I have. I'm making myself a Milo,' he said, getting up.

'Do you think we should share our plans with the girls?' Howard called to Elsie seated in her recliner, hands wrapped around her glass of sherry, as the kettle roared behind him.

'I don't think we'd better. If the police get involved for some reason it would be best for them to know nothing, right?'

'Oh, yes, good point. Proving they didn't know anything or didn't help us, whichever way we chose to go, could be tricky.'

'And traumatic,' Elsie added.

'Yes, I imagine they'll be annoyed enough at any rate.'

'Hmm. Or grateful we spared them the horrors that some friends and parents go through.'

'It's hard to have conversations with them. I don't like us being so guarded. It's not how we've always been and certainly not how we raised them to be.'

'No, it's a bit of a mess. And we haven't even done anything yet.'

'Before I forget, about the jumping out of a plane: not workable, either – unless we spent a fortune on lessons to be able to jump ourselves, no, thank you. And anyway, if we could get through that to jump on our own, we'd get the company in trouble and it would involve the coroner, et cetera – major ruckus to cause some poor small-business operator.'

'Yes. I see what you mean.'

'Oh. Oh. I forgot to tell you. That show I finished watching – the one with the fighting family of rogues?'

Elsie looked over at Howard, eyebrows raised.

'Well, right at the end they had a scene where the old bloke – the patriarch, most evil of them all – killed himself by drinking from a small vial of what turned out to be liquid potassium, supplied by the family doctor. You can imagine the excitement I had.'

'And ...?'

'Nothing. I googled the shit out of the iPad and damned if it wasn't a bum steer. I was so disappointed – for the obvious reason – but that show, right the way through, seemed so realistic. Well, up until that point. It was quite the letdown all round, I can tell you.'

'Yes. No, that's no good. On either front. I'm sorry, I know how much you were enjoying that show.'

'Ah, it's all so bloody complicated,' Howard said.

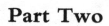

Part Two

Chapter Twelve

'Here we are, see what you think of this,' Howard said, coming over to the table, having just retrieved the pages from the printer and stapled them together.

'It's rather long, isn't it?' Elsie said, accepting the document and flicking through it.

'Probably. But we need to make ourselves clear, and also ensure there won't be any police investigation.'

'You're right. I'll give it a full read-through – just in case.'

'Well, don't get too picky – just look for any typos I might have done.'

'I know some of the lines and rhymes are a little wonky – it was a joint effort, remember? And I'm not about to go changing things around – I'm a little over the whole thing, to be honest. I'm quite certain the girls will have zero appreciation for the fact we left them this.'

'True. But it has kept us entertained for a while. I enjoyed doing it. I can't think why I haven't dabbled in poetry during retirement – or some other writing for that matter …'

'I enjoyed doing it too. Now, Howard, my love, can you please let me read in peace for a bit.'

'Roger that, dear.' Howard linked his hands and waited while Elsie read.

To our darling daughters, Corinne and Janine,
Please forgive us, we're not doing this to be mean.

Howard and Elsie want to die,
They've had enough of this life-is-good total lie.

We've left this earth before turning seventy-nine,
Before life plays its cruel tricks and we're less than fine.

We made a pact, you see,
Many years ago, that never apart we would be.

You know we lost all our parents before this age,
So it's time for us to escape this awful cage.

Without quality of life, we're not prepared to take the chance,
We're keen to go, without a backwards glance.

We haven't taken this decision lightly,
But needed to while still relatively sprightly.

We've known each other right from the start,
And couldn't bear to be apart.

It's something we won't contemplate,
Our heartbreak would really be too great.

Daughters, we love you both — you've been the best we could have asked for.
You've made us very proud, and being your parents has never been a chore.

Please, you're not to blame,
So, no guilt — that is not our aim.

There has been no coercion involved,
This is equally our choice, we are resolved.

We've given this decision a lot of thought,
Please don't think we're feeling fraught.

Not with this, on this we're clear and calm,
And hope this knowledge will provide a balm.

We're not ill or depressed, the spark has just left these old folk,
Though there's also a chance we'll soon be broke.

Though before we go, we need an extra little mumble,
About the state of things, we'd like to grumble.

You see, being an oldie even when things are relatively hunky dory,
It's still not much chop for our era with the kids flouting their glory.

We scrimped and saved and carved out a great life,
Only to find discrimination and criticism to be rife.

We elderly are invisible in the world, we go completely unseen,
Which I'm sure you can imagine causes life to lose its sheen.

We get pushed and shoved out of the way,
By all and sundry, each and every day.

Whether it's physical or just being forgotten,
By young ones or the government, it's all rather rotten.

There seems to be a general loathing,
And we're discarded, just like old clothing.

The environment is ruined, everything's a mess,
It's too much to bear, we must confess.

Too much waste and lack of care,
Has made everything seem beyond repair.

All and sundry with their fancy needs,
Have ruined this earth, so much it bleeds.

We've lost our friends, too – there's barely any left,
Going to so many funerals, leaves us really quite bereft.

These are the best years of our life, they say,
Because we have all day to play.

But with interest rates at next to nil,
Life as an oldie is quite the bitter pill.

Resources are getting low,
So it's really time to go.

We're sorry to not be leaving you with more,
But you've done well and will continue to, we're sure.

We wish we could be shot off into space,
But, alas, that's not the case.

We've tidied and sorted, put everything to rights,
So our passing will be less of a blight.

Our affairs are in order, with all details on the thumb drive,
To make everything easy for when you arrive.

If you are reading this we have moved along.
We've shuffled off, completely gone.

For Howard and Elsie, it's time to snuff out the flame,
It's our choice, and no one is to blame.

Just please don't be mad,
All our love, Mum and Dad.

'Other than being a little long and unwieldy, and repetitive in spots, I think that works – covers everything, anyway. Do you think in the first line we should have included mention of Stephen and Sonia? They are like family?'

'Hmm. Why didn't we think of that before? It's a valid point, but it'll muck things up no end. No, let's just leave it as is. I'm a bit weary of it too. And if we start changing things again, we'll be doing it forever.'

'Okay. Fair enough. They'll understand, I'm sure.'

'I'm not sure about anything to do with how they'll react, Else,' Howard said. 'Probably best we won't be here to know.'

'So, we're signing – our full signatures – down the bottom, for further clarity?' Elsie said, picking up a pen from the table.

'Yes, I think so. Though it's unlikely anyone will think a drug cartel or some such organisation will have left a calling card of this ilk,' Howard mused as Elsie scribbled.

Elsie chuckled. 'At least you watching all those detective shows hasn't been in vain, dear. Here you go – your turn,' she said, handing over the pen.

'Right,' Howard said, adding his signature. 'Good job, dear. I'm rather proud of our poem,' he added, holding up the document and gazing longingly at the first page.

Chapter Thirteen

'Darling, what's that you've got there?' Howard asked as Elsie dragged a small basket into the car and onto her lap.

'Snacks,' she said.

'We're not going on a picnic, my love. We're not going anywhere. Remember?'

'Of course I remember. But we have no idea how long this is going to take. And as you know, I like to be prepared.'

'Righteo. I guess. Probably a good idea. We could be here for minutes or hours.'

'Ready, then?'

'Yes.'

Howard turned the car on and sat back with his hands loosely linked in his lap and his eyes closed. Elsie did the same, though her hands were resting on top of the basket in her lap.

Some time later – Elsie wasn't sure how much time had passed – Howard began shuffling about, clearly bored. Elsie was trying very hard not to shuffle as well. She kept her eyes closed and tried to ignore him.

'I'm not sure I have the patience for this,' Howard said. 'I need a distraction. What have you got in the basket?'

'I thought you'd never ask,' Elsie said, grinning at him. 'Right. Books to read — a light novel or a self-help type one. Chosen for no other reason than their small size.' She held them up. 'Your choice.'

'No, you choose — I'll take the one you don't want,' Howard said.

'Okay. Here.' She handed over the self-help paperback.

'It's a little late for this, isn't it, dear?' he said, looking at her with his eyebrows raised. 'Being as we're here and all,' he said.

'Next time bring your own choice of book.'

'Well, I'm hoping there won't be a next time.'

'True.' Elsie opened the novel and began to read, quickly becoming engrossed. She turned the pages, settling into the rhythm of the story.

'Nope, I'm not feeling it,' Howard said beside her, letting out an exasperated grunt and folding and unfolding his arms, causing the car to move slightly underneath him.

'Turn the radio on and listen to the music, or something,' Elsie suggested without looking up. *Just be still and quiet!* she shouted in her mind.

The sound of classical music filled the car — the mournful tunes of a string quartet.

'Please, not that — it's depressing,' Elsie said.

'I thought it quite appropriate, given the situation. But I can change it. What would you prefer? Something cheerful?'

'I don't really care, my love. I'm happy reading.'

The station was changed and a burst of pop music came through the speakers. Just as Elsie thought, *Oh I don't mind that,* and before she could utter these words, the dial was moved again. Talkback now blasted out.

'No crusty old men inciting division in the community,' Howard muttered and leant forward again to turn the knob. What sounded like the voice of a preacher was up next.

Elsie closed her eyes and mentally shook her head with exasperation.

'Let us pray,' said the voice.

'How about we don't,' Howard said. And then the cabin was silent except for the hum of the car's engine outside. 'Shouldn't we be feeling sleepy by now?' Howard asked.

'I have no idea,' Elsie said. 'You're the one who came up with this idea. You did do some research, didn't you?' She closed the book and looked at Howard.

'Not really, no. I didn't think it was warranted. Attach a pipe to the exhaust, pop it through the window and Bob's your uncle. I would have thought.'

'But you always do research.' Elsie turned in her seat – first one way and then the other. 'And, which window?' she asked.

'Sorry? What? Oh.' He turned around to look towards the back. 'Shit. I must have forgotten that bit. Damn it.'

'I'll do it.' Elsie got out and went to the back of the car. There was a slight smell of exhaust fumes in the large space, but it was barely oppressive. She stood looking down at the exhaust, her hands on her hips, shaking her head and frowning.

A moment later Howard was beside her, his mannerisms mirroring hers.

'How in the world do you think it's going to work using the garden hose, anyway? Forget that you haven't actually directed it into the vehicle – it's got to go through, what is it, fifteen metres of hose? – before it goes anywhere. I thought you were all over this, Howard.'

'Hmm.' Howard scratched his head. 'All very good points. I'm losing my sharps. Sorry.'

'I thought you would have done some measuring, bought a length of pipe the correct size of the exhaust pipe, connected it, tucked the other end into the window, and sealed it up with duct tape and plastic. Isn't that what everyone else does?'

'No idea. Yes, you're quite right. I have rather made a mess of things. Do you want to abort mission, then?'

'Well, we're here now – let's just open the car windows and do it that way,' Elsie said, pulling the end of the garden hose from the much larger exhaust pipe.

'It'll probably just take longer than however long it was going to take before,' Howard said.

'Which we don't have a clue about, anyway, remember? Oh, Howard, really?'

'Sorry, dear.'

'Let's just get back in the car. I'm actually quite enjoying my book. I must have read it before, but can't recall the story it all. Come on.'

They resettled in their seats.

'I don't think we really need a seatbelt, either,' Howard said. 'But, oh well. Force of habit and all that,' he said, the device giving a loud click. 'Wind the windows all down.' He pressed one button after the other. 'There we are.'

'Please, my love, can we do this without the running commentary?'

'Actually, I'm not sure I can. I'm bored. What else is there in that basket?'

Silently Elsie handed him the basket, keeping her eyes on her book.

'Ooh, cheese and crackers. Goodie,' Howard said. 'Want some?'

Elsie took several deep breaths while staring at the last line she'd just read for a few moments. Then she closed the book. 'Oh, go on, then, may as well make a day of it.'

'You've done well with this, my dear. Bravo,' Howard said, fossicking through the basket.

Better than you did with your allocated task, Elsie thought. But the last thing she needed was to die annoyed. Beside her was her best friend of seventy-odd years. This was their last mission together. 'Sorry I was a bit crotchety,' she said, smiling warmly at Howard.

'That's okay. I understand. Not to worry. I'm sorry I've become ditsy when you counted on me having my act together. Let's just enjoy this, shall we, since you've gone to the effort with the treats. Again, bravo.'

'Thanks. Yes. Good idea. Actually, forget the cheese for me for a bit. Pass the liquorice, will you?'

'Your wish is my command.'

They sat there devouring their sticks of liquorice, staring out the windscreen at the back of the garage wall.

'Oh, I need the loo now,' Elsie said as she wiped her hands on a tissue she'd dragged out from her sleeve. 'Back in a sec.'

'Okay. Oh. I think I'll go too. We don't want to leave a mess. I'm not sure if we will or not when we go.'

'I think we'll, um, evacuate everything.'

'Yes, that's right, I've read about that along the way.'

'Still, I don't fancy sitting in a wet patch,' Elsie said. 'We'll want to leave the car running, remember?'

'Oh, yes. Of course. It really goes against one's instincts, doesn't it?' Howard said, turning the car back on.

'This whole thing does,' Elsie said, opening her door.

'That's true.'

Out of the car, Elsie turned her nose up at the stench of exhaust fumes around her. She walked into the kitchen, followed by Howard. They separated – Elsie ducked into the powder room and Howard carried on up the passage to their ensuite.

After flushing and washing her hands, Elsie waited in the hall for Howard.

'Shall we carry on?' he said, picking up her hand as he passed.

'Right,' Howard said, settling back into the car. 'Can never be too safe,' he chuckled as he did his seatbelt back up again.

'Exactly,' Elsie said, clicking her own buckle closed and grinning at him as she did.

'Okay. Where were we? Chocolate next?'

'Good idea. It should be right at the bottom, under the thermos. We don't want to make ourselves queasy, though, do we?'

'I hardly think it matters if we do, my love.'

'Yes, of course, silly me. In that case, hand over a whole row, dear.'

They munched and sucked on their squares of rum and raisin chocolate, moaning and groaning with pleasure.

'I say, this is the life,' Howard said.

'Or death,' Elsie said.

'Quite. Yes, quite right.'

'No regrets?'

'No regrets.' He clasped her hand briefly before letting it go. 'That's better. I feel more relaxed now. I'm going to try reading again,' Howard said.

'Good. I will too. Just pop the basket on the back seat if it's in your way,' Elsie said. 'Or pass it here. It makes quite the good book rest.'

'That's what I've just discovered, actually. Or would you rather have it to use for that purpose?'

'No, I'm all good.'

'Okey-dokey, then.' He leant over and gave her a peck on the cheek. 'Sweet reading. Sweet dreams.'

'And you,' Elsie said, patting his hand and then opening her book again. She let out a long sigh as she sank back into the story.

Sometime later Elsie looked up and frowned. She glanced across at Howard, who was engrossed in his book. *We seem to have been quietly reading for ages. How long does it take to die like this? Or at least slip into a coma? Or have I already? Maybe this is what being dead is like. No different to living, really, though.* She concentrated on listening. Something was definitely different. Ah, it was quieter than before.

'Howard?'

'Yes, dear?' he said, without looking up from his book.

Elsie noticed he'd read about a third of the paperback. She checked the novel in her own hands. She was about a third the way in as well. Oh, yes, that's right, the husband in the story had just confronted his wife over her affair.

'Are we dead?' she asked.

'No, I don't think so. I'm not sure, now you ask.' He closed his book and looked at her.

'This is taking an awfully long time.'

'It is,' he said. 'I agree.' They checked their watches in unison.

'Oh,' Howard said, now staring at the instrument panel on the dash, perplexed.

'What?' Elsie said and leant across to follow his gaze.

'I think the car has stopped.'

'Oh. That's what's different. You're right. Shit. What now?'

'I think we've run out of fuel.'

'Oh, Howard. You're kidding?'

'No, unfortunately not.'

'Why didn't you fill it up?'

'Because that would be a waste of money, what with us no longer needing it and all. I've really ballsed this up, haven't I? Sorry, my dear.'

'It's okay.'

'What shall we do now?'

'Abort mission, I think. Find another way. I wouldn't mind finishing this book now I've started it,' Elsie said.

'We can call the RAA and get them to bring fuel later. Oh. Except we can't because I cancelled the membership.'

'Of course. And we can't go out and get any, because the car won't go. You didn't cancel the registration on the car, did you?'

'No. Nor the insurance – again, so the girls can use the car. I've left the house and contents covered too.'

'Good thinking. Thank goodness one of us is on the ball. Let's go in then.'

'Windows up.'

'Yes. We don't want next door's cat getting in and peeing on the upholstery.'

Howard turned the ignition off after putting all the windows back up, and they got out. Howard with picnic basket in hand and Elsie with her book and handbag. At the door into the house Howard clicked the car's remote.

'I know it can't be driven, but can't be too careful,' he said.

'Quite right. Now, cup of tea. I'm parched,' Elsie said. 'Get the thermos out – no point wasting it.'

'Oh, yes. Here we are,' he said, dragging it out and placing it on the bench next to the basket.

'I'll put all this away later,' Elsie said.

'Okay. Perfectly fine with me.'

'Should we find a movie to watch?'

'Yes. Good idea.'

'I'll start looking. Bring the chocolate, will you?' she said, taking the thermos over to her recliner.

'Okay. In a bit. I need the loo again. Bloody prostate, bladder, or whatever it is. I swear, just the mention of tea,' he muttered as he left the room.

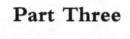

Part Three

Part Three

Chapter Fourteen

'I think it's my turn,' Howard said as they heard the doorbell at the front door ring. He put the paper on the coffee table, placed his reading glasses on top, closed the recliner, and got up slowly.

'God, it takes so bloody long to do anything these days,' he muttered to himself as he made his way to the hall, hoping the person wouldn't get tired of waiting and leave. Or, worse, ring the bell again. Though when the last person had knocked on the door, unsolicited, he couldn't recall.

People dropping in unannounced had largely ceased during Covid and not really started up again. That was one thing Howard and Elsie often remarked upon; that no one ever really popped in anymore. Though they didn't do any dropping in anywhere themselves either. Everyone seemed so into being in their own personal space and privacy. He couldn't say he missed the cold-calling salespeople. Gone online and infested the email instead, he supposed.

Struggling to keep his slippers on his feet, he realised, made him shuffle more than his age should have. When he had proper shoes on, he could get up quite a clip, when he wanted to. It still wasn't the same without Maisie by his side – when would he get used to her absence? – not that she'd been able to take much exercise near the end. He looked down at his slippers and frowned. He probably should have slipped on the leather ones. Actually, why weren't they here at the door? He paused before reminding himself he was meant to be doing something. *Oh yes. Concentrate. I'm answering the door.*

'Coming,' he called. He wondered if he was leaving little lines of track marks in the carpet that he'd vacuumed earlier, taking great care to leave it looking smooth – all one colour. He liked the whole surface to look perfect, and often got lost tending to it. A bit like a white gravel Japanese garden he supposed. Or snow. They'd done plenty of snow trips in the early days. And spent a bit of time in Japan wandering the pristine tranquil gardens. Each time they'd come home and discuss putting one in. But they'd never got any further than that. It would mean reorganising everything and pulling up roses and well-established shrubs. It all seemed a waste of time, energy and money, and in a couple of weeks the topic would fall by the wayside. Oh well, it was all too late, they'd be gone soon. Hopefully. Though, they'd had to go back to the drawing board with that plan. He opened the door.

'Hello there,' he said, nodding to the small child of about eight or nine standing in front of him holding a plastic domed container he could see held some sort of brightly coloured something underneath. 'Hello,' he repeated, now raising a hand to the person standing behind her, who must be her father – a young chap, early to mid-thirties, Howard suspected. Though age of people was a bit of a mystery to him these days. Everyone seemed young.

'Hello. I'm Millicent Wynter – that's Wynter with a Y, not an I. And Milly for short, to my friends – also with a Y and not an

I. Ha!' she said lightly, grinning. 'Anyway, I think we're going to be very good friends,' she added, her tone and expression serious again. 'And this is my dad, Daniel Wynter.' She indicated to the left and slightly behind her with her head, to which the accompanying man responded with a raised hand and a nod.

'We're your new neighbours. We've just moved in next door. Over there. On that side,' Milly continued, seemingly without a breath. She indicated to her right with her head. 'So, I made you some cupcakes to celebrate. Do you like cupcakes? I looove cupcakes. All cakes, really, but maybe cupcakes the best.'

Howard blinked as he struggled to keep up with the fast pace of words. He wondered if her father – Daniel, was it? – too was trying to stifle laughter or perhaps he was too used to her to be so affected.

'Oh, yes, very much. I like cupcakes too. Yum,' he added for emphasis, in an effort to hide his amused bewilderment and the fact he was quite lost and definitely a little behind in the conversation. He found himself smiling, though he was holding back the urge to let out a joyful guffaw.

'Here you are.' Milly pushed the container towards Howard. He placed his hands on either side of it in order to accept it from her. But then she paused and looked at him with narrowed eyes and mouth in a serious, slightly puckered line. 'You're not gluten-free are you? Or allergic to anything else?'

Howard shook his head. 'Um,' he said as he felt his cracked old leathery heart moving inside his chest. *Oh, what a lovely young lass.*

'Anything that might be in cakes, that is? Not medications and that sort of thing. There are no nuts. Nuts are a big no-no all over the place, so I rarely use them in baking for other people anyway. You have to be sooo careful. So many rules,' she added with such an exaggerated roll of her big brown eyes that Howard almost lost control of the bubble of amusement growing inside him and had to fold his lips in on themselves in an effort to keep his composure.

He cleared his throat in order to try to speak. 'No. No allergies of that nature, that I'm aware,' he finally managed. He was beginning to feel buoyant, so much so that he wouldn't have been surprised to look down and find he was floating a foot or more above the ground.

'They're chocolate with pink icing. I hope that's okay,' Milly said.

'That sounds just perfect,' Howard said, beaming at her.

'Brilliant,' she said. 'Well, here you go – they're all yours,' she said joyfully and pushed the container towards him a little more before letting go.

'Thank you very much, Milly. I'm Howard. Howard Manning, by the way,' he said, finally realising he hadn't said that already. Well, he didn't think he had. The last few moments – had it only been that long? – had been a whirlwind.

'I'm Daniel. Daniel Wynter,' the man said. 'I'm just the sous-chef and escort,' he added, moving forward a little and giving a nod.

'It's lovely to meet you both. Would you like to come in?' Howard asked, beginning to feel more like his previous self again.

Though he had the strangest feeling – more comforting than concerning – that something had shifted within him and he wasn't quite that same person he'd been deep inside before he'd opened the door mere moments ago. His mind drifted as he tried to pinpoint what he was feeling. It was like the reverse of déjà vu, wasn't it – not feeling you'd been there before, but the feeling that you were going somewhere important, only you didn't know where, how or why? No, probably nothing like déjà vu in reverse at all, he thought vaguely, letting it all go.

'Oh. Well, we don't want to intrude,' Milly said, bringing Howard fully back. Her hands were linked together in front of her denim shorts overalls, a bright pink top visible underneath that matched what he could see of the icing on the cupcakes he held.

'You wouldn't be intruding it all,' Howard said, beaming. 'But please don't feel you have to stay.'

'Yes, please,' Milly said, stepping forward confidently, causing Howard to have to step aside in case she bumped into him.

Daniel smiled at Howard, nodded his head, and followed his daughter.

'Would you like us to take our shoes off?' Milly asked, pausing just inside the door. She hadn't moved more than a step into the hall and Howard almost collided with her. Daniel was beside her, clearly awaiting the answer to Milly's question. He had one foot lifted slightly and was partially bending down while holding onto the architrave with one hand.

'Ah, no, that's okay. Lovely of you to ask, though,' Howard said. *What beautiful manners.*

'Are you sure?' Daniel said.

'Perfectly.' Howard enjoyed a little sigh of contentment to himself as he closed the front door behind them. 'This way,' he said. 'Elsie, we have visitors,' he called loudly, to give her time to prepare. Though she had about two seconds. Too bad if she'd suddenly decided to rip off her bra, or her top, or was doing something risqué.

What Elsie was doing was still extracting herself, with difficulty, from the plush confines of her recliner when Howard, Milly and Daniel exited the hall into the main area.

'This is my wife, Elsie,' Howard said to the newcomers. 'Elsie, this is Milly and Daniel Wynter. They've moved in next door. On that side.' He pointed. 'Milly has made us cupcakes. Isn't that lovely?'

'Wonderful. Hello there, Milly and Daniel. Lovely to meet you.'

Howard noticed Elsie's hand extend a little before retreating again to grip her other in a clasp.

'Sorry, no hand-shaking,' she said, cringing. 'I did okay with remembering during the pandemic, but now everything's back to sort-of normal I keep reverting to old, well-established habits,' she explained. 'And I'm rambling. Sorry. Would you like a cuppa and one of these lovely cakes?' She peered through the lid. 'Yummy.'

'They're chocolate with pink icing,' Milly announced.

'My favourites,' Elsie said. 'Did you make them?'

'Oh, yes. Though Dad supervised. I have to be careful with using the microwave. I had to melt some butter. And, I'm not allowed to use the oven yet, so Dad had to put them in and then get them out again when they were cooked.'

'Brilliant. You're very clever. Come over and sit at the table.'

'I'll put the kettle on,' said Howard. 'What can I get you, Daniel?'

'Tea, if you have it, thank you. White with one sugar. However it comes, strength-wise.'

'Any preference for variety? We have quite a selection of loose teas, you see ...' Howard stopped, telling himself, *Just the tea, Howard, he doesn't need a lecture too.*

'Oh. Something like English breakfast. Really, whatever you're having along those lines.'

'That's what we like – an easy-going guest,' Howard said. 'I'm hit and miss with remembering to take out the leaves. I have a tendency to forget and get lost in my own thoughts.'

'I can help,' Milly said, leaping up from the chair she'd just that moment sat down on and rushing to Howard's side.

'Brilliant. Thank you. Tea and coffee are in that cupboard, along with mugs and spoons there,' he said, pointing. 'The tea we want is in the blue tin with the swirls. Can you reach okay?'

'Yes, thank you. This is a pretty tin.'

'Thank you. We've had it many years.'

'I like that you don't use tea bags,' Milly said, peering into the tin of loose tea leaves.

'Yes, we very much like tea and are quite particular about its quality. Tea bags are very convenient, but, um …' He stopped, aware of the impressionable child beside him hanging on, and most likely soaking up, his every word. He didn't want to come across as a pompous old git.

'An unnecessary burden on the environment?' Milly said.

Howard almost lost his composure, his shock the only thing that stopped him bursting into laughter. 'Yes. You're quite right,' he said sagely.

'They both pollute *and* require the use of chemicals to produce. Yucky.'

'Exactly.' *We're going to be great friends, Milly*, Howard thought, smiling to himself.

Howard filled the kettle, put it back on the base, and turned it on.

'Would it be okay if I have Milo?' Milly asked, turning back from the open cupboard. 'I'm too young for caffeine,' she added.

'Of course. Yes. Milo it is. There's hot chocolate in there, too – probably at the back – if you'd prefer.'

'I'm good, thanks.'

'So, if you don't like tea bags, either, you'll know how to put the tea in one of these, then?' Howard said, holding up one of the three single-cup infusers he'd just got out of the drawer along with a handful of teaspoons.

'I sure do, Mr Manning,' Milly said, accepting the diffuser, which she deftly opened. 'Fill them to here?' she asked, pointing.

'Yep,' he said and then watched, impressed and slightly mesmerised, as Milly carefully filled each diffuser with tea, avoiding spilling even a leaf, and then placing them into mugs, followed by level spoons of sugar.

'Like that?' she asked, looking up at him.

'Perfect,' he said, smiling down at her.

They then stood together, side by side, watching and waiting for the kettle to boil. It seemed unusually loud and Howard felt the need to say something in the stretching absence of voices.

'Actually,' Howard said, 'I think I'm going to have Milo too. You've inspired me, Milly. Elsie? Daniel?' he called. 'Would you rather Milo or hot chocolate instead?'

'I'm good with tea, thanks, dear,' Elsie said.

'Me too, thanks, Howard.'

'Righteo.' He turned back to see Milly taking the diffuser out of the mug and then carefully opening it and tipping the tea back into the tin.

'Sorry to upset the applecart,' he said.

'It's no problem at all,' Milly said. 'Do you want sugar still or shall I tip it back into the jar, too?'

'Yes, please tip it back. You're a very good helper.' As soon as he'd said the words, he cursed sounding like a patronising old git. But he'd wanted to say something. The kid was a cracker – in the best possible way.

'Thank you,' she said cheerfully, without a hint of annoyance.

'Right. How much Milo do you like, Milly?'

'How much can I have?' Milly asked.

'Milly,' Daniel called in a warning tone.

'As many as you like,' Howard said. 'I do three rounded teaspoons.' He held up the loaded spoon with his hand cupped underneath to show Milly and so Daniel could also see.

'Okay, that's fine,' Daniel said.

'Good with you, Milly?'

'Yep. Sounds good to me, Mr Manning. Can I do it?'

'You sure can,' Howard said, stepping back a little.

'This one's yours – like this?' she asked, holding up a teaspoon mounded with Milo.

'That's perfect.'

He waited silently while she counted out two more spoons into his mug and then three into the other mug, noticing her lips moving – either counting or from being deep in thought – as she did. 'There we are,' she said, putting the lid back on the Milo tin and pressing down hard.

'Brilliant. How about I pour the water? I might have made it pretty heavy. And you can tell me when. When to stop, that is.'

'Okey-dokey, sounds like a plan, Mr Manning.' Howard and Milly grinned at each other.

'Now, I like my Milo half and half – half water and half milk, that is,' Howard said. 'How about you, Milly?'

'Would it be okay if I had it like that too?'

'Of course.'

'Dad?' Milly called.

'Fine with me, if it's fine with Mr Manning.'

Howard watched her shoulders do a little jig, like part of a dance, and while she didn't say anything, imagined her saying 'yay' or 'cool'. No, 'yay' was what the young ones said these days, wasn't it?

'Now, the other thing we need to decide is if we want the milk or hot water to go in first. It's serious business, this Milo making, Milly,' Howard said.

'Oh, yes, I know,' Milly said, matching Howard's solemn tone.

'So, what's it to be?'

'Um. Water first, I reckon,' Milly said with a decisive nod after a moment's consideration. 'Definitely.'

'Good choice. Okay, ready? Tell me when.' He poured slowly.

Milly stood on tippy toes peering into the mug from a safe distance. 'When,' she said. 'Right there, thank you. That's perfect, thanks, Mr Manning.'

Howard felt the sudden urge put an arm around Milly's shoulder and give the darling kid a squeeze. But he stopped himself. The world was rife with stories of dirty old men and being inappropriate with youngsters, preying on children, the whole stranger-danger messaging and what have you. Was one allowed to or not allowed to show any affection these days? Christ, what a minefield.

'Righteo, Milly, do you think you can manage to carry two, or should I get a tray out?'

'I'll be all right if you will be,' she said, smiling up at him. He took in the serenity plastered across her face. She reminded him of their daughters Corinne and Janine – those precious years after toddler tantrums and before puberty hit. Lots of joyful times, he remembered. And then, as if in just a few years, they'd left home.

'Okay, Mr Manning?' Milly said, dislodging his thoughts.

'Yep, good to go,' he said.

'This looks like a perfect cup of tea, thank you, Howard and Milly,' Elsie said.

'Yes, thank you,' Daniel said. 'Good job, kiddo.'

'Great job, Milly,' Howard said, beaming at her.

'Thank you,' she said.

'Would you like to do the honours with the cupcakes, Milly?' Elsie said.

'Sure thing, Mrs Manning.'

'Thank you,' Howard and Elsie both said when a cupcake was deposited in front of them on a folded serviette.

'You come prepared, I'm very impressed,' Howard said.

'I'm a thinker,' Milly said sagely.

Howard again had to pull his lips together in on themselves to stop the laughter bubbling up inside him from escaping.

With her task complete, Milly sat back in her chair with a satisfied expression on her face – like a queen surveying her subjects, Howard thought. He then noticed out the corner of his eye Milly carefully placing her hands in the same way around her own mug of Milo as he had his. *Aww, darling thing.* To test his new shadow, he lifted the cup to take a sip. Sure enough, Milly followed. *Sweet,* he thought. But his heart went out to her as he wondered if she was desperate for grandparent-like figures in her life. Did she have any grandparents?

'It's a very good cup of Milo, Mr Manning,' Milly said as she put the mug down, again in the same way Howard just had.

'Why thank you, Milly, though you did most of the work – so you should be congratulating yourself.'

Milly smiled up at him.

He took another sip from his drink to distract himself, but as he did, realised it might be a bad idea – he was at risk of spitting it out and embarrassing himself if she became any cuter or more precocious.

'So are you going to be a baker when you grow up?' Elsie said after she'd peeled the paper off and taken a bite through the pink icing and swallowed her first mouthful. 'This is delicious. And very moist.'

'I'm glad,' Milly said. 'I'm not sure yet – I like lots of different things. Maybe I'll do something to do with the environment or waste management. The planet is a disaster and needs some serious help.'

'Yes, I quite agree,' Elsie said.

'I like to help,' Milly said.

'I can see that,' Elsie said.

'Anyway, I have plenty of time to decide. And it's not like the old days when you stayed in one job forever, is it, Dad?'

'Exactly, kiddo. No need to get set on a path too soon,' Daniel said.

'There's too much pressure on them at school to decide, I think,' Daniel explained, looking from Howard to Elsie. 'It's why I do what I do. I'm a teacher – science – and career counsellor,' he said. 'I was a carpenter before – I'm not long out of uni after getting my teaching degree.'

'That's fantastic. I'm sure you'll be brilliant,' Howard said.

'We'll see. I start next week.'

'Are you from Adelaide?' Elsie asked.

'No. Sydney – so, we're brand-new imports, you could say.'

'Fabulous,' Elsie said. And then she and Howard said at the same time, 'Well, welcome.'

'Thank you.'

'Is it just the two of you?' Howard ventured, and then a beat later, 'Sorry, there's me being nosey. Don't feel the need to answer.' He waved his hand dismissively.

'Not at all,' Daniel said. He paused and then opened his mouth to speak, but Milly got in first.

'My mum's name was Amy and she died when I was a few days old, but Dad tells me all about her,' she said in a volley of words, clearly having said this exact thing many times before.

'Oh, Milly. Daniel, I'm so sorry,' Elsie said. Her heart clenched.

Howard experienced a wave of sadness. 'Yes. I'm really sorry to hear that,' he said, cursing the inadequacy of his words and ability to adequately convey his true feelings. He wanted to wrap the darling little kid in his arms and never let her go. He ached inside.

'Thank you,' Milly said.

'Yes, thanks. It's been hard, but we're doing okay, aren't we, kiddo?'

'Totally. And I think we're going to be even better now we're living at number eighteen Mercy Court. I can feel it! Um, would you like plain or maybe carrot cake next time?' Milly asked a beat later. 'I can do the proper cream cheese icing, which is super yum,' she added, proudly.

'Oh, that's very generous of you, Milly,' Howard said, a little lost for words. 'But please don't feel you have to bring cake whenever you visit. It will be lovely just to see you,' he said, stammering slightly.

'We don't want to crowd Mr and Mrs Manning, Milly,' Daniel warned.

'Sorry. Yes.' Milly looked a little downcast and Howard's soul reached out to soothe her.

Elsie wanted to stroke the child's cheek, tell her it was okay, that they didn't mind a bit – that she was a darling, just the way she was. But Milly wasn't their child and they had to respect her own parent's views and teaching.

'It's quite all right. And I love all varieties of cake, I think. Thanks for asking,' Howard said quietly, causing her to brighten again. He leant down to Milly. 'And you're welcome to visit anytime. You're quite the breath of fresh air. Right, Elsie?'

'Oh, yes. Absolutely. To all of the above.'

'So please do feel free to pop in anytime. You've simply made my day,' Howard said.

'And mine,' Elsie said.

'You're welcome to visit us anytime, too, right, Dad?' Milly said.

'Absolutely. Yes, please feel free to drop in anytime, to visit or if you need anything,' Daniel said.

'Okay. Great. Thanks,' Howard said. 'We look forward to it.' *I think we're going to be firm friends*, Howard thought, beaming. He had the urge to clap his hands in glee, but kept them wrapped around his mug. He took another sip, as did Milly.

'So, are you retired, Elsie and Howard?' Daniel asked.

'Yes. We were both accountants, running our own business, until around fifteen years ago.' Feeling so at ease with the delightful newcomers, Howard almost added: *And now we're sitting around looking for a way to die because we're bored and jaded with it all*. He bit his tongue. Maybe Daniel could help with that. Except that would break one of the most important rules – not involving others. Damn. Oh well, things were certainly brighter today, anyway, that was for sure, thanks to this delightful interlude.

'Do you have grandkids?' Milly asked.

'No. We don't. We have two daughters. But they haven't had kids.'

'Okay,' Milly said, nodding thoughtfully.

'They both live interstate – in Melbourne,' Elsie said.

Howard searched for a safe topic for discussion, and suspected Elsie was doing the same – he could practically feel her cogs turning from across the table. They were out of practice with meeting new people, especially children. Actually, he couldn't remember when they'd last met a child for the first time. Thankfully at that moment Daniel spoke, breaking the silence. He didn't know how long they'd been sitting there not speaking – hopefully not too long, though time did quite often tend to morph and do weird things.

'Well, thank you so much for your hospitality, but we'd better get back to our unpacking, hadn't we, Milly Wynter?' he said, pushing back his chair and getting up once they'd finished their drinks and cake.

'Would you like to take the rest of your cakes with you?' Elsie said, getting up.

'No, that's okay. I have some more at home. You can keep them. Unless you don't want to?' Milly looked at them.

'Oh no. We'd love to keep them, wouldn't we, Howard?'

'Yes. Yum. It won't be long before I'll be keen for another.'

'Cool,' she said, smiling. She stood up. 'Shall I tidy up for you?' she asked, looking down at the table.

'Oh no, just leave everything there, thanks,' Elsie said.

'Okay.'

'Would you like to take your container? We can easily get one out to put the cakes in,' Howard said.

'That's okay, Mr Manning. I can get it another time. I'm right next door,' Milly said, carefully tucking her vacated chair back under the table.

'You can come back anytime, Milly. I really mean that,' Howard said.

'Yes,' Elsie reiterated. 'And thank you again for the wonderful cakes. But please don't think you have to bring anything when you visit – just your delightful self or selves would be lovely.'

'Really?' Milly said, her eyes big, making her young again, rather than the old soul that seemed to poke through sometimes.

'Yes, really and truly,' Elsie said, smiling warmly.

They all got up and walked through the kitchen and down the hall. Out on the step beyond the open front door, Milly threw herself against Howard for a hug and then did the same to Elsie. And then without a word, but a huge smile, exited in front of her father, and skipped out onto the driveway.

'Thank you again,' Daniel said. And then in a quieter, lower tone, 'And please do tell me if she becomes a bother. Here, let me give you my number.' He pulled out his phone from his back pocket.

'Hang on, I'll just get our phones and give you our numbers too,' Howard said and headed back inside.

'It's a good idea to swap numbers, just in case. But not because we think for a second Milly will be a bother. Honestly,' Elsie said quietly. 'She has completely brightened my day,' she reiterated as they waited in the hall for Howard to return. She peered out and saw Milly twirling around in the driveway, her arms spread wide, giving the impression of a ballerina. Daniel turned to follow Elsie's gaze. 'We truly do mean it that she's welcome to drop by anytime,' she said.

'She really is a great kid,' he said. 'Most of the time. But careful what you offer – she can be a bit tornado-like,' he added with a laugh.

'Well, we'll see how we go. I promise we'll have a quiet and gentle word with you if we need to. But I'm sure we won't.'

'Right, here we are. Sorry about that. Forgot I put them both on to charge – and in different rooms.' Howard appeared again, looking a little flustered and frowning and shaking his head. 'Here, probably easiest if you put the numbers in – I have the speed and dexterity of a sloth these days,' he said. He stabbed in the code and then handed the first device over to Daniel with a grin.

'Right. There we are,' Daniel said when he'd finished putting his number into Howard's and Elsie's phones and Howard had read out theirs for him to put into his own before tucking it back into his back pocket.

'Great,' Howard said.

'Well, you know where we are if you need anything,' Daniel said. 'Do feel free to call anytime.'

'Same goes for us,' Howard said.

'Yes. Absolutely,' Elsie added. They stood in the open doorway watching Daniel make his way down the driveway to Milly.

Howard and Elsie smiled as Milly turned and waved, which they returned, before turning back around and moving close to Daniel as they carried on down the driveway.

Howard waited until they were out of sight before closing the door behind him and Elsie. 'Well,' he said, turning to her. 'How absolutely delightful!'

'Yes, a wonderful interlude.'

'I feel quite energised after that. But also exhausted, if that makes any sense,' Howard said as they tidied up.

'Completely,' Elsie said. 'Because I'm a bit the same way.'

'Fancy cooking on her own like that at that age,' Elsie said.

'Yes, she'll go a long way in life,' Howard said. 'Good head on her shoulders, and delightful to boot,' he added.

They settled back into their recliners. Howard squelched around as if having trouble getting comfortable, his movements accompanied by grunts and groans. After a few moments the only sound was the hum of the fridge. Elsie had picked up her crossword but couldn't seem to get re-focussed, so just stared at the page. Milly and Daniel's visit had left her feeling both buoyed and unsettled. She frowned to herself as she tried to unpack it: *It's nice to have such lovely new neighbours. But having a small child in such close proximity brings with it certain obligations, doesn't it? No, obligations isn't quite the right word. Complications? Yes, that certainly fits. But that's not what I was after. It's ... Damn. What is that word?* Elsie scrunched up her face in order to dislodge the word she could feel she almost had. *Considerations! That's the one. We can't very well ...* The clunk of the fridge startled her slightly and she listened to the usual long groan and gurgle then final metallic shudder as it fell silent again.

At that moment Howard spoke. 'Elsie?'

'Yes, dear?' Elsie looked up and over at him.

'I've been thinking.'

'I hope you didn't strain anything,' she said, smiling with her eyebrows raised.

'Very funny. I'm being serious.'

'Okay. Go on.'

'You know how we haven't found a decent exit solution yet?'

'I do.' Elsie sat up a little straighter.

'I'm again going to look into getting a robotic vacuum cleaner – seriously this time.'

'Oh.' That wasn't at all what Elsie thought he was going to say. 'Okay.'

'If that's okay with you?' Howard asked, picking up on the slight surprise in her tone.

'Of course. We've talked about this, Howard, and it's up to you.'

'I know, but you'll have to put up with it buzzing around. I think I might get one, actually – for getting under things, so I don't have to bend down so much.'

'You don't have to sell the concept to me, Howard – vacuuming is your territory. As long as you can make it work with the budget.'

Howard gave a decisive nod and began extricating himself from his chair.

Chapter Fifteen

Elsie sat cross-legged on the lawn at the edge of the rose bed, pulling weeds. She was grateful she still could, though standing up again was where the issue would be. She had moved a little far away from the gardening kneeling seat that she could use to hoist herself up. It was a glorious late autumn day to be out. She looked around, forgetting for a moment Maisie wasn't here anymore, expecting to see the darling form curled up or stretched out nearby or snuffling around amongst the roses.

Elsie looked up every time she sensed or heard movement beyond their property, ready to welcome or greet a passer-by – there weren't many due to it being a cul-de-sac, which meant no through-traffic; foot or otherwise. Most people who passed by the houses without front fences and with lawns and low planting growing right to the kerb were neighbours or those who had missed the delineation that it was a court and driven in by mistake. Three people had walked past, but not one had returned Elsie's wave. It made her sad to think how things had become – no one really knew anyone anymore. No one simply popped in for a cup of tea, either. Though no doubt she was being unusually morose and hard on society, thanks to her grief over Maisie, who should have been beside her.

Milly and her dad were delightful, and had seemingly ignored this modern convention. That thought made Elsie smile. She tilted her face into the sun for a moment, ignoring the threat of UV rays – though she had on plenty of sunscreen under the broad-brimmed hat she wore.

Back to her weeding, movement again caught her eye. A car. Oh, speak – well, rather *think* – of the devil. She raised her hand to Milly and Daniel as they pulled into their driveway a few metres away and then disappeared on the other side of the thick pittosporum screening. She smiled at Milly's enthusiastic waving as she returned to her task. The heavy cloak of sadness and loneliness still hung around her, but she was significantly buoyed.

Lost in her rhythmic pulling of the short weeds and putting them aside in a neat pile, Elsie was slightly startled to again see movement beside her – this time human. A pair of small shiny black shoes and white socks were in view. She then saw bare legs and a chequered blue and white school dress as she looked up to find Milly standing nearby.

'Hello, Mrs Manning,' Milly said.

'Hello, Milly. How was school?'

'Okay. Nothing exciting happened, but that's okay because nothing bad happened either,' Milly said and gave a nonchalant shrug. Elsie's whole heart expanded and peace swept through her. She ached to reach out and pull the child close.

'Well, that's good,' she said instead.

'May I sit down?' Milly asked.

'Of course. Will your dad mind if you get a bit dirty?'

'I don't think so. I'll be careful. And, really, it's only dirt, isn't it?'

'That's true,' Elsie said.

'Would you like some help, or would you prefer to do it by yourself?' Milly was now seated cross-legged beside Elsie. 'We can just keep each other company, if you like.'

'I'd love some help, thanks. Thanks for asking,' Elsie said, smiling at Milly.

Side by side, they silently pulled the weeds.

'Can I ask you something, Mrs Manning?' Milly asked a little while later. 'You don't have to answer.'

'Oh. Okay. Sure. Go ahead.'

'Why are you sad?' Milly asked.

Oh. 'Today? Or in general?' Elsie asked.

'Um. Today?' Milly said. 'It's just … You seemed really down just before – or were you thinking or concentrating or something?'

'Bit of both, Milly. I was thinking how much I was missing the company of our dear old dog, Maisie. She was very old and died a little while ago. So, yes, I am a bit sad, generally. She was wonderful company. Especially when I was gardening.'

'Was she a creamy coloured dog with black and brown bits?'

'That's right. She was a German Shepherd.'

'A beautiful dog.'

'Yes, she was wonderful.' Elsie's eyes filled with tears and she struggled to swallow the lump suddenly present in her throat. When Milly got onto her knees and wrapped her arms around Elsie's shoulders, she thought she might weep. When the little girl put her head on her shoulder, she did. Neither said a word for the next few moments.

Elsie smiled when Milly began to rub her back and then said, 'Do you feel a little better now?'

'Yes, thank you. I'm sorry about that,' Elsie said, wiping her eyes with her sleeve and then blowing her nose after locating a tissue up the second sleeve she checked.

'You should never apologise for tears,' Milly said sagely. 'They're important. Well, that's what my dad says.'

'He's a very smart man, is your dad,' Elsie said, smiling at Milly.

'Yes. I know. Though sometimes he can be very annoying.'

'Ah, but that's sometimes a parent's job,' Elsie said, leaning over and giving Milly a quick hug. 'Keeps you on your toes, I bet.'

'Oh, yes. Did you have any brothers or sisters growing up? I don't have any sisters or brothers,' Milly said.

'No. Neither Mr Manning nor I have any siblings.'

'Snap.'

'Yes, snap. Do you mind not having any brothers or sisters, Milly?'

'I don't think so. I don't know what I haven't known. Does that make sense? I think that's how Dad says it.'

'Sounds about right to me.'

'Maisie had a great life with you and Mr Manning,' Milly said, abruptly changing the subject.

'Honestly, I think we were the lucky ones,' Elsie said. 'She brought a lot of joy to our lives.'

'Will you get another dog, do you think – when it's not too soon? Dad says that about meeting someone else – a lady. He needs to not be sad anymore about Mum.'

Elsie nodded, searching for the right thing to say. Thankfully Milly continued before it became awkward.

'I don't know how long that takes,' she added with a shrug.

'As long as it takes, I think, Milly. Grief – losing someone – changes you forever. You can come to terms with it, but things never completely feel the same as before.'

Milly nodded thoughtfully, in the same manner Elsie had a moment ago, while staring at the ground in front of her.

'I still miss my two grandparents who died when I was little. I don't remember them very well. But I remember they made me feel good. My gran's hugs felt like yours do.'

'I'm glad, Milly. Though I'm sorry to bring the mood down. I hope I haven't made you sad,' Elsie said.

'It's okay. I like thinking about them, even if it makes me sad. Does that make sense?'

'It sure does.'

'And, anyway, it's my fault,' Milly said. 'I asked you about something sad first. Guess what?'

'What's that, Milly?'

'We're getting three chooks – reddish-brown ones. They'll lay brown eggs, apparently. Or, that's what Dad says. We'll see.'

'I think he's right about the brown eggs coming from brown chooks,' Elsie said. 'We had some growing up and that was certainly the case. White eggs from the white chooks, too.'

'I meant they might not lay eggs at all.'

'Oh?'

'They're rescue chooks, so they might be too upset. We'll see, I guess. I don't mind. They'll be good company. I just hope they don't peck.'

'No, that would not be very good,' Elsie said. 'I'm sure it'll be fine.'

'Do you and Mr Manning like eggs, Mrs Manning?'

'Oh yes. Very much. Do you, Milly?'

'Yes. My favourite thing for breakfast is a poached egg – especially when the yellow yolk is runny and the white is set.'

'Me too. I love them boiled as well,' Elsie said.

'Me too. Runny, and with toast soldiers. Actually, I think I like eggs any way they come.'

'I'd agree with that.'

'How about pavlova?'

'Oh yes – that's a very good use for eggs. Have you made one yourself, Milly? They take some patience to get just right.'

'No, I haven't made one yet, but my gran used to make a yummy one that was soft and squishy inside and crunchy on the outside. Cream and fresh berries on top. Yum.'

'Yes, yum,' Elsie agreed. 'My mouth is watering now.'

'Mine too,' Milly said.

'When are you getting your chooks?' Elsie asked.

'In a few days, when Dad has got the proper house set up. He said there might be cats out at night, not foxes, so they have to be locked up safe. He says I'm not allowed to have them in my room.'

Elsie laughed. 'That's probably a good idea,' she said. 'Chooks can make quite a mess.'

'Yes, they have runny poo. I'm going to work on Dad,' Milly said with a decisive nod.

'Good for you, Milly.'

Milly and Elsie shared a smile.

Elsie noted the gleam in the small child's eye and thought her father didn't stand a chance.

'We're also going to do dog fostering, or puppies, or whatever, when we get more settled,' Milly said.

'That's a lovely idea. You don't think you'll get too attached? I think I would,' Elsie said.

'I know what fostering is. I have a friend at school who has foster parents. He has a real mum too – it's *complicated*,' she said dramatically. 'I don't know, maybe it'll be fine knowing they're going off to make other people happy.'

'True. That's a good way to look at it.'

'Well, we'll see,' Milly said again, sounding like a much older person.

Milly returned her attention to the weeding and they fell silent.

After a few more minutes, she sat back on her heels from the clear garden bed around the roses and said, 'Are you going to plant something in here now or leave it bare?'

'Bare, I think,' Elsie said, sitting back with Milly.

'I have an idea,' Milly said.

'What's that?'

'You don't have to agree – it's just an idea, really.'

'Okay?'

'Well, you could plant some forget-me-nots flowers to remember your dog Maisie – that's what Dad and I do every year in our garden; to remember my mum and my grandparents. They are really pretty.'

'I think that's a wonderful idea, Milly. Thank you.'

'You're welcome. Also?'

'Yes?'

'Do you think I could have your weeds and household scraps for the chooks when I get them?'

'Yes, you absolutely can. You tell me when you get them and maybe we can leave a container outside for you to help yourself.'

'That's a good idea, too.'

'We'll work it all out later.'

'I hope they'll be happy with us. They've had a tough life.'

'I'm sure they'll love living with you and your dad, Milly.'

'I'd better go and help Dad with dinner,' Milly said getting up. 'Would you like a hand getting up?' she said, holding out a hand to Elsie.

'Perhaps if you could just pass that thing, thanks, that would be a big help. I might be too heavy for you to help.' She pointed towards the device.

Milly brought the stand over. 'Here?' she said. 'Is that the right spot?'

'I think so, thank you. I'll give it a shot,' Elsie said.

Milly stood with her hand on the edge of the stand just out of the way.

'There we are,' Elsie said, with slight relief, when she was back on her feet. 'Thank you very much for your help with this, and the weeding,' Elsie said.

'You're welcome.' Milly gave Elsie a quick hug and then skipped off down the driveway. Elsie waited until she'd disappeared around the corner and then carried the stand into the garage.

'How was the lovely Milly today?' Howard asked from the kitchen table where he sat with the newspaper spread out in front of him. 'I poked my head out before when I heard voices, but you looked deep in conversation, so didn't think I would disturb you.'

'She really is a delightful little girl. I might have to change my view on the younger generation.'

'Yes. Quite.'

'They're getting three chooks soon.'

'Ah, lovely. I do rather like the sounds of busy chickens.'

'She also suggested planting some forget-me-not seeds out there under the roses to remember Maisie.'

'Oh, that's a lovely thought. You did have quite the chat, then, didn't you?'

'Yes, it cheered me up no end.'

'I'm glad. Cup of tea? Then I'll see to firing up the slow cooker for dinner.'

'Perfect – times two. Howard?'

'Yes, dear?'

'Milly wouldn't have seen the photos of Maisie, would she? They came right through, didn't they?'

'Why do you ask?'

'It was just something she said. She seemed to know what Maisie looked like.'

'Oh, she's probably psychic, or something. Maybe Maisie's ghost or spirit, or what have you, was out there with you in the garden.'

'Really, Howard, you do say the most extraordinary things.' Elsie let out a stifled laugh.

'Come on, that's exactly what you were thinking, wasn't it?'

'I was, actually,' Elsie said, sitting down at the table. 'I just had the strangest feeling. I can't describe it.'

'Don't they say lots of kids are psychic, or have metaphysical abilities, before adults drum it into them that they're being silly? Same thing with creativity; we – adults, generally, I mean – make them self-conscious with all our judgement rather than just letting them have fun.'

'Hmm.'

'Don't think about it too much, dear. Some things can't be explained and you lose some of the magic by trying to fit them into boxes.'

'Listen to you being all mystical.'

Howard shrugged. 'Just making an observation, my dear. Anyway, if it makes you feel any better, she might have caught a glimpse of the photos of Maisie over on the shelf – her vision would be a damned sight better than our old peepers.'

'True. You're right, though, it doesn't matter.'

Chapter Sixteen

Elsie had just finished a sudoku and was deliberating whether to start another or get herself a cup of tea when the doorbell rang.

'I'll get it,' she called to Howard, who was ensconced in the study tapping away at the keyboard, squinting at the screen in front of him and frowning. She smiled. It was impossible to know if he was frowning because of what he was reading or because he was having trouble making out what was on the screen. Or if that expression was set for the day. He waved his hand in acknowledgement but kept on with whatever he was doing. Sometimes Elsie thought she should take an interest, but also figured he could equally include her if he wished. She'd invited him to help with sudoku in the early days of her doing them but he decided they were not for him. She'd refrained from reminding him of the similarity to his many spreadsheets of their budgeting and expenses and household schedules. *Howard does so love a spreadsheet, and numbers generally! Apparently though not when they're in someone else's format and must only add up to nine*, she thought, as she made her way up the hall.

'I'm coming. Just give me a few moments,' she called. Elsie opened the door tentatively, wondering as she did if it would be a collector for some charity or other. She didn't think they had a delivery due. Though Howard didn't always declare what he had ordered and when. Nor did she, for that matter – if it was from her own account. Her face immediately began to beam at seeing Milly standing in front of her.

'Hello there, Milly,' she said.

'Hello, Mrs Manning.'

'Are you collecting for something?' Elsie asked, noticing the child had something tucked under her arm and her hands were demurely clasped in front of her. 'For the Girl Guides or Brownies, or something else?' she added in response to the slightly frowning face and slowly shaking head.

'Oh!' Milly finally said. 'You mean biscuits or donations? I'm not a member of a group like that. I joined back at our old place, but the girls weren't very nice, so I left.'

Elsie tried not to laugh at the child's forthrightness and serious tone. *Good for you*, she thought. 'Girls, well lots of people, actually, can be very unkind,' she said.

'Yes. Unfortunately, that's what happens when they aren't happy inside and don't like themselves very much,' Milly said matter-of-factly before letting out a sigh.

'Sorry, here's me not being very polite,' Elsie said. 'Can I help you with something?'

'Yes. I have a favour to ask.'

'Oh. Okay.'

'It's all right. It's not a very big one.'

'And would you like to come in?'

'Yes, please, if that's okay. I'm not interrupting anything, am I?' Milly said.

'Not at all. It's really lovely to see you.'

'Thank you. It's very nice to see you too.'

'How's your dad?' Elsie asked as she closed the front door while Milly waited in the hall.

'He's very well, thank you.'

'Right, come on in. Howard,' she called, 'we have a visitor. Milly from next door is here.'

'Hi, Milly, don't mind me. I'm fighting with the computer,' Howard called, leaning back from the desk in his chair to see where Milly now stood with Elsie just behind her.

'Is there anything I can help you with, Mr Manning?' Milly said. 'I'm quite good with computers.'

'Oh. Now that's very useful to know. Would you, by any chance, know how to change the screen back? I've accidentally pressed something, or a series of somethings, and my screen is now blank. It's never happened before − well, if it has, I don't remember.' He held up his hands in a gesture of helplessness and frustration.

'Oh yes,' Milly said. 'I've done this loads of times. It happens to Dad quite often − drives him bonkers too. Shall I look?' Milly was now standing beside Howard.

'Yes, please. Just watch your foot and I'll back out of the way. Would you like to sit?'

'No, I'm good, thanks. It'll take two seconds,' Milly said.

'Okey dokey.' Howard rolled his chair back and glanced at Elsie. They grinned at each other.

Elsie would bet Howard was feeling just like her; that the wintry gloom had just become radiant, thanks to the cheerful presence of young Milly.

After a couple of taps on the keys, Milly said, 'There you go,' and stepped out of the way.

'Brilliant! Thank you so much!' Howard said. 'That was quick.'

'You're very welcome.'

'You can drop in anytime, Milly,' Howard said.

'Thanks. And you can ask me anytime, if you need help.'

'Would you like a Milo as a thank you, or anything else?' Howard said.

'Um. I actually came in to ask a favour.' Milly looked from Howard to Elsie.

'Go ahead, dear,' Elsie said.

'Yes, anything. You've just saved my sanity,' Howard said.

'Well … I was wondering …'

Suddenly the earlier confidence seemed to leave Milly and she became shy and demure, and even cuter, if that was possible, Elsie thought.

'Yes?' Howard and Elsie prompted at the same time.

'Um. Dad likes to supervise my reading, not because we *have* to for school or anything, but because … well, I'm not sure, really. But we both like doing it — we take turns reading, actually. Anyway, he's a bit busy at the moment — school stuff. So, I was wondering if you'd like to keep me company while I do it. If it's a bother, it's fine, I can wait until he's available. But I just thought I'd ask.'

'I would love to,' Elsie said.

'Me too,' Howard said. 'Unless three's a crowd,' he added, grinning in an effort to put the little girl at ease. 'I'd be happy to take a turn too, if you like.'

'You would?' Milly said, her cheeks flushed.

'Yes. Absolutely.'

'I'm really not disturbing you?'

'Not at all. At our age we're thrilled to be given something to do, aren't we, Elsie?' Howard said.

'Yes, this is true.'

'Thank you very much. It won't take long.'

'Milly, we've all the time in the world. Honestly. Your dad knows you're here, though, doesn't he?' Howard said, suddenly concerned.

'Yes, I left a note. As I said, he's a bit busy. And, just between us, he can get a bit cranky when he's marking,' Milly said conspiringly.

'I can relate to that,' Elsie said.

'Well, you've really brightened my day,' Howard said. 'I'll make us some hot drinks. A Milo like you had it last time, Milly?'

'You remembered?' Milly said, her wide eyes glued to Howard.

'I did.'

'Yay. Just like that, thank you.'

'Coming right up.'

They sat in a row across the main couch, Milly in between Howard and Elsie, mugs of Milo in hand. Milly had a small pile of books on her lap.

'I'll drink my Milo first, if that's okay. I don't want to spill anything,' Milly said.

'Good idea. Yes. Books were very precious in our house growing up too,' Howard said.

'Do you enjoy reading, Milly?' Elsie asked.

'Oh yes, I love it.'

'And how's school?' Howard asked.

'Okay. I like my teacher and I don't mind my classes.'

'Have you made some new friends?'

'Howard, dear, don't badger the poor child,' Elsie said.

'Sorry. Yes, you're quite right. Anyway, I'm not convinced making friends is the be all and end all.'

'I don't know what that means,' Milly said.

'He means, making friends might not be the most important thing in the world,' Elsie explained.

'Exactly. Though everyone talks about it like it is,' Howard added. 'Do they still, Milly? That's what it was like growing up for us. Sometimes keeping friendships going can be difficult, especially when they leave or let you down for whatever reason. Still is, if I'm being honest.'

'Howard, don't depress the poor thing,' Elsie said.

'Oh, no, I'm okay. I think people on the whole are quite disappointing. And I've decided that having loads of friends isn't my main priority,' Milly said. 'I don't have trouble making friends but I'm getting a little picky about how I spend my time. I'm not fussed about being in the *cool* or popular group. Did they have that when you were at school?'

'They most certainly did,' Elsie said. 'And it took some navigating, I can tell you. Well, nothing has changed there, then.'

'I reckon some things never change,' Howard said.

'Yes, Dad says that all the time,' Milly said.

'Your dad being a teacher must make things a bit difficult,' Howard said. 'But at least he's not the principal.'

'I think it helps that most of the kids seem to like him,' Milly said. 'As far as I can tell, so far he's considered one of the cool teachers.'

Elsie blinked at the words and tone coming out of the small child beside her. She had to bite the inside of her bottom lip to stop from smiling too broadly. And she was definitely avoiding catching Howard's eye over top of Milly. From what she could see out of the corner of her eye, he looked to be in a struggle of his own. He was wiping his mouth, most probably after almost spitting out a mouthful of liquid Milo.

'Sounds like a good plan to me,' Elsie said.

'What *is* your main priority, if you don't mind me asking?' Howard asked and Elsie wanted to slap his arm or tell him to stop mocking Milly, or whatever it was he was doing.

'Well, getting a decent education and not getting too distracted,' Milly replied. 'Oh, and having fun. You make very good Milo, Mr Manning.'

'Thank you, Milly.'

Milly leant forward, holding her books with one hand, and put her mug down carefully on the coffee table. 'Actually, would you mind if I wash my hands first?'

'Of course. I mean no, that's perfectly fine. Here I'll show you where,' Elsie said, clamouring up with all the grace and speed she could muster, which wasn't much.

'It's okay, just tell me where,' Milly said.

'Through into the hall and it's the second door on the left,' Elsie said, pointing. 'The first is the toilet, if you need it.'

'Okay. Thanks.' And with that Milly was gone.

'Isn't she precious?' Elsie said quietly.

'Adorable,' Howard said. 'She's quite made my day,' he added with a sigh. 'What a cutie.'

'All better?' Elsie said as Milly came back towards them.

'Yes, thank you.' Milly settled herself between them again.

'Now would you like to go first, or Mr Manning or me?' Elsie said.

'I will,' Milly said, opening a book.

'Any instructions for us, Milly?' Elsie asked.

'Yes, it's a long time since we helped anyone with their reading,' Howard said.

'I don't think so. Please correct me if I muck up any of the words. Though I am quite good at reading.'

'Right. Got it,' Howard said.

As she listened to Milly read, Elsie's mind went back to homework with Corinne and Janine and the fights they'd had over it. Nothing major, just frustration bubbling over – more about having to do homework and it eating into their leisure time than the actual work itself. Thankfully both girls were intelligent and neither one lazy.

'You have a lovely reading voice,' Howard said, 'if you don't mind me saying. Am I allowed to say that?' He looked to Elsie, cringing.

'Yes. Thank you,' Milly said.

'And you really don't need any help at all, though I am very happy to sit and listen,' Elsie said. 'I enjoyed that book.'

'I did too. Let's do another. Shall I take a turn reading?' Howard said.

'Yes, please. And then you can take a turn, Mrs Manning. If you want to. I've got five books. But if it gets too much, just tell me and we can stop.'

'Oh, that's the washing machine screeching at us to get the clothes to hang out. You two carry on here and I'll see to that,' Elsie said, getting up.

'Are you sure, Elsie? It can wait for me to do in a bit,' Howard said.

'I can help,' Milly said. 'I'm good at hanging up washing. And getting it in. And folding it.' She finished with a loose shrug.

'Oh. That's very kind. I'll do it – that way it might be dry before it gets too late,' Elsie said, carrying on with getting up.

'This can wait a few minutes,' Milly said, putting the stack of books on the coffee table and getting up. 'Unless I'll just be in the way,' she added, pausing and looking from Elsie to Howard.

'Not at all, though you might struggle to reach the clothesline.'

'I can pass the things up to you to save you having to bend right down,' Milly offered. 'If that would help?'

'Oh, yes. It would, actually.'

'Okay. Come on, let's all go and then come back and do some more reading,' Howard said as they got up.

'You're a very good helper,' Elsie said, trying to ignore the hint of embarrassment at Milly handing her her large full-brief knickers. Though the child really didn't seem it all perturbed at spying either hers or Howard's smalls – not that they were. *Ah, to be a confident youngster before life knocks the stuffing out of you.*

Inside again, before they settled back into reading with Milly, she suggested to Milly they send her dad a text to let him know they might be late, which they did.

As they saw Milly to the door, Elsie wondered if Howard was feeling as reluctant as her to say goodbye to the little girl.

'Would you like us to walk you home?' Howard asked.

'No. That's okay, thank you.'

'Please just get Dad to text us to let us know you got back inside all right. We know it's right next door, but still ...' he said, shrugging.

'Okay, I will. You can never be too careful or safe, right?' Milly said.

'Exactly,' Howard said.

Elsie smiled at the pair going about their exchange.

'Thank you very much for your help,' Milly said at the door.

'You're very welcome. Anytime,' Howard said.

'And thank you for helping us out with the washing,' Elsie said.

'And the computer,' Howard added.

'You're welcome too,' Milly said. 'And it's an anytime from me too.' She grinned.

'Okay then. Great,' Howard said, grinning back.

As they stood there, Elsie wondered if Howard was also toying with whether to hug her or ruffle her hair, or how you were meant to say goodbye to a child that you were no relation to but liked very much. But the answer came in the form of Milly hugging first Howard and then Elsie, throwing her arms around them and pressing her face into their stomachs momentarily, trapping their arms by their sides, before releasing them.

'Hang on a sec. You took me a bit by surprise. I can give a better cuddle than that,' Elsie said, holding out her arms to Milly, who seemed coy again. Embarrassed, maybe. 'Oh, that's better,' Elsie said, holding on tight to the little girl and then giving her hair a stroke.

'Thank you,' Milly said. 'You're very good at hugs too.'

'As are you,' Elsie said.

'Well, don't leave me out,' Howard said holding his arms out wide. He sighed deeply as he luxuriated in the comfort of Milly's arms around him. He hadn't experienced this since their own girls and didn't know until that moment how much he'd missed it, or that he had at all. 'That's lovely. Thank you.'

Outside, Milly turned back and grinned at them.

'Come over anytime,' Howard and Elsie called.

'You too,' Milly said and then skipped off down the driveway.

Howard and Elsie remained leaning against each other after losing sight of Milly.

'I'm not sure who's more attached – us or young Milly,' Howard mused, putting his arm around Elsie.

'No. I was just thinking that.'

'She's rather put the pep back into my step.'

'Yes, and mine.' Elsie let out a long sigh of contentment.

'Elsie?'

'Yes, dear?'

'I couldn't bear to cause her any upset. Or Daniel, for that matter.'

'No. Me neither.'

'Are you thinking what I'm thinking?'

'That you're glad we're still here and don't fancy leaving now?'

'Yep. That's exactly it.' Howard squeezed Elsie tightly to him.

'How are the finances?' she asked.

'Okay for about another seven months. We'll find a way — we always have done.'

'I'd live on beans for weeks on end for Milly,' Elsie muttered.

'Me too, but I don't think it'll come to that, my love. Come on, time to go in — I'm getting cold,' he said, shepherding Elsie inside and closing the door.

Chapter Seventeen

'Hello, I'm back,' Howard called, entering the kitchen from the hall.

'This, I notice,' Elsie said, not looking up from her book of puzzles.

When she sensed more movement and sounds of exertion coming from Howard than his usual arrival from an outing, she looked up.

'What's that? What are you doing?' she asked. He'd just placed a large, flat box on the bench and fossicked in the kitchen drawer for a knife.

'I'll show you in a second,' he said and proceeded to extract a lump of white polystyrene, a booklet, and then a selection of bits and pieces from the box, putting each aside. 'Here we are,' he mumbled. 'I've got us a new helper, Elsie. What do you think?' he said, holding up a large, round disc-like object.

Elsie knitted her brows and squinted as she tried to ascertain what it was that was made out of shiny black plastic. She'd seen such a thing before. *Oh. It's a ...* She realised what it was at just the same time Howard spoke again.

'It's a robot vacuum cleaner,' he said, holding it up with a proud expression something like you would expect from a hunter-gatherer bringing home a decent catch.

Given vacuuming was his domain, Elsie thought he was justified in feeling excited about his purchase. She didn't share his excitement, though. 'Good-o, then. Lovely,' she said, returning to her puzzle, the tiniest touch of sadness settling within her.

They'd discussed getting one of these things every so often over the years and resisted for several reasons. The main reason was that they hadn't wanted Maisie to be frightened by a strange whirring electronic monstrosity wandering around in her vicinity and quite possibly beeping and bumping into her. What stirred up her sadness now was the reinforcement of Maisie's demise and their moving on.

She knew Howard was missing Maisie's company, as she was, and the appliance was a better idea than a drone, which had been considered on and off, too. They'd started out as toys, but had become so much more, and with rules attached, which Howard had concluded made it all too hard.

'It's controlled by an app,' Howard announced, clearly thrilled with his purchase.

Elsie nodded and mumbled, 'That's good, dear.'

'Don't worry, I haven't weakened on the home smart system device thingy. That's a bridge too far, in my opinion. I'm not ready to accept that all and sundry won't be listening in. Take all those times footage from nanny cams has reportedly been found on public online sites. Hell, no,' he added in a mutter.

Elsie could tell by his tone that he was reading the instructions; his voice had dropped an octave and he sounded like he was more talking to himself, or thinking aloud, than addressing her. He'd call her name if he wanted Elsie's opinion or a more considered reply.

'There's a camera in it, which I admit is a little disconcerting, but it's apparently helpful for diagnosing problems, so it must remain turned on. Might be useful if we're not here. Though probably not wise to run it unsupervised, at least until we know each other better,' he added. 'And, actually, come to think of it, there's not much a camera looking around the place at just a few inches above ground level will see that could be put to nefarious purposes. It'll all be skirting boards and the legs of furniture and the like, I should imagine,' he muttered on.

Elsie smiled to herself as she pondered the next crossword clue, tapping her pencil against her lip.

'What are we going to call it, do you think?' Howard said suddenly.

'Sorry, dear, what's that?' Elsie looked up.

'I said, what are we going to call it. Shall we give it a name?'

'Why would we give it a name?'

'I don't know, seems the polite thing to do to be able to address it, since it'll be in our home.'

'It's a machine, Howard. And wouldn't it, by your logic just there, make more sense for it to be speaking to *us* – will it know our names, is it capable of learning them?'

'Sadly not, no.'

'Well, there you go, then.'

'What? So, no name? Oh. Sorry, young chap.'

Elsie looked over to see Howard stroking the device. She almost laughed at noticing the disappointed pout of his lips. Instead, she shook her head slowly. She didn't roll her eyes, because, as odd as it was, Howard's interaction with the device was rather cute. And, sadly, another indication of how much they missed their darling Maisie, she thought, as a wave of intense sadness swept through her soul, causing her eyes to water.

Perhaps in some ways they *had* been missing not having grand-children, not that there was anything they could do to remedy that. And, really, could you actually miss what you didn't know the ins and outs of? Elsie pondered. Was it yet another of the many ideas wider society put in your head or set you up to compete with others on, which only served to keep people miserable in their inability to win? *Ah, all too deep*, she thought, shaking her head. Elsie looked back up at Howard. As she did, another random thought struck.

'How about Brian?' she called.

'What's that you say?' Howard said, looking up from reading the instructions.

'I said, if you'd like to name it, how about Brian?'

'Oh, I like that! So, then it's a he, is it, do you think?'

Yep. Elsie didn't say the words out loud, because they didn't apply to her darling Howard, and he was clearly feeling extra-sensitive and may misconstrue, but of course the device would be a male! Because she'd put money on the fact that it wouldn't listen or do as it was told. Again, from anecdotal evidence, not necessar-ily lived, men by many accounts were often considered to be quite useless in these two areas. Evidenced by the regular occurrence of a meme that said something along the lines of: *If a man says he'll fix it, he will – there's no need to remind him every six months.* She had a feeling this would apply to Brian, sitting over there motionless on the bench. Though operator error could well be part of the problem at some point. She didn't mind, really, it was just good to see Howard engrossed in something. Since Maisie's passing, when he wasn't doing his usual chores and after finishing the paper, far too often he wandered aimlessly and morosely about the house.

'Well then, Brian, let's pop you down and see how you go,' Elsie heard Howard say lovingly. She looked up in time to see him place their new friend on the floor and gave it a final pat. He was smiling, which sent a ribbon of warmth weaving through her.

But don't you always have to charge the batteries for new devices before using them? she wondered, though stayed silent. She shrugged to herself.

'Right, so apparently he's going to roam about and map the place,' Howard said, standing back with his hands on his hips. 'So just ignore him,' he added, glancing at Elsie.

'Okey-dokey, then, have fun, Brian,' she said, and had to admit to herself that she rather liked the idea of having someone other than Howard to chatter nonsense to. Maisie had been a wonderful listener, not that Elsie thought for a second this device they'd called Brian would show any intuition or affection where human emotion was concerned. She wasn't stupid.

Howard came over and sat down, phone in hand and watched while Brian skittered back and forth in front of them.

It's a bit loud, Elsie thought, but kept it to herself.

'I think he's rather cute,' Howard said fondly.

'And a little mesmerising,' Elsie said. She found herself closing the book and letting her attention follow Brian, who did the cutest little spin when he turned. Though how else he would change direction, when he was round in shape, she didn't know. She smiled. It was rather good fun, as far as distractions went. She resisted getting up to follow when Brian finished the lounge space, or a half-hearted effort, more like, though she didn't know how much time had passed. Her mind had drifted. She might even have fallen asleep for a moment or two, such was her feeling of serenity.

Howard pushed himself out of his chair. 'I'll just go and keep an eye on him while he finds his way.'

'Good-o,' Elsie said and returned to her puzzle, chuckling to herself as she heard Howard chattering to Brian up the hall. She couldn't hear what exactly he was saying, most likely pointing out a spot he'd missed or telling him he was a good boy.

Elsie let out a long, contented sigh as she acknowledged some of the previous lost equilibrium and energy might be returning to the house.

'That was quick,' Elsie said when the machine tootled back into view, Howard in tow.

'Yes, he's flat – he's coming home for a rest and recharge,' Howard said, a little deflated.

'I thought you would have had to charge it fully, like when we get a new phone,' Elsie said.

'Yes, ordinarily we would, but I got Brian as floor stock, so he was already up and running. Well, that's that then,' Howard said, sinking into his chair, his shoulders and stomach seeming to fold in on themselves.

'Only a temporary setback, I'm sure,' Elsie said.

'Yes. We'll have to decide when we want him roaming about and when we don't.'

'I'm sure it'll take time to get into the swing of things. We can play it by ear, can't we? That is, we don't have to decide right away, do we?' Elsie said.

'Oh yes. No. We can keep reprogramming him to suit us. He is rather loud, though, isn't he?' Howard said with clear disappointment. 'He didn't seem so rowdy in the shop.'

'No doubt that's because it was a bigger space, and fully carpeted?'

'Maybe. Yes, it was.'

'We'll get used to it. *Him*,' she corrected, in an effort to cheer Howard up. 'We *are* going from relative silence, don't forget.'

'Oh yes, of course,' he said brightening.

'Just enjoy getting to know each other. It might take a little time to adjust.'

'Yes, you're quite right. I'm not sure how good a job he'll do – I'll still probably have to vacuum the same amount, but at this point the novelty value is a bonus.'

'I quite agree.' Howard and Elsie shared a smile and then let out little sighs in unison.

'Right, then, cup of tea, since Brian is out of action?' Howard said.

'Yes, please.'

'I'll make some sandwiches, too, while I'm up. It's not too early for lunch, is it?'

'No. Good idea.'

'Then I'll pop a load of washing on and then re-read Brian's instructions and have a play with the app.'

'Sounds like a good plan to me, dear,' Elsie said, already engrossed back in her crossword, tapping the tip of her pencil against the page as she searched her memory for the right word.

Chapter Eighteen

There was a knock on the door. Elsie climbed out of her chair. She quite liked answering the door these days, in case it was young Milly. *Fingers crossed*, she thought, smiling, as she made her way down the hall.

'Milly, how lovely!'

'Hello, Mrs Manning.'

'What's that you've got there?' Elsie asked, looking down and over at the small toy stroller beside Milly, which contained what looked like a bundle of towels. At that moment the red comb and then sleek red-brown speckled feathered head of a chook popped up and looked around. 'Oh. Wonderful. Hello there.'

'This is Two. We've come on an adventure to visit you and Mr Manning.'

'Two, did you say?'

'Yes, Two, as in the number. She was the second one out of the box. And she also happens to be the friendliest. She follows me everywhere. I thought you might like to meet her.'

'Well, thank you. I'm very pleased to meet your Two. Hello there, Two,' Elsie said, bending down and peering at the chook, who had stretched her neck out further. She rubbed her head. 'Aren't you lovely?'

'Is Mr Manning here? And if so, would he like to meet her too, do you think? If he's home, that is?'

'He is, and I'm sure he'd love to meet Two. Howard,' Elsie called. But she received no response. 'I know. How about we go out the back to the garden? He'll see us then, or we can bang on the window and try to catch his attention, if necessary. Then you can get Two out and we'll be able to have a proper look at her, if you like.'

'Oh yes. That sounds like a good plan.'

'Come on, then, this way.' Elsie walked with Milly around the side of the house, unlatching the gate and then closing it again behind Milly.

'I don't think she'll want to escape. She really likes being with me,' Milly said.

'I'm sure you're right. Just best to be certain.'

'Okay.'

Elsie opened the back sliding door and called for Howard. 'Dear, come out here and meet Milly's chook.'

Howard appeared. 'Hello there, Milly.'

'Hello, Mr Manning. I'm sorry if we're interrupting you,' Milly said.

'You're not interrupting. Not at all. I'm doing nothing that cannot wait. It's lovely to see you. What have you got there?'

'This is Two. She's a very friendly chook. You can pat her if you like.'

'She won't peck me?' Howard said.

'Oh no. Here, I'll get her out.'

Howard and Elsie shared warm grins either side of Milly as they waited for the child to gently untuck the chook from the towels and bring her out.

'Well, aren't you a beauty?' Howard said. He put his hand out and stroked the chook. 'Did you say her name is Two?'

'Yes. The number. She was the second one we got out.'

'Ah. I see now.'

'One and Three stayed home. They're not quite as friendly.'

'Two follows Milly everywhere, Howard, isn't that lovely?' Elsie said.

'How wonderful. The others might as well, once they've settled in,' Howard said.

'I don't mind. They're individuals. They're still nice, just not as shadowy as Two.'

'Do you know what breed they are?' Howard asked.

'Oh yes. They're ISA browns.'

'Fabulous. They're an excellent breed – both for laying eggs and making great pets. We had some when our daughters were young.'

'You did?' Milly's eyes were big.

'Yep. Sure did.'

Milly shifted the chook as it now struggled a bit in her arms. 'Would you mind if I put her down? She's getting a little restless.'

'And heavy, by the looks,' Elsie said. 'Yes, pop her down.'

'Will she run away?' Howard asked.

'I don't think so. But we shut the gate behind us just in case,' Milly said.

'Good idea.'

The three of them stood watching as the creature shook and fluffed her feathers out, stretched her neck and wings, then strutted off across the lawn towards the garden bed.

'Would you like a Milo or a glass of water, Milly? Or do you have to rush back home?' Elsie said.

'A glass of water would be very good, thank you. Would you like me to get it?'

'No, that's okay, thank you for offering, though. How about you and Mr Manning keep an eye on Two, and I'll be back in a jiffy?' Elsie said.

Howard settled himself on the wooden bench seat and Milly climbed up beside him. 'She really is a beauty, Milly,' Howard said, clasping his hands in his lap and stretching out his legs.

'I love watching them,' Milly said. 'It's relaxing,' she added, also stretching out her legs and linking her hands in her lap.

'Oh yes, I quite agree.'

'I hope you don't mind if she makes a mess,' Milly said as Two scratched in the dirt, sending bits of mulch and leaf litter flying onto the lawn.

'Not at all. She's having a lovely time,' Howard said.

'Yes, I was telling Mrs Manning, we're on an adventure.'

'Good for you.'

'Do you and Mrs Manning go on adventures, Mr Manning?'

Howard racked his brain for how to answer. What constituted an adventure in the eyes of a small delightful child these days? Certainly not funerals and his daily treks to the supermarket. 'Hmm. Not so much these days.'

'That's no good. Sounds to me like you need an adventure, Mr Manning,' Milly said brightly.

'You might have a point there, Milly.'

'Right,' Elsie said, putting down a tray with glasses of water and a plate of cheese and crackers on the low outdoor coffee table in front of them. 'Here you are,' she said, handing a glass to Milly.

'Thank you very much,' she said, accepting the glass and then taking a sip.

'Bikkie?' Howard said, holding out the plate to Milly and Elsie.

'You have very good snacks,' Milly said.

'Why, thank you. I agree. Brainwave idea, Elsie.'

The three of them sat in a row across the bench, watching Two. Elsie couldn't have said if she'd been there like that for two minutes or an hour when the chook wandered over to them.

'Hello there,' she said, reaching down to stroke the bird when it appeared at her feet, looking up with its head tilted slightly.

'She likes you,' Milly said knowingly. 'I knew she would.'

'Well, the feeling's very mutual,' Elsie said.

'Absolutely,' Howard said. 'Can I pick her up and have a hold, do you think, Milly? Would Two mind, or you, for that matter?'

'No. Well, I don't. I think you'll soon know if Two does – that's what Dad always says.'

Howard chuckled. 'Quite right.' He reached down and carefully picked the chook up. 'Ah, you really are a lovely creature,' he said as Two tucked her feet under her and settled onto his lap.

'You're a good chook, Two,' Milly said, reaching over and stroking the bird.

'Would Two like some cheese and bikkie?' Elsie asked.

'Oh, could she?' Milly's eyes became enormous.

A flood of warmth roared through Elsie's insides. 'Sure can,' she said and broke a piece of biscuit and cheese off and offered the items to the bird in Howard's lap.

'Oh, she likes that, I think,' Howard said.

The bird hopped across onto Milly's lap, where she stretched her neck towards the glass of water Elsie had just picked up and was about to take a sip from.

'Two. Manners,' Milly said, causing both Howard and Elsie to laugh at her schoolmarm tone.

'I guess you're thirsty, too, um, Two,' Elsie said with another laugh and held out her glass, tilting it towards the bird. 'Go on, then.'

She stroked the sleek glossy feathers glistening bright red and brown in the light as Two moved.

Having had a couple of dips of her beak into Elsie's water, the chook sat down on Milly's lap and tucked her feet underneath her, taking a few moments of shifting and squishing about before she was fully still.

'You're a good girl,' Milly cooed, stroking the chook.

'What a wonderful interlude,' Howard announced.

'I don't know what that means,' Milly said without looking up.

'A most excellent interruption to my day,' Howard said, by way of explanation.

Milly nodded. 'I'm glad you like her,' she said, beaming up at Howard and then Elsie.

'Oh yes, she's wonderful,' Howard said.

'I agree. I look forward to meeting One and Three, as well, when they fancy or are ready,' Elsie said.

'Look,' Howard whispered. 'She's fallen asleep. Her eyes are closed.'

'Are they?' Milly said. 'I can't see from here. And I don't want to disturb her.'

'No. Good idea.' Elsie's heart swelled.

Howard muttered something Elsie didn't hear. She looked across at him. 'Don't move, Milly,' he whispered. 'I want to take a photo.' With his phone in hand, he carefully twisted himself around and snapped a few pictures. Elsie wasn't sure if she was in the shot or not. She didn't mind either way. Milly smiled at Howard. 'Perfect,' he said triumphantly, and held the phone out for Milly and then Elsie to see.

'That's a great shot, dear,' Elsie said.

'I'll just send it to your dad, Milly.'

'Oh, thank you, Mr Manning.'

'My pleasure.' *Having a wonderful visit with your gorgeous daughter and her chicken, Two,* Howard wrote, attached the best pic, and pressed send. He sat back in his chair with a contented sigh and wondered when he'd felt this relaxed. And when was the last time he'd simply sat and watched the clouds? Beautiful fluffy white figures moved across an otherwise brilliant blue sky. The sound of distant traffic hummed in the background, along with the low drone of a plane overhead. *Ah, this is the life.*

He was brought back suddenly from his tranquillity by his phone signalling a message had arrived. It was Milly's dad, Daniel, thanking him for the photo.

'I'd better go now, actually. I've got some homework to do before dinner,' Milly said suddenly, shattering the silence. She sighed. She got up and wrapped the towel back around Two and put her into the pram.

Howard and Elsie got up and stood back, arm in arm. They chuckled as Two snuggled down and then disappeared into the folds.

'She likes that, by the looks,' Howard said.

'Yes, she does,' Milly said. 'Oh! I almost forgot!' She stuck her hand into the pocket of her denim overalls, brought out a purple envelope and held it out to Howard and Elsie.

'What's this?' Howard asked, accepting it and opening the envelope.

'You are both invited to my eighth birthday party. It's next week. At the park. You don't have to decide right this minute – you can just text Dad later.'

'Oh. How lovely. Thank you,' Howard said.

'Yes. Thank you.'

'Is that a robot vacuum?' Milly asked, pointing towards the glass door.

Howard and Elsie turned.

'It is, but he's not supposed to be up and about right now. I've only just got him. He is programmed for the morning, you see – well, he's meant to be. Brian, what are you up to?' Howard said, scratching his head.

Elsie and Milly grinned at each other.

'Cool. Hi, Brian,' Milly said, waving to the machine just inside, which seemed to be peering out at them. 'And great name, by the way,' she added, grinning at Howard and then Elsie.

'Thanks. But he's a very naughty boy.'

Milly giggled. 'I'll leave you to it,' she said. 'It's been a lovely visit, but I really had better go now.' She positioned herself behind the stroller with her hands on the handles.

'Okay. I agree, it's been lovely. But we don't want you getting into trouble,' Elsie said.

'That's right. Thank you so much for bringing Two over to meet us,' Howard said.

'You're welcome. Thank you for the snack and water.'

'I'll open the gate for you,' Howard said, hurrying to get ahead of Milly with her stroller.

'Thank you for having us, Mrs Manning,' Milly said, turning back before carrying on around the side of the house and through the gate.

'You're very welcome, Milly. Thanks for visiting.'

'Bye,' Milly called again, as she disappeared with Howard.

'Thank you,' Milly said to Howard as she went through the gate he held open for her. 'Bye, Mr Manning. Good luck with sorting Brian out.'

'Ah, thank you. I've clearly gone wrong somewhere along the way with setting him up.'

'Let me know if you need any help with the app.'

'Okay. Thank you. Goodbye, Milly. See you again soon.'

A few minutes later Howard was back beside Elsie. 'She offered to help out with Brian.'

'Of course she did, bless her.'

'It might come in handy, having a young person at call. Though I am rather determined to solve it myself.'

Howard clasped Elsie's hand, then raised it to his lips and gave it a kiss before lowering it again. They sat in companionable silence.

Once again Elsie wondered if he was thinking what she was; that maybe she was missing not having grandkids after all.

'She really is such a treat,' Howard said and popped a Jatz with slice of cheese into his mouth whole. 'What a perfect day,' he added, stretching his legs out and settling in to watch the clouds again.

'I wonder what dear old Maisie would have made of Two,' Elsie said.

'Barked her head off, most likely. Or gone in and tried to hide under the bed, perhaps.'

'Yes. True. I miss her.'

'Mmm. Me too.'

'Let's look at this invitation, to distract us,' Elsie said, opening the envelope and pulling out the paper. She read it through to herself, smiling as she did.

'What's the gist of it, dear?' Howard said.

'Well, it's at the park just across the way – there's a map. It's on Sunday, and only for an hour in the afternoon.'

'It's quite late notice. Do we have anything on then? I imagine it's been organised for ages and she might have had to suss out whether we'd like to attend,' Howard said.

'We haven't had anything on on a Sunday for yonks. We'll check when we go inside, but I'm sure we'll be free. And, it being late notice might be because she's only recently arrived at the school and met some people her age.'

'You could be spot on there, my dear. I keep forgetting we've only just met her. Doesn't it already feel like she's been part of our lives for quite a while?'

'It sure does – in a good way. So, continuing on … We're to bring nothing, just ourselves. There are also a couple of notes at the bottom – I wonder if it's just for us, or everyone who's invited. It says, "Please no presents. If you wish, a donation to a charity of your choice would be perfect, and very much appreciated."'

'Aww,' Howard said.

'But wait, there's more,' Elsie said, holding up a hand. 'This is on the last line: "Milly cares deeply for the environment, so please no balloons, no single use plastic, or similar – nothing that could harm our precious planet."'

'Goodness, is that all handwritten? By an eight-year-old?' Howard was impressed but a little aghast.

'No. Typed.'

'I like her directness and clarity. And her apparently low-maintenance predisposition towards herself. What a kind and sensible kid. How lovely,' Howard said.

'Yes.'

'There's something written on the back, too,' Howard said.

Elsie turned the page over. 'Oh. It's a list of suggested charities – a comprehensive selection, by the looks.'

'I would expect nothing less,' Howard said proudly.

At that moment Howard's phone chirped again. 'It's another text from Daniel. Great, Milly got home safely. And he's inviting us for dinner at their place for her actual birthday. It's this Friday evening. What do you think? Yes, to both functions? I think so. Shall I reply straight away, to that effect?'

'Yep. Go on, then.'

Chapter Nineteen

'Right, what are we going to give Milly for her birthday? I don't care what the invitation says – we're giving her *something*,' Elsie said.

'I agree. But I have no idea what kids like these days.'

'I don't think we need to. We could bring back something from the old days.'

'Oh! I know.'

'What?'

'Remember the stilts the girls loved at around that age? How about some of those?' Howard said.

'Now there's a thought. But it's been a long time since we've bought anything in tins big enough.'

'True.' Howard tapped his lip with his finger thoughtfully.

'Or we could tizzy up a broomstick as a hobby horse for her,' Elsie suggested. 'She might like that.'

'Yes. That's another good idea. But I like the first one better. We just need to figure out ...'

'And I can easily run up some wide-leg pants on the machine.'

'Hang on. Shoosh for a sec.'

'What is it?'

Howard had his eyes closed and face scrunched up in deep concentration.

'I'm sure I know where there are some large tins. It's right here,' he said, tapping his head. 'I just need it to come that bit further ...'

'You know, we could just buy two tins of Milo. Given how much we're going through these days.'

'I'd rather not,' Howard mumbled. 'I know there's two here somewhere already. Just need to ...' He got up without another word and Elsie watched as he went through the kitchen and out into the garage. Quietly she rose and followed him. Standing beside him, she copied the direction of his gaze up to the shelving above the workbench against one wall.

'There.' Howard pointed. Above them was a row of tins, most likely large Milo tins – minus their green labels – and probably some from old Sunshine milk powder from decades before.

'They're a bit old and crappy, though, aren't they? And they're in use. Do you want to sacrifice those?' Elsie squinted slightly in an effort to read the black marker announcing the contents within. 'It's also so beautifully uniform,' she added.

'I know, but I think it's worth it. I'm sure Milly would love it. And you said yourself you want to make pants like the girls had. Just make them long and wide enough to go over and cover the tins, okay?'

'We could get some paint and pretty them up. Or even some colourful contact – that stuff you wrap books in,' Elsie suggested.

'Oh yes, brilliant idea, dear.' Howard clapped his hands. 'Though the sticky stuff, if it's made for attaching to books, might not be suitable for slightly rusty metal. Let's go with painting them. And ... I do believe, my love, we have ourselves a mission!' He moved the nearby step into place, stood on it and reached up and brought down a tin marked 'nails', which he held out for Elsie to take. And then reached up for a second tin, marked 'hooks', which he also handed to Elsie before stepping back down.

'Right. Next question,' Elsie said. 'What are we going to do with the contents?'

'For now, make use of all that plastic in the cupboard inside, that we've so recently sorted?'

'Good idea. We're on a roll. Come on. Let's make a list and then head out.'

Armed with their list, they locked the house, paused in the porch to run through their inventories a second time – keys, wallet, phone, list, backpack with bottle of water and a couple of extra carry bags inside – and headed to the bus stop.

'Perfect timing,' Howard said just a few minutes after they'd arrived at the stop, nodding his head to the approaching bus. Being the middle of the day, it was almost empty.

'When were we last on a bus together?' Howard asked as they settled into their seats after greeting the driver and validating their tickets. 'What fun.'

'Yes. It was before Covid.' Elsie tried not to think about the last time she'd been alone on a bus – the day Maisie died. She was glad for Howard's sake he hadn't remembered this.

'Oh yes – the good old days.'

'Quite.'

'We do live in a very convenient spot, don't we?' Howard said a few minutes later, now beside the bus and holding out his hand, if needed, for Elsie to alight. They were almost right outside the entrance to the large hardware store – their first stop.

Howard carried the backpack, already becoming a little heavy and clinking occasionally with the three small cans of paint, including primer, that they'd deliberated over until Howard said if it was worth doing it was worth doing properly and he wasn't having the paint rub off the tins he was sacrificing.

'I felt like a naughty teenager, having to get them to unlock the cabinet,' Howard said as they waited for the bus again. This time to take them to the big store selling party supplies and fabric. 'I feel so energised, too. When did we last have a mission?'

'The other week, dear, when we were trying to find a way to die,' Elsie pointed out.

'Oh, yes. Gosh, that feels like months ago now,' he muttered to himself.

'And, more recently, your many hours of research and subsequent purchase of Brian,' Elsie added.

'Egad! Am I losing my mind?'

Elsie tried not to sigh out loud. It seemed Howard asked this same question nearly every second week these days. 'Possibly. We're still saving the apple seeds for just in case, remember?' *How could he possibly forget; they're in a jar on the bench, in plain view, and we add the seeds each day after they've dried on a sheet of paper towel on the window sill. Granted, it's now more about keeping up with a well-honed routine, and something to do, than actually using them – though there are quite a few. But still …* 'Other than that, we were all out of inspiration. And now we've become rather attached to Milly. Ring a bell?'

'Yes. All good.' He shook his head and frowned. 'Hard to believe we used to run a successful business and employ people. Oh well.'

'Yes, oh well,' Elsie said. 'No point agonising over it. It is what it is, as the young ones say all the time.'

'They do, yes. Did we used to say that?'

'I don't recall so.'

'No. Me neither. You know, it's one of the few current bits of lingo, if that's the right terminology, that I can say I actually approve of,' Howard declared.

'Me too. It's a good one. Most likely recycled or come back around, or what have you.'

'Probably. Ah, here we are.'

Elsie followed Howard's gaze up the street to where a bus was approaching.

'Too easy,' Howard said as they got on and bid good afternoon to the driver. 'We probably should have got the paint last – on the way back. This backpack is getting heavy already,' he said, taking it off and putting it at his feet.

'Have I ever been in here?' Howard asked looking around the large discount department style store.

'I have no idea. Probably not. I only used to come here for fabric when I sewed,' Elsie said. 'Which hasn't been for years. Ah, here we are – patterns.'

'Are you sure you want to make the pants? We could go somewhere and buy them.'

'I'm not so sure we could. When did you last see really wide flares? They haven't been in for a decade or so, from memory, and probably haven't really been as wide as we'd need since the seventies. We have to take the tins into account, remember,' Elsie said. 'As it is I'll have to alter the design a bit – see.' She held out the packet and pointed to the shape of the leg in the illustration.

'Righteo. Lucky one of us is up with it all,' Howard said. 'Ooh, look, sequins. Glitter.'

'We're not using them. I don't think they're very environmentally friendly, so Milly wouldn't approve.' Elsie moved up the aisle. Howard ambled along beside her.

'Ah, good point. Isn't she a great kid, our Milly?'

'She's not really ours, Howard.'

'Oh, I don't know – she seems to have taken as much a shine to us as vice versa.'

'I'd agree with that.'

'Buttons,' Howard pointed out.

'Yes, that's why we're in this aisle. I'm just looking. I have an idea in mind.'

'Okay, I will leave it to you – your department, and all that.'

'I'm happy for you to chime in, just don't get all crotchety if I don't answer because I'm deep in thought. Okay, this way, I think. Fabric.'

Howard followed in a slow meander, picking up and touching this and that on his way past.

'What do you reckon about this?' Elsie asked, pointing to a bolt of colourful fabric on top of a pile of material of all sorts on a table – bright, patterned, and plain shades, different textures.

'Is that jellybeans?' Howard asked.

'It is. Or, look. There's balloons.'

'And this one is spots.'

'They're all great – nice and bright. Which one do you think?' Elsie asked.

'I don't know,' Howard said. 'We don't want to go too clown-like, I don't think. I hate clowns.'

'Yes, I know you do. I'm not too fond of them myself. As long as we don't involve face paint and a bright curly wig, I reckon we're fine. Other than that, the brighter the better,' Elsie said.

'Hmm.'

'Let's just do eeny-meeny-miney-moe or close our eyes and pick that way.'

'Oh!' Howard said.

Elsie followed Howard's gaze as he turned towards a young girl and her mother nearby, and then back to her again. She shrugged as he raised his eyebrows, aware of what he had silently suggested.

'Excuse me,' he asked, 'could I ask your advice, please?'

'I don't work here,' the woman said tersely.

'No. I know. Perhaps advice isn't quite right. Your *opinion*. Both of you, if you wouldn't mind.' He addressed the child, who was around Milly's age, Elsie thought.

'If someone was making you some groovy pants for dress-ups, which pattern would you prefer? This one or this one?' Howard said, pointing to the fabrics.

The girl moved closer. 'For fun dressing up?' she asked.

'Exactly,' Howard said.

Elsie nodded.

'Out of the jelly beans or the red and white stripes?'

'Yes. Or any of them, really,' Howard said, nodding.

'For someone my age?'

'Yes.'

'Cool!' She pursed her lips, which reminded Elsie of Milly when she was deep in thought. 'This one,' she said decisively, putting her hands on one Howard and Elsie had missed, which was poking out from underneath. She then started trying to pull it out. Howard stepped in to help. What was revealed was a swirling pattern of rainbow colours.

So, seventies fashion is almost back again, Elsie thought. She was sure she'd had a dress in something similar back in the day.

'Oh, that's perfect. Thank you so much,' Howard said, grinning.

'You're welcome. Mum, can we get some?' The child said.

'No. We're getting the letters you want for your bedroom, remember?'

'But Muuum.'

'Come on. We don't want to keep your dad waiting.'

'Sorry,' Howard muttered to the woman who had just glared at him on her way past.

Elsie also offered a repentant cringe.

'Bye. Thanks again,' Howard and Elsie said.

'Bye,' the girl said with a big smile and wave of her hand, as she hurried to catch up with her mother, who had stalked off.

'How much do we need? And I assume we take this to the counter for them to cut?' Howard said, grabbing the bolt of fabric and looking around.

'Pace yourself, Howard, we need to get some elastic and the stuff for the braces. Check the list. And we can leave that here for now to save carrying it.'

'No way. Now we've decided, I'm not letting it out of my sight.'

'Okay, but don't say I didn't warn you. Or you can just wait here with it,' Elsie said.

'Nope this shop is too much fun. I want to take it all in. I can't believe you haven't brought me here before.'

They went back to the buttons where Elsie explained about attaching the braces. 'In case she wants to take that part off,' she said to Howard, who nodded in response. They also found proper braces, but by then Elsie was flagging, so stuck with her choice of bits and pieces to make their own and threw the ready-made ones into their basket in case this all went pear-shaped. She remembered all too well how sewing could do your head in.

'I enjoyed that,' Howard announced after they'd paid and were heading back to the bus stop.

'Me too. Now fingers crossed I can remember how to use the sewing machine.'

'Like riding a bike or falling off a log, I should imagine,' Howard said. 'I have full faith in you, dear.'

Back at home, Elsie went through to the spare room. Howard stood with his hands on his hips watching as she took the cover off the machine. 'Are you going to do it now?' he asked.

'Yes, I thought I might. Any reason why I shouldn't?' she said, half turning and looking up at him.

'No. No reason, I suppose. Shall I get to work on the tins, then?'

'I reckon so. If you like. Unless you want me to help.'

'No, not particularly,' he said and turned around to go.

'Just make sure you leave plenty of the cord so Milly can adjust them to suit,' Elsie called.

'Got it,' he said, raising his hand as he left the room. 'Before I get stuck in, can I get you anything to eat or drink?'

'No, thanks. I'm too engrossed here.'

'Okey-dokey. See you in a bit.'

'They look fantastic,' Elsie said what seemed just minutes later when she entered the garage. Though enough time had passed for Howard to have sprayed on undercoat and decide on a diamond pattern, which he'd drawn up on a piece of card as a template ready for painting.

'What do you think?' Elsie said, holding up the tiny pair of pants with braces attached. She'd gone with the ready-made braces in the end, having decided there was no point having them sitting around not utilised.

'Perfect. Wonderful,' Howard said, looking at them. 'That was quick.'

'Yes, it all came back to me. I'd forgotten how much I enjoyed sewing, too. Why did I stop, do you remember?'

'You ran out of projects? Could that be it? No girls around needing costumes and that sort of thing, no dress-up events for us to go to and us not needing cushions and the like for the house?' Howard offered.

'Yes, I suppose. Could have just taken a break and not thought to resume, like most everything else we used to do at some point, I guess.'

'True. You're probably right.'

'I vaguely recall something about having trouble,' Elsie mused.

'Most likely with threading the needle.'

'I didn't have any trouble today – well, not a huge amount.'

'Perhaps that's because you were so enthusiastic with the partic- ular project. I must say, I'm dead keen to put the colour on these,' Howard said, turning back to his tins on the bench. 'I'm resist- ing ignoring the instructions of leaving it to dry for the adequate time. What do you think of this design?'

'Great. Should work well with the pants, not that you'll actually see them underneath. Probably didn't need to paint them at all, really.'

'Well, we're covering our bases. In case she doesn't want to wear the pants, or whatever. And we didn't want to give her ratty- looking tins speckled in rust, remember?'

Elsie nodded. 'I hope Milly likes all this.'

'I think she will. I have no concerns on that score,' Howard said. 'Actually, I've had another idea.'

'Oh?'

'Yes, I'm on a roll. What do you think about getting some photos printed and going and getting an album for her as well? I loved going through ours – on the whole – and seeing all the things I'd forgotten about that we and our kids got up to. Particu- larly given how rarely everyone seems to print the pictures out these days. And it does fit with our retro theme – not that that's either here nor there.'

'That's a great idea, Howard. And it's probably not a bad plan to hedge our bets across a couple of gifts.'

'We can add to an album, too, if we remember to take photos at the party.'

'Yes, let's do that. It'll save Daniel remembering – he might be too busy wrangling all the children.'

'We could be official photographers.'

'Yes. I'm not sure how I'll be with a stack of rowdy kids, so it'll be a good excuse to keep out of the way.'

'We can do that tomorrow. Later I'll look into which bus goes to Kmart and the times.'

'Righteo. I'm putting the kettle on. Are you coming in?' Elsie said.

'Yes, I still have to wait a bit to paint,' Howard said.

Chapter Twenty

'Howard, have you noticed Milly seems to prefer being outside when she visits?' Elsie asked. She was sitting down at the table while Howard stood beside her, wrapping their gifts for Milly.

'No, not especially. I guess she's aware we wouldn't want a chook loose to poop on the carpet.'

'True, but not just about that. I don't know. I could be barking up the wrong tree. Just a feeling.'

'Well, go with it – it's always right.'

'Have you noticed she looks strangely at the couch?'

'No. But then I've never been as observant as you – I'm a man, remember? We're known for our lack of attention to the finer details. There we are. All wrapped! What do you think?' he asked, holding up the box containing Milly's birthday gift – the tins, pants and photo album, with some images already inside – freshly wrapped in bright pink paper.

'Perfect, dear. Never let it be said you don't take care of the little things.'

'Why thank you.' Howard pecked Elsie on the lips.

'Voila. Done here too,' Elsie said, her hands around the plate of miniature pavlovas decorated with cream and fresh strawberries, lifting it slightly. She'd made them that morning after the conversation she'd had with Milly in the front garden while weeding had come back to her over breakfast.

'Magnificent. Almost too lovely to eat. Right, are we all ready to go?'

'I think we are. Present – check. Dessert – check. Keys, wallet, phone – all, check.'

'Are you happy carrying that or would you like the present instead?' Howard asked.

'I'm good.' Elsie smiled to herself as she stood behind Howard at the front door while he opened it and then waited for her to pass through first. She paused for a sigh of contentment, thinking how wonderful it was to be going next door for dinner for Milly's birthday.

'I wonder if she'll have candles and how they'll be extinguished,' Howard mused aloud as they made their way down the driveway. 'People won't just go back to blowing on cakes again, will they, do you think?'

'That's a good point. I hope not. I shudder now at thinking that's how we all did it all those years.'

'Makes you wonder how many people got crook from it and never knew, doesn't it?'

'It sure does. But don't worry, I'm sure Milly and Daniel will have something covered. Or you can tactfully put them right. Remember that auntie of yours who always flatly refused to blow on a cake and instead would wave one of her birthday cards quickly across the top?'

'Oh yes! I'd quite forgotten that! Well remembered, dear,' Howard said.

Milly must have been watching through a window, because the door was opened as Howard was preparing to put down his load in order to free up a hand for knocking.

'Hello there, Milly. Happy eighth birthday!' Howard and Elsie said the same time.

'Thank you. Hello, Mr and Mrs Manning,' Milly said and wrapped her arms around each of them, despite them still holding their respective goods. 'You're right on time. Come in.'

'This is for you,' Howard said, offering the parcel.

'You didn't need to bring me anything. But thank you very much,' Milly said, accepting the box, clearly delighted.

'Hello,' Daniel said, standing in the kitchen. 'That's very good of you. And I truly meant you didn't need to bring anything for dinner. Just pop them down there on the bench.'

'We know you did. But I fancied doing these. I hope you don't mind,' Elsie said, glad to have put down the platter.

'Are you kidding? It's very much appreciated. I didn't do a cake for tonight because of the party on the weekend,' Daniel said.

'Great. We can stick some candles in them if you fancy, and you have some, that is. And, anyway, consider these as in-part returning the favour of the wonderful eggs,' Elsie added.

'I hope it's okay that we brought a gift,' Howard said. 'We took the instruction to apply to the party. It's not a real birthday dinner without a present,' he added, looking at Daniel.

'Perfectly fine. All good,' Daniel said.

'Can I open it now, Dad?' Milly said, clutching the present.

'Is it your birthday today?' Daniel said, grinning.

Milly nodded enthusiastically.

'Well, then … If it's okay with Mr and Mrs Manning …' Daniel said.

'It sure is,' Howard said.

'Oh yes, absolutely,' Elsie said.

Milly sat on the floor in the lounge room area, which was similar to Howard and Elsie's space, though with more clutter, Elsie thought, taking things in while trying not to look too nosey. No, not *clutter*, she revised, more *life*. Everything was neat, but there was more colour and more stuff than in their place next door.

'Are you coming, Dad and Mrs Manning?' Milly called.

'Oh, sorry, are you waiting for us?' Elsie said, looking over to where Milly was sitting cross-legged on the floor with her large present in front. Howard was already settled on the black puffy leather couch.

'Okay, all ready,' Elsie said as she sat down next to Howard. She clasped his hand, which he squeezed. They shared a conspiratorial grin. Under her hand she felt Howard loosen his grip and cross his fingers. She patted his hand reassuringly.

'Righto, kiddo, all set,' Daniel said, also now seated beside Elsie.

Out of the corner of her eye, Elsie saw him extract his phone from his pocket and bring the camera up. She hoped for both their sakes, but mostly for Howard's, that Milly liked the gift, or at least had concealing-of-disappointment down pat.

Elsie found herself holding her breath as Milly carefully picked at the sticky tape.

'Oh, just tear it, Milly,' Howard said. 'Presents are for ripping open, I say. Go for it.'

Milly grinned and, with concentration and joy plastered across her face, put a finger under the edge and tore a big hole in the paper wrapping. More slowly she peeled back the top of the box and then peered in. She brought out the pair of brightly coloured pants and held them up.

'Wow, how cool are these?' she said, now standing up and holding them against her. 'Did you make them, Mr and Mrs Manning?' she asked, looking from Howard to Elsie.

Elsie nodded, a little flutter of something she couldn't quite place – joy? Gratitude? – rippled through her at Milly's lack of assumption that she had been the seamstress. Maybe one day there really would be gender equality.

'I'm not quite sure what they are, but I love them!' Milly said, looking a little perplexed. She twisted her mouth slightly and then carefully laid them on the floor and returned her attention to the box.

'We'll explain in a bit,' Howard said. 'Keep going,' he added, nodding at the box.

Milly brought out the photo album next, and opened it. 'Aww, look at Two and me. Oh wow. Thank you so much,' she said, holding it to her chest for a moment and sighing happily before putting it down beside her and diving back into the box.

Next Milly brought out the first of the two brightly coloured tins, a look of pure confusion across her knitted brows. 'So pretty,' she said, stroking the item that was now in her lap.

'Fantastic!' Daniel said, clapping his hands and grinning widely. Milly looked up at him.

'You know what it is?' Howard said to Daniel.

'I do,' Daniel said, nodding.

Milly got the second tin out. She was fiddling with the cord attached and turning the tin around in her hands, clearly still none-the-wiser.

'Hop up, kiddo,' Daniel said, vacating his seat. 'Right, put these on,' he said, holding up the pants for Milly to step into.

Elsie clasped her hands to her chest as she saw what a perfect fit they were, as Daniel adjusted the braces.

'Cool,' Milly said, looking down and running her hands over the bright fabric.

Daniel then lined up the two tins in front of Milly. 'Now, put your hands on my shoulders, if you need to steady yourself, and then pop your feet onto the tins, one at a time. Okay?'

'Okay.' They all watched as Milly carefully, using Daniel as support, climbed onto the tins.

'Wow, I'm tall. Yay!' she said, looking down.

Howard and Elsie smiled at her.

'Hold up, there's more,' Daniel said. 'You lift the cords up, and your feet, so you can move.'

'Really?' Milly frowned with scepticism.

'Yep.'

'You might need to adjust the length,' Howard said. 'I had to take a guess. The knot is under the lid,' he added, pointing.

'Stand up straight, Milly,' Daniel said. 'Now grab these.' He held the cord loops up and waited for Milly to take hold of them before letting go himself. 'And you lift the tin with this, as you lift your foot. And, voila, we have stilts to walk with! Brilliant. Perfect length, too, Howard. And then, Milly, you pull the bottoms of the pants down to hide the tins – then people will think you're just tall,' he added. He again clapped his hands gleefully. 'What a fantastic gift.' He beamed at Howard and Elsie.

Howard was a little concerned Milly wasn't quite sharing her father's enthusiasm.

'Like this?' Milly asked a moment later, carefully lifting a foot and a hand and then the second foot and hand. As the tins moved, Milly moved on top of them.

Elsie was glad the Wynter's house had wall-to-wall carpet where their house had tiles, otherwise there'd be quite a din going on.

'That's it, Milly, you've got it. My, you're a quick learner,' Howard said. 'Just take it easy so you don't fall off.'

'This is so cool,' Milly said, now striding confidently around the room.

'Well done,' Elsie said, clapping.

'There you go, you're getting up quite a clip. Bravo,' Howard said, clapping his hands.

'Yes, good job, Milly,' Daniel said.

They all watched as Milly made her way around. And then she was back in front of them.

Milly hugged Howard, who was closest, and then Elsie. 'Thank you so much, I love them! Best birthday present ever! So cool,' she added in a mutter, and took off again.

Howard and Elsie exchanged more grins. Elsie suspected Howard glowed inside just as much as she did. What a priceless moment. How lucky were they?

'Again, thank you both, so much,' Daniel said.

'Our pleasure,' Howard and Elsie said at the same time.

'I'm glad you knew what they were, otherwise it could have gone very differently,' Howard said.

'Oh no, you would have just had to demonstrate,' Daniel said with a cheeky grin.

'Yes, well, we're a little past that.'

'Yes, that ship has well and truly sailed – long ago,' Elsie said.

'Look, Two likes them,' Milly called, turning her head back to the small group of adults seated behind her. Howard, Elsie and Daniel looked over to the glass door leading out to the garden. 'And even One and Three,' Milly added.

'Oh, aren't they cute?' Elsie said.

'Magnificent birds,' Howard said. They chuckled at seeing the three chooks lined up, peering in, twisting their heads from side to side with curiosity.

Just as Elsie thought they all looked the same and she couldn't tell which was which, Daniel said, 'You might get visits from all three now, Milly has managed to worm her way into all of their hearts — she's a real little chook whisperer.'

'I'm sure that'll mean you'll get lots of eggs,' Elsie said.

'Yes. Happy chooks lay lots of happy eggs, don't you?' Milly said, waving to them. 'Can I go out and show them my stilts? Is that what they're called?' she added, turning back to look from Howard and Elsie.

'Yes, that's right,' Howard and Elsie said, together, and nodded.

'Sure can,' Daniel said. 'Just please don't walk back inside on them without checking they don't have any chook poo underneath, like you do with your other shoes,' he said. 'Go on, off you go.'

'Thanks,' Milly said. She opened the door and then carefully stepped out. 'Look, One, Two and Three, how cool am I?'

'Shut the door behind you, Milly,' Daniel called, as the first step clanged on the pavers. Milly did as she was told.

'You've absolutely made her birthday,' Daniel said, beaming. 'Again, thank you.'

'Thank *you* for including us. The pleasure is all ours, I can assure you, isn't that right, dear?' He clasped Elsie's hand and turned and looked into her eyes, smiling warmly.

'Oh, yes, truer words never spoken,' Elsie said. 'She really is a wonderful girl.'

'I think so. But I can understand if she's an acquired taste,' Daniel said, smiling, his eyes on his daughter outside. 'Right, can I get you a drink of something?' he said, slapping his hands on his thighs and getting up. 'I'm having a beer. But I have red and white wine and sherry too, if you prefer. Or even a shandy, actually — there's some lemonade as well.'

'Oh, a shandy would hit the spot,' Elsie said. 'I haven't had one of them for a long time.'

'Yes, please, that sounds perfect,' Howard said.

'Great. Coming right up. Dinner shouldn't be far away,' Daniel said, checking his watch. 'Pizza for the birthday girl – her choice, so I hope that's okay.'

'Oh yes – wonderful,' Elsie said.

'Yum,' Howard said. 'I haven't had pizza in donkey's years.'

'No,' Elsie said. She tried to remember the last time, but became a bit distracted by the sudden rumble in her stomach and the salivating going on in her mouth.

Daniel had just finished pouring the drinks and handing them to Howard and Elsie when the doorbell rang. While he went to answer it, Elsie and Howard watched Milly playing with the chooks outside, striding up and down across the lawn, a chicken, which Howard thought might have been Two, following close behind. The other two sleek beauties had lost interest and were kicking up dirt and fossicking in the garden bed nearby. Again, Howard reached over and gently clasped Elsie's hand. She gripped it firmly and gave it an extra squeeze, knowing he'd be feeling exactly what she was at that moment: that life didn't get much better than this. Their shoulders lifted and then subsided in unison as they both took a deep satisfying breath. They then raised their noses slightly, detecting a whiff of pizza, garlic bread and warm, damp cardboard.

'Can you please just tap on the glass and let Milly know?' Daniel said. 'Ordinarily, I'd shout,' he added with a laugh.

Howard did as asked, and Milly looked up and smiled and waved at Howard as he beckoned her in.

At the door she carefully stepped off the stilts and turned them over to check underneath them. Then, with some difficulty, she gathered the strings to lift off the ground, and raised her pants at the same time.

Howard got up and went over to open the door for her and to keep Two, who was right on her heels, from following her inside. 'Sorry, Two, you can't come in,' Howard said, gently holding the chook back with his foot. 'Well, I'm assuming not,' he added, his silent question answered immediately by Milly.

'Stay, Two,' Milly commanded, in a tone that surprised both Elsie and Howard. 'Good girl,' she added, recognisable as the gentle Milly again.

'You're very good at that,' Howard said.

'Yes, I'm bossy.'

'Oh, no, it wasn't a criticism,' Howard said.

'I know,' Milly said cheerfully, 'there's nothing wrong with being a little bossy.'

'Oh,' Howard said, looking a bit lost.

'Good for you,' Elsie said, a wave of awe sweeping through her.

'She won't listen if I'm too meek and mild,' Milly explained.

'Quite right,' Howard said.

'Dad, where shall I put these? I didn't see any poo.' She had one tin tucked under each arm inspecting it again, turning her head to check carefully.

'Perhaps just there on the mat, in that case.'

'I want to leave my pants on, if that's okay. They are so awesome.'

'Well, mind you don't trip over them,' Elsie said. 'Would you like me to roll them up a bit for you?'

'Oh, yes, please. That's a good idea.' Milly appeared in front of Elsie, who bent down and carefully folded the bottoms up.

'You could also hoist them up and secure them with a hair tie or one of those scrunchie things you wear,' Howard said. 'That's what our girls used to do.'

'Did they?' Milly said, eyes big.

'They did,' Howard said. 'Though their pants weren't as bright as yours. I think Corinne had red and white striped and Janine black and white polka dots, from memory.'

'That's right. Well remembered, Howard,' Elsie said.

They sang happy birthday and then Milly followed Howard's gentle suggestion and instructions on how to extinguish the eight candles Daniel had stuck into individual mini pavlovas. Though she frowned with scepticism as she swiftly waved her birthday card back and forth a few times just above the flames.

'Oh wow, it works! And no germs!' Milly exclaimed, wide-eyed, a moment later. 'Thanks, Mr Manning, that's a really cool trick,' she added as Daniel carefully removed each candle.

'Yes, thanks for that brilliant solution, Howard. Much appreciated,' Daniel said.

'Glad to be of assistance,' Howard said, beaming.

'These are really yummy, Mrs Manning,' Milly said, after she'd had her first bite of pavlova. 'Do you think you could bring some of these to my party on Sunday?'

'Millicent Wynter!' Daniel cried.

'What?' Milly said, looking up.

'It's not polite to impose on people.'

'I don't know what that means,' Milly said innocently.

Elsie tried not to smile. Poor Daniel, he looked a little lost.

'It's not polite to expect people to do things for you,' Daniel said.

'But ...' Milly looked genuinely confused.

Elsie thought she couldn't blame her.

'Mr and Mrs Manning were not put on this earth to be at your beck and call.'

'Oh. I get it. Sorry.' Milly looked downcast. And then, after appearing as if in deep thought for a moment, raised her head and said, 'How about you supervise me while I make them? Would that be okay? Dad?'

Howard almost laughed out loud at recognising the defeat in Daniel. Ah, the number of battles of wills of this nature he'd had with his daughters, who far too often had exhibited the ability to outwit and outthink him … He dared not look at Elsie, lest he actually burst out laughing, which would be completely inappropriate right now.

Oh, you don't have a chance with this one, Elsie thought, mentally shaking her head while being careful to keep the broad smile she wished to display hidden. *Give up now, Daniel, you won't win this one.* She's quicker than you, and one step ahead.

'Daaad?' Milly urged. 'You can't tell me off, anyway, because it's my birthday,' she pointed out. 'Dems the rules, remember?' She now looked at him with her lips pursed and her head tilted slightly.

Could the kid look any cuter? Howard thought. *Clever little scamp.*

'It's perfectly okay with me,' Elsie said quietly. 'I'm both happy to make some to bring to the party and/or do so with Milly's assistance – or vice versa.' She really hoped she wasn't overstepping, but she also wanted to break this deadlock and not have Milly's birthday dinner ruined by a battle of wills. This age was precious – for both father and daughter – and before long their stoushes would be on much larger issues. Though maybe it was important to set firm ground rules now in order to prevent later skirmishes. She was well out of the loop with wrangling small children. *Oops. Bit late now.* She offered Daniel a cringe.

'Seriously, Milly, you do my head in sometimes,' Daniel said and let out a defeated sigh. But he seemed to Elsie to be relatively jovial.

The look on Milly's face, which was a combination of innocence and triumph, was priceless. She looked at him expectantly.

'Now, I'm agreeing to this because Mrs Manning has said it's okay ... And, Mrs Manning is free to change her mind at any time ...' At this he looked at Elsie.

Elsie nodded, hoping her expression was stern enough.

Milly clapped her hands. 'Goodie.'

'Let me finish, Milly,' Daniel continued, hand raised. 'And I'm letting your impert ... um ... cheekiness slide because, as you pointed out, it's your birthday. But please don't make a habit of putting people on the spot and asking favours of them.'

'Okay. Got it. Sorry.'

Yes, son, good move. Pick your battles, and probably best to let this one go by the wayside, Howard thought, chuckling to himself.

'And I'll be chief taste tester – quality control, if you will?' he said. He was hoping to wrest back the previous buoyancy which he considered was at risk of dwindling. And it was the kid's birthday. *Birthdays are everything at her age, well, they should be, because life isn't carefree for long before it becomes all too hard.*

'Oh yes,' Milly said, cheerful again.

'Honestly,' Daniel muttered, shaking his head as he tucked back into his pavlova.

Chapter Twenty-one

'Happy birthday again, Milly,' Howard and Elsie said on Sunday when they met on Daniel and Milly's driveway, ready to go over to the park for Milly's birthday party together.

'Thank you. Good afternoon, Mr and Mrs Manning,' Milly said, giving each a hug.

'Groovy pants,' Howard said, grinning and giving Milly a gentle nudge.

'Yes, I love them. I'm not taking my stilts, though. I don't want one of the others wrecking them.'

'That's probably a good idea,' Howard said.

'Hi, Elsie. Hi, Howard,' Daniel said. 'It's not too late to back out – it might be a raucous, exhausting hour or so.' He puffed slightly and was a little red in the face.

'We consider ourselves forewarned and are, as they say, all in. Aren't we, Elsie?' Howard said.

'Absolutely. We're here with bells on.'

Milly looked them both over, her brow furrowed.

'Not with actual bells on, Milly,' Elsie said with a laugh. 'It's just a saying to suggest we're excited to be here.'

'Oh. Okay,' Milly said, looking both confused and disappointed.

'Are you excited, Milly?' Howard asked.

'Yes. And ...' She seemed to be carefully searching for words, or had thought better of continuing. 'Well, I'm going to miss One, Two and Three. They can't come. They have to miss out.'

'That's probably for the best,' Howard said.

'Yes, you don't want to have to worry about them,' Elsie said.

'That's true,' Milly said. 'I really hope everyone has a good time.'

'I'm sure they will,' Elsie said.

'Yes. And if they don't, you know that's not really your problem, don't you, Milly?' Howard said. 'They might have had a bad morning, or be sad or upset about something completely unrelated to your party.'

'I guess,' said Milly, sounding unconvinced.

'I know you want everyone to be happy all the time, kiddo, but you can't control other people's emotions. We've talked about this,' Daniel said, putting an arm around her shoulder.

'It's your birthday – the most important thing is you having fun,' Howard said.

'I suppose.'

Elsie frowned at how out-of-sorts Milly sounded. She was smiling, but the child didn't seem to at all exude the joy that Elsie thought a carefree eight-year-old embarking on a party with her friends should be. She caught Howard's eye over Milly's head and could tell by his pursed lips that he was thinking the same thoughts as her.

'It's not too late to cancel,' Daniel said. 'If you really don't want to do this, you don't have to.'

'No. It's okay, my friends are counting on me. And it is only for an hour.'

'They would understand if ...'

'I'm not so sure about that, Dad,' Milly said and bestowed such a withering expression on her father that Elsie had to look away lest she burst out laughing. Looking down, she noticed Howard shuffling his feet and again knew they were very much on the same page.

'Oh, you're too smart for me, kiddo,' Daniel said, squeezing her to him. 'Seriously though, if you want out, just say the word.'

Elsie's heart melted, watching the two of them.

'No, come on, let's get going,' Milly said, clapping her hands and easing out from under Daniel's arm.

'What can we do, Milly?' Elsie asked.

Milly thought for a moment. 'Nothing. We're all good, thanks, Mrs Manning. Aren't we, Dad?'

'Yes. We just need to bring the esky out. Then we're all done and ready to go.'

'Would you like a hand with it?' Howard asked.

'Actually, that would be great, if you wouldn't mind. It shouldn't be too heavy – just a bit cumbersome.'

'Here, dear, you take this,' Howard said, passing over to Elsie the stack of Tupperware containers filled with mini-pavlovas that they'd made yesterday, under Milly's careful observation.

'We'll hop into the car so we're all ready to go. Okay, Mrs Manning? If you get in first, I can take those for you and then pass them to you when you're in, if that would help,' Milly said, holding open the door for Elsie.

'That's a good idea – thank you, Milly. They're a bit awkward, but not heavy,' she said, handing the stack over, and then climbing into the car. Milly waited until after Elsie had put her seatbelt on to return the Tupperware.

'All set,' Elsie said, positioning them on her lap. Milly closed the door with a clunk and went around and climbed in beside her.

'I hope you don't mind sitting in the back with me, Mrs Manning,' Milly said.

'Not at all. It's very comfy back here. And I'm honoured to have the birthday girl all to myself.' Milly smiled at Elsie and then busied herself with putting her seatbelt on.

'That's very good of you to leave the front for Mr Manning,' Elsie said.

'Oh. Well ...' Milly looked a little bashful. 'I'm not actually allowed to sit in the front yet – because of the airbags. I'm too small. I think I might be allowed when I've turned nine. So, a little while yet.'

'Oh, yes, of course. Sorry, I forgot.'

'That's okay.'

'We were the same with our dear old dog. Maisie.'

'Yes, I know Maisie.'

'Right.' Elsie sucked in her breath quietly. Here was the opportunity she'd been waiting about a month for. The time and circumstances had never quite coincided where she'd felt comfortable enough to broach the subject, but here they were, sitting quietly, just the two of them and Milly had all but handed it to her on a platter. 'Can I ask you something, Milly?'

'Okay.' Milly turned and looked at Elsie intently.

'Did you see her ... um ... her ... ghost that day in the garden when you helped me with the weeding?'

'I did.'

'Do you see other things?'

'Sometimes.'

'And have you seen Maisie again?' Elsie experienced a strange sense of wistfulness – a mix of happiness, hope and sadness – surge through her.

'No. I think she just needed me to tell you goodbye for her. Or something. I'm sorry. I hope that doesn't make you sad.'

'It's okay,' Elsie said, her voice a croak as it pushed past the lump that had suddenly formed in her throat. 'Maybe just a little,' she added.

Milly nodded. 'You don't have to hide your emotions. They're a natural part of life,' she said.

'Thanks, Milly,' Elsie said and squeezed Milly's hand, which was resting to her right on the seat between. 'I just miss her, that's all,' she added, wiping a stray tear with her left hand while continuing to clasp Milly's hand.

'I know. I miss my two grandparents that died too. But I know they're okay – I saw them. Just the once. I think they were saying goodbye properly too. It was quite nice, really.'

'That's good, Milly,' Elsie said. Milly nodded thoughtfully and turned to face the front.

'So, you're not so keen on your birthday or your party?' Elsie said, eager to change the subject. She smiled gently over at Milly. 'Do you want to talk about it? It's okay if you don't.'

Milly shrugged. She fiddled with the edge of her t-shirt, looked down at the floor.

'Are you, maybe, missing your grandparents? Or your mum?' Elsie prompted carefully.

'I don't think you can miss what you've never known, can you?' Milly said, looking at Elsie again and frowning.

'I think you can miss what your friends have, without knowing how that something feels, if you know what I mean?'

Milly nodded thoughtfully. 'I really do miss my grandparents, actually,' she said quietly, picking up Elsie's hand and putting it in her lap and holding it with both of hers.

Elsie thought her heart would break into two. She bit her lip and snuck a look at Milly. But Milly was now looking out of the window away from her.

'I remember them, but not as much as before. That's what makes me sad,' she said, now looking up at Elsie. Big wet teardrops hung from the long lashes surrounding her enormous brown eyes.

'Oh, darling.' Elsie undid her seatbelt. 'Come here,' she said, opening her arms wide and then welcoming Milly to her. 'You know, in my experience, the best and strongest memories – the ones of the things that made you feel the happiest at the time – come back when you least expect. When you feel that you've quite forgotten them. It's a bit like how a wave at the beach comes in and then goes back out, leaving the wet sand behind. Perhaps that's not a very good example.'

'Do you mean like a rock pool – that the wave comes in and the water gets trapped in the gaps and can't get back out, so it stays?'

'Yes. Exactly. That's a great way of putting it, Milly. What the waves do is called ebb and flow. Some memories you might think have gone forever, but then they slip back in when you least expect. Like with our dear Maisie dog. I'd forgotten how her feet sounded on the carpet. And last night I could have sworn I heard her. No, that's not really a good example, either.' Elsie frowned.

'Don't worry, Mrs Manning, I think I know what you mean,' Milly said. 'But it still hurts. Right in my tummy. It's like being hungry. But, also, not like that at all. Here,' she said and pushed her fist into the top of her stomach.

'I know it does, Milly. Unfortunately, the things that mean a lot keep sending reminders. Some are painful and some not quite so much.'

Milly nodded and then they slipped into silence.

Elsie wondered what was taking Howard and Daniel so long.

'Thank you,' Milly said quietly, bringing Elsie's attention back into the car.

'What for, darling?'

'For being you. And for being here with me.'

'Oh, darling girl. It's my pleasure. You've become very special to Mr Manning and me,' she said, reaching over and stroking Milly's hair.

'And you're very special to me,' Milly said, smiling up at Elsie and blinking.

'I'm glad,' Elsie said, beaming back.

At that moment Howard and Daniel appeared carrying the esky, one handle each. They put it in the boot and closed it with a thump.

'Right. Ready to get this show on the road?' Daniel said from his driver's seat, looking in the rear-vision mirror at Milly.

'Yep, all good, Dad. Seatbelts on,' Milly called in a much more cheerful voice.

'Oh yes, good remembering,' Howard said, snapping his on and then giving a salute.

'These chairs are for you, Mr and Mrs Manning,' Milly said, unfolding two chairs and setting them up. She patted the seats. She'd already taken the containers of mini pavlovas and placed them on the small table that Daniel had set up, with Howard's help.

'Oh, we could have brought our own,' Elsie said.

'We absolutely could have. Are you sure there are enough to go around?' Howard added.

'Yes, perfectly sure,' Milly said.

'Thank you, then, that's lovely of you,' Elsie said. 'Are you sure we can't do anything to help?'

'Yes, is there anything else to do?' Howard said, looking around.

'Nope.' Daniel said. 'Not yet, anyway. We've gone very low-key, haven't we, Milly?'

'We have,' Milly said.

'Sounds like a good plan to me,' Howard said.

'But not boring,' Milly said reassuringly.

'Oh, nothing with you involved could ever be considered boring, Milly, I'm certain of that,' Howard said, patting Milly's shoulder before sitting down on the indicated chair.

Elsie sat down also.

'Well, we'll see,' Milly said, again giving a glimpse of being well beyond her eight years, complete with hands on hips.

'I know! Would you like me to push you on the swings before everyone arrives?' Milly asked.

'Do you mean us, Milly?' Howard said, looking up at Milly and then over at Elsie.

'Yes.'

'Oh, well … well, yes, actually. I'd love that. I haven't done that for donkey's years,' Howard said, getting to his feet again.

'Oh, go on, then. Why not?' Elsie said, also getting up.

'Come on, you're never too old to swing,' Milly said, holding out her hands to be grasped by both Howard and Elsie. Elsie caught Daniel's eye and returned his wink. She grinned.

'It's okay, I won't push hard,' Milly reassured, as they made their way over to the play equipment.

'You might not be able to, Milly,' Howard said with a chuckle. 'I'm probably quite heavily.'

'Well, I am quite strong,' Milly said.

'Yes, I'm sure you are.'

'You know, Milly, we should be pushing you, since it's your birthday,' Elsie said when they'd settled themselves on the curved rubber swings that were actually really quite comfortable.

'It's not my birthday today. And I do it all the time. And you need adventures, remember? Though, I'm not sure this really counts. Oh well,' she added, as if to herself, before shrugging. 'Ready?'

'Yes. Good to go,' Howard said.

'Yep, and me,' Elsie said.

'This is fun,' Howard said a few moments later as they gathered pace.

'Okay?' Milly asked.

'Oh yes,' Elsie said.

'Absolutely. Whee,' Howard said.

'Tell me if you need to stop,' Milly said.

'We're going to wear you out, Milly,' Howard said.

'Yes,' Elsie agreed.

'That's okay,' Milly said, though Elsie detected a slight puff to her voice.

'Here, let me help,' Daniel said, appearing behind Howard. 'You push Mrs Manning, Milly.'

'Cool. Thanks, Dad.'

'How's that?' Daniel asked Howard.

'Perfect. I feel a bit of a fool, but I also don't give a hoot what anyone thinks.'

'Yes, me too. But I'm having far too much fun to care,' Elsie said.

'We both swing whenever we come over here, don't we, Milly?' Daniel said.

'Yes, you're never too old to swing,' Milly said again.

'Exactly,' Daniel said. Then a few moments later, he added, 'Sorry, folks, but our first guests have just arrived. We'd better go and greet them, Milly.'

'Sorry. We can do some more later, if you want,' Milly said, letting the swing go and heading off after her dad.

Despite saying they didn't care what anyone else thought, Elsie and Howard quickly vacated their positions as soon as the swings had stopped. They went and sat down on their allocated chairs and watched as two young kids headed towards them, with a mother in tow. Howard couldn't tell if half the kids were boys or girls, in their bright clothes and long hair, not that it mattered, he told himself. *Why did everything need labels?*

'Mr and Mrs Manning, this is Joey and Ethan – they're twins, but not identical,' Milly said. 'And this is their mum, Mrs Taylor.'

'Hi,' Mrs Taylor said, raising a hand.

'Hello,' Howard and Elsie said, nodding and smiling.

'Mr and Mrs Manning are our next-door neighbours, and my very good friends,' Milly announced proudly.

'Okay, off you go,' Mrs Taylor said, making shooing motions towards her kids with both hands.

'We'll be singing happy birthday and having cake soon,' Milly called, as they ran off towards the jungle gym equipment. They each raised a hand in acknowledgement. 'Is it okay if I join them?' Milly asked, looking at her dad.

'Of course, kiddo,' Daniel said.

'Will you be okay, Mr and Mrs Manning?' Milly asked.

'We absolutely will, thank you, Milly,' Howard said.

'Yes, don't you worry about us,' Elsie said. Milly hesitated, clearly not too sure about leaving them. 'Go on and have fun with your friends,' Elsie urged. 'We'll be right here if you need us.'

'Yes, right here,' Howard said, mirroring Elsie's gentle tone.

'Okay,' Milly said and skipped off after the boys.

'I'm Rachel,' Mrs Taylor said, having unfolded a chair and set it up beside Elsie. 'Sorry, but I don't do handshakes anymore – Covid,' she added by explanation and shrugged.

'Fair enough. Howard and Elsie,' Howard said. 'Pleased to meet you.'

Elsie was just about to ask Rachel if she lived far away, to start a conversation, when the woman got her phone out and began furiously texting, her phone beeping in between bouts, which were clearly replies. Though the speed at which her fingers moved, seemingly without pausing, made it look to Elsie as if she was typing a novel or essay – definitely something long. Except she did see a series of bubbles containing texts out of the corner of her eye.

She cast a glance at Howard and received raised eyebrows in return. Invisible again, Elsie thought, clasping her hands in her lap and leaning back into her chair to watch Milly at play. This time she was happy to be left alone, though couldn't help wondering if Rachel's kids felt the same, given the number of times they appeared to look over in their direction, seemingly trying to catch their mother's attention.

Gradually the park filled with children and their parents or guardians. A couple of people were introduced as nannies. Howard and Elsie lost track of who was whom and which child belonged with which adult. What mattered to Elsie was that Milly seemed okay. She wasn't racing around like most of the others, who seemed to be playing chasey in between darting back and forth to grab morsels of food and drinks from the table, but she was at least off interacting with her peers.

Elsie kept an eye on Howard, who was a few steps away, taking some photos. She was relieved when her attention was caught by

Milly, whose eyes had just lit up at seeing a little boy with similar dark hair and features, accompanied by an older woman, walking towards her. She smiled at seeing Milly grab hold of the boy's hand and drag him towards where she was sitting. Howard materialised beside her, just as Milly and the boy arrived.

'Mr and Mrs Manning, I'd like to introduce you to my friend Connor. We're having a sleepover at my house tonight,' she added proudly.

'Oh, that's wonderful,' Howard said. 'Hello, Connor,' he added.

'Fantastic, Milly. Hi, Connor,' Elsie said to the shy-looking child.

'Hello,' Connor said, smiling weakly.

'And his foster mum, Mrs Draper is …' Milly looked around. 'Oh. Well, she's over there,' Milly said, pointing.

Both Elsie and Howard looked over towards where Milly was indicating, ready to introduce themselves, but Mrs Draper had her back to them and was moving away. Elsie thought she appeared to be talking on the phone; she certainly had one hand up by her ear.

'You're just in time for cake, Connor. Dad! We can do cake now – Connor's here.'

'Okay then,' Daniel said to Milly. And then in a loud voice, his hands around his mouth, he called loudly, 'Kids! We're cutting the cake now. Come on. Over here, everyone.'

Gradually all the kids came together from all directions and, in a swarm, headed towards the table of food. The accompanying adults moved over and stood back behind the throng of children now gathered close around Daniel, who had lifted the lid from a cake with shiny chocolate icing sprinkled with coconut and thin pink candles sticking out of it.

Milly and Connor stood side by side behind the cake, waiting while Daniel lit the candles. Then everyone sang happy birthday to Milly and cheered.

'Have you made your wish, Milly?' Daniel said.

Howard saw Milly close her eyes tight. She then appeared to be concentrating intently for a moment, before opening her eyes again and nodding to her dad. Then Howard experienced a wave of pride go through him as Milly looked up at him across the table and gave a reverent nod before picking up the card lying beside the cake and beginning to wave it deftly above the candles. He practically surged with importance at hearing all the utterances of awe coming from the kids gathered around watching Milly make a show of extinguishing the candles.

'Bravo, Milly,' Howard called, unable to stop from praising his young protégé as she finished her performance with a small bow complete with hands outstretched, palms up.

Elsie chuckled beside him and gave him a gentle nudge.

Utterances of 'awesome', 'wow', 'that's cool' gradually petered out as all the candles were carefully removed and set aside.

Elsie wanted to laugh at the rapturous attention being paid to the cake by the children gathered around Daniel, some standing with their elbows resting on the table watching closely as he cut it into pieces.

Howard was thrilled when Milly brought the first pieces over, sitting on a paper napkin, and offered them to him and Elsie.

'Oh, how lovely. Thank you, Milly,' Howard and Elsie said at the same time. They exchanged broad grins and tucked into their cake.

Howard and Elsie declined Daniel's offer of more food and drink, and before long the park around them was emptying and Daniel was starting to pack up. Elsie was pleased to look over and see Milly and Connor sitting side by side on the platform of the play equipment, their legs dangling down, feet swinging. She wondered if they were deep in conversation or sitting in companiable silence.

Elsie got up to help Daniel and Howard followed suit.

'It's okay, thanks,' Daniel said. 'I'm just tossing everything into the esky and the car to deal with back at the house. Though a hand carrying the esky again would be great, thanks, Howard,' he added.

'No problem,' Howard said, folding up his and Elsie's chairs and leaning them against his leg. 'If you give me the keys, I can take the chairs across to the car, if you like.'

'Yes, thanks. Here you go,' Daniel said, handing the keys over.

Gradually everything was packed into the car. Milly and Connor were called over and then they all clambered into the vehicle. As they drove away from the kerb beside the park, Howard thought he was pleased to see there was no sign they'd been there, except the grass was a bit flatter than when they'd arrived.

'Mr and Mrs Manning?' Milly said on their way back home.

'Yes, Milly?' Howard and Elsie said in unison.

'Could Connor come and meet your robot vacuum, Brian, when we get back? If you're not too sick of noisy children, that is. We'll be very quiet, won't we, Connor?'

Connor was nodding enthusiastically.

'But it's okay if it's not okay with you. We can come another time.'

'I don't see why not,' Howard said. 'Elsie?' He couldn't see her sitting in the seat right behind him.

'Yes. It's perfectly fine with me.'

'Cool,' Milly said. 'Connor hasn't seen one before. How's he been behaving, Mr Manning?'

'Quite well, recently, thank you, Milly. No major problems.'

'That's good.' Howard wondered if Milly had sat back hard into her seat with her arms folded. He suspected she had.

'Here we are, folks,' Daniel announced a few minutes later as they pulled up in his driveway.

They all piled out of the car and accepted armfuls of items and carried them inside until the car was empty again.

'Thanks for a lovely time, Daniel,' Elsie said as they headed out, having both eschewed the offer of a hot beverage or something stronger.

Howard had almost said aloud that he didn't dare accept more hospitality from Daniel, and further delay his and Elsie's return home, with Milly and Connor hovering nearby, clearly waiting for them to leave.

Chapter Twenty-two

'He's this way,' Howard said, striding across the open-plan living space, phone in hand, to the office where Brian's charge station was located. 'Here we are,' he said, pointing. 'This is Brian. Brian, meet Connor.'

'Hi, Brian,' Connor said.

'He's recharging at present. I'll see if I can get him going again – he's programmed to start tomorrow morning, you see,' Howard explained, prodding at his phone, plainly aware that he probably looked and sounded old and incompetent to the quiet little boy who, thanks to his shy and slightly sad manner, made his heart ache. He was also, as ridiculous as he told himself it was, keen to impress the child. No, perhaps not *impress*, as such – cheer up.

Brian, with his LED lights, seemed to blink to life slowly and look around. Then, after performing a complete spin, and emitting a little electronic mutter to himself, the machine took off out of the room, passing very close to Howard's and Connor's feet as it did. They turned as if joined at the hip and watched Brian go.

'Cool,' Connor said and followed Brian out of the room, followed by Howard.

Howard smiled. This ritual of Brian's never failed to amuse and delight him, either.

According to the instructions, once on his mission, Brian was supposed to follow the map or pattern he'd established the first time. But far too often he seemed to do a completely random series of criss-crossing movements to cover the space. This is what he was now doing.

Howard often told him he didn't blame him for wanting a change – the same way day in, day out would be boring as hell. Well, if Brian had a brain. Howard often forgot the device didn't and couldn't think for itself. Though far too often it did seem to answer him when he spoke to it. He could see how people feared machines taking over the world.

Connor laughed and clapped his hands. 'That's awesome,' he said.

'See, told you,' Milly said, pulling Howard away from his thoughts and back out to the action. He sat down in his chair and watched the children watching Brian. A few times he noticed they deliberately moved to stand in his path. And each time the machine would, just in time, change direction and swivel its way around to avoid them.

'Can I get you kids anything?' Elsie asked from the kitchen, having disappeared up the hall for a bit upon arrival. To use the loo, most likely, Howard thought.

'I'm good, thanks, Mrs Manning,' Milly said.

'Yes, me too, thank you,' Connor said, though with less certainty and volume than Milly.

It seemed like just a few moments later that the kids had lost interest in Brian and were hovering by the arm of Howard's chair.

He immediately recognised the mannerisms. It may have been eons since their girls were this age and since he'd had anything to do with kids, but he could see they were itching to ask him something.

'What is it, kids?' Howard asked. 'You look like you've got ants in your pants, which, in my experience, means you might want to ask something but aren't quite sure how or if you should. Am I right?' he added gently, looking into Milly's eyes while smiling kindly. Partially hidden behind Milly was Connor, who Howard couldn't see much of, though imagined he was probably clutching his hands in front of him nervously, or had them tucked deep into his pockets.

'We do, actually, Mr Manning,' Milly said. 'You're very smart.'

Flattery, flattery, Howard thought with a silent chuckle. The kids knew which way was up. 'Yes?' he urged.

'Well ... we were wondering ...' At this moment, Milly, as if in one smooth movement, stepped aside and gently pushed Connor forward. The poor kid was now blushing the shade of a pomegranate.

'Connor,' Milly urged, now standing with her little arms crossed, in a stance reminiscent of a schoolmarm pose, with matching vocal tone, though slightly softer. Howard tried not to smile too broadly. The kid was bloody awesome. And then he did laugh, though managed to keep it to a stifled croak, when she sighed with obvious exasperation and lifted her arms, still crossed, leaving no doubt as to her vexation. 'Mr Manning?' she said.

'Yes, Milly?'

'You know my stilts, which I absolutely love?' she said emphatically.

'I do. What about them?' Howard said.

'Welllll, Connor loves them too.'

'Right?' Howard was catching on, but keeping himself back. He figured it was probably a good life lesson for them to have to ask for things, push through their awkwardness, rather than for him to let them off the hook by jumping in and offering.

'Well, we were wondering ...'

Connor was nodding, the redness having retreated, as if he'd found some courage now he didn't need it.

'... if you could make Connor some,' Milly concluded.

'Oh,' Howard said, his mind already taking him into the garage and up to the shelves and scanning the contents for another pair of decent-sized tins. But his demeanour and slight exclamation seemed to have been interpreted to be negative by the pair of small people in front of him. Connor had shrunk back into himself and his big brown expressive eyes – really, he could be Milly's brother they were so alike, now Howard thought about it – had gone quite dull. Even young Milly appeared somewhat deflated.

'It's okay,' Milly said quietly. 'I'm sorry if it's not appropriate to ask.'

'Oh no. It is. It's quite okay. It's me who should be apologising.' Howard clambered to ease their discomfort. 'My response to your question wasn't because I don't want to, it's because I was trying to remember if I have any more of the big tins we can use. You'd want them nice and tall like Milly's, wouldn't you? Then you're at a fair advantage if, and when, you race each other.'

Connor was nodding furiously now.

Milly was practically bouncing up and down on her feet. 'Could we help you look in the garage maybe?' she ventured carefully.

'That's a good idea. Come on, then,' Howard said, leading the kids out to the garage.

Elsie, who had been leaning against the kitchen bench observing goings-on, wondered where they could put the contents of the tins Howard was about to sacrifice – because of course he was going to, that wasn't in question. Knowing there weren't any more Tupperware or similar containers big enough in the pantry cupboard, Elsie thought for a moment before remembering the stack of buckets with lids in the laundry.

She went to the laundry and then opened the cupboard underneath the sink and retrieved two with matching lids. Like the Tupperware, they seemed to multiply over time. But at least these were all the same size so the lids were instantly found. She took them to the garage just in time to see Howard descending the step with a large tin in hand. Another one was already on the bench. He was looking at them as if wondering what to do – no doubt deliberating over whether he could bring himself to upset the order of the space by simply emptying the contents onto the bench, Elsie thought, smiling to herself.

'Here, tip it into these,' she said, holding out the buckets and lids. The boyish grin of appreciation suddenly in his eyes and face was something that never failed to send a surge of affection through her.

'Thanks, love, glad someone's on the ball,' he said, accepting the buckets and the lids.

Bless the woman's cotton socks, Howard thought. She was always a step ahead of him. They would deal with reordering the space later. For now, it was about making a little boy happy. Priorities.

The fact that Howard was willing to upset his space, which he prided himself on, was testament to his big, generous heart, Elsie thought, and felt the sudden urge to wrap her arms around him from behind and lay her cheek against his broad back.

'Okay. Let's see what we have for holding them up,' Howard said. 'We might be lucky and have enough of the same cord we used for Milly's. Let's check, shall we?'

The kids crowded in close, nodding.

'You'll also need some pants to go with your stilts, won't you, Connor?' Elsie said. Milly and Connor turned towards her and looked on with apprehension. 'Or not?' she added, eyebrows raised. 'It's entirely up to you.'

'We'd love some, but we don't want to put you to any trouble, Mrs Manning,' Milly said. 'It's a lot more work than attaching the strings to the tins.'

Connor, nodding, looked downcast.

Bless the little darling – she could read him like a book, Elsie thought.

'Would you like pants, Connor?' she asked. 'Though they won't be the same as Milly's because I don't have enough of that fabric left. But I have some other leftover bits and pieces that I could put together. What do you say?'

'Oh, yes, please,' Connor said.

'But only if it's not too much trouble,' Milly said in a tone reminiscent of Corinne, being the elder sister and taking charge.

'Not at all. I would love to make you some.'

'Then you can have races *and* look groovy,' Howard said, looking up from where he was measuring cord. He gave Elsie a wink and a grin, which she returned.

What's a few seams run up on the machine when I can bring such joy to two small people. 'You wait here and I'll get my tape measure.'

As Elsie retrieved her tape measure and pulled the lid off the machine, she thought how glad she was that she'd so recently used it and wouldn't have any time lost in getting up to speed again.

It was strange how things turned out, she thought, making her way back to the garage. No time spent even thinking of sewing for a decade and now here we are twice in a couple of days. It did feel good to be useful. And appreciated. Not that she felt unappreciated by Howard, or anyone else, specifically. It was just general – like being invisible – as an oldie.

Elsie dictated Connor's measurements to Milly, who wrote them down. She wanted to involve her while Connor was busy with Howard. The small boy was currently holding one tin ready for Howard to hammer a nail through to make a hole for the cord. Milly couldn't get a look-in, though – she was crouched close, but off to the side, as Connor stood on the one available step, with his head close to Howard's.

'Milly, would you like to come inside and help me choose the perfect bits of fabric to join together?'

'Oh yes. I can do that,' Milly said.

'Let's go, then,' Elsie said.

They made their way into the office where Elsie retrieved a stack of fabric offcuts from her stash in the sewing cabinet. Milly sat swivelling on Howard's desk chair, waiting.

'How about you go through this pile, Milly, and choose some pieces and lay them out on the floor to see which order they should go in?'

'Okay. Can we use any of them?' Milly asked.

'Yes, any you like and think Connor would like. Do you think we should check with him, or do you think we should surprise him?'

'Um,' Milly said and thought for a moment. 'Let's surprise him.'

'Good idea. Remember, we'll need enough for both a front and a back, in the size we have written down – okay?' Elsie said, hoping she'd made sense.

'I think so.' Though she seemed a little doubtful.

'You choose the fabrics, and then we'll worry about the size. The golden rule to remember with making pretty much anything – well, anything involving cutting – is to measure at least twice before cutting. Got it?'

'Yep. Got it,' Milly mimicked.

'And with the big pieces – we can cut bits out, rather than using the whole piece, if you like. So, fold anything to the size you want if there's a big piece. Do you know what I mean?'

'I think so, yes.' She thought for a moment before speaking again, this time a little surer. 'You mean like patchwork, rather than all the same like mine are, don't you?'

'Exactly. You're very clever, Milly.'

'I know what patchwork is because I have a quilt like that that my grandma made before she died.'

'That's a lovely keepsake,' Elsie said lightly and carried on quickly before the mood could turn. 'Okay, then, off you go,' she urged. 'I'll get the machine set up ready.'

Elsie pretended to be busy with the machine, but was instead watching Milly, sitting on the floor, choosing fabric colours and patterns several times before finally leaning back on her heels. Beside her she'd carefully folded the discarded bits and piled them up neatly.

'That looks like the perfect choice to me, Milly.'

Milly beamed up at her. 'This is really fun, Mrs Manning.'

'I'm glad you think so, Milly.'

'Thank you so much for doing this.'

'It's my pleasure.'

'Connor's going to love it,' she said enthusiastically. Then she added, in a quieter, more serious tone, 'He doesn't have much.'

'Oh. Okay,' Elsie said. She wanted to know more, but also didn't want to press and pry.

'Things aren't easy for him at home.'

Elsie suspected this was a phrase Daniel had used. The tone seemed more grown-up. 'I'm sorry to hear that, Milly,' she said.

God, what does one say to kids in response to this? Hell, what would I say to an adult, for that matter, in the same situation? Things will get better? But, will they? How would I know? Hang in there? Oh dear.

'He's lucky to have you,' she said.

'He's a good friend to me too,' Milly said.

'I'm glad, Milly. Do you know, Mr Manning and I met on our first day of kindergarten – all the way back when we were four.'

'You did?' Milly said, her eyes suddenly enormous. And then her brow was slightly puckered.

'Yes, a *veeeerrry* long time ago,' Elsie said with a laugh.

'Wow,' Milly said.

'And we even have the same birthday.'

'Double-wow!'

Probably best I don't tell her we got married on our nineteenth birthdays – that might completely blow her mind. 'Yep. And we're still best friends, all these years later.' Aware time was marching on and she didn't want Milly to lose focus, she returned to the task at hand. 'Okay, now we're going to measure out the bits,' she said. 'Do you remember what I said the golden rule was?'

'Measure twice before cutting anything,' Milly said triumphantly.

'Exactly. Good job, Milly.' Elsie beamed. There was something rather wonderful about having someone hanging on her every word and action. 'So now we're going to pin the bits together. We do them with the patterns – the good side, that is – together so the seams are inside the pants when we're done.

By the twist to Milly's mouth, Elsie thought she'd probably lost her. It was a lot to take in.

'It will make sense in a minute, I'm sure,' she explained.

Milly nodded.

Elsie thought she probably should demonstrate how, before sewing, but was keen to get it done. It was getting late – and her stomach had just growled, as if reminding her of the hour apparently being close to dinnertime. She really did want to finish this for Connor before they had to leave.

Elsie surprised herself with how quickly she ran up the pants and popped in the elastic. As she made the braces, she marvelled at her inadvertent forethought in deciding to purchase both the bits and pieces and ready-made braces at Spotlight that day.

Finally, she held up the pants for Milly to see, turning them around and showing her the back and the front – not that it really mattered which was which – and checking the braces were adjusted to about the right length.

'They are absolutely brilliant, Mrs Manning!' Milly said, putting her hands together under her chin and wiggling her bottom half back and forth.

'Thanks, Milly. You did a brilliant job choosing the fabric and the order of placement. So, it's been a great team effort. Fingers crossed Connor likes them.'

'He'll love them! No doubt about that,' Milly said. Elsie grinned.

'Where do you think they are?' Elsie said, cocking her head to listen. At that moment a chorus of chooks started up.

'Yay, someone has laid an egg,' Milly said, clapping her hands. And then, sounding a bit concerned, she added, 'They're quite loud. Do they bother you and Mr Manning?'

'Oh no, we love them,' Elsie was quick to say. 'Especially when they sound so pleased with themselves, as they do now. We find them very joyful to listen to, Milly.'

'Oh, that's good,' Milly said with obvious relief.

'Thanks for checking, though, Milly,' Elsie said. 'That's very considerate of you.'

'I think they might be outside, at the front – Mr Manning and Connor, that is,' Milly said.

'Yes, perhaps they're giving the stilts a test-run.'

'Let's go and see.'

Sure enough, Connor was out on the front lawn, with Howard standing nearby, supervising, arms folded, offering him words of encouragement: 'You're a natural, Connor. Well done,' he said.

'Ooh la la, aren't they the business?' Howard said, turning around and noticing Milly and Elsie standing there, the pants draped over Elsie's arm. 'That was quick.'

'Yes, I had a fabulous helper,' Elsie said, resting her hand on Milly's shoulder.

'For me? Really?' Connor said, bug-eyed, making his way over slowly, on account of the stilts. 'Oh, wow.'

Elsie held up the pants for him to see.

'Are they for me?' he asked again.

'Yep,' Milly said.

'Sure are,' Elsie said.

'Really? To keep? To take home?'

'If you would like them,' Elsie said. 'Here you are.' She held them out to him.

'Oh, wow.' He seemed too overwhelmed to take them from her – just stood stammering with disbelief.

'You'd better try them on,' Milly said, arms folded across her chest in the now familiar stance. 'In case we need to adjust them.'

Howard caught Elsie's eye and they shared a smile.

'You'll have to get off the stilts first,' Milly commanded, as Connor looked unsure how to proceed. A moment later he had the pants on and then the stilts. In a move that caused Elsie's heart to jump, Milly leant down and straightened the folded bottoms down over the stilts. 'There you go. Perfect,' she said, standing back up again and looking at Elsie, who nodded in return.

'Well, that's the business,' Howard said approvingly. 'Oh,' he said as suddenly Connor thrust himself into his chest and hugged him.

'Thank you very much, Mr Manning.'

'You're very welcome, Connor,' Howard said. And then he was released and it was Elsie's turn for a hug around the stomach.

'Thank you very much, too, Mrs Manning.'

'It was my pleasure, Connor. I'm glad you like them.'

They stood in a tight huddle, hugging, Milly having joined in too. Howard's heart swelled.

'Is it true you and Mr Manning have been best friends for*ever*?' Connor said, looking up at Elsie, when they'd finished hugging and moved apart a little.

'Yep. It sure is. Well, *almost* forever – we met when we were four; even younger than you two.'

'Wow,' Connor said.

'See, told you,' Howard gently ribbed.

'Yep. A lot of water has passed under the bridge since then, hasn't it, Mr Manning?' Elsie said.

'It sure has, Mrs Manning,' Howard said.

'What's going on?' Daniel called loudly and jovially from the driveway. They all turned to face him.

'Mr and Mrs Manning made me stilts and pants. Look, aren't they awesome?' Connor said.

'They sure are. That's very good of Mr and Mrs Manning. Aren't you lucky?'

Connor nodded furiously.

'Thank you,' Daniel said, turning to Elsie and Howard.

'I hope it's okay,' Elsie said quietly to Daniel, suddenly not sure they'd done the right thing.

'Yes. I hope we haven't overstepped,' Howard said, moving closer to Daniel.

'Oh, not at all. It's fine with me. And very generous of you. I just hope you weren't badgered into it,' Daniel said, quieter, and raised his eyebrows.

'No, definitely not,' Howard said.

'They've been a pleasure to have,' Elsie reiterated.

'Okay then,' Daniel said, smiling, and then turned back to Milly and Connor. 'Are you guys ready to come in now?'

'Yes. But do you need me to help tidy up in the sewing room, Mrs Manning, or in the shed, Mr Manning?' Milly asked.

'Do you need me to help tidy up too?' Connor asked, looking up at Howard.

'It's okay, Milly. But thanks very much for asking,' Elsie said.

'Yes, good thinking, kids, but we're all good in that department. You run along. It's been really lovely to have you both.'

'Please feel free to come anytime,' Elsie reiterated.

'Thank you. It's been really fun,' Connor said.

'Yes. It's been a great day. Best day ever, Dad!' Milly said.

'Glad to hear it, kiddo.'

'Thanks, Mr Wynter,' Connor said.

'My pleasure, Connor. Come on, then. I think there might be some eggs to collect,' Daniel said.

'Cool,' Connor said.

'Oh, yes,' Milly said. 'We heard them.'

'Thanks again, Howard and Elsie,' Daniel said. 'I'd better get these two calmed down so we get some sleep tonight, after such a big day.'

'Ha ha, yes. Bye for now,' Howard said.

'Bye, Mr and Mrs Manning. Thank you very much for having us,' Milly said.

'And me, Mr and Mrs Manning. And thanks very much for the pants and stilts,' Connor said.

'Yes, goodbye, Daniel,' Elsie said. 'See you, and you, kids, again soon,' she said, ruffling the hair on Milly's and Connor's heads.

A moment later Milly and Connor had waved and were running down Howard and Elsie's driveway.

Daniel headed off after the kids, lifting his hand in a wave as he did.

Howard put an arm around Elsie's waist and drew her to him.

'Well, wasn't that fun?' Elsie said.

'Best day ever!' Howard said, mimicking Milly.

Elsie laughed. 'Touché. Priceless.'

Chapter Twenty-three

'Hi, Sandy, long time no see!' Howard said, chuckling and grinning broadly as he stepped past Sandy, who was holding the door open, and into her house.

'Hi, Sandy,' Elsie said with an exaggerated eye-roll. 'Oh dear. Don't mind him,' she added with a laugh. 'We caught a cab, so he hasn't had twenty minutes of getting stressed in the traffic and cursing ridiculous drivers. There could be all sorts of mischief.'

'Good to know,' Sandy said, grinning. 'You both seem chirpier today, which is the main thing,' she added. 'You're not late, but everyone else is here. I'm pretty sure you'll know them all, more or less. Come on through.'

'Sorry. Our taxi took us the long way. Can I help with anything?' Elsie asked.

'No. Please, sit. Everything's ready to go.'

'Hello, everyone,' Elsie said before taking a seat beside Howard. It was clear she'd arrived in the middle of a conversation Howard was having with Larry Coventry – or rather, trying to. Others must be interrupting because Howard seemed a little exasperated.

Ah, she realised, *it's about sorting photos*. Someone must have asked what they'd been spending their time on recently, or something.

'At least with the time before digital we only took what we needed, not this endless snapping we do now. I have literally dozens of the same shot and have to sit there squinting and turning my head this and that way as I try to decipher which one is the best to keep,' Linda Rutherford said from across the table.

'Oh yes. I know what you mean. It reminds me of when I'm at the optometrist trying to figure out the prescription. It's a case of choosing between one or two, and sometimes I think I've decided and then I blank just before I do it again, and it's nope, I have no idea – we'll have to do that again. Sorry, I interrupted. Anyway it drives me mad. You were saying – photos,' Evelyn Jarvis said.

'Yes. It was quite fun too …' Howard said.

'In that case, you can come and do ours, if you like,' Chester Jarvis said with a laugh.

'No thanks. I'm glad to have it finished …'

'God, well done. Big job. I think I'll be going through ours for the next decade. I've got lost along the way on what I've duplicated and saved separately here and there,' Chester said.

'Well, at least they're somewhere. We lost two decades' worth due to a malfunction, didn't we, Larry?' Susan Coventry said from beside her husband.

'Yes,' Larry said.

'I'm sorry to hear that. Bloody technology,' Chester said.

'I was pretty annoyed to start with but what can you do – no point getting all het up about it after the fact. Actually, it's a little liberating, too, in some respects.'

'I can see how that might be the case,' Chester said, nodding knowingly.

'Garlic bread, folks – one at each end of the table please. And then help yourselves,' Sandy said, placing two baskets down, the contents thereof wrapped in foil. 'Back in a sec with mains – lasagne and salad,' Sandy said.

'Can I help carry?' Linda said.

'Yes, and me?' Susan said.

'No, please, it's easier if you stay seated. It's just a couple of trips.'

'Anyway,' Howard persisted. 'Larry and Susan, I was looking at pictures of that party you held for 1980 New Year's Eve. The fancy dress shindig. We were Fred and Wilma – the theme was The Good Old Days.'

'Oh, we loved dressing up,' Susan said wistfully.

'The good old days indeed. Before we knew just how bad things would get – referring to the stock market crash of 1987 and insane interest rates, that is,' Larry said.

'Christ. Wasn't that a time to be trying to buy a house? The kids of today don't know how easy they've got it,' Dennis said.

'Don't get me started,' Linda said. 'Avocados, anyone?'

'Folks. Lunch is served,' Sandy said, appearing carrying three plates in one hand and one in the other.

Elsie was glad the conversation had been swiftly ceased. They'd got off track and she could see it becoming heated.

The meals were gradually delivered and after a round of expressions of thanks and then murmurs of how tasty the food was, the conversation started up right where it had left off and continued on amidst the eating and drinking.

'So, you were saying, Howard, Elsie, about our New Year's Eve party?' Larry prompted.

'Oh, yes. We had a wow of a time – well, judging by the bizarre photos Howard took,' Elsie said with a chuckle.

'Yes,' Howard continued. 'There's a whole roll of strange angles and heads cut off, views of ceiling, light fixtures and the tops of curtains,' he said, rolling his eyes. 'Nothing like what I was seeing – or *thought* I was seeing at the time. The person developing them must have wondered if I was all right in the head.'

'Yes, they're very … ah … trying-to-be-arty-but-failing-miserably,' Elsie said with a laugh. She found herself grinning at the memory of Howard's expression of dismay upon opening the packet of photos he'd just paid for and waited a week to be developed.

'That's an accurate description. The mystery is how the hell they made it into an album,' he said, and took another sip of wine. 'It was the time you had the magic mushrooms. I completely lost my head in a good, fun, but also very disconcerting way.'

'One of the parties with the mushrooms, you say?' Larry mused. 'That night must have been one of the last, from memory. And I think you said you kept the photos to remind you of the experience. I vaguely remember you bringing them to some lunch or other soon after, and us all heaving with laughter – though my memory isn't what it probably should be. Could be all the mushrooms along the way.' He guffawed.

'What? I thought that night was a one-off,' Howard said.

'Oh no. One has had to retain some free form of fun as the wowsers have systemically taken away every other form through legislation. Though, everything in moderation. We still grow them – just a few to keep us going,' Larry said, tapping his nose with his index finger.

'Really?' Linda said.

'Yes. You're never too old to experience a little break from reality, or you shouldn't be. In fact, it's a necessity,' Susan said.

'God, I feel so dull. So out of touch,' Howard said.

'Yes, me too,' Elsie said.

'And me. I've never so much as had a joint,' Linda said.

'You did too – well, one puff. Don't you remember that time by the campfire?' Linda's husband Dennis said with a laugh.

'Oh, yes. First and last time camping, too. I wandered off for a wee and ended up upside down in a bush not knowing which way was up. Dennis had to send out a search party.'

'Yes, we heard this whispering.' He laughed. 'Sorry, dear, but it really was very funny,' Dennis said.

'It was funny the next day when I was safely back in the car heading home, yes,' Linda said, grinning widely.

'Staying in three-star hotels is the closest we've ever got to camping since,' Dennis said.

'Not in reference to camping – I've never seen the point in that, and no offence to those who do enjoy such pursuits – but wasn't life fun once?' Evelyn said.

'Yes, it was,' Sandy said.

'What happened?' Linda said.

'Old age,' Chester said.

'Didn't we have this moan with you the other week?' Evelyn said.

'No, not us. We haven't seen you guys since just before the whole Covid fiasco. Speaking of the eclipse of fun. We were keen to try our first cruise until then. Now it's, hell no!' Larry said.

'Yes. Same with us,' Chester said.

Elsie idly wondered how many luncheons or dinners, depending upon where you were in the world, were taking place right now where a group of elderly citizens were sitting around whinging about life and reminiscing about the old days – or, mourning for them, to be more precise.

'We've missed our chance – not mobile enough these days,' Dennis said, nodding towards the walkers in the corner. Elsie looked over. She hadn't noticed them there when they'd arrived and Dennis and Linda had already been seated.

'I have to say, I do miss not being able to constantly scowl now the masks have gone,' Susan said.

'Oh, I still do,' Evelyn said gaily. 'I don't give a hoot what anyone thinks. If someone is pleasant, I'll smile. If not, I'm fine with resting witch face – I don't like to use the B word.'

'I'm looking forward to giving anyone who tells me to smile a piece of my mind, to make up for the compliance and lack of confidence and mouthiness in my younger self,' Linda said.

'Yes. Actually, that's one thing about being seemingly invisible, as an oldie,' Evelyn said. 'I haven't had anyone say, *smile, it might never happen*, for ages.'

'Oh god. That reminds me. All those utterances from leering men on building sites in the street – everywhere, really – saying, *you'd look pretty if you smile*. Like that's our only aim in life – to look pretty. Pulease! But we women all smiled in response, didn't we?' Linda said.

'That's what annoys me the most – if we're talking about reminiscing and the old days – all the bloody compliance: rearranging my expression to suit, my clothes, hair, wearing makeup. Oh, what a waste of energy – in the sense it was easier to just go along. Sorry, I'm on my high horse now. You can tell there's some residual resentment left after all the therapy, can't you?' Evelyn said.

Awkward chuckles roamed around the table before everyone took a sip from their glass.

'At least the young ones are putting their foot – feet – down, though it should have happened eons ago,' Susan said.

'Yes. It's frustrating that we – women of our era, that is – only set the ball off on a gentle slope, as it turns out,' Sandy said, moving around the table collecting empty plates.

Elsie and several others offered to help with the plates but Sandy said, 'Seriously, it's just easier for you to stay put – the house is too small. Fine for just me, but …'

They all nodded and carried on with the conversation.

'The world wasn't ready to listen – or take up the ball and run with it, if we're sticking to that metaphor. And they wonder why so many of us are bitter and disappointed,' Linda said.

'Yep.'

'Well, that's cheered us all up no end,' Howard said, slapping the table.

'Sorry. But you brought up the old days,' Evelyn said.

'Here's to the memories and your very fun parties, particularly care of magic mushrooms,' Howard said, raising his glass.

'To the memories, getting old and once being young and fabulous,' Susan said.

'And to weird arty photos,' Elsie added, trying to lighten the slightly gloomy mood.

'*And* to having to wait a week to see if you got any good shots,' Chester said. 'And to the digital era of not having to do that anymore.'

'I kind of miss the nervous anticipation. It gave it all an exciting edge,' Susan said.

'Ha ha, living on the wild side. Don't tell anyone – oh, I don't suppose it matters now, anyway – but I once had to get a bride and groom to do a re-enactment after they got back from their honeymoon …' Chester said.

'Sorry to interrupt, Chester. Here we are. Please pass these around,' Sandy said, placing bowls of fresh fruit salad and cream with decorative shards of meringue sticking out, this time having carried them all on the one tray.

'Yum,' Linda said, setting off a chorus of agreement before they all began to eat again.

'I didn't know you did wedding photography,' Larry said. 'Did I know that once?'

'Yes, probably. Well, I did,' Susan said.

'I only did it for close friends and family, really,' Chester continued.

'Ah, because you were a journalist. Of course,' Larry said.

'Yes,' Chester said.

'Keep up, dear,' Susan said.

'See, just relegated to being an old person now,' Chester said sardonically.

'Sorry, I didn't mean that,' Larry said.

'Ah, it's okay. Anyway, they'd been away for a few weeks and the bride's dress was figure-hugging to begin with and they'd been on a cruise and over-indulged a bit on all the food. Or maybe she was pregnant, but they didn't say. She had to have it pinned at the back because it wouldn't close properly in parts. Luckily it was a favour to them so they couldn't be too annoyed.'

'What happened with the photos from the day that meant you had to redo them?' Sandy asked.

'Oh. The photo lab lost them, or something, I can't recall now. I think that was the one. What a nightmare.'

'Though not your fault,' Sandy said.

'No. But it did prove to be a curse – they got divorced a few years later. Though I could have everyone muddled up. I vaguely remember having to redo a couple of events.'

'Oh. Remember that bride who fell into the five-tier wedding cake? Someone's child had crawled under her dress thinking it was a tablecloth or something and she tripped over?' Evelyn said.

'Oh god. Yes. I got that on film – the pile of cake. The bride scowled at me for doing that, but I thought it made a lovely shot – speaking of arty, Howard. And the groom. He was a friend of a friend and she was a ... that B word you don't like to use ... an absolute diva piece of work. He left her on their honeymoon, if I recall. No, not left her there – he was too well mannered for that. I might have done. Ah, good times. I keep expecting to see footage of that appear in my Facebook feed – it was captured on video, too. I'm sure someone will have digitised it by now and/or be seeing the funny side of things.'

'Inability to delay gratification, that's what's wrong,' Evelyn blurted suddenly.

'Sorry?' Larry said.

'Yes. Or at least an unwillingness to,' Elsie said.

'The problem with the young ones. I've been trying to think of the term,' Evelyn said.

'True. That's why everything is about *bingeing* – especially TV shows. I remember how exciting it was to look forward to our favourite show – to wait a whole week. It made for a true feeling of occasion,' Chester said.

'Oh yes. I remember *Doctor Who* being a particular favourite of ours,' Larry said.

'All well and good, except if your TV reception was crappy – you'd wait a whole week, only to then have to try to peer through the snow. That was our viewing life – very hit and miss,' Susan said.

'Speaking of zero delayed gratification, it's impossible to buy anything for anyone these days when they just do it themselves, whenever. Have you found that?' Evelyn said.

'Yes, but that's also the fault of all the cheap imports. When we made everything here that we needed it was a different story,' Larry said.

'Ah, hindsight,' Dennis said.

'Yes. Hard to get that genie back into the bottle, along with the zero interest for delayed gratification one,' Howard said.

'The young ones seem to have zero interest in quality or longevity, too, if you ask me,' Evelyn said.

'If I had my way, I would have kept this island self-sufficient and only import goods and luxury products we couldn't make ourselves,' Larry said.

'Yes, but luxury in whose eyes – that would be the difficult question? I see people bragging online about this and that and often think but that's tacky,' Linda said.

'Oh, god, the whole online presence is pretty tacky all round, in my opinion – all the bragging. But best I don't get started,' Susan said.

'Who's for tea and coffee? Sandy asked, getting up again and then moving around the table collecting the bowls.

There was a pause in conversation while drinks orders were taken.

'I must say it's been lovely to catch up and have a good whinge,' Evelyn said, leaning back in her chair.

'Yes, we're meant to be thrilled with life because we're not working. But those who say that don't take into account the health issues, lack of funds, lack of mobility, memory and mental faculties,' Chester said.

'Yes, we're to pipe down and be grateful,' Dennis said.

'At least you men know now what we women have had to endure our entire lives,' Linda said.

'Well, that's us told,' Larry said, cringing.

'Well, I, for one, am sorry about that. And unfortunately I can't say I would have done things differently if I'd been in charge, because we're all a product of our times and I was always meek and mild and not prone to causing a ruckus,' Howard said.

'Thanks, Howard,' Linda said.

'I'm not bitter, well, not much. What would be the point? All in all, things aren't too bad,' Susan said.

'If you don't scratch the surface too much,' Evelyn said.

'True,' Linda said.

'Shall we declare the cranky old gits' meeting closed, and change the subject to a more cheerful one?' Chester said.

'Sure. You can try,' Dennis said jovially.

'Yes, go ahead. But what happy subject do you have to offer?' Larry said.

'Exactly,' Dennis said.

'I got a significant discount on my new hearing aid last week. That cheered me up no end,' Chester said.

'Oh. Write the details down for me, will you? Or, better yet, text them, will you?' Larry said.

Gradually the day wound up.

'I enjoyed that immensely,' Howard said when they had said goodbye to Sandy and were seated in the taxi heading home.

'Yes, me too,' Elsie said.

Chapter Twenty-four

'Oh,' Elsie said. They were in the hall hanging up their coats on the hooks, and just before she did, Elsie had put her hand in the pocket of hers for a tissue to wipe her suddenly drippy nose and had felt something else.

'What is it, dear?' Howard asked.

Without answering, Elsie brought out a piece of paper and unfolded it. As she scanned it, her eyes became wide and the corners of her mouth turned up. With a cheeky grin, she handed the paper over to Howard.

'Well, I say. *Shh, don't tell anyone*,' he read aloud. 'Is that an instruction or the name of the recipe?' he muttered, before reading on. '*Special mushroom risotto*. Not much use without said *special* mushrooms, is it?' He let out a humph of disappointment and a cringe as he handed it back and returned to shedding his layers by unwinding his long scarf.

'Hang on,' Elsie said, fossicking in her deep coat pocket, having to stretch her hand right down into it and hoist her shoulders at the same time in order to get all the way to the bottom. Her fingers felt something cool and smooth — two cool and smooth somethings, actually. She closed her grip on them and dragged out the items. She held up two small bags, just like you saw on the news or a TV show about drug busts.

'Oh, well, I say.' Howard peered at them. '*Our special mushrooms*,' he read out. 'So, what's that, in the other bag, then? Looks like dried grass clippings.'

'I think you're quite right,' Elsie said, frowning as she scanned the pink sheet of paper again and for the first time noticed that below the typed recipe in neat handwriting was a note: *use sparingly or liberally — as you wish — in brownies or cupcakes or tea*. Included was a hand-drawn smiley face. 'Ooh, I say. Looks like we might be getting that adventure young Milly says we need.'

'I'm pretty sure this is not at all what she meant, Elsie,' Howard said with a laugh.

'No,' Elsie said, also chuckling. 'But being serious for a moment, I think we'd really better hide that, given we have a policeman living across the way, not to mention impressionable children dropping in willy-nilly.'

'Yes, good point. You can do that while I'm off getting arborio rice. What else do I need?' He accepted the recipe.

'I think I've had quite enough excitement for today.'

'Not necessarily for today — just to have on hand for … whenever.'

'Okay. Good idea.'

'A packet mix to make some brownies, too, do you think?'

'No, I think we can scrounge up enough ingredients for a batch in the pantry.'

'Good-o, then.' He took his scarf back off the hook and began winding it around his neck.

'Are you going right now?' Elsie asked.

'I thought I might, before I forget or completely run out of steam. I'm flagging fast. It's a pity you didn't discover these items ten minutes earlier, when we still had hold of the cab. Oh well. Anything else we need?'

'No. You went this morning, remember?'

'Oh, yes. One day merges into the next. I wasn't sure if it was yesterday or last week.'

'I know what you mean. Perhaps check the fridge for milk and veg and the stock of bread in the freezer. I need to sit. I'm suddenly very weary,' Elsie said. 'All that food, as lovely as it was.'

'All that moaning takes its toll, too,' Howard pointed out.

'True.'

'It was fun, though.'

'It's always such a good feeling to be amongst like-minded people. And it's so rare these days.'

'And getting rarer. Well, I'm off,' Howard said.

'Careful crossing the road.'

'Will do, dear.'

'Have you got everything?' Elsie asked when Howard returned a little later.

'I think so. And I'm rather keen to get into it. What do you think?'

'There's that disinterest in delayed gratification everyone was talking about at lunch,' Elsie pointed out.

'Oops. You're quite right. So, shall we or not?'

'I think so, yes. Let's at least make the risotto. It says on the recipe it can be frozen,' Elsie said.

'Ah, yes, good point. I hope if we do it tonight, it gives me a rest – I'm quite weary.'

'Well don't run out of puff yet, we have to make the risotto.'

'I'm stuffed if I know why we can't just bung it in the microwave like most other things,' Howard said.

'Because a big part of risotto is the love that goes into it via time spent stirring in the stock slowly.'

'But does it? Does love really go into it when one is cursing and moaning about how long it's bloody well taking?'

'Really, Howard? It's never you actually doing the stirring of the risotto,' Elsie said, rolling her eyes.

'Okay, point taken. I'm just keen to try it, now I've got the idea in my head.'

'I get that – that's rather obvious. You're behaving like a spoilt child or drug addict salivating over the next impending fix.'

'God, you're right. Sorry.'

'Oh, I am too – I'm just not voicing it like you are. And only because I can't. You got in first and I haven't had much of a chance. Anyway, remember what expectation does – that is, having too high expectations? Makes us ripe for disappointment,' Elsie said.

'Oh, yes, true.'

'Open mind, dear.'

'Roger that. I'll simmer down, get back in my box and all that,' Howard said.

'Anyway, we don't have to do it now. There's no rush,' Elsie said.

'True, but haven't we learnt that there's no point putting off a potential source of enjoyment?'

'Also true. Good point. I'd hate to actually cark it without having given it a whirl.'

'That's highly unlikely, dear, given our lack of success in that department,' Howard said.

'Yes, but remember our dear old friend Murphy?'

'Well, fat lot of good he and his law have done us!'

'Maybe it only works when you are least suspecting, or don't want whatever it is to happen,' Elsie pointed out.

'Well, then it probably won't have been so bandied about as it has, I suspect,' Howard said.

'Or maybe he's been working right alongside us, given the car fiasco – what could go wrong there, did. Oh, I don't know. You've lost me,' Elsie said.

'Don't worry, dear, I've lost myself!' Howard said. 'Right, let's get this show on the road. It says it can be successfully frozen, so we can make it and decide afterwards if we're going ahead with the next phase this evening or not,' Howard said, leaning down and peering at the recipe with his brow knitted.

Elsie looked at Howard. *I said two minutes ago it could be frozen. Are you losing your mind?* But she kept the words to herself. What was the point in correcting him? 'Something to do for the next little while anyway,' she said instead. 'Unless you need a rest.'

'A nap, or are you proposing huffy-puffy? Because, if that's the case, I don't think I have it in me.'

'Howard, since when, recently, have I been suggesting huffy-puffy when inquiring after your state of energy? Get your mind out of the gutter. Wherever has that suddenly come from?'

'I have no idea. Sorry, it's taking me quite by surprise, too.'

'What has? Just the thought, I hope,' Elsie said, looking at him sideways.

'It must have been seeing the sausages in the window of the counter of the butcher on my way past. Twigged the far-off memory of something.'

'Oh, Howard,' Elsie said, shaking her head and then sighing. Though she was smiling. He was loveable – right now in a very Mr Magoo way. She rubbed his shoulder. 'On a serious note, are you okay – with that side of things, I mean?'

'As in not being remotely interested? And do you mean me or the old fella down there?' he said, looking down and nodding.

'Well, both.'

'Are you?'

'Oh yes. I would suggest a trip to an adult shop for a vibrator, or other such device, if not,' Elsie said, 'or head to one myself. Well …?'

'I'm good if you're good,' Howard said.

'Really? You're not just saying that?'

'No. Since when have I ever just paid you lip service – we made a pact during our marriage vows, to always be open and honest. I've always held up my end of the bargain. I hope you have too,' Howard said.

'Of course.'

'And to answer your question, if I really thought you were missing out in the huffy-puffy department, I would be suggesting a purchase from said store.'

'As long as we are in the same boat?'

'Absolutely,' he added, putting his arm around Elsie and giving her a squeeze.

She leant into him. 'I love you, Howie.'

'And I love you, my darling. Every day I feel blessed that we are together.'

'As do I.'

Howard kissed Elsie on the top of the head before releasing her. 'Right, shall I start chopping the onions while you heat up the stock?' he asked.

'You hate chopping onions,' Elsie said.

'But I'll do it for you. My love for you has no bounds.'

'So I see. It's okay, though, I'll do it,' Elsie said. 'You can deal with getting out the pots and pans.'

They worked away side by side, several times catching each other's eye and smiling.

'I'm so glad we get along so well still,' Howard said.

'Yes, lucky that.' Elsie gave in to the tears brought on by the onions, as she thought about how truly blessed she was to have her best friend beside her. Though there was also an unpleasant accompanying ache telling her how much losing him would hurt. She shoved it all aside as she tipped the onions on the board into the pan and then smiled as Howard produced a wet face cloth and carefully wiped her face before kissing her on the end of her nose.

'All better?' he asked.

'Yes, thanks.'

'Shall I start the first shift stirring?' he asked.

'If you like. Bloody arthritis.'

'Yes, but at least we can tag team it.'

'It looks perfect, dear,' Howard said around forty minutes later when they'd stirred the cream and grated parmesan cheese through. 'Should I dish us up a couple of bowls?'

'I think so. The smell of onions frying always makes me hungry. And the note there says it takes around twenty minutes to take effect. Let's divvy up the rest and pack away in the freezer in case we lose the plot or become completely useless or something — would be a shame for it to go to waste,' Elsie said.

'Providing it's an enjoyable experience,' Howard pointed out.

'I'd be happy with exciting or unusual — it doesn't even have to be enjoyable.'

'Yes, good point.'

'Okay, what shall we mark the containers with for the freezer?' Elsie said, black marker now poised ready above the lid of the container.

'How about: Larry and Susan's special mushroom risotto.'

'Bit long-winded — won't fit. How about *L and S's SM risotto*? We want it a bit distinguishable from the other batch that's in there.'

'True. That will do — otherwise we're overthinking it. Are you getting nervous?' Howard asked.

'Yes, I am a bit. It's been a long time since we did anything like this. What if it causes a heart attack or stroke or something?'

'Great, if we go together!'

'But it's unlikely when we're healthy — barring the general malaise of old age — according to all the doctors we see,' Elsie said.

'Should we leave a note on the bench, just in case? And turn on the outside light?'

'No. We don't want young Milly popping in from next door to tell us we're wasting electricity.'

'Good point. And let's leave the blinds and curtains down so no one disturbs us — they can think we're taking a nap or gone to bed early, or watching a movie or something.'

'Again, might I remind us we're overthinking?' Elsie said.

'When have we ever not, really? If we hadn't all the years, where would we be? It's not such a bad trait to have — especially when we have each other to rein it in.'

'That's true.'

'It really is a lovely risotto,' Howard said a little later when he pushed his bowl away from him slightly across the table.

'That's because of the cream, I think, not the special ingredient,' Elsie said. 'Remember, we haven't used cream in ours for years.'

'True. I think we should revisit that idea next time,' Howard said, standing up. 'I'll just rinse these,' he added.

'Uh-oh.'

Elsie's words and concerned tone caused him to stop midway to the sink and turn back to look at her.

'What is it?'

'I've just remembered why we stopped putting cream in – it was because dairy was upsetting your stomach, Howard. Remember?'

'Oh, shit. Literally!' he said.

'Well, let's hope not.'

'Oh well, it's a little late now. And we might not know now if it was that or the special mushrooms, if I get the runs.'

'What we need is a carer. I'm probably going to be no help if it happens, depending of course what happens,' Elsie said.

'Like a babysitter? Can you imagine how that could come about? Excuse me, could we pay you for a couple of hours to just sit and keep an eye on us while we take an LSD trip?'

Elsie laughed. 'And they'd have to be here for six hours – we probably couldn't afford the fee.'

'No, especially if we paid extra for them to keep silent about it all. A quagmire indeed! Oh well, as I say, it's too late now. I'm going to try and forget about the cream – mind over matter and all that – and go and sit and see what happens.'

'Take your phone over in case we need to call an ambulance. God forbid! And a glass of water. Oh. And we'd better use the loo first, too.'

'Good thinking.'

'Right,' Howard said after they'd both returned from using the toilet. He checked his watch and then put his recliner back and clasped his hands on his stomach. 'See you on the other side, Elsie. I'd say *sweet dreams*, but I'm not sure what it will be.'

'Yes, see you on the other side of whatever is about to happen.'

Howard and Elsie lay in their respective reclined plush leather chairs, hands laying on their stomachs, waiting.

'I feel like that time on the plane when they announced we couldn't land and that they *thought* we had enough fuel,' Elsie said.

'God, that was an excruciating wait.'

'At least we can't fall out of the sky now, unless one of us thinks we can fly at some point,' Howard said.

'True.'

'Should we have got some rope and tied us down, do you think?'

'No. Let's just go with it. We're overthinking again,' Elsie said.

Howard watched Elsie raise her hand. 'What?' he asked.

'The colours, look.' She pointed.

'I don't see them.'

'Soooo pretty. We could have saved all that money all those years ago seeing the northern lights. Here they are.'

'Why are the lights on the ceiling laughing at me?' Howard asked. He waved his hands, swatting away the bulbous faces hovering, just out of reach, above his face. 'Cheeky buggers,' he muttered. He grabbed his phone – needing several attempts, as it kept moving in the cupholder and eluding his grasp. Finally he had it and somehow got the camera activated, and snapped a few photos. But he couldn't focus on the objects or his phone. Everything kept moving and his hand seemed not a part of him. Instead of getting frustrated, he began to laugh.

Elsie joined in. Soon tears streamed down their faces. And then they began to hiccup, causing another bout of hysteria.

'What are you doing, Howard?' Elsie asked, turning her head slightly, when they'd stopped gurgling and choking on their laughter.

'I'm waving to the palm. Just being polite. Look, its fingers are waving. See, it likes you.'

'It's poking out its tongue at me,' Elsie said, returning the gesture. 'Nasty plant. I'm the one that remembers to water and fertilise you, you ungrateful beast. Thanks very much for the appreciation. He's never so much as given you a second thought.

'Oh,' Elsie said, shifting her gaze away from the palm and looking towards the kitchen. The previously plain round clock on the wall caught her eye. It was shimmering; watery, glittery, and multicoloured, its hands waving, as if to attract her attention. *Huh, well look at that.* She stared at it. *Ooh, aren't you pretty?* She tried to raise her finger to point it out to Howard, but couldn't move her arm. She seemed to have lost her voice, too. *Oh. Am I paralysed? Or maybe just very, very relaxed? Oh well. All part of it, I guess.* She was comfortable sitting watching the kitchen clock – oh. Several kitchen clocks were now flying about the original one. She tried to count how many there were, but they were darting this way and that, dipping and diving.

She closed her eyes to have a long blink, in an effort to regain some clarity. When she opened them, she was disappointed the clocks had become one again and it was back in place on the wall, and just as ordinary as it had been before. She tried to focus on it. Could it really only be that ten minutes had passed? No, surely not. *Twelve hours and ten minutes? Ah, who would know. And does it matter?*

'Butterflies, so pretty,' Howard said.

Where was he? To Elsie, he sounded like he was in a tunnel or a long way away. Another dimension. Like Doctor Who, maybe. She giggled.

Howard chuckled. 'You're tickling me. Funny butterflies,' he said, dragging Elsie's attention back to him.

Elsie tried to follow his gaze and waving hands, but couldn't see whatever it was he was seeing.

'No, not butterflies. They're ... they're ... oh my god, *frank-furters* ...' he said and cracked up laughing. Finally, after he'd wiped the tears of laughter from his eyes and stopped spluttering, brought on by having attempted to speak several times, he continued '... floating about – beady eyes and tiny hands and pudgy feet, dear little things. Very cute.' *Are they clapping?* 'Listen.'

'What?' Elsie mumbled.

'I can hear them clapping their little hands. Oh, wow.'

'No, that's the palms waving at me. Rude palms. They're giving me the finger. Gee, thanks a lot. Give him the finger, I'm the one who feeds and waters you,' Elsie said.

'So how do you feel? Okay?' Howard asked, some time later, when they had mostly returned to their normal selves. 'And what did you think?'

'Weird. Fun times. I feel fine, though my stomach hurts from laughing,' Elsie said.

'Mine too. And the muscles in my arms from protecting my face and swatting away all the flying things. I don't remember what they were.' Howard frowned. 'I think it's normal not to remember details – I read that somewhere.'

'Butterflies,' Elsie said. 'They were enormous, apparently, and lots of them.'

'Oh. Wow.'

Elsie began to laugh. 'You were also seeing mini frankfurters, complete with arms and legs. That's what you said.'

'Really?'

'Yep.'

'Oh, god, where did that come from?'

'The recent discussion about huffy-puffy, most likely. Hope there's nothing you aren't telling me about that.'

'Not on that score,' Howard said. 'Why can't I remember any of it – the LSD experience, that is? That's a bit disappointing. I do remember laughing and I have sore stomach muscles, so it must have been fun.'

'Yes. I'm sure it was.'

'Oh well. Nice to go on a trip without leaving the house.'

'True. I do feel beautifully relaxed, actually,' Elsie said.

'So do I, come to think of it.'

'And at least nothing went wrong and neither of us freaked out.'

'Yes. Thank goodness for that. And I didn't get an upset stomach … Oh. Did you know it's one am?'

'What? Really? Are you sure?'

Howard checked his watch again and then his phone. 'Yes. Positive. Wow. That means we've lost around six hours. That's about the time the effects last, so that's normal.'

'It's a morning after we took it – we haven't lost a week or something, have we?'

'No, all good.'

'Phew. I wouldn't have been surprised to learn we had – I feel all out of kilter.'

'Yes. I'm rather dishevelled myself. But wide awake.'

'Me too. I won't sleep now.'

'Oh well, it's not like there's anywhere we're meant to be today, or have to do. A quiet day at home, methinks,' Howard said.

'Yes, I concur. I probably need a wee. Well, I should do. Did I have one along the way?'

'No idea, dear.'

'God, I hope I haven't wet myself.' Elsie tried to move in her chair to check, but found she couldn't. A quiver of fear jangled inside her. 'I don't want to alarm you, Howard, but I seem to be a little paralysed.'

'What's a little paralysed? You're either paralysed or not, dear, I would think. And actually, I can't move either.'

'Don't panic.'

'I'm not. I actually quite like how I feel right now.'

'And to clarify – when I said a little, I meant that to soften the delivery. I know there's not degrees of paralysis.'

'Oh, I think I'm coming out of it,' Howard said. 'I have a case of pins and needles.'

'I think it's not from the mushrooms, as such, but from being sat for so long – immobile. Okay, feeling is coming back for me now too. Next time I vote we don't stay seated.'

'That could be dangerous. But let's not worry about that yet. And who's to say we didn't move around last night? There's a lot I don't recall.'

'That's true. I just hope we didn't leave the house and embarrass ourselves.'

'At our age I think we can get away with most things.'

A few minutes later, Elsie was stretching her fingers and legs and twisting her neck this way and that checking she had a full range of movement again. 'I think I'm all good now,' she said. 'I'm going to have a shower.'

'Okay. I'm going to wait here a bit longer. Then I'll get us a cuppa. Actually, I'm hungry. Is it meant to give us the munchies, like they say marijuana does? I don't recall seeing a note about it. I'll get us some cheese and bikkies,' Howard said, hoisting himself up. 'What fun – a midnight feast.'

Elsie came back to the loungeroom in her bathrobe, sat down, and picked up a cracker and popped a bit of cheese on it. 'I'm disappointed I didn't see Maisie,' she said.

'It was an out-of-body experience, not a seance, dear.'

'I know. But still. I miss her.'

'I do too. Oh, don't go getting all sad on me, Else.'

'I can't help it.' Tears rolled down Elsie's face. 'I want to go back,' she snivelled. 'I was at least having fun before. I want more of that.'

'Another day, my love. Let's see how we recover from this time first,' Howard said.

Chapter Twenty-five

'Hello there, you two,' Howard said, holding open the front door to let Milly and Connor in.

'Yes, hello, Milly and Connor. It's really lovely to see you,' Elsie said.

'Hello Mr and Mrs Manning. Thank you so much for having us,' Milly said. 'Dad says thanks again too.'

'Hello. Thank you for having me,' Connor said.

'It's our pleasure, isn't it, Howard?'

'It sure is. Now, Milly, your dad did say you might have some homework. Do you?'

'Yep. Some reading and some maths.'

'Okay. Can we be of assistance?'

'Yes, please. Can you help with both?'

'Sure can,' Howard said.

'How about you, Connor?' Elsie interjected. 'You're in the same class, do you have homework, too?'

Connor nodded shyly.

'Would you like some help?' Elsie said.

'You wouldn't mind?' Connor said.

'Not at all. In fact, it would be my pleasure,' Elsie said.

'Exactly,' Howard said.

'I'm not very good at reading. Or maths,' Connor said.

'That's why you practise, then, right – to become better?' Howard said.

'I guess.'

'Connor, no one's perfect at anything right off the bat,' Howard said, desperate to say the right thing, but also not dither or be silent for too long and have the poor boy further unsettled.

'Sometimes we're not at all very good – at lots of things. And that's okay, as long as we give whatever it is a shot,' Elsie added, a little earnestly, for which Howard was grateful.

'We only have to do our best – like *really* do our best. Not pretend, right, Mr and Mrs Manning?' Milly said.

'Exactly right, Milly. Our best is always enough,' Howard said.

'Yes, because we actually really can't do any more than our best,' Elsie reiterated.

Milly gently nudged Connor with her shoulder, as if to reinforce the point.

The sudden memory of Howard doing the same to her at a similar age while standing behind the corrugated iron water tank, consoling her after some girls had been mean – pushing her over in the playground on purpose, if she was remembering correctly – caused Elsie to gulp slightly in shock. Still, seventy-odd years on. It was so true that it often wasn't the words someone said but how they made you feel that was most important.

She smiled at Connor, who was nodding and starting to look a little more comfortable.

'How about you and I take your bag outside, Connor, and set to work? It's nice out there, perhaps a bit chilly, but you just say if you need a blanket, or to come back inside,' Howard said. 'Then Milly and Mrs Manning, you stay in here. That way you won't be bothered by my voice when I muddle up the words,' Howard added for Connor's benefit.

'Sounds like a good plan, Mr Manning,' Milly said. 'Okay, Connor? We'll be right here – you'll be able to see us through the window. See ...' Milly pointed.

'Here's an idea,' Howard announced. 'How about we swap halfway through?'

Howard thought Connor still didn't seem convinced, though wasn't sure what the actual problem was and therefore had no clue how to go about remedying the situation. He was thankful when Milly stepped in.

'There's nothing to worry about, Connor,' she said, hands on hips. 'To start with I'll sit with Mrs Manning, inside, and you will sit with Mr Manning outside. And then we'll change over a bit later. There'll be no faffing about,' she added.

Ooh, Milly, that was maybe a little sharp, dear, Elsie thought, cringing. Though her concern stopped her from giving into the laughter tickling her lips.

Connor nodded, picked up his bag and led the way outside.

Howard smiled at Elsie and Milly before raising his hand in a wave and following the boy outside.

'Sometimes he needs to be told,' Milly said as she took her backpack to the kitchen table and proceeded to unpack it. 'Not to be mean,' she continued, 'but because he gets *stuck*. He tries too hard. Oh, I don't really know,' she added, looking a little unsure, before flapping a hand. 'Dad says it's because of his, um, situation at home. He's been in foster care. His mum is in prison. She might be back soon – I'm not too sure. It's about drugs,' Milly added matter-of-factly, opening her green fabric pencil case and fossicking in it. 'The people he's with, Mr and Mrs Draper, are nice, as far as I know, but the house is full. Very busy and much too loud,' she said, extracting a pencil with apparent satisfaction. 'So Connor's staying with us for a few nights – not just sleepovers; Dad's his official sort-of foster carer. What I mean is, not full-time; for emergencies and when people like the Drapers need a bit of a break. Which kind of makes us brother and sister. But, also, not really at all. I guess,' she added with a shrug.

'Ah, I see,' Elsie said.

'He had lots of people around him, but he still, um … It doesn't really make sense, but he said he still felt sad and lonely.'

Elsie nodded. Milly shrugged again and then returned to her pencil case, from which she extracted a pen, which she lined up with the pencil before diving back in for more. Elsie became a little hypnotised by her careful, slow actions. She was also still thinking about what Milly had said about Connor's home life – mainly marvelling at the insight he had for such a young child. Insecurity would do that, she suspected, as would being exposed to things kids shouldn't be exposed to. Poor kid might even have had to see his mother after an overdose or something. Her heart began to ache for him.

'At least he has a lovely friend in you, Milly,' Elsie said, for something to say in the silence that was at risk of becoming uncomfortable.

Milly nodded. 'He's a good friend to me too. I reckon we're going to be best friends forever, like you and Mr Manning. Well, I hope so, anyway.'

'Me too,' Elsie said.

'Though boys are a bit weird, aren't they?'

This time Elsie did laugh out loud, the comment, so out of the blue, taking her by surprise.

'Well, they *are* different, that's for sure. I like to think we complement each other – I mean, suit each other.'

'Um. It's okay, Mrs Manning, I know what complement means – like two sides of the same coin; different but necessary, sort of,' she added, scrunching up her face.

Close enough, Elsie thought. 'Yes, very good.' She was grateful for not having to find a way to explain it to the child herself.

'I'm reading above my grade now,' Milly announced.

'That's fantastic. Well done.'

'You know how you said, that other time, that when you love reading you can never be lonely, Mrs Manning?'

'Yep. I do.'

'I told Connor ...'

Okay, great, but where are we heading with this?

'... but it made him sad.'

'Oh. Why's that?'

'Because he can't read very well and he doesn't think he will ever be able to.'

Oh. Elsie searched her mind for something useful to say, but as she did, thankfully, Milly continued.

'I'm so glad he could come today. Reading with Mr Manning will be a big help, I reckon. And with you, if you'd done it with him,' she hastily added, looking up at Elsie with a slightly sheepish expression on her face.

'Milly, you never have to worry about choosing Mr Manning over me or me over him. Okay?'

'But ...' Milly seemed unsure. And then she brightened, and declared: 'Because you're two sides of the same coin – different but necessary!'

Elsie chuckled to herself. *Very clever.* The kid was a sharp one. 'Yep, that works.'

'So, shall we do your reading or maths homework first?' Elsie asked a few moments later. Milly was silently staring out the window. For the first time, Elsie realised why she'd chosen to sit in Howard's chair – she could see Connor and Howard through the sliding glass doors, which is where her attention was now concentrated. 'Would you like to check on them?' Elsie asked.

'Um.' Milly seemed to give the question considerable thought before saying, 'I would. But I also don't want to disturb them if they're getting on okay.'

Elsie turned fully around in her chair to look. 'They seem fine to me,' she said.

'Yes. Connor looked a bit frustrated just before.'

'Oh. Well, then, let's leave them be for now. You can go out and offer them a drink and a snack a bit later, if you like. That way it won't look quite so much like you're checking up.'

'That's a good idea. Thanks, Mrs Manning.'

'Mr Manning is very patient, so I'm sure they'll be fine, Milly. You're a very good friend,' Elsie said, again disappointed to not conjure up anything more profound or original.

Milly nodded. 'But I need to also give him space to be himself and make his own mind up – even when he takes ages. That's what Dad says. But he takes *forever* sometimes – Connor, that is,' Milly said theatrically.

Again, Elsie tried not to laugh. Instead, she carefully said, 'We all need to go at our own pace, Milly. Hurrying never helps anyone or anything. That's something that took me many years to learn.'

'Patience is a virtue,' Milly said with a sigh, surprising Elsie. 'It's something my gran used to say. A lot. I think. I don't really remember, but she must have because Dad says it too. It means it's good to learn to have patience – it's important too.'

'It sure is.'

'But it's not always easy. Actually,' she added thoughtfully, and a beat later, 'it's really hard sometimes.'

'Yes, I agree with you there, Milly.'

'I'm ready to do my reading now, if that's okay. Can you please make sure I don't make any mistakes?' Milly asked.

'I sure can.' Elsie leant closer so she could read the words in the book Milly now had open in front of her.

'How did you go?' Elsie asked a little later when Connor came in alone and stood beside the table, followed by Howard.

'Really good,' he said, beaming. 'I did it, Milly. I read the whole book through with only a few mistakes.'

'But we got them licked easily, didn't we?' Howard said from behind Connor, his hand on the boy's shoulder.

'Sure did. But now I need a wee. And a little break before we tackle maths,' Connor said, looking a bit uncomfortable.

'Just down the hall – first door on your left for the toilet, young fellow,' Howard said.

Connor bolted.

'How are you girls going?' Howard said, moving around the table and putting a hand on Milly's shoulder. She smiled up at him.

'He looked pleased. Did he really do okay, Mr Manning? Connor struggles with reading.'

'He sure did, Milly. A couple of false starts, but we got there at quite a clip in the end. We practically galloped home. How about you?'

'Milly tells me she's a class ahead with her reading now,' Elsie said.

'That was quick. Well done, Milly. Though I'm not surprised to hear that at all,' Howard said.

'We're about to tackle maths, aren't we?'

'Yes,' Milly said with little enthusiasm. 'I'm definitely not a class ahead with maths.'

'Well, we can't all be good at everything.' Howard said.

'Connor is better at maths than me.'

'See, swings and roundabouts,' Howard said.

'I don't know what that means,' Milly said, frowning.

'Hmm. Well ...' Howard searched his mind for a better way to explain. 'Ah, I know,' he said, as if to himself. 'You know how a seesaw goes up and down – sometimes you're at the top and sometimes you're at the bottom?'

Milly nodded.

'Well, it's like that – life, or being good at something or not so good at things, is like that. Do you see?' As he said the words, Howard wanted to kick himself for not using the seesaw instead. Damn all the idioms and clichés he had stuck in his head that fell out all too regularly.

Milly nodded again, this time a little more thoughtfully. Then she said, 'You can also be in the middle on a seesaw too, though – balancing.'

'True. You're quite right,' Howard said.

Elsie smiled on, enjoying the ever so slight butting of heads.

'All better?' she asked, noticing Connor appear out of the corner of her eye. He had his hands in front of himself, in a manner she recognised, and he looked very upset. *Uh-oh*, she thought, noticing the darker patch spread beyond what his small hands were able to cover.

What do we do now? Should I help – or best Howard does? Elsie wondered.

Thankfully, in the couple of seconds she'd been dithering, Milly had accurately read the situation. She was already up and out of her chair, had crossed the space, and was standing with an arm around Connor.

'It's okay,' Milly cooed. 'These things happen.' Milly looked up plaintively at Elsie.

'They sure do,' Elsie said, getting to her feet.

'Oh,' Howard said, catching on. 'Has a miscalculation occurred?' he said. His heart sank for the boy, as he was transported right back to the same age where a similar event had occurred – only, worse, it had happened in front of everyone at school. Thankfully he'd had his best friend Elsie, like Connor now had Milly. Elsie had even had to venture into the boys' toilets – a terrifying prospect.

Connor and Milly were nodding.

'Hey, it's okay. These things happen, mate,' Howard said. 'Well, it did to me when I was around your age.'

'Yes, absolutely, and really not a huge deal,' Elsie said. She knew Howard was telling the truth, because she'd been there with him. She'd had to go and find a teacher to help and, shudder, go into the boys' toilet. She'd retained a bit of a fear of male toilets, and had always been thankful she'd had daughters and not sons.

'I'm sorry,' Connor bleated, two stripes of tears now making their way down his cheeks.

'There's no need for tears, young fellow,' said Howard. 'We'll clean you up quick smart and all will be right with the world once again.'

'Yes, please don't cry, darling. It's okay,' Elsie said.

'We don't have any spare clothes here,' Milly said quietly, 'and our house is locked up.'

'That's all right. We can easily wash these,' Elsie said.

'Would you?'

'Of course. No trouble at all,' Howard said. 'And they'll be dry in a jiffy – it's actually quite breezy out there.'

'And we have a dryer we can pop them into, if they look like they're taking too long,' said Elsie.

'Good thinking, dear,' Howard said. He was pretty out of his depth on this one.

'The only thing is, what we can pop on you while they're getting sorted. Any ideas, Milly?'

'I've got my stilt pants that you made me, in my bag,' Connor said, brightening.

'Oh, well, that's perfect. Good thinking. We're all sorted, then,' Howard said.

'I'll get them,' Milly said, going outside and then returning with Connor's backpack, which she opened and extracted the pants from.

'But I don't have any undies,' Connor said quietly.

'Ah, don't worry about that,' Howard said, waving a hand. 'We can all survive with you not wearing any undies for a few hours.'

'Yes, we won't tell anyone,' Milly said.

'Exactly. No problem at all,' Elsie said.

'How about a shower first?' Howard said. 'But only if you want to.'

Connor nodded.

'Would it be best if I help?' Elsie said.

'Um …' Again, Howard cursed the paedophiles who meant all this additional palaver.

Thankfully, Milly seemed to have sensed the awkwardness, because she said, 'I'll help, Connor. Come on. This way.' She clasped his hand and dragged him towards the hall.

'I'll just come and get you a towel – hang on a sec,' Elsie, hurrying after them.

Howard ran his hands through his hair. Poor kid, he thought. He longed to help, and hated feeling so helpless. He also hated that the kid hadn't felt at ease enough to pipe up earlier that he needed the loo. *Oh well, too late to worry about that now.*

While he felt sad and helpless, his heart also glowed at seeing Milly being so caring and calm and capable in a crisis. It really was a beautiful reminder of him and Elsie as youngsters.

He went over and busied himself with putting on the kettle and getting the things out of the cupboard for a cuppa. This he could do.

As the kettle roared to life, he thought, *You'll do well, kids, if you stick together, like us.*

He leant against the bench and became lost in memories of them as kids – a flickering montage of images of them laughing together and standing consoling each other at various times. The thing that had never changed was that they never failed together. Not once, well, that he could recall, had they both fallen apart at the same moment. Always one had been there to pick the other up – rescue them both. It was probably what he loved most about their partnership – if he had to name just one thing.

'Are you okay? It's not your fault,' Elsie said, crossing over to him and giving him a gentle nudge with her shoulder.

She'd been doing that since the beginning too – it was an action that had many meanings: sometimes meanings that only they were aware of.

'Everything okay out there?' Howard said, dragging himself from his reverie and the past. He looked up. 'Sorry, I was miles away. Did you say something?'

'I said, don't blame yourself.'

Howard nodded. 'I'm sad that the poor little chap didn't feel able to interrupt our reading to tell me he needed to go.' He folded his arms across his chest.

'Maybe he didn't need to go then,' Elsie offered. 'Maybe it was after coming in and being excited about doing so well,' she said, leaning her head against his back.

Howard nodded again.

Elsie eased her hand under his arms and threaded her arm through, and tugged gently. 'Don't take it on. It's unlikely to be simply about the here and now.'

'Yes, you're probably right,' he said. 'Thanks.' He patted her hand. 'Isn't Milly a gem?'

'Yes, she sure is. She's got everything under control. I'll go back in a sec and see if they're ready for me to rinse out Connor's things. I just wanted to check on you.'

'I can do it, if you like.'

'No, that's okay. You take care of the refreshments.'

'Thank you, my love. I am feeling a little fragile, to be honest. I know, I'm a silly old fool.'

'Well, you're my silly old fool. And if you are, then I am too. And there's nowhere I'd rather be and no one I'd rather be with,' she said.

Howard leant down and kissed her nose. 'I love you, Elsie Manning-nee-Stokes.'

'And I love you, Howard Manning-always-Manning,' she said smiling. 'I'll have a Milo, thanks. And I bet so will the kids.'

Howard nodded and turned back to the bench while thinking how many times had they said *I love you* to each other over the years – a million by now, surely. And yet it never failed to buoy him. When they were kids – before adding 'old' – it had been 'silly sausage'. Oh how he loved them, he thought, his heart lifting.

'We're all good now,' Milly announced, arriving in the space and making her way over to the bench.

Connor trailed behind.

'Thanks, Milly. Well done. You okay, young fellow – not too bothered by things, I hope? As I said before, it happens to the best of us,' he added, attempting to sound jovial.

'Really?' Connor said, brightening.

'Oh yes. Every one of us has been in your situation at one time or another, I reckon.'

'Yep,' Milly said. 'See, Connor, I told you. I'll just go and help Mrs Manning. You stay here with Mr Manning.'

Connor nodded.

'Can I help at all, Mrs Manning?' Milly asked from the doorway to the laundry.

'Thank you, but I think I'm all good right now, Milly. I won't be a jiffy,' Elsie said. 'You can carry some pegs for me in a minute, if you like.'

'Thanks so much for all this. And for not making a fuss,' Milly said.

'Oh, there's no fuss needing to be made,' Elsie said, half turning from her position with her hands in the sink where she washed Connor's tiny jeans and undies.

'We're really lucky to have you and Mr Manning as friends,' Milly said, leaning against the doorframe and rubbing on it like a slinking cat.

'We feel blessed to have you as our friends too, darling. Listen,' Elsie said, pausing and cocking her head.

'Another egg!' Milly said. 'Good chookies.'

Elsie smiled and returned to her task, grateful to the chook for the disruption.

'There we go,' Elsie said a few minutes later, standing back from the clothesline where Connor's two pieces of clothing now flapped in the breeze. 'I think they'll be dry in time.'

'Good job, Mrs Manning. And I think you're right. The wind will do the trick,' Milly said, causing Elsie to chuckle to herself.

'Thanks for your help, Milly. I think we've earned ourselves a Milo and a bikkie.'

'Sounds like a plan, Mrs Manning.'

'Do you think we need to say anything more to Connor, Milly?'

'No. He's okay. He gets it.'

'Okay. Promise you'll tell me if that changes?'

'I promise,' Milly said sagely and gave a decisive nod. 'Come on. Then we have to finish my maths homework, Mrs Manning.'

'Oh, yes. Please don't let me forget. We have plenty of time. And after that, there might be a surprise for dinner,' Elsie said as they left the laundry and made their way down the hall.

'If you mean pizza, Dad asked me to choose something Connor would like too.'

'Ah, okay then.'

They were about to get to the end of the hall and turn into the open door to the kitchen when Milly paused and said, 'But Connor doesn't know. He'll be surprised and really excited. He loves pizza but he never gets to have it. Mrs Draper doesn't get takeaway. When he's with his mum she loves getting drive-through burgers,' she added, and then in a whisper, 'but just between us, he's not a huge fan of those.'

'Right. Good to know.'

'It's a bit complicated. I'll tell you another day,' Milly said.

'Okay, then.' Elsie smiled to herself at Milly's grown-up tone.

'Here they are,' Howard called. 'Milo time? We're all ready to go here.'

'Yes, please and thank you. But I'm going to have mine at the table while I finish my maths homework. If that's okay?' Milly said as she crossed to the kitchen where Howard stood with Connor beside him.

'That's perfectly fine with me,' Howard said.

'Good thinking,' Elsie said, picking up a mug and taking it to the table.

'Shall we take ours and go back outside and carry on, Connor?'
Howard said.

Connor nodded.

'Come on, then.'

Connor looked at his mug, seemingly a little unsure.

'Shall I carry that for you, if you're worried about spilling it?'
Howard said. 'I might have made it a bit full.'

'Yes, please,' Connor said, handing it over.

'How about you get the door for us, then, Connor?'

Connor nodded. 'Okay. I can do that.'

'Great. Well, lead the way, young chap,' Howard said, raising
the mugs.

Chapter Twenty-six

'Oh my goodness,' Howard said, looking up at Elsie from his newspaper spread out before him on the table. 'Larry and Susan Coventry have died. It's here in the paper.'

'What? Both of them? No, surely not.'

'Apparently. There's a death notice.'

'But we only saw them the other week. Gosh. Perhaps it was that car accident over the weekend. How awful.'

They sat in silence for a few moments before Howard said, 'Is it really bad that my first thought was *Oh no, there goes our supply of fun times elixir*?'

'Yes. Truly terrible. But I have a confession to make: it was the first thought I had too. So, we can both be terrible together.'

'Damn. I enjoyed their mushrooms. And their company at that lunch wasn't half bad, either. Hey, you don't think they were jacked up on something then, do you?'

'No idea. Maybe.'

'They didn't seem at all strange and they would have if they'd been on something, wouldn't they?' Howard said.

'I suppose. Though don't plenty of people carry on in life under the influence of some thing or other? You hear about that all the time, don't you?'

'Do you?' Howard said.

'Oh, you know, Howard – like functioning alcoholics, I mean. They apparently hold down jobs and must come across as normal enough – whatever normal is, anyway – to be able to do so. I imagine it's the same with drugs – the illicit ones *and* the prescription ones.'

'Yes, mother's little helpers. Probably half the people dropping off and picking up their kids from school are on something legal, or otherwise,' Howard said.

'It's all too depressing to think about. And scary. Thank goodness we've decided to give up driving,' Elsie said.

'Yes, good idea that.'

'Though just crossing the street still holds plenty of danger,' Elsie mused.

'That's true. And I do that at least once a day. Do you think we should go back to home delivery, like during the pandemic?'

'That's up to you, dear – you're the one traipsing back and forth, mostly. I will say, though, we might never leave the house if we give up those little trips, given how many friends we've lost now.'

'And by *we*, you really mean royal we – as in *me*, right? Are you trying to tell me something? Like, I've put on weight or something?' He looked down his chest.

'Don't be ridiculous, Howard. Since when have I ever not just come out with something? It was me who educated you on the men-don't-get-hints factor all those years ago when we first started running the business.'

'Oh, yes. I remember. And a very good lesson to learn too. Thank you.'

'You're welcome. And back to the topic at hand. No, you have not put on weight and, even if you had, you know damned well I wouldn't say anything and wouldn't give two hoots anyway. Honestly, Howard, you would think we had just met, with a comment like that, not that we're approaching our sixtieth wedding anniversary.'

'And seventy-five years, is it, since we met?'

'I think so, yes. But that's exactly my point.'

'Sorry. I'm not sure what's wrong with me this morning,' Howard said.

'You're *shook*, as the kids would say, upon reading of the loss of Larry and Susan. Poor things. I really hope, for their family's sake, they weren't under the influence, or the cause of whatever happened.'

'I must say, I am very disappointed. I wonder if they'll have a son or grandson willing to take up the slack in the illicit substances department. Do you want to go along to the funeral and do some sleuthing?' Howard said.

'Yes. But, no, better not.'

'But, seriously, for reasons of respect and offering our condolences, do you want to go along?'

'When is it?'

'Friday, two pm.'

'Let's think about it. We've got the week. Though, we barely knew them – and, bearing in mind, it will involve taxis or carpooling with someone.'

'True. I'd forgotten about the inconvenience of not driving oneself for a moment there.'

Elsie looked up at Howard and her brain crackled. Was he losing it? Like, in a way where she ought to seek help or intervention, or what have you? How many times lately, and how often, was she having this very thought?

'I know,' he said, flapping his hand, 'we just mentioned not driving. I haven't *completely* lost my faculties. I think I'm just distracted and a little unsettled by this morning's news. Perhaps, instead of attending, we stay here and celebrate – I mean commiserate – their passing by using the weed they gave us. We could bake some brownies or something.'

'That's a good idea. I'm glad you didn't say eat the rest of the risotto, because I kind of feel like saving that for later – for a time when life is too dire to contemplate and we really need to escape for a bit.'

'Yes, good plan, dear. After I've finished with the paper, I'm going to see if I can find out something about the relatives – see if anything flags as a possible source.'

'As you wish,' Elsie said, her attention already back on her crossword.

'It fairly boggles my mind, Elsie. There's so much to think about. One doesn't even need to leave the house to have things happen.'

'Hmm.'

'Never dull moment.'

'Well, I wouldn't go that far, Howard.'

'Though, certainly, there are a lot less dull moments now young Milly's on the scene.'

'Yes, dear little thing. I miss her when she's at school.'

'I hope she's giving the teachers hell,' Howard said. 'Both of them. Connor's a good kid, too.'

'Mmm. I think it's a given that Milly would be at least keeping them on their toes,' Elsie said. 'Oh, listen, it sounds like someone's just laid an egg.' They lifted their heads and smiled at hearing the earnest clucking and cackling of a proud chicken or two.

A moment later, in unison, they sighed and returned to their respective parts of the newspaper.

After a few minutes, Howard's mobile pinged. 'Oh,' he said as he read the text message that had just come through.

'What is it?' Elsie asked.

'It's Thomas Radcliffe, he's invited us to go on a bus to Larry and Susan's joint funeral. He's wanting a decent delegation from the tennis club to do a guard of honour. Shall I say we'll go, Else?'

'I don't see why not, since that's the transport issue solved.'

'That's what I was thinking. I'll let him know straight away.'

Chapter Twenty-seven

Howard and Elsie had just left the house and were walking down their driveway to go and meet the minibus to Larry and Susan Coventry's funeral when Milly and Daniel's car reversed out of their driveway. It stopped in front of Howard and Elsie, and the front passenger and back passenger windows rolled down.

'Hello,' Daniel and Milly called.

'Hi, Daniel, Hi, Milly,' Elsie and Howard said at the same time.

'No school today, Milly?' Howard said.

'I'm off to the dentist.'

'Oh, sorry to hear that. I hope you get a good report.' Howard moved towards Milly as Elsie walked closer to hear Daniel repeat something they'd both missed.

'I'm milking it. But don't tell Dad,' Milly said in a loud whisper, and tapped the side of her nose.

'Got it,' Howard said, nodding and tapping his own nose. He then pretended to lock his mouth with a key and toss it over his shoulder, causing Milly to grin.

'Are you off somewhere interesting?' Milly asked.

'Milly Wynter, don't be nosey,' Daniel said, partially turning in his seat.

'It's okay, Daniel. We're off to a funeral, Milly, of some old friends,' Howard said.

'Old, as in lived a long time? Or old, as in you've been friends for a long time?' Milly asked.

'Um.' *Bit of both?*

'Or, is it *complicated*?' Milly added, wrinkling her nose, which gave her a very serious-looking expression.

'Yes. That's the one – option three,' Howard said. 'We'd lost touch and not seen them in recent years – though saw them again not long ago.'

'Okay. Did they both die? Together?'

'Yes. Apparently.'

'Oh. That's unusual.'

'That it is, Milly,' Howard said.

'Milly, enough with the questions. Please.'

'Sorry, Dad. Sorry, Mr and Mrs Manning.'

'It's okay, Milly,' Howard said. 'We're not actually sure what happened.'

'But they'd had a long life, and were happy enough, by all accounts,' Elsie added, keen to put Milly's mind at rest in case it was about to stray into dark places.

'Oh, yes,' Howard said, clearly catching onto Elsie's wavelength. 'They were older than us – well into their eighties, which is reasonably old.'

Milly nodded, as if thoughtfully digesting the information.

'We'd better keep going, kiddo. Don't want you to be late,' Daniel called from the front seat.

Milly rolled her eyes theatrically at Howard, causing him to laugh.

'Are you sure you don't want a ride out to the main road?' Daniel asked, looking from Howard to Elsie, eyebrows raised.

'We're fine, thanks,' Elsie said.

'Yes, it's very kind of you to offer, but we're keen to stretch the legs before being sat on a bus for the next while,' Howard said.

'Okay, then, bye,' Daniel said.

'Bye. Good luck with the dentist, Milly,' Elsie and Howard chimed.

'Thanks. Good luck at the funeral.'

'Thank you,' Howard said.

Elsie smiled and nodded.

Howard and Elsie stood and waved until Daniel's car had disappeared.

'Oh, she's a breath of fresh air. I feel much buoyed,' Howard said as they set off along the neat footpath in front of their neighbours to the left.

'You say that every time you see her.'

'I know.'

'It's true, though. I feel the same.'

'I wish we could have taken her with us as our personal merriment maker,' Howard said and then fell silent. It was a bit of an unspoken rule with them that they not talk too much when walking and instead focus on where they were putting their feet. They often remarked at how poor their balance was nowadays and how their feet seemed to be not always where their brains led them to believe they were. The mildest of uneven surface was positively dangerous and the smallest of trips on a footpath or edge of a paver, or even a stick left lying about, was quite literally life-threatening. The cars whooshing by at speed didn't help, the sound messing with their equilibrium.

'Here, do you think?' Howard finally said, stopping. They were out on the main road just beyond their nearest bus stop. 'I did say this stop, didn't I?'

'Yes, I think so. Oh, I'm hot,' Elsie said, flapping her cardigan edges a little to move the air. 'It really is proving to be a very warm winter.'

'Sorry, is there anything I can do to help?' Howard said.

'No. I'll be all right in a minute.'

'I spoke too soon about the weather. That's raindrops I feel. I'm glad we brought a brolly,' Howard said, putting the umbrella up.

'Yes. That was good thinking on your part, Howard.'

They stood close together under the large, golfing-sized umbrella, looking up the street for sign of the minibus.

'I feel a little awkward about this now,' Howard said.

'What about – going to a funeral under false pretences?'

'Well, yes. That.'

'We probably wouldn't be if not for Thomas Radcliffe wanting a rent-a-crowd.'

'Right you are. So, it's officially a win-win, then, I suppose.'

'And it's not like we're complete strangers,' Elsie pointed out.

'Yes, but we're not really going to offer our respects.'

'Well, we *are*, as well as the other. Aren't all funerals about a sense of curiosity in some respects – to listen to the eulogy and learn something you might not have known about the person, or to see who's there and who you know in common?'

'I suppose.'

'It's the ultimate reunion, really, isn't it? Especially with Adelaide being never more than one degree of separation.'

'True. They shouldn't be fun, but it is, really, to see who's who in the zoo that you might not have seen for ages.'

'Or since the last funeral,' Elsie pointed out.

'Ah, yes, there's that,' Howard said. 'A far too regular occurrence for us these days.'

'Yes. Saves us having people around quite so often, though.'

Howard chuckled. 'I love that you can always find a silver lining, dear. Just make sure I don't snore. I'm sure I nodded off at the last one,' Howard said.

'You did. You gasped when I nudged you.'

'Shit. That's right.'

'Oh well, it wasn't too noticeable and not *too* out of place. Thankfully.'

'And at our age, one is prone to nodding off if the space is nice and warm. And not giving too many hoots about it, which is a good thing. Everyone must know it's par for the course in our age bracket. It's not like falling asleep during a wedding. Can you imagine the horror?'

'Oh dear. Yes. Doesn't bear thinking about,' Elsie said, shaking her head. Though the conversation had left her feeling amused.

'Look. We're right on time,' Howard announced a moment later. 'Here we are, I think.' He nodded with approval. 'Brilliant.'

'Hello,' Howard and Elsie said to the woman bus driver who had got out to help them on. 'Thank you,' Elsie said, accepting the arm offered to her, in lieu of a handle.

'I can take that for you, if you like,' the woman said, nodding at Howard's hands – one clutching the umbrella, now closed, and the other holding the handle of a small chiller bag containing four bottles of water and a large container of nuts and dried fruit. They'd discussed earlier that having to lug it around – depending upon if the bus would be staying the whole time at the funeral or leaving and coming back again later – was preferable to them becoming faint with hunger or low blood sugar, and/or thirsty. They'd brought a decent-sized pile of treats and two extra bottles of water so as to be able to, if not share with *everyone*, at least offer out of politeness. They figured it was worth the extra inconvenience of the weight to carry to be well mannered and well prepared. As they'd packed, they'd also discussed how back in their day they must have drunk very little water – there was no carrying around drink bottles at all times like now. This was a conversation they often had.

'Thanks very much for helping make up numbers,' Thomas said, partially standing up from his seat and extending his hand to Howard and then to Elsie, to which they simply raised theirs.

'No problem. Thanks for including us and organising everything,' Howard said.

'Yes,' Elsie said, smiling and nodding. *What Howard said.*

'Shocking business – bloody kids driving while on their bloody phones.'

'Oh, was it? We haven't caught up with what happened,' Howard said.

'Yes, a young lad in a hotted-up sportscar ran the red light and ploughed straight into them as they were crossing the street on their way out to the movies. It was that accident in Norwood late Saturday afternoon that was all over the evening news. Poor things didn't stand a chance. Just terrible,' he said, shaking his head.

'No. How awful,' Howard said.

'Yes, horrific,' Elsie agreed.

'Everyone, you remember Howard and Elsie Manning?' There was a chorus of mumbles and grunts and quite a few heads nodded. 'Howard and Elsie, this is … er, everyone,' he said, waving a hand, before sitting back down.

'Hello,' Howard said, giving a general wave. Most faces were familiar.

Elsie did the same.

They then turned to face the front and sat in the last pair of seats, which was right up the front and caused them to feel a little left out of things, physically and otherwise, mostly due to being newcomers to the busload.

Howard, having forcibly pushed aside from his mind the terrible news he'd just heard, found himself itching to raise the topic of illicit substances with the others and find out who else might partake. It fairly blew his mind to think their tennis club gatherings all those years ago might have been dens of iniquity and he longed to get the lowdown. Though, what if it wasn't still going on and his and Elsie's gift from Larry and Susan had been on the down-low. Things could get embarrassing. He wondered if the others were partly going along, like he and Elsie were, to see if there was a possibility of an alternative supply. As much as he wanted his curiosity to be satisfied, it wasn't exactly something one ought to enquire about, was it? He strained to try to hear the topics of conversation behind them, but all he got was a dense rumble of voices. He gave up, stuck his legs forward, crossed his arms and settled in for the journey.

Elsie stared out the window as she tried to tune into the rabble of voices behind her. The mood seemed buoyant for a funeral – especially considering the tragic circumstances involved. Though it wasn't necessarily a symptom of a lack of disrespect for the occasion but one for the dullness of their days generally and the volume of recent similar events in their lives.

Howard wanted to ask Elsie if she was having the same thoughts as he or if she was off on another tack. Or perhaps she was just having a snooze, he thought, sneaking a look sideways at her and finding her eyes closed and her head lolling and threatening to bump into the window.

Howard's musing took him all the way to the big wrought iron gates of the suburban cemetery about forty minutes away and continued when they'd all got out of the bus.

'What is it, Howard? Are you okay?' asked Elsie beside him, snapping him back to attention.

'Sorry. Oh, yes, just thinking too hard.'

'Well, stop it,' she hissed, before raising her hand and waving to someone off to the right of the group that Howard assumed to be the immediate family. He smiled and raised his hand in acknowledgement, not wanting to appear rude. Except he couldn't for the life of him place the couple he thought Elsie had waved to. Though, to be fair, they were standing in the shade and quite a way off. He felt his shoulders slump slightly as they made their way over.

At that moment, Howard heard Thomas calling from somewhere behind him, 'Come on, folks, this way.' Howard knew he'd be making herding motions with his hands, if he chose to turn around and look. A stab of annoyance rose in him. He now remembered what tennis club had been like with this guy as president. Dull. Too serious.

He struggled to recall if he and Elsie had left for that reason or another – before or after arthritis had taken hold in his knees and in Elsie's hips and elbows. He did recall being disappointed that when he'd stopped playing it hadn't felt welcoming to stay at the club as just a social member, especially after he'd declined the invitation – or rather coercion – to play lawn bowls instead.

No wonder they'd been invited to make up numbers. Thomas had probably struggled to find enough people who took his calls these days. *Sucker*, Howard remonstrated with himself, as he settled into the chair at the end of the row.

'Are you sure you're okay?' Elsie said, leaning in close and whispering.

No. I'm feeling like a fool, or at least a charlatan for being here and being accosted by Thomas bloody Radcliffe. But Howard, knowing he had a habit of stage whispering when he was trying to actually whisper, and recognising the now reverent hush occupying the space as people took their places, just nodded and gripped her hand before gazing down to the folded sheet containing the order of service and details of the deceased they'd been handed on their way in.

He felt a tap on the shoulder and turned in his chair. And immediately wished he hadn't – it was Thomas Radcliffe holding up a couple of spare sheets, waggling them.

'Oh, you've got one?' Thomas said.

Howard nodded and held up his own, wriggling it in mimicry. He then turned back and closed his eyes at the sudden rush of annoyance.

God, it's like being on a school bloody excursion!

After taking several slow breaths, he told himself to relax and reminded himself that his motives for being here were less than authentic, so he was in a glass house and couldn't throw stones. They were here now. And he had to behave. And anyway, it wasn't like they had anywhere else to be – except home, which was beckoning more and more loudly by the minute.

Hopefully they would be served tea and biscuits later, at the very least. If they were lucky, they might get a full stand-up luncheon – ribbon sandwiches, mini pies and quiches ... *Oh yes.* His mouth began to water, until he reminded himself not to get his hopes up on that score, either.

It seemed to take ages for everyone to get seated and for the service to begin. Howard was already starting to feel drowsy, while pondering that it was just as unruly as herding small children, though definitely in slow motion. There was no racing off after said small children, instead it was about trying to shuffle the poorly mobile into tight spaces and struggling to make room for all the walkers and manoeuvre around walking sticks – not get battered in the shins nor whack anyone else with your own.

Having been assured the bus was staying, he'd left his golf umbrella on the seat. He now wished he had it to hold onto as something familiar to fiddle with. He wasn't sure where that thought, nor the ball of anxiety that had just grabbed his chest and then let go, had come from. He'd been taken by surprise and only just stopped himself in time from clutching his chest and gasping.

Oh. Okay. All good, he told himself. *Just muscle memory or what have you from previous funerals.*

Howard and Elsie had often discussed that they thought grief never really went away – that it compounded, a whole new layer added with each loss. Perhaps it meant they hadn't adequately dealt with previous episodes. Though, other than crying, living through the pain, talking about the deceased – not deliberately erasing them from experience or memory, like some seem to – what else was there to do?

Oh. No. Not layers as such, here's a better metaphor: It was more like already rain-sodden ground receiving another drenching and the water running off due to there being nowhere more for it to soak in – that was what all the layers of grief were like. Or was it more like layers getting heavier? Or like an onion?

Howard's mind began to swim. He started to sweat under his armpits in his dark grey suit. He reached up and loosened his tie slightly. It was becoming really stuffy. He closed his eyes and then forced them open again, pinching the skin between his left thumb and forefinger in an attempt to keep himself focussed.

He muttered his way through a couple of hymns – once two of his favourites, though ruined long ago, thanks to their prolific funeral usage and now being associated with mourning.

Howard sat up straighter to listen to the oldest son. But then his shoulders drooped again at the eulogy seeming to be just like any other and containing nothing that could be said to reference Larry and Susan's enterprise – even incognito.

When the grandson mentioned what great meals his grand-mother had made, and how her risotto was a favourite, for which she was renowned, Howard came close to letting out a loud guffaw, but managed to catch it part way up his throat and shove it back down quick smart.

No one else seemed in on the joke, he thought, as he had a quick look around the assembled crowd. And, anyway, the kid up front looked about twelve – like, *really* twelve – not the same twelve he and Elsie used, glibly, to refer to anyone more than a couple of decades younger than themselves.

He felt Elsie nudge him. He bit the inside of his cheek and dared not look at her. He could feel the heat of private conspiracy radiating between them. He cast a glance at the guy – the son – who had just spoken, standing a little away from the youngster currently speaking. He was smiling – almost grinning. Was that because his kid had dropped a family secret into his speech or was he just smiling in sad support and encouragement? The annoy-ance of not knowing grew in Howard, until he again reminded himself he was being ridiculous. What was this fixation all about? Was he becoming, or had already become, addicted to the drugs?

No, he pondered. If that were the case, he'd have devoured the rest of the risotto in the freezer. No, he thought again, it was about having something interesting on which to focus. That was all. These episodes were few and far between – these *adventures*, as young Milly had put it. Not that this was what she would have meant. Maybe, though, when she was older ... Who would know? Thoughts of Milly made him instantly feel better – lighter.

Elsie looked at Howard in surprise as he gently nudged her.

'Come on. That's us,' he whispered, tilting his head towards the aisle.

Elsie nodded and followed him. She felt dishevelled – a little stunned, even – and wondered, as she made her way along the emptying row of recently vacated chairs, if she'd fallen asleep. She couldn't remember anything after the eulogy and speeches by several people.

Gosh. She hoped she hadn't embarrassed herself, or anyone else. She must have had quite the nap, she thought, as they lined up at the end of the chairs beside the aisle, because now the shock and bewilderment were wearing off she was feeling very refreshed. She longed to raise her arms above her head and have a good stretch, give in to the several yawns she could feel backed up in her oesophagus. She carefully took several deep breaths and closed-mouth yawns that were so big they made her eyes water. She wriggled her toes and focussed on her limbs and muscles – tensing and releasing them where she stood as an alternative attempt to stretch out the cricks and luxuriate in the lovely afternoon post-nap glow.

She almost laughed aloud when a small child appeared out of the corner of her eye and curled up on the plush burgundy hall runner, before being scooped up by the nearest adult.

There was growling and whispering as the kid protested and wriggled and Elsie thought, *I hear you, kid*.

She smiled at the child now peering at her, glassy-eyed, over someone's shoulder. They responded with jamming a fist into an eye socket and rubbing rhythmically. The cadence was soothing and Elsie had to look away.

Oh, to be able to take a nap. She indulged in a private sigh.

Thankfully her thoughts were dragged back to the occasion as the first of the two caskets, hoisted above the shoulders of friends or relatives, began to move slowly down the aisle towards them, the rows of people providing guards of honour along the sides – a variety of sporting and social community groups, Elsie assumed – lowering their heads in a reverential send off.

Soon everyone was milling about and then slowly, by some unseen force, being herded after the contained bodies. And then the caskets went one way and the guests flowed in another and Elsie and Howard found themselves in a room laid out with after-noon tea things.

'Goodie,' Howard said quietly and rubbed his hands together.

Elsie smiled back and nodded energetically, before again becoming lost in trying to recapture what she must have missed. She could recall no mention of afternoon tea being served. Losing track was very disconcerting and Elsie didn't like it at all.

Am I having a stroke? She glanced around to check no one was watching, and then, putting her hand in front of her, as a shield, poked her tongue out. She pushed it left and then right, to check it did so in a straight manner – remembering a health service announcement about the symptoms of stroke. On Facebook, was it? If so, it was one of few actually useful memes, or whatever they were called, floating around on the thing. She tried to remember what was next. *Ah, speech! There was a phrase, wasn't there?* She couldn't remember it if there was. Anyway, saying it in your head wasn't much use and she couldn't very well say it out loud here, amongst everyone.

She raised a hand again, and now prodded at her cheeks – first one and then the other. *All good.* Both were soft and squishy, but she could feel herself prodding them, which was surely a good sign. She relaxed slightly. *Okay, so, it was just a nap. Whoops. And a very good one at that. Double-whoops.*

Elsie held back near the corner of the room they'd all been swept into, which was laid out with tables containing plates of sweets – pastries, cakes and scones with jam and cream – and savouries – more pastries, sandwiches, scones with cheese and tomato and cheese and gherkin. Howard would bring her a cup of tea when he'd made his way through the throng, she thought, again appreciating the wonderful man she was proud to call her husband.

He always took care of her at events like this – not that she couldn't herself, but his extra bulk and gentle but firm forcible presence, when necessary, was always effective for politely making his way through masses of people.

She watched with awe, as usual, at how quickly he managed to navigate a space and get to the heart of the matter. Whenever she was in the situation of doing so, she always managed to get stuck, unseen, behind a bunch of much larger people – the only way through requiring quite rough nudging and the impersonation of a bulldozer or military tank, if her need was urgent.

Oh. Elsie frowned slightly as Howard took a detour away from the tea and coffee station on the far side of the space. *Damn it, you're almost right there. And I'm parched. What are you up to now?* She leant forward to look past him to see where he seemed to be heading with such purpose. *Ah. The family.* Huddled in a group seemed to be several generations of friends and relatives. *Now I remember! They're the people who had spoken earlier.* Her thought was confirmed by all the back-slapping now going on and the clear signs of relief across the faces – she'd been to enough funerals, and other events, to recognise the signs of relief and congratulations, and post-event releasing of nerves and tension. And she recognised two of the people as those who'd been up in front speaking earlier. *Before I must have fallen asleep*, she thought, the heat of slight shame flowing through her.

Just as Howard got close to the people, there was a flurry of activity and the group moved en masse – like a swarm of bees – off to the left and disappeared out a side door. No doubt off for ciga-rettes or beers or both. She noticed a cloud of frustration cross Howard's face before he turned back around.

At that moment Elsie realised she was right beside a table laden with goodies and a pile of empty plates was by her arm. She'd moved away every time she'd been bumped and jostled, but hadn't quite realised she'd been propelled so close to the food – she'd been too busy keeping an eye on Howard.

She picked up two plates, carefully adjusted them until she held them both securely in one hand, and then gathered a selection of delicacies before slowly retreating to the corner of the room, where she managed to catch Howard's eye as he made his way back through the crowd carrying two cups on saucers.

As he passed one of the tables of food, Elsie smiled at noticing him collect two brandy snaps filled with cream, with barely a pause in his stride, and place one on each saucer. As he pressed on, he caught her eye, and winked.

'Well done,' she said when he arrived in front of her. 'My favourites.'

'I know, my love. Swap you for a scone, since they have jam on the top – you won't want that, will you?'

'No, I got it for you. It's an abomination, and I will have no part in it!' she declared.

'Noted. I will very generously take it off your hands. I'm good like that.'

'You are. You're the best,' she said. They performed a perfectly choreographed manoeuvre – honed through their six decades or so of doing this very thing – to end up with a plate and cup and saucer each.

'Thank you, dear,' Elsie said.

'The pleasure is all mine. Thank *you*.'

'You're welcome.' Elsie loved that they had melted a little away from everyone – the group they'd come with was scattered around the room – and could indulge in their own little picnic, albeit slightly awkwardly due to standing up.

Out of the corner of her eye she noticed movement, and followed the source with her gaze. She nudged Howard and, through the last remnants of a mouthful of brandy snap, said, 'I wouldn't mind doing that.'

Howard turned to where she was looking.

She nodded at the same small child from earlier who was now under one of the food tables – the sparkles on her little black patent shoes just visible under the long white linen tablecloth.

'Ah, yes,' Howard said, 'to be a carefree kid again.'

'And to be able to fit into small spaces, out of the way, like that.'

'True. And that.'

'I think I nodded off during the service – I feel quite refreshed,' Elsie said.

'Yes. Me too, to both of those things,' Howard said. 'It's been quite the perfect afternoon, really, other than not getting intelligence on the matter of substance procurement.'

'So, no luck there, then?'

'No. I apparently had my invisibility cloak on again.'

'Yes. I saw that. Oh well.'

'I suppose it's time to let it go and enjoy this food. It is what it is.'

'Hmm. Better hold on to that risotto until we're desperate, though,' Elsie said.

'I agree. How's the tea?'

'Perfect, thanks.'

'Mine too. No mean feat when done for the masses in urns and pots – and not even a tea bag in sight!' Howard declared.

'Yes, marvellous,' Elsie said, taking another sip.

When they had finished their food and nodded hello and acknowledged a few vague acquaintances across the crowd – the seemingly unspoken agreement amongst everyone being that it was easier to simply do that and stay put than trying to move – it was time to put down their plates and cups and saucers.

Like a mob of sheep, they were rounded up and herded outside and back onto the bus by Thomas Radcliffe.

'Sorry to rush you, folks, but we only have the bus until four,' he said.

There were murmurs of agreement or disappointment – Elsie couldn't tell which – as they all resumed their seats and seemed to give a collective sigh of contentment more akin to leaving a tournament than the funeral of two people killed tragically though reasonably late in life.

The bus completed several turns, negotiating its way out through the suburbs and onto the main road.

Before long, Elsie couldn't resist the warmth of the sun shining through the window, nor the hypnotic effect of the gentle whoosh of traffic around them and the gentle rocking and rolling of the vehicle. She leant in to Howard and closed her eyes.

Howard kissed Elsie on the head and closed his eyes and let himself be drawn into the chorus of snoring already going on behind them.

'Righto, folks, first stop. Howard? Elsie? This is you.' Howard tried to ignore the female voice prodding at his semiconscious, but they pushed their way through. He'd definitely heard his name. And there was a strange continuous buzz-buzz, buzz-buzz sound, as well. Gradually he came fully to and opened his eyes to discover the bus was stopped. Ah, and the strange buzzing noise now became clear – it was the indicator. The driver was outside the open door, standing on the pavement, waiting for them to alight. He checked outside to establish exactly where he was and to confirm this was in fact their stop.

He gently nudged Elsie, who still had her eyes closed.

'Hmm,' she murmured.

'We're here, Else, time to hop off,' he said, gathering their things.

Howard nudged Elsie again, a little too firm this time.

Elsie awoke with a jolt and turned and stared at Howard, blinking.

'Sorry, that was a bit hard. We're at our stop, dear. Time to get off the bus,' Howard said.

She stretched her eyes wide open as she stumbled, slightly dazed, out of the seat, past Howard and down the aisle to the front, where she could see the door was already open.

'Bye, everyone,' she said, turning, just remembering the others on the bus, and her manners. But everyone else was still asleep.

Howard did another quick inventory and checked the space around their seat was empty.

'Thanks, folks,' he said quietly, turning and nodding in lieu of a wave, his arms too weighed down by the carry bag and umbrella. A few murmurs were heard and some shuffling in seats occurred but, other than that, the little group snoozed on.

'Thanks very much,' Howard said, nodding to the driver.

'Yes. Thank you,' Elsie mumbled.

Howard and Elsie stood on the pavement and watched as the bus pulled back onto the road and then gathered speed.

Howard could tell Elsie was out of whack – she looked dazed and was turning her head this way and that. Her voice was also slightly slurred. He was feeling rather doughy himself, though one of them had to be fully compos mentis. Knowing Elsie would be blinking in the sunlight, despite already wearing sunglasses – because he was too – he put the carry bag down and undid the strap of the umbrella.

'Here, the sun's a bit fierce,' he said, opening the huge umbrella over them.

'Golly. That's two naps in one day,' Elsie said in a sleepy voice. 'Both lovely, but I'll never sleep tonight.'

'No, me neither. Are you okay to walk?'

'I think so. My toes are a little sleepy. Anyway, what if I'm not?' she said brightly, clearly coming fully to now. 'Are you offering to carry me?' She looked up at him, the cheeky glint in her bright blue eyes that he loved so much sparkling animatedly.

'Would if I could, my love. But probably best not to try, though,' he said. 'I can call a cab?'

'Or an ambulance, if you did try to carry me,' Elsie said.

'Yes, that. I have no doubt it would be necessary – and meant in no way as a criticism about your weight, but rather my ineptitude, or rather *aptitude* as a weakling of an old codger. Come on, let's get home, Else, before that black cloud heading our way gets us,' he added, picking up the carry bag and putting the strap across his body and tucking Elsie's hand around his arm, which he bent to accommodate her. He patted her hand and leant in to give her a quick peck on the nose before moving off slowly.

'Oh, look,' Howard said as they came around the corner into the cul-de-sac. 'Looks like our men in uniform are moving out.' Up ahead what looked to be a furniture removalist truck was parked on the grassy verge across the road from Howard and Elsie's house.

'Yes. I see. I feel a little bad we didn't have any more to do with them after they were so helpful that day.'

'Hmm. I think they'd understand. They probably have too many interactions with dithering old folk at their respective jobs as it is to be quite happy to not have it at home as well, I should imagine.'

'That's true. Should we at least pop in to say goodbye, do you think?' Elsie asked, peering up ahead.

'Can do, though they're probably very stressed. And exhausted. Remember what moving day is like?'

'Oh yes.'

At that moment, Philip and Joseph's hatchback became visible from behind the truck and accelerated towards them.

Howard and Elsie paused and raised a hand each. They received waves in return as the car, with windows up, drove past.

'That answers that then,' Howard said, easing forward again.

'Yes. Oh well. All the best, Philip and Joseph,' she muttered.

'Brian, we're home,' Howard called.

Chapter Twenty-eight

'Milly?' Elsie asked. She and Milly were doing a jigsaw puzzle at the table.

'Yes, Mrs Manning?' Milly looked up from the partially completed puzzle, a piece poised between her fingers.

'Can I ask you something?'

'Sure.' Milly put the piece aside, linked her fingers and looked intently into Elsie's eyes.

Elsie found Milly's earnest expression amusing, endearing and a little disconcerting. 'But please don't feel you have to answer, if you don't want to,' she said.

'Okay.' The lack of concern in the child's face, the open serenity, spurred her on.

'Do you see our dog, Maisie, on one of the couches or recliners over there?'

Milly frowned. 'No. She wasn't allowed on the furniture,' Milly said. 'She knew that. It's okay, she didn't mind.' As if thinking that was the only question forthcoming, she returned her attention to the puzzle, picking up the piece she'd placed down and immediately putting it into position.

'Okay. Thanks, Milly.' Elsie was further disconcerted. A series of questions about Maisie flooded into her mind, tumbling over each other as the debris caught in the floodwaters of her soul. Her chest and heart became tired and she could feel the tension of tears gathering behind her eyes sharpen.

'Sorry, me again …' she said after a few moments and then frowned at her strange choice of words. The child was right in front of her!

'Yes, Mrs Manning?' Milly looked up again.

'Why do you look strangely at the furniture over there, then, whenever you come in. You do, don't you – you avoid them? You prefer to sit over here at the table, or outside on the bench, don't you?'

'I do,' Milly said, nodding. She twisted her features, as if trying to find the right thing to say.

'Is it something to do with Maisie, or do you … well … um … see something or somebody else? Other spirits.'

'No. And no.'

'Which is it? I don't want you to be bothered by anything here.'

'I'm not, Mrs Manning. Um. Well, not really. I love coming here. I love being here, Mrs Manning. I wouldn't come over so much if I didn't.'

'That's good. And we love having you here.'

Milly nodded.

Silence continued and Elsie watched Milly staring at the jigsaw puzzle, frowning slightly and nibbling on the inside of her bottom lip. She hoped the child was searching for the right words, or any answer really, and not the next piece of the puzzle.

And then Milly looked up, fixing her huge brown eyes on Elsie and, after a couple of heaves of the chest, as if taking several deep, fortifying breaths, said, 'Welllll …' More deep breaths.

'Yes?' Elsie prompted when Milly didn't seem about to speak again. 'What is it? You can tell me anything, Milly.'

Milly nodded and then said, 'Are you and Mr Manning going to die soon?'

Elsie found herself gripping the edge of her chair with both hands.

What?

'Sorry? What was that?' Elsie blinked as she rewound a little in order to ascertain if she had in fact heard correctly.

'Are you and Mr Manning sick? Do you have cancer?'

Oh. What? Elsie was too stunned to do anything but blink a few more times. What shocked her the most about the question was the matter-of-fact delivery.

'No, not that I'm aware,' she finally said. 'Do you know something we don't?' Did the child really know things? Or was her gift, or her curse, or whatever it was, confined to the souls, or what have you, of deceased pets? *God, where to start to unpack this?* Elsie now regretted giving in to her curiosity and peeling the lid off what appeared to be a can filled to the brim with wriggling worms.

'Oh, no. I'm not psychic, Mrs Manning. Or anything like that,' Milly said. 'Well, I don't think so. Maybe I am. Just a bit.' She shrugged.

'Okay, but why did you ask that?'

'Sorry, it was a bit abrupt of me, wasn't it?' Milly said.

'Maybe. But I was being nosey first. Sorry, I shouldn't have said anything.'

'No. I think you were being concerned,' Milly said. 'Thank you.'

'Oh. Okay. Well, you're welcome.' Elsie wondered if that was the end of the conversation. She was left feeling confused and unsatisfied. But she couldn't badger the child. Maybe she'd imagined Milly had a problem with the couches. Howard hadn't noticed what she had. She picked up a puzzle piece and searched for a place to put it.

Out of the corner of her eye she noticed Milly look down at the table and, after two more deep breaths, which caused the whole of her upper body to rise and lower again, she said: 'Both my grandparents – on my mum's side – died just after getting recliner chairs like that,' Milly said, nodding towards the lounge area.

'Oh. I see.' Elsie tried to reel herself in from the shock and say something more appropriate. 'I'm so sorry to hear that, Milly.'

'Thank you.'

Elsie looked over at the recliners. 'So, do you think Mr Manning and I are going to die soon, too, because we have some similar chairs?'

Milly nodded. 'Do you think that's silly of me, Mrs Manning?'

'No. Milly, I think, if it makes sense to you, then it's very reasonable. But I can assure you Mr Manning and I are not planning on going anywhere, except to the shops and the like.' She mentally crossed her fingers. *Oh god, is Milly picking up on our plans? Has she had visions of what we've been planning, our discussions? But we haven't talked about it much since meeting Milly, if at all, have we? Even the child isn't sure if she's psychic, but there seems to be something mystical going on with her.* Elsie wouldn't be surprised to learn Milly had all sorts of unusual abilities – she was a delightful, remarkable child who sometimes seemed closer to Elsie's own generation when Elsie heard her and wasn't looking at her and didn't have the stark reminder of her true age and size.

'Were they sick, Milly? Your grandparents?' Elsie asked.

'Yes. They both had cancer. But they were fine before they got their special chairs.' Suddenly Milly seemed her true, vulnerable age.

'Have you been worried all this time that we're going to die, Milly?' Elsie said gently.

'Yes and no. Not *worried*. Or, maybe just a bit. But we have to face things when they happen – there's no point worrying about something before it does, right? Because it might not happen at all.'

'That's right.'

'It's not always easy, though – not worrying, that is,' Milly added.

'No. Tell me about it,' Elsie said, sardonically, letting her guard slip for a moment.

'But I would really miss you and Mr Manning,' Milly suddenly said. 'You're both really lovely.'

'Oh. Well, thank you, Milly. We think you're really lovely too.' Milly smiled up at Elsie.

'I'm *back*,' came Howard's booming voice, just before the door opened and he clattered in, his arms full of groceries, his face red. Elsie beamed up at him, silently thanking him for his impeccable timing. 'Hello there, Milly, how's the jigsaw going? Ah, very well, I see.' He placed a hand on Elsie's shoulder and one on Milly's, joining them all together. 'Who wants a cuppa and ham and cheese toasted sandwich? Shall I text your dad to let him know you're staying for lunch, Milly?'

'Oh, yes, please.'

After Daniel replied, Milly leapt up to help Howard. Elsie watched them leave the table together, thinking she was pleased at having the conversation with Milly, and any residual awkwardness, cut off swiftly. Though she also couldn't wait to take Howard aside and tell him about it.

Chapter Twenty-nine

The doorbell rang and Howard checked his watch before easing himself out of his chair. 'Are we expecting anyone, Elsie?' he asked.

'No, I don't think so.'

'The kids?'

'Pretty sure not.'

He made his way down the hall, his brain churning over who it might be and what they wanted. He really hoped it wasn't that dear old lady with dementia who had appeared that other time. Not that she wasn't nice enough, he just didn't really have the energy or the patience, to be honest, to deal with that today without the reinforcements of the others from the lunch.

He opened the door to find Milly and Connor standing in front of him.

'Hello, Mr Manning,' Milly and Connor said at the same time.

'Hello there, you two. Have we forgotten you were coming today?' he said, scratching his head.

'No. We're not meant to be here,' Milly said.

He looked at Connor standing, fidgeting, a little behind her.

'Well, would you like to come in?'

Milly and Connor looked at each other. Connor shrugged.

'Is everything okay?' They didn't seem it. Both were nervous or apprehensive.

'Oh yes, don't worry,' Milly said, regaining some of her usual boldness. 'When I said we're not meant to be here, I didn't mean not *allowed*. I meant you and Mrs Manning aren't expecting us to be. If that makes sense?'

'Perfectly, yes. Right, so what's up?' Howard said.

'Um …' Connor, now beside her and blushing furiously, said, fidgeting with his hands, 'We are here because we have a question to ask.'

'A favour,' Milly said.

'Oh, I see,' Howard said.

'It's a biggie, Mr Manning,' Milly said.

'Yes, enormous,' Connor said.

'Right. Well, consider me prepared. Is it a question for just me or for Mrs Manning too?'

'Both of you,' Milly said.

Connor nodded beside her like a dashboard toy.

Howard took a fortifying breath while thinking, *Crikey, it's like drawing blood out of a stone.*

'And is it a question for out here, or would you like to come inside?' he asked.

'Inside please,' Milly said.

More nodding from Connor.

'Right you are, then, in you come,' Howard said, stepping aside, smiling to himself with bemusement. 'Elsie,' he called as he closed the door, 'we have guests.' But when he turned back around the kids were gone, already out in the main room.

'Hello there, Milly and Connor,' Elsie said.

Howard could tell from her tone that she was a little confused and concerned. 'It's okay, dear, we haven't messed up. They're here to ask us – both of us – a big favour,' he said, raising his eyebrows to Elsie.

'Oh, I see.' She put her pencil in her puzzle book and closed it. And with hands lying on top of it looked expectantly at the two children standing nearby. 'Got it. Go ahead,' she urged. 'You have my undivided attention.'

'And mine,' Howard said, standing beside the kids. He shoved both his hands in his trouser pockets. But when no words were forthcoming from the kids and they began shuffling their feet and looking antsy, he said, 'Oh. Do I need to sit?'

Both kids nodded.

'That might be a good idea, Mr Manning,' Milly said.

'Yes,' Connor said, nodding again.

A ripple of curiosity and concern raced through Howard as he resettled into his still-warm chair. It seemed very strange to have them being so formal when just last week they had practically been part of the place – part of the furniture and coming and going as if a member of the family. What was going on?

'Here we are. Just how big is this favour?' he asked, trying to stem his nervousness.

'Huuuuuge,' Milly said.

'Oh, well, do you think perhaps you two should sit as well?' Elsie said.

'Um, maybe in a bit,' Milly said, frowning slightly.

'Yes,' Connor said.

Elsie observed Connor seemed to the more nervous of the two and longed to wrap her arms around him and tell him everything was and would be okay. Though really, she didn't know that was true. Maybe things weren't and wouldn't be.

Milly took a deep breath, causing her shoulders to raise close to her ears and her cheeks to puff. Elsie found herself copying her mannerisms and then holding her breath when the child spoke.

'You know how we don't have any grandparents of our own, anymore?' Milly said.

Well, I know you don't, Milly, but we really don't know much at all about Connor, here, but go ahead, Howard thought. 'Yes,' he said, nodding.

'We do,' Elsie said, also nodding.

'Well ... Mr and Mrs Manning. We, uh, we were wondering. Would you do us the honour of coming along to our school's Grandparents' Day as our, um, sort of, er, pretend grandparents?'

'Yes. And mine, too,' Connor said.

'I said *our*, Connor,' Milly said, glaring at Connor.

Oh. The wind was knocked right out of Elsie. And without looking at Howard, she knew he was experiencing the same sensation. The phrase *could have knocked me over with a feather* – used a lot by both her parents – rumbled through her, being the appropriate utterance for one of very few occasions in her seventy-eight years on this earth.

'It's okay if you don't,' Milly continued, 'If, you know, you don't think it's appropriate or ... whatever ...' She shrugged.

Shit, Howard thought, *the poor kid is misreading our silence. Say something, you old git. Say the right thing, and quick smart.*

Thankfully, Elsie recovered swifter than Howard. 'Oh, Milly, Connor, I, for one, would love to be your sort-of-pretend grandmother, or grandma, or nanna, whatever term you prefer,' she said, stumbling over her words slightly.

'You would?' Connor said, eyes big. 'Really and truly?'

Howard was nodding furiously. Suddenly he realised he hadn't actually given his answer. 'Oh yes,' he said, 'it would be a great honour.'

Milly and Connor beamed and looked from Howard to Elsie, all hint of embarrassment gone.

Elsie didn't know if they had made a pact over who would hug whom, but suddenly she had Connor clambering into her lap and then wrapping his arms around her neck and burying his head into her shoulder, while, out the corner of her eye, she could see Milly doing the same with Howard.

'Thank you,' Connor mumbled.

'Thank *you*, Connor, for asking,' she said, stroking his hair.

After a few moments the kids had clambered off them and were seated, side by side, on one of the lounges.

'Thank you so much,' Milly said. 'It means a lot to us, doesn't it, Connor?'

'Yes, it really, really does.'

'Tell me, do we need to do anything for this Grandparents' Day of yours?' Howard ventured carefully. *Is it one of those things where we have to go along and talk about ourselves and our previous careers? And, at an assembly or in front of the class?* Should he remind them he and Elsie had both been accountants, so were probably considered pretty boring in the scheme of things and would most likely put everyone to sleep with tales of their working life? That was, if they could even recall any tales worthy of sharing. Or could they talk about their travels, put together a PowerPoint slideshow perhaps? That would be more interesting, though it all depended on the theme or what the teacher wanted to achieve.

'Oh, no, you don't need to do *anything*, well except come along for afternoon tea. And it wouldn't be for longer than an hour,' Milly said.

'Yes, there'll be cake and tea and coffee,' Connor said. 'Maybe Milo. I'm not quite sure about that one,' he added, frowning deeply.

'It's all about celebrating the older people in our lives who are really special to us,' Milly said.

Connor nodded.

'Oh Milly, you darling girl. And Connor, bless you. Well, I can assure you both, you've become very special to us too,' Howard said, almost choking on the last word, such was the sudden appearance of a lump in his throat. He dared not look at Elsie.

'Exactly. How lucky are we to have met you both?' she said. 'We feel very blessed.'

'So you'll come?' Milly asked, suddenly seeming unsure again.

'Of course. But when is it?' Elsie asked.

'Oh, sorry, I forgot the most important bit,' Milly said, blushing slightly. 'It's Friday of next week – at two to three. In the afternoon.'

'Okay …' Howard mused as he racked his brain for anything they had on.

'Can you still come?' Milly asked, eyes bunched up and brow wrinkled.

'Let me just get the diary to check,' Elsie said and started to ease herself out of her chair.

'I can get it for you,' Connor said, leaping up and standing to attention in front of her.

'Oh, yes, please. It's that black book over there on the bench,' she said, pointing.

Within seconds, Connor had returned with the diary and handed it to Elsie.

Out of the corner of his eye, Howard saw Milly wringing her hands. He knew she must be desperately hoping. She actually looked a little constipated. Maybe she was. He silently urged Elsie to hurry up.

'Next Friday, you say?' Elsie said, her eyes on the diary. 'That's the second, right?'

Both kids were nodding furiously.

'How are we situated, dear?' Howard asked.

'All clear. I can confirm that we can and would love to attend your Grandparents' Day at two next Friday the second. I'll write it in right now,' Elsie said, making a note in the diary.

'Oh, goodie!' Milly cried.

'Yes, yay!' Connor said.

'Where is it? At the school?' Elsie asked, pausing, pencil aloft.

'Yes,' Milly said. 'And Dad said he will come and get you.'

'Oh, that's not necessary. It's a bit out of the way for him.'

'Yes, quite a lot of unnecessary rigmarole, I would have thought,' Howard reiterated.

'He's very happy to. Really and truly,' Milly said. 'He's going to text you and tell you all about it.'

'And we don't need to bring anything? Cake, maybe?' Howard asked.

'Oh no, nothing at all,' Connor said.

'Yes, only yourselves. You are guests of honour. You just need to come along. We'll look after you,' Milly said.

'How wonderful,' Elsie said.

'Yes, sounds like a great deal to me,' Howard said.

'Exactly. Thank you, kids, we're absolutely delighted,' Elsie said. 'And can I now get you a Milo or glass of water or milk, or something?'

'No, thank you,' Milly said.

Connor shook his head, though Howard didn't think he looked very sure he wanted to answer in the negative.

'Thank you for offering, but we have to get back,' Milly said. 'I need to feed the chooks and collect the eggs and then we have to have dinner before Connor goes home.'

Connor looked downcast.

'Hopefully you'll be back again soon, Connor,' Howard said, trying to reassure the child.

Connor nodded. And then he looked up, frowning, as if something had occurred to him. 'Mr and Mrs Manning?' he asked.

Milly, who had her hands on her chair, ready to get up, settled back down again.

'Yes, Connor?' Elsie said, getting in before Howard.

'Is that apple seeds in the jar over there?' he said, pointing over to the bench where the jar of apple seeds still sat, Howard and Elsie continuing to add to them out of sheer habit.

'Connor. Don't be nosey,' Milly said as they all turned to where he was looking.

Connor dropped his head again. 'Sorry.'

Oh, Howard thought.

Um, Elsie thought.

'Yes, you're quite right, Connor, they are,' Howard said.

'Why?'

'Connor,' Milly warned.

'But I want to know. Apples are very good for you, but the seeds are poisonous,' he rambled. 'It's okay to sometimes eat your apple core, including the seeds, but the seeds, the brown bits, on their own can be very very bad for you.'

'Good to know. Thanks, Connor,' Elsie said. She dared not look at Howard.

'I'd be really sad if you got sick. Or, um, died,' Connor said.

'Yes, I would be too – really, really sad,' Milly said, softening her mannerism slightly and sticking out her bottom lip.

'That's lovely, kids, thank you. Connor, you know lots of interesting information,' Howard said, a little pathetically, he thought. He was avoiding looking at Elsie while struggling to find a way around this.

'So why do you have them?' Connor persisted.

Oh dear, Howard thought.

So, no getting out of this one then, Elsie thought.

'Oh my god. Connor, stop! If you don't, I'm going to tell Dad you were a pain,' Milly said, folding her arms across her chest tightly.

Connor responded by mirroring her posture, with the addition of an icy glare. He then looked from Howard to Elsie.

'Um, well, er …' Howard began. He desperately searched his mind for something suitable to offer against the thought rolling over and over in his mind of *Damn it, why didn't we hide that away?*

Elsie sat up a little straighter. She too was keen to see what Howard came up with. *Better you than me, thanks, dear.*

'We … er … we started collecting them for a … um … oh, yes, that's right. I remember now … a craft project. Something different to do. We saw online that someone had used them for art – a collage – so we thought we might give it a shot. You need quite a few though,' he added a little helplessly. 'Do you know what collage is?'

'Oh yes, it's sticking things on,' Connor said. 'We learnt about that just the other day, didn't we, Milly?'

'We did. It's fun.'

Oh bravo, Howard, Elsie thought, wanting to actually cheer and clap.

'Would you like me to help you with your project?' Connor asked. 'You might have enough seeds now – there's a lot there.'

'I'd love to help too,' Milly chimed in, sitting up straighter in her chair.

'Oh. Well, thanks for the offer, Connor, Milly, but we've rather lost interest in it now. Haven't we, Elsie?'

'Yes, we have.'

'Can I have them, then? To use for art. Or do you still want them?' Connor said.

'Oh, um …'

'It's okay, I know they're poisonous, remember – I definitely won't eat them,' Connor said.

'Well, I suppose you can have them if you'd like them. What are you going to do with them?'

'I don't know yet, but thank you so much!' Connor jumped up and raced over to the bench where he pulled the glass jar to him. 'I'll return the jar when I'm finished.'

'Oh, that's not necessary, but entirely up to you – it's only an old gherkin jar,' Elsie said.

'We'd *really* better go now,' Milly said, getting up. 'Dad will be in touch soon about next Friday. Come on, Connor,' she said, grabbing his hand and all but dragging him off the couch after her. 'We can see ourselves out.'

'Yes, please don't get up, Mr and Mrs Manning,' Connor said.

'Hang on for just a minute,' Elsie said. 'Connor, Milly, if you want us to be your honorary grandparents for your special school day, would you like to call us something other than Mr and Mrs Manning?' She looked at Howard with raised eyebrows and nodded in response.

'That would be fine with me,' Howard said.

'Oh. Could we?' Milly said.

'Yes. I don't see why not,' said Elsie.

'Well, I guess it depends what,' Howard said with a gentle chuckle. 'Sorry, that's me being silly,' he added, waving a hand.

'Any ideas?' Elsie said.

After barely a moment's thought, Connor said, 'Can I call you Granny and Grandpa?'

'Sounds good to me,' Howard said, warmth spreading through him, marvelling as it did at the power of one simple word. Who would have thought?

'Granny and Grandpa sounds perfect to me too,' Milly said.

'Brilliant, so that's settled, then,' Elsie said.

'I concur,' Howard said.

'So, can we call you that from now on? And always?' Milly asked.

'Yes, can we?' asked Connor.

'Yep, fine, with me,' Howard said.

'And me,' Elsie said.

The four of them beamed at each other and then Connor raced back and hugged Howard and Milly did the same with Elsie.

'Okay, well, bye, Granny and Grandpa,' Milly said, beaming.

'Yes, goodbye, Granny and Grandpa,' Connor said, also smiling broadly. 'And thanks for the apple seeds,' he added.

'You're welcome,' Howard said.

'Yes. See you later, Milly and Connor. Thanks for the quick visit and lovely invitation,' Elsie said.

'We'll see you both then, if not before,' Howard said.

The four of them grinned at each other. Milly and Connor left, giving a final wave as they did, before turning around and practically skipping down the hall.

'Well, I say,' Howard said, looking at Elsie wide-eyed.

'Yes, that about sums it up.'

'I really didn't see that coming. The invitation *or* Connor's inquisition,' he added with a chuckle.

'No, it's quite knocked the stuffing out of me – one part in a good way, the other not so much. Oh dear.'

'Yes, exactly.'

They sat back in their chairs, silently taking in their new status.

What a gorgeous pair of kids, Elsie thought.

What marvellous youngsters, Howard thought. *How lucky are we?*

Could life be more perfect than at this very moment? Elsie thought.

Ah, to be appreciated, now that's the elixir of life, Howard thought.

Perhaps not so invisible now.

Chapter Thirty

'Right, all ready?' Howard asked Elsie.

'Sure am. Oh, what fun. Well, I hope so. I'm not entirely sure what to expect,' she said.

'No, Grandparents' Day is a novel concept to me too,' Howard said.

'It's very good of Daniel to be picking us up.'

'Yes, let's head out and wait for him. He'll be here any minute, I'm sure,' Howard said.

Howard did their usual inventory when leaving the house. *Lights off, phone wallet and keys in hand, door locked and pulled closed behind us*, he thought as he held the door open for Elsie to exit first.

'Ah, perfect timing,' Elsie said, waving to Daniel as his car pulled into their driveway.

'Oh, I say, this is service,' Howard said as Daniel stood holding the back door closest to Elsie open.

'I have been instructed to have you both sit in the back, like a proper chauffeured vehicle,' Daniel said after saying hello. 'And the kids are waiting at the end, so we'll have to comply. I made a promise, hope you don't mind.'

'No, not at all. I think it's lovely,' Elsie said, climbing in.

'Yes, very special indeed. Bless those kids, they really are treasures,' Howard said. 'It's okay, though, I'm happy to at least get my own door. Save you the extra effort. We can keep it to ourselves, if necessary.'

'Okay. I won't say if you don't,' Daniel said with a grin, closing Elsie's door behind her and then getting back behind the wheel.

'And you are to take special note of how clean the car is,' Daniel said into the rear-vision mirror as he carefully reversed out.

'Oh, okay,' Elsie said, looking around her. 'It was perfectly clean last time when we went over to the park for Milly's birthday.'

'Well, please make mention; they worked so hard, both Milly and Connor – washing, wiping, cleaning, everything. It was all them – I didn't even have to ask.'

'Aww, bless them,' Howard said.

'Yes, they're very excited to have you both as their guests.'

'We're thrilled, too,' Elsie said.

'And very honoured,' Howard added. 'Any other instructions, or anything we need to know?'

'No, not really. I don't think. It's an afternoon tea, set up in the hall. I've just come from there and it's all organised. The kids have been great with pitching in. I hope you won't feel too smothered, though. I know they can both be pretty full on ordinarily and today they are at another level. It's not for long, though.'

'Okay. Forewarned,' Howard said.

'Don't worry, Daniel, I'm sure it's going to be perfect,' Elsie said.

'Yes, and we're old and ugly enough to gently put them in their place, if necessary. Well, Elsie not so much the ugly, but you know what I mean,' he added. Nervous tension rose up in him. He forced his mouth closed. *You're babbling, you silly old git.*

He felt Elsie's hand close over his on the seat between them. *Ah, you beautiful woman, you always know what I need.* He gave her a squeeze in return, shot her a tense smile, and settled back into his seat to enjoy the ride and watch the buildings pass by the window. *Nothing to be nervous about.*

Elsie wondered when they'd last been somewhere or done something they had never experienced before. It was natural that Howard was a little nervous. And he was; she could tell just by the sound of his breath and rise and fall of his shoulders. She was somewhat too, but hers was more excitement rather than trepidation.

She watched out the window and up at the clouds. Big fluffy specimens. Not many, though. She wondered who they might know there today. Most of their remaining friends had grandkids – were they a similar age to Milly and Connor? Someone might be familiar from one of their groups of fellow travellers or various sporting or service organisations they'd kept vaguely in touch with. In Adelaide the whole population was pretty much a Venn diagram, with everyone overlapping to varying degrees on at least one point.

'Here we are, folks,' Daniel called from the front.

Howard blinked. *Already?*

'That was quick.' Elsie wondered if she'd nodded off momentarily in the beautiful sun streaming in the window. Daniel's voice had startled her slightly, so perhaps she had. Her gaze was still on the clouds, though – well, pointed towards the otherwise bright blue sky while her head was raised, anyway.

'You're a very smooth driver,' Howard said and then wanted to kick himself for being so patronising. Daniel was a man in his thirties, not a sixteen-year-old first-time driver, damn it.

'Thank you, I aim to please,' Daniel said, smiling and thankfully not seeming to have taken offence.

'There they are,' Howard said, spying the kids standing together at the edge of the car park area as soon as they turned in.

'Little darlings,' Elsie said. She could see them wringing their hands and bumping each other. No doubt Milly was issuing instructions to Connor and Connor was replying, 'I am.' Elsie's heart began to flutter with additional excitement.

'Oh, this is exciting,' Howard said, by which Elsie knew he meant *this is a little scary*. She gave his hand another squeeze. Sometimes she wondered how they'd had the confidence with clients and all the networking activities they'd done, back in the days of running their business. So much of life, and strong self-esteem, relied on practice, and boy, were they out of it. In so many areas. Though this was just like going to a funeral, really: approaching a sea of friendly faces and following the cues they were given. She wanted to lean in and tell Howard this, but didn't want to risk Daniel hearing and getting the wrong end of the stick.

'Now, Howard, please wait for me to get your door after I've done Elsie's,' Daniel said when they had pulled up in front of Milly and Connor, who were now practically dancing on the spot. 'Then I'll leave you with them for a minute while I park the car, okay?'

'Roger that,' Howard said.

'Remember, I'm under strict instructions,' Daniel reminded them. 'And so are they. None of the kids are allowed off that concrete there. Because of the cars. Obviously. Sorry, didn't mean to teach you both how to suck eggs.'

'All good,' Howard said as Daniel got out and opened Elsie's door.

'Thank you, kind sir,' Elsie said, hoping she'd been loud enough for the kids to hear. While Daniel dealt with Howard, she went over to Milly and Connor and hugged them. 'What a truly special day. Thank you, kids,' she said.

'Did Dad drive really smoothly?' Milly asked. 'I asked him to take extra care.'

'He most certainly did. It was a perfect drive. So smooth I might actually have fallen asleep for a moment,' she said, smiling warmly at Milly and Connor.

'Hello there, you two,' Howard said, scooping up both kids at once.

'Thanks so much for coming to our Grandparents' Day as our special guests,' Milly and Connor said in unison in a clearly rehearsed speech.

Elsie cast her eyes along the line of people exchanging greetings, the timing of which seemed almost choreographed, too.

'Well, it's our pleasure,' Howard said formally.

'Yes, thank you very much for inviting us,' Elsie said.

'What do we do now?' Howard asked.

'We just wait here for a moment until Dad has parked the car,' Milly said, looking across the car park. 'Don't worry, we're going to look after you both very well,' she added.

'Yes, we won't leave your side once. Oh, except when we have to get your cups of tea and food,' Connor said.

'That sounds perfect, dear Connor,' Elsie said.

'Yes, sounds good to me, too,' Howard said. The kids returned Howard's and Elsie's broad smiles, with the addition of several hundred lumens of brightness. 'And I hear you two washed and cleaned the car for us. Is that right?' Howard said. He was still fluttering with slight nervousness and talking seemed the best antidote while they waited for Daniel. He knew he should be safe in Milly's and Connor's hands, and all those other kids and adults and the teachers hovering, but he was a little uneasy. It was a bit like being in a foreign country where you didn't speak the language and couldn't be sure of what to do and when. He didn't want to put a foot wrong and embarrass anyone.

'We did,' Milly said.

'Yes, we spent ages,' Connor added.

'And it shows,' Elsie enthused. 'Well done.'

'Right. Sorry about that. Here we are now,' Daniel said, appearing beside them. 'Now I have to head in and help the other teachers. Are you okay, Milly and Connor, to look after Mr and … Granny and Grandpa by yourselves?'

'Oh yes,' Milly said, nodding furiously. 'All good, Dad.'

'Totally,' Connor said, copying Milly's head display. 'All good, Mr Wynter.'

'Howard? Elsie?' Daniel said with raised eyebrows.

'Yes, thank you, I think we're in very capable hands,' Elsie said.

'I second that,' Howard said. He looked down at feeling a hand, which he immediately knew was not Elsie's, tugging gently at his hand that was clenched beside him. He opened it, accepted Milly's tiny paw and smiled down at the girl who beamed back up at him. He snuck a look at Elsie, who grinned and winked at him.

Stop being so nervous, old fellow, he told himself, *you're going to ruin this for yourself – and Milly and Connor too – if you don't get your act together. And you don't want that, do you?*

No, definitely not. He took a deep breath.

'This way, Grandpa. Follow me,' Milly said, taking a decisive step forward.

'Yes, this way,' Connor said, with less confidence than his friend, and followed Milly.

Through wide-open glass doors, they entered a hall with wooden floors and were greeted by a sea of round tables adorned with posies of flowers in glass jars. Elsie wouldn't mind betting this was a project that kids had done – there was that wonderful rustic nature about the arrangements.

'We're on table thirteen,' Milly said over her shoulder. 'Over here.'

She led them deftly around the edge of the hall, avoiding the milling people. The kid was clearly on a mission, Howard thought to himself, smiling.

Milly pulled a chair out for Howard and, after looking at Milly, Connor followed suit for Elsie.

'Thank you,' Howard said, nodding to Milly.

'Thank you, darling Connor,' Elsie said. Elsie and Howard were seated together, side by side, with Milly beside Howard to his left and Connor to the right of Elsie.

Gradually their table filled with two more children and four older people. Elsie smiled and nodded hello to them before looking around the room at other tables. Some had more grandparents than kids and others vice versa – an even mix, she decided. She pulled her attention back as she heard Milly clear her throat.

'Granny and Grandpa, this is Heidi and her grandparents,' Milly said, pointing to the girl across the table. 'And this is Jacob and his two grandads.' The adults nodded and muttered hello to each other.

'Howard and Elsie Manning,' Howard said. He thought the others had offered their names too, but couldn't be sure in the din that was ensuing due to all the various-sized feet on the wooden floor.

Gradually everyone was seated and the noise reduced until only earnest whispers remained. Then a teacher was standing on the stage up the front and a voice came through the speakers around the room. *That's nice and clear*, Howard thought with approval. And then he frowned to himself. Should he have his hearing checked? Elsie hadn't complained he was ignoring her or having her repeat herself too often. Oh well, might be a good idea to check. When had they last done that? Yet another appointment to make and keep. Damn the maintenance phase of this being elderly business. He returned his attention to the voice.

'Thank you all for being here. The kids have worked really hard, so we hope you have a lovely time and feel appreciated. We know life takes over and we can all feel a bit forgotten at times. So we all hope you take this little reminder with you when you leave and at those times when life takes over you remember today with fondness.

'In front of you are a couple of gifts from the children – made with their own hands and out of love: a posy for each of you and a piece of art with some words of what you mean to them.

'I'm sure you'll feel as proud as I did when I saw how much they think of you, their grandparents and those they think of as their grandparent figures, even if you're not actually related. Families come in all shapes and sizes – what's important is the mutual love and support within them.

'Shortly, our kids will wait on you with tea and coffee and serve a selection of cakes, sandwiches and pastries. But before they do … Now, kids, please.' She raised her hands.

Howard was a little shocked at the noise as all the kids on all the tables pushed their chairs back at once. Daniel, holding a microphone, appeared behind Milly and handed her the device.

'Three cheers for our special older people,' Milly called loudly, her voice echoing around the space. 'Hip, hip, hooray. Hip, hip, hooray. Hip, hip, hooray!' she cried, all the children joining in.

Elsie felt a rush of tears well in her eyes. Thankfully no one noticed due to the clapping and cheering going on around her, the loud round of applause seeming to go on forever before the children gradually pulled in their chairs again and sat down.

'Thank you, Milly, that was wonderful. All of you, good job,' the teacher up the front said. 'And that's the formalities. We hope you have a lovely time here with us. Please feel free to open the scrolls now, which are the children's art pieces.'

'Well done, Milly, that was great,' Elsie said, leaning over past Howard.

'Yes, good job, Milly,' Connor said.

'I didn't know we were going to be on the extra extra special table, Milly,' Howard said. 'What an enormous privilege. And yes, great job,' he said, putting an arm around her shoulders and giving her a squeeze.

'Open your scroll thingies,' Connor urged. 'There's one from each of us. The flowers are from both of us – though there's one for each of you,' he babbled excitedly.

'Wow, isn't that lovely,' Howard said, having pushed the raffia tie off the first rolled painting and unfurled it. He was a little surprised to see no apple seeds had been incorporated. He read the printed words *My grandparent is special because*, and then the handwritten, slightly higgledy-piggledy, ones underneath: *patient kind reading Milo*. He tried not to frown too hard or move his head from side to side as he tried to figure out what the picture might be of. Oh dear. Um?

Thankfully, Connor came to his rescue, leaning in so far around from beside Elsie that he was practically climbing onto the table.

'It's us on your bench outside doing homework,' he said before sitting back down in his chair.

'Oh, I see that. It's fabulous. Good job, Connor,' Howard said, leaning around Elsie and giving the kid's shoulder a squeeze.

How very diplomatic, Elsie thought, having unfurled Connor's painting to her, which contained the same words as Howard's, in the same order. The painting was very different, though.

'Is this us at the table inside?' she asked. She wasn't sure she'd have got that far if not for having heard the explanation of Howard's painting from the artist himself.

'Yes, that's right,' Connor said, nodding. 'Wow, you got it. That's awesome.'

Milly leant over the table, turned to Howard and then Elsie, and said sagely, 'Connor likes to go a bit abstract.'

Elsie couldn't tell if her expression was one of disapproval or appreciation.

'Let's see what you have done, Milly,' she said, gently sliding the loop off the scroll. 'Oh, isn't this lovely?' The words on hers were: *helpful caring lovely welcoming.* Elsie snuck a look over at Howard's painting from Milly. Again the same words were replicated, and in the same order. Good thinking, kids. 'Which chicken is this?' Elsie asked, pointing to the image that was clearly a chook on the lawn with three people, two adults and a child, watching.

'That's Two.'

'Ah, of course,' Elsie said, nodding.

'I've got all three here,' Howard said proudly, turning his picture towards Elsie.

'That's right. You have,' Milly said. 'And that's me on the stilts you made.' She pointed.

'Yes, I see. It's very good, Milly,' Howard said.

'How wonderful. I shall treasure this,' Elsie said.

'Yes. Fantastic,' Howard said.

'I'm going to roll mine back up so they don't get anything spilt on them,' Elsie said.

'Oh, yes, good idea, dear,' Howard said.

'Would you like some help?' Milly said. 'They're a little fiddly and we've done it before. Connor, help Granny,' she instructed.

Over their heads, Howard snuck a look at Elsie, who winked back as the kids busied themselves with rolling up the paper and slipping the ring of raffia back over the ends.

'Would you like a cup of tea now?' Milly asked.

'Yes, would you?' Connor said.

'Yes, please,' Elsie said.

'I would, too, thank you. I'm a bit thirsty,' Howard said.

'Please help yourself to the water, too,' Milly said, pointing to the filled glasses in front of them.

'I can't guarantee the tea will be great,' she added quietly to Elsie, now on her feet.

'I'm sure it will be lovely,' Elsie said, smiling at Milly, who nodded.

'Yes. And however it comes is fine by me,' Howard said, causing Connor to look a little relieved.

Howard and Elsie watched as both kids skipped off, along with their classmates on the table, the names of whom completely now escaped Howard, and he and Elsie were left with the other grandparents. He thought they should be polite and converse, but it was rather impossible with such a racket caused by all the kids racing about. He gave up that idea. Anyway, the adults were now concentrating on the pictures in front of them.

He turned to Elsie. 'Isn't this rather fun?' he said quietly.

'Very special. Fabulous. I feel a bit like royalty ...'

'Sorry about slopping it in the saucer,' Milly said mere moments later when she reappeared carrying a teacup and saucer, followed by Connor.

'Yeah, sorry, I slopped it too,' Connor said, placing the cup and saucer onto the table, causing the saucer to dispense most of its liquid onto the tablecloth.

'All good, kids. It looks like an excellent cup of tea,' Howard said.

'Yes. Well done,' Elsie enthused.

'I hope it's okay,' Milly said, frowning slightly. 'You don't have to drink it, if you don't want.' Though the actions of the two littlies didn't quite match their words, Elsie thought, noticing Milly and Connor standing there, seemingly with anticipation, waiting for them to try their tea.

Elsie did and then gave an exaggerated, 'Yum, it's a good cuppa. Thank you both.'

Milly and Connor then turned to look at Howard who, noticing, and realising they were waiting for something – approval, most likely – took a sip of his tea and said with great enthusiasm, 'Ooh, yes, now that's hit the spot. Very good, thank you.'

Having achieved their goal of approval on the tea front, Milly said, 'Great. We'll get you a selection of things to eat now.'

Connor nodded.

'Is there anything you don't like?' Milly added.

'Yes, anything? Or allergies?' Connor said, mimicking her serious tone.

'No, no allergies. Surprise us,' Howard said, smiling at them.

'Yes, that sounds good to me, too,' Elsie said.

'Okay, back in a sec,' Milly said and raced off, with Connor in hot pursuit.

'Aren't they adorable?' Elsie said.

'Priceless. Though it's a bit tricky to say what we don't like when we have no idea what's on offer, don't you think?' Howard said. 'There's no menu anywhere, is there?' he added, looking over the table. 'Anything we've missed?'

'No. I don't think so,' Elsie said, also scanning the area. 'You're right about that. And we'll have to eat everything, so as not to cause a ruckus,' she added.

'I agree. God, I hope no one has done sandwiches with fish paste or pâté on crackers,' Howard said.

'Hopefully it's simple, recognisable fare. Positive vibes – send positive vibes, Howard,' Elsie said.

Howard closed his eyes and pictured scones with various toppings – a nice, safe bet, he figured.

'Here we are,' Milly said, placing a plate in front of him. 'These are scones and tomato and cheese, a mini bacon pie, a chicken ribbon sandwich, a scone with jam and cream, and a mini-pavlova. That's probably not nearly as good as the ones you make,' she added with a shrug. 'Oh well, enjoy.'

'Thank you. That's a great selection.'

Elsie looked at the plate Connor had just placed in front of her. He proceeded to point out the items, which looked exactly like what was on Howard's plate beside her.

'Milly, what's that thing called again?' he said, pointing.

'Mini bacon pie,' she said.

'Thanks,' he said to Milly. 'And that's a mini bacon pie,' he repeated to Elsie.

'It's actually a quiche,' Milly said, leaning around carefully to Elsie, 'but it's too hard to say for most of the children.' She raised her eyebrows and lips to create an expression of well-what-can-you-do? Elsie laughed.

'What do you have there, Milly and Connor?' Howard asked.

'Plain chocolate cake,' Connor said.

'Fruitcake,' Milly said. 'We can swap, if you like,' she added.

'I'm good, thanks,' Howard said, 'but you've given me quite a lot, so feel free to help me out if you would like.'

'Oh, can I?' Connor said, his eyes big.

'Sure can.'

'And me,' Elsie said, holding her plate out to him. He took the scone with jam and cream.

'Yum. Thank you very much.'

'We were only meant to have cake – chocolate or fruit,' Milly explained before picking up her piece and taking a bite.

'Ah, I see,' Howard said.

They ate in silence, as did the others on their table.

After what seemed only a few minutes, the teacher was back on the stage and speaking into the microphone again. 'Thanks, everyone, that concludes our little afternoon tea party. Thank you for coming. Thank you, children, for being so well behaved and taking such good care of your guests. We're going to pack up now. Kids, please escort your guests out when you're ready.'

There was another mass scraping of chairs and rowdy clatter of footsteps on the timber floor as they headed back out the way they'd come.

'Don't forget your pictures and your posies – you're allowed to take the jar, too, so it doesn't drip,' Milly said. 'Actually, I can carry that for you,' she added, reaching across and grabbing the jar.

'Wasn't that just lovely?' Howard said as Connor, clutching his hand, led him out. He had the two scrolled pieces of art tucked under his arm.

Elsie was beside him, hand in Milly's, also clutching two pieces of art. Howard wondered, as they made their way, if the kids had formed an agreement to swap grandparents this time around.

'How was that?' Daniel asked, suddenly appearing beside them amidst a swarm of other adults and children in uniforms outside the hall under the verandah. 'I'll just get the car,' he added before Howard or Elsie could speak. 'Milly, Connor, you wait here and look after Granny and Grandpa.' Milly and Connor stood so straight, Howard thought they might be about to salute. He was almost disappointed when they didn't.

'Wait. Where are your school bags?' Daniel said, turning back around.

'Oh. Still in our lockers?' Milly said, looking at Connor, who nodded. 'I'll get them – I'll get yours too, Connor, if you stay here with Granny and Grandpa. Okay? I'll be quicker.'

'Okay. Thanks.'

'Sorry, Granny, can you please hold this for me?' she said, handing Elsie the glass jar.

'Sure can,' she said.

'Yes, thank you, Milly,' Daniel said. Though Milly had already ducked through the throng and was out of sight.

In a matter of just a few minutes, a puffing Milly reappeared lugging two backpacks with dangling nametags, just as Daniel's car appeared in front of them. They all clambered in, this time Daniel holding the doors open, copied by Connor, and Milly putting their bags in the boot.

'Good job, kids,' Daniel said when they were all strapped in and on their way.

'We've had the most wonderful time,' Elsie said.

'Yes, a most excellent afternoon,' Howard said.

'We're so pleased,' Milly said. 'Thank you again for coming along.'

'Thanks again for inviting us. It was very special. And thank you, Daniel,' Howard said.

'Yes, what a wonderful afternoon,' Elsie reiterated.

'Great, and it's my pleasure.'

They made the journey home in silence.

'Thank you again for a truly special afternoon and the wonderful gifts,' Elsie said when they had arrived home.

Milly leapt out, followed by Connor, and opened the doors.

'Here, I'll hold that while you get out,' Milly said, holding out her hand for the posy that Elsie handed over.

Connor was beside Howard, holding out his hand too, though hadn't said a word. Howard wasn't sure whether to hold his hand out to him or what, so he handed him the scrolled artworks and said, 'Thank you, kind sir.'

'Have a lovely evening,' Milly and Connor said at once, another clearly rehearsed phrase, Howard thought. He and Elsie waved and, when neither Connor nor Milly made any move to get back into the car, went to the front door and opened it. They stood on the stoop waving as Daniel's car backed back down the driveway and then pulled into the Wynters' driveway.

'Luckily we can't see, thanks to the pittosporums,' Elsie said. 'Otherwise it would be a little comical standing here waving at each other from our respective front doors.'

'Yes, quite. Too funny. Wasn't their formality cute?'

'Very. I'm a little exhausted, though.'

'We're old. Of course we are. No surprises here,' Howard said. 'Come on. Oh, it's actually quite chilly out,' he said, putting an arm around Elsie and shepherding her inside.

Chapter Thirty-one

'Here we are,' Elsie said. 'Hello there, kids.'

'Hello, Granny, hello, Grandpa,' Milly said. 'Thanks very much for having us over.'

'Yes, hello, Granny and Grandpa. Thanks very much for having us,' Connor mimicked.

'Our pleasure. How was school?' Howard asked.

'Good,' Milly said.

'Good,' Connor said, though clearly less sure about that than Milly, Elsie thought.

'Do you have any homework you need to do?' Elsie said.

'No, not today,' Milly said.

'Nope. That's partly what made it a good day,' Connor said.

'Cool, you've put the pictures we gave you up on the fridge,' Milly said, going over to the appliance.

'You really kept them,' Connor said, looking incredulous.

'Of course!' Elsie and Howard said in unison.

'They're very good pictures that deserve pride of place,' Elsie said.

'Exactly,' Howard said.

Howard loved how they dumped their bags at the end of the bench and went over and slumped onto the chairs at the table, exactly as their own girls had done all those years ago – just like they belonged. Granted, it was more Milly who seemed at ease, as if she belonged, but Connor was doing a fine impression of imitating her.

Elsie smiled at the kids. One thing that hadn't seemed to change over the generations was the exhausted relief at being home from school, yet also the energy the same situation seemed to instil. These two – while looking completely different to their girls, who had worn strict quite formal uniforms compared to these kids' casual loose pants and polo tops – were behaving in exactly the same way as Corinne and Janine had when coming in from a day of school. Elsie knew which uniform she – or rather, Howard – would have preferred. How many hours had he spent ironing those dresses and soaking the silly white collars they'd had?

Her heart swelled again at remembering how he'd insisted on continuing to do their washing in the final few years of school so they had less on their plates while studying so hard.

God, those last two years had been touted as the be all and end all. According to the school, their whole lives hinged on those final grades. She'd been careful to say, 'Just do your best', as often as possible while also being encouraging.

No mental health and self-care awareness back then in the wider community. Or at least not named as such. And, really, self-care would have only been about going for a walk in the sunshine. Elsie had been so pleased to hear from Milly that their class started the day with guided meditation. But she couldn't help feeling sad for the generations of students who had gone before who hadn't even been encouraged to stop and breathe. How many had suffered as a result?

'You look bushed,' Howard said.

'I don't know what that means, Grandpa,' Milly said.

'Tired,' Elsie said.

'Oh, yes, we're very tired,' Connor said.

'Well, would you like a drink?' Howard said.

'Maybe in a bit, thank you,' Milly said.

Howard and Elsie both took a seat at the table.

Connor nodded. 'I nearly forgot!' He went back to his bag, opened it, brought out an object wrapped untidily in brown paper, and carried it over to the table. 'This is for you, Granny and Grandpa,' he said, holding the item out over the table.

'Oh, how lovely,' Elsie said, accepting it, as she was the closest.

'Wonderful. Thank you, Connor,' Howard said.

Elsie carefully removed the wrapping and held up what looked like a cardboard cylinder covered in apple seeds. 'Oh, wow. How clever of you, Connor,' she said, turning the object around. 'Isn't this something, Howard?'

'Yes, it sure is,' Howard agreed, nodding. *How very diplomatic of you, dear.* He carefully accepted the object Elsie held out and then turned it around, wondering as he did if it was a functional piece of art or not, and what he ought to say next.

'It's a pen holder,' Connor said proudly. 'For, um, keeping your pens and pencils in, in your office by the computer or over there by where you charge your phones,' he said, pointing. 'Or you could put anything tallish in it, I suppose,' he added with a shrug. 'But not anything wet or damp, because it's made of cardboard. I wanted to use the glass jar instead, but the glue was not suitable for use by children,' he added a little despondently.

'That's okay, young man, I think it's perfect just the way it is. Look, Elsie, how well Connor's lined them all up neatly.' He was actually genuinely impressed by the precision and care Connor had clearly taken in placing each seed just so.

'Oh, I see. Wow. You've really done an incredible job,' Elsie said. Her awe was sincere – there's no way she would have had the patience. 'Good job, Connor.'

'Yes, bravo, young fellow,' Howard said.

'Thank you,' Connor said, beaming.

'I'm going to put it by the computer right now so it doesn't get damaged,' Howard said, getting up.

'See, perfect,' Howard said, now standing in the doorway into the study and holding out the pen holder, which he'd put a pen into.

Connor grinned back and nodded.

'Cool,' Milly said, smiling at Connor and giving him a gentle nudge.

'Now, tell us about your day,' Elsie said when Howard had returned and sat back down at the table.

'We have to be in a school play,' Milly said, catching Elsie's attention. Or, rather, it was more the unenthusiastic tone that did. Elsie looked up. Any opportunity to get a chuckle from a Milly mannerism.

'Ooh, that's exciting,' Howard said. 'Or not?' he added, noticing Milly's frown and Connor's wrinkled nose.

'No, it's not, Grandpa. We don't want to do it. But we have to,' she said, folding her arms tight across her chest.

'Yes. They're making us be part of it,' Connor said, mirroring Milly's action.

'What's it about?' Elsie said.

'And, is it *that* bad? Do you have to say much – learn too many lines?' Howard said.

'It's about a group of singing vegetables. And, yes, I think it will be as bad as anticipated,' Milly said. 'The only very, very small good thing about it – this big,' she said, holding up her forefinger and thumb, a fraction apart, 'is we only have to sing, and only as part of a chorus.'

'Which I think is bad enough. I can't sing,' Connor said.

'Don't worry, mate, I can't hold a tune,' Howard said. 'But you'll be right, hidden amongst others, by the sounds of things.'

'Yes, so, what's the play about?' Elsie asked again. 'Singing vegetables, did you say?'

'Yes. More brainwashing,' Milly said.

Elsie bit her lip to stop from laughing. She dared not look at Howard.

'Well, vegetables are, er, very important,' he managed.

'Yes, we know. But do we really need to do a play about it? I think not,' Milly said.

Oh, Milly, you're too cute, Elsie thought, but kept the words to herself. It was perhaps best not to encourage wilful dissent in children that were not one's own.

'Did you know that the thing about carrots being good for your eyesight is a proper from the war? The Second World War,' Connor said, finding some confidence.

A proper? Huh? Oh! 'Do you mean propaganda?' Howard said.

'Yes. Sorry,' Connor said, looking downcast.

'No need to apologise. Tell me more.' Howard knew about the ploy to get people to dig up their gardens and plant vegetables, which is where the carrots-equal-good-eyesight thing came from, but he wanted to give Connor his moment in the spotlight.

'Well, we learnt about it at school. Maybe because of the play. I'm not sure. During the war ...' Connor told them the story.

'Wow. Really? That's so interesting,' Elsie said when he had finished.

'Yes, and you told the story very well,' Howard said. 'How fascinating.'

'Exactly,' Milly said, 'so you can't just accept what they say – groups, authorities, adults in general.' She waved a hand around. 'No offence, Granny and Grandpa,' she added.

'Oh, none taken, Milly,' Elsie said.

'I think you're quite right,' Howard said.

'Howard,' Elsie warned under her breath.

'That is to say, adults should be listened to, mostly,' Howard added, falling over his words slightly.

'It's okay. I get it, Grandpa,' Milly said. 'You're not allowed to encourage us to buck the system. We have to earn that right ourselves.'

'Which doesn't even really make sense,' Connor chimed in, and then twisted his mouth. 'Because how does having your head filled by what other people say teach you to think for yourself?'

'That's a very good question. Hmm,' Howard said.

'Connor, maybe that's another one of those *we'll find out when we're older* things or an *it's complicated and best left to figure out later*, right, Granny and Grandpa?' Milly said.

Howard could have kissed the child for her impeccable timing and successfully letting him off the hook. 'Yep. Spot on, Milly,' he instead said.

'These things often become clearer on their own later,' Elsie offered.

'Makes my head hurt just thinking about it,' Milly said with a big sigh.

'And mine,' Connor said, also letting out a loud sigh.

'Don't ever grow up, kids,' Howard said, grinning at them.

'I don't think that's actually possible, Grandpa – we're growing every day,' Milly said.

'Yes, Mum says I'm much taller now, since ...' Connor said and stopped.

Howard chuckled. 'Yes, you're quite right,' he said.

'I think what we need is a homemade biscuit or two,' Elsie said. 'That might help clear up any immediate confusion and give you two the energy to tell us more about this play you have to do.'

Or at least buy us some time to catch our breaths – good thinking, Elsie, Howard thought.

'Oh yes, that would absolutely help,' Milly said, her eyes opening wide.

'I agree,' Connor said, nodding enthusiastically.

'So, what vegetables are you for the play?' Howard said when they were again all sitting around the table with their drinks and a plate of biscuits in front of them. 'Do you get to choose yourself? Or do the teachers choose?'

'A bit of both,' Milly said. 'We get to choose, but there are only a few things left – we can't all be carrots, for instance.'

'Oh, I see. Yes, that wouldn't be too exciting – unless the play was about a bunch of carrots.'

'Which it isn't. It's assorted vegetables,' Milly said. 'I want to be broccoli. Well, I don't want to be *anything*, but that's not allowed.'

'What's that?' Connor asked.

'You know, don't you – green and looks a bit like a tree?' Milly said.

'Um,' Connor said. He didn't look further enlightened.

Elsie got up and went to the fridge and pulled out a head of broccoli and took it over to the table. 'Connor, let me introduce you to broccoli,' she said.

'Oh. Yes, it does look like a tree. A bit. Oh, I can't be that as well. We have to be different things,' he said.

'I started off wanting to be a tomato, but it's apparently not a vegetable. It's a fruit,' Milly said.

'Oh, they're being picky,' Howard said.

'It's educational, so I suppose they need to be correct,' Elsie pointed out.

'Right. An ear of corn could be fun to do,' Howard said.

'Does corn have ears? How weird,' Milly said, frowning.

'No, not ears. That's what the fresh corn, from the vegetable section in the supermarket, is called.'

'Is corn a vegetable?' Connor asked, frowning deeper than Milly. 'I've had popcorn and cornflakes, but ...' He shook his head.

Elsie held her breath slightly, hoping Milly wouldn't jump in and rock his confidence. Thankfully she seemed too stuck on the corn and ears factor.

'Dear, since you're still up?' Howard said, nodding to Elsie.

'Oh. Do we have any? We don't, do we?'

'We do, as it happens.'

'Oh, right you are, then. I didn't see any there a second ago.'

'Just to the left of the carrots.'

'Here we are.' Elsie held up the corn, complete with sheath, having replaced the broccoli. She pulled back some of the outer green leaves and fuzz inside to expose the yellow kernels.

'Cool,' Connor said. 'I'll be corn.'

'Hang on. If you said you can't be any old vegetable, do you have a list of what things are left that you can choose from?' Howard said.

'Yes,' Connor said.

'Well, we'd better check that before we go getting too excited, don't you think?' Elsie said.

'Yes, that's a very good point, Granny,' Milly said. 'It's in my bag.'

'Me too.'

The kids jumped up and went to the end of the bench where they'd left their school bags.

'Oh. We can only be things that can be standing up, too,' Milly pointed out. 'Sorry, I forgot to mention that bit.'

'Ah, that makes more sense now,' Elsie said. 'I suppose that's so no one falls asleep, is it?'

Howard laughed. 'That would be it. Pity,' he said.

Elsie grinned.

'It's actually because it's difficult to sing when you're lying down.'

'Of course. Silly me,' Howard said.

'I think that's why there won't be any avocados. I love avocado,' Milly said, now rooting around in her backpack.

'Well, they're a fruit – technically a berry. It was in a crossword I did recently,' Elsie said.

'Oh,' Milly said, pausing and looking back at Elsie. 'Maybe *that's* why. I don't remember.'

'No zucchinis, either, I suppose, because they're not really of the standing up variety – though they're definitely a vegetable. Well, I'm pretty sure. Rules out quite a few things,' Howard muttered. 'I'm guessing they also have to be obvious – not too obscure. Hmm. I see,' he added, thoughtfully.

'I don't know what that means,' Milly said.

'No, me neither,' Connor said.

'Strange – unknown – the opposite of obvious. Familiar,' Howard said.

'Okay. Nothing weird,' Milly said to Connor, as if translating another language.

'Found it,' Milly finally said, returning to the table with a piece of paper in her hand.

'Me too,' Connor said a split second later, also coming back to the table and sitting down.

Both kids held out creased, folded pieces of paper – Milly's less crumpled than Connor's. Howard took one and Elsie the other.

'Gosh, it's a lot to wade through,' Elsie said, scanning the front quickly and then turning the page over. 'Howard, it's one of those take home and have Mum and Dad deal with it type things.'

'Oh, yes, you're quite right,' Howard said, squinting. It began with *Dear parent/guardian*, and then there was a whole heap of printed text about the play. He just wanted the facts, not all the preamble. He went to the bullet list at the bottom.

Milly and Connor munched on their biscuits and drank their drinks while they waited.

'Oh, I remember now,' Milly said, breaking the silence. 'The main people – or vegetables – have been chosen. They're the ones who have to say lines. But those of us just singing in the chorus, it doesn't matter if there's more than one of us – you know, more than one capsicum, or whatever. I'm a bit confused. I think we'd better not fully decide until we've checked on Monday.'

'Hang on,' Howard said. 'There must be instructions on the back about the choices.'

'Yes, there is,' Elsie said.

'Ah. Here it is. Finally. They don't make things easy, do they? That hasn't changed over the decades, has it, Elsie?' Howard muttered.

'No, it hasn't,' Elsie agreed, now also squinting at the printed page. 'Oh, here we are. They must be the names of all the kids in the play, with some options. Those circled must be the ones already assigned. It's actually quite confusing.'

'Adults often are, I find,' Milly said matter-of-factly as she took another biscuit from the plate.

'Yes, I quite agree, Milly,' Howard said. 'Right. It looks to me like Milly, you get to be either an onion or a mushroom. But mushrooms aren't even a vegetable. Oh well, let's not let the facts get in the way ...' he mused.

'I guess they can't be too picky, otherwise they wouldn't have enough for a decent assortment,' Elsie said.

'Oh. But I want to be a broccoli. Bum,' Milly said.

'Well, Connor here seems to have the option of being bok choy or broccoli. Could you swap?' Elsie said.

'Yes, would that be upsetting the applecart too much?' Howard said.

'Apples aren't vegetables – they're fruit,' Connor said.

'Yep. That's true. Um ...' Howard wasn't sure how to explain.

'That's another one of those things adults say,' Milly said to Connor. 'It kind of means to be a bother – be a pain,' she translated.

'Thanks, Milly. Quite right.' *Sort of.* 'So, could you change, do you think? Unless you want to be the broccoli, Connor?'

'No, that's okay,' he said under Milly's piercing glare that Howard thought might be strong enough to burn paper. *Oh dear.*

'Who would have thought there were so many vegetables to choose from?' Elsie said. 'Even when the lying down ones are taken out.'

'Actually, I'd quite like to be a mushroom,' Connor said. 'Then I could probably have a hat. That's what I like about the green one that Milly's going to be.'

'Broccoli,' Milly said.

'Yes. That one,' Connor said.

'You could both have hats,' Elsie said.

'Goodie. Could I put red spots on it – like in the book we read?'

'Well, then you'd be a toadstool – not a mushroom. And you can't eat them – well, you shouldn't because they're poisonous,' Milly said.

'Huh?' Connor said. He looked to Howard.

'Yes, Milly's right. The edible ones are usually plain white or brown. They could still make for an interesting costume.'

'Are you making your outfits at school – as part of class – or at home?'

'At home, unfortunately,' Milly said, rolling her eyes. 'Dad says we're not spending money on hiring anything because he's made the chicken pen.'

'We'd love to help, wouldn't we Elsie?' Howard said. 'To make something, that is,' he added.

'Really?' Milly said. 'That would be awesome.'

'Oh yes. I'd love to help,' Elsie said. 'As your honorary grand-parents, I feel it our duty.'

'Or, rather, our right,' Howard said.

'Yes,' Elsie agreed.

'Oh yay,' Milly said.

'How long do we have?' Howard asked.

'A few weeks – it's the last week of term.'

'The date is on the sheet you have there, Howard,' Elsie said.

'What fun!' Howard said.

'I'm glad you think so, Grandpa. Personally, I think it's a pain. Like book week,' Milly said.

'I never dress up,' Connor said with clear disappointment.

'Well, how about you tell us in plenty of time and we'll help you sort something out,' Howard said.

'Would you?' Milly said.

'Really?' Connor said.

'Of course,' Howard said.

'But, first things first,' Elsie said, her eyebrows raised at Howard.

'Yes, there's me getting ahead of myself. The play. On in a few weeks. I think for the broccoli and mushroom, crepe paper would be the best bet. Do they still make that stuff?' Howard asked.

'I don't know,' Milly said.

'Is there any rule that you have to make your own costume, or can adults do it for you?' Elsie asked.

'I don't think it matters,' Milly said.

'Goodie. This is going to be fun,' Howard said, rubbing his hands. At that moment the doorbell rang.

'Gosh, that'll be your dad already. Where did the time go?' Elsie said.

'I'll get it,' Howard said, getting up.

'Guess what, Dad?' Milly said when Daniel appeared.

'Yes, guess what, Mr Wynter?' Connor said.

'What's that?'

'Granny and Grandpa are going to help us with our costumes for the play,' Milly said.

'Are they? I hope you haven't badgered them into anything. Please don't feel obligated, Howard and Elsie.'

'Oh no, we don't,' Elsie said.

'No. It will be our absolute pleasure and privilege. My brain is already swirling with ideas,' Howard said, tapping his head with his finger.

'Yes, mine too,' Elsie said.

'Well, there's plenty of time,' Daniel said, still seeming a little dubious.

'We're keen to be organised. And it'll roll around pretty quickly, I'm sure,' Elsie said.

'Yes, none of this stress of the last minute or teething problems, with us,' Howard declared proudly. 'It's actually quite wonderful to have a project to sink our teeth into.'

'Goodie,' Milly said, clapping her hands.

'I'm going to be the best mushroom on stage ever,' Connor said.

'Okay, then,' Daniel said. 'Who am I to argue?'

'But we're not doing it alone – you two will need to be fully involved. Okay, kids?' Howard said, earning a nod of approval from Daniel.

'Oh yes, absolutely. Can't wait,' Milly said.

'How about a working bee on the weekend, unless you have other things on?'

Connor looked downcast.

'Um, Mr Wynter, can I stay some more with you?' Connor said. 'Can you sort it out with … whoever …?'

'I sure can, kiddo. I'll have a word. I'm sure it will be fine. You're not to worry about it. Okay?'

Connor nodded, looking relieved.

'Sorry, Howard and Elsie, I almost forgot. I have some eggs for you, if you'd like them,' Daniel said, offering the half-dozen cardboard egg carton he'd been holding.

'And we have some scraps in exchange,' Howard said. 'Doesn't seem a fair deal, really,' he added, going over to behind the bench and collecting one of the scrap buckets in use, bringing the second out from the cupboard under the sink to put in its place.

'Brilliant. Thanks. I think the chooks would disagree with you there, Howard. Scraps are welcomed most heartily, aren't they Milly?'

'Oh yes, they especially seem to love yours,' Milly enthused.

'Come on, you two,' Daniel said. 'Thanks again for having them.'

'The pleasure is all ours,' Elsie said.

'Yes, they're great kids,' Howard said.

'That's good to hear. It's a huge help to me. Right, got everything?' he said as he herded Milly and Connor up the hall.

'Bye, Granny and Grandpa. Thanks so much for having me,' Milly said, pausing to hug Elsie and then Howard.

'Yes, thank you for having me, too,' Connor said, hugging them.

'See you both soon. Thanks again for the brilliant pen holder,' Elsie said.

'Ah, good times,' Howard said, standing with his arm around Elsie on the porch outside watching the trio meander down the driveway, Milly and Connor bumping into each other deliberately and playfully.

'It was rather helpful of Connor to give us back our apple seeds,' Elsie said.

'Yes, quite!' Howard said, chuckling.

Chapter Thirty-two

'Hi Corinne,' Elsie and Howard said at once when the call had connected. They sat at the table.

'Hi, Mum. Hi, Dad,' Corinne said.

'Yes. Hello. It's both of us,' Janine called.

'Hello there. How's things?' Howard said.

'So, what's new with you two?' Elsie said.

'We've booked to come and visit on the twentieth.'

'Of this month, as in two weeks away?' Howard said.

'Yes. That's the one,' Corinne said.

'Oh,' Elsie said before she could stop herself. She looked at Howard.

'What's that mean?' Janine said.

'Um. Well, we're rather busy that weekend?' Howard said.

'Doing what?' Corinne said and then added, 'Sorry, I didn't mean that to sound quite so incredulous. It's just you guys have spent all year telling us you don't do anything anymore because all your friends have died or are dying.'

'Corinne,' Janine said.

'Sorry, that was harsh.'

'It's true, though, Mum, Dad. You've made it very clear your lives are rather boring,' Janine said.

'Dears, I don't recall saying lately that we're bored,' Elsie said.

'Well, I suppose not, not recently,' Corinne said.

'Anyway, semantics,' Janine said. 'That's great you're busy. I guess.'

'Yes, what are you up to?'

'You know how we've got the new neighbours – Milly and Daniel …?'

'The ones with the chickens?' Janine said.

'The little girl, Milly, is eight? With the friend that is Connor, also eight?' Corinne said. 'Those neighbours?'

'Yes, exactly,' Howard said.

'They're great,' Elsie said.

'Anyway, young Milly and Connor are in the school play. And we're going along to watch,' Howard said.

'Yes. And we've even made their costumes,' Elsie said.

'Oh, wow,' Janine said.

'That's some … um … some serious involvement,' Corinne said, sounding a little wary.

'They're eight, dears,' Elsie said.

'And playing vegetables – it's a propaganda play,' Howard said. 'They're brainwashing them.'

'Right. But the play will only be for a couple of hours on the Friday or Saturday evening, or during the day, won't it?' Corinne said.

'Yes, you won't be tied up *all* weekend, will you?'

'We're going to go to each session – the Friday evening and then the Saturday daytime one, the matinee.'

'Why?' Corinne said.

'To support them,' Elsie said.

'Yes. And be there in case they need some moral support. Milly's dad will be busy behind the scenes, as he's a teacher. And Connor's home life is … well, complicated. Apparently.'

'Yes. So, we want them to look out from the stage and see two friendly and familiar faces – even if they can't actually see us because of the bright lights,' Elsie said.

'We'll tell them where we'll be sitting and they'll know exactly where we are.'

'That's lovely of you, Mum, Dad,' Corinne said.

'Yes, I agree,' Janine said.

'One of the strongest memories I have – generally – is you both being there for every play, presentation, major assembly,' Corinne said.

'Yes. I really appreciated that too. Perhaps not as much then as I do now.'

'Hmm. And if I didn't convey that, because I was a snotty teenager, then please hear me now: Thank you. Both. For everything,' Corinne said.

'Oh, Corinne. That's not necessary. But thank you. I don't recall you being all that bad as a teenager.'

'Now, Janine, on the other hand,' Howard said with a laugh.

'Ha ha. Thanks a lot. But all jokes aside, thank you from me too. I don't think I quite understood the juggling act that would have involved,' Janine said.

'Well, we did lose a couple of clients along the way who didn't understand we had lives outside of them and work,' Howard said.

'But – swings and roundabouts – I'm sure there were others who appreciated our love of family and commitment to family values,' Elsie said.

'True. But back to that weekend. Why don't you come along to the play? In the words of Milly and Connor, it is pretty silly. But they really are delightful,' Howard said.

'Yes, they're fabulous. And neither kid has any other family, so I'm sure they would really appreciate a bigger cheer squad than just us two old fogies,' Elsie said.

'Well ...' Janine said.

'Sorry, don't let us pressure you. It'll probably be boring as all get out. At least come to the afterparty – well, it's just lunch.'

'For a bunch of eight-year-olds? No, thanks,' Corinne said.

'Yes, really? It's a hard no from me too,' Janine said.

'No, it'll be just Milly and her dad and Connor,' Howard said.

'And maybe Connor's mum,' Elsie said.

'Yes, um, depending on how, er, *complicated* things are with her at the time.'

'She's having a few mental health issues,' Elsie said. 'Anyway, we're taking the kids to the Italian cafe down the road to celebrate after the Saturday show.'

'Wow, you're really invested,' Janine said.

'It's nice you've found some new friends,' Corinne said. 'Oh, god, how do I sound?'

'Just like us when you started a new school, I should imagine,' Howard said with a laugh.

'Yes,' Elsie said, also laughing.

'And the circle is complete,' Janine said.

Corinne laughed. 'Yes. We've become you,' she said.

'I hope not,' Howard muttered.

'So, is there a reason for the visit that particular weekend?' Elsie said. 'Could you perhaps change your dates, if you don't want to do the play or you want to see more of us?'

'Yes, sorry to be difficult,' Howard said.

'You're not. It's us who should be apologising – for taking you for granted and not checking first,' Corinne said.

'Yes, exactly. We're the ones who assumed you wouldn't have anything on. There are a couple of things I want to discuss with you,' Janine said.

'Ooh, that sounds ominous,' Howard said.

'All good, I promise.'

'Yes. And me,' Corinne said. 'Also, nothing to worry about. Good excuse to visit, though, I thought.'

'I got cheap tickets, so they're tricky to change. So, count me in with going to the play,' Janine said.

'Me too. I reckon I could sit through an hour or so of kids being kids.'

'Great,' Elsie said. 'We'll get two extra tickets.'

'Fantastic,' Howard said. 'The kids will love having you there, I'm sure.'

'You never know, it could be a hoot – given the unpredictability of the little darlings.'

'Oh yes. Remember that clip of the kid singing the Christmas carols really loudly – the wrong song and completely out of tune?' Corinne said.

'Yes, it's bloody hilarious. Every. Single. Time. And it's been making the rounds of social media every Christmas for years,' Janine said.

'Oh, I know the one. It's adorable,' Elsie said.

'Yes, utterly priceless. The poor person holding the phone or video camera trying not to laugh and get the shakes,' Howard said. 'Oh, the unbridled confidence of children.'

'Maybe we'll get a clip to send viral of Milly and Connor,' Corinne said.

'Mmm, one can always hope,' Janine said. 'Though now we've said that we've jinxed it. Most likely.'

'True. Anyway, Mum, Dad, I for one would be delighted to head along and support the school play and a couple of kids you've become fond of and who have put a pep in your steps; which they so clearly seem to have,' Corinne said.

'Absolutely. Well put, sis,' Janine said.

'Oh, that's great,' Elsie said.

'Yes, it means a lot,' Howard said. 'Which time would you prefer?'

'Um. What do you think?' Corinne said.

'Well, it would rather depend on your flights. If they're Friday, you might be cutting it a bit fine,' Elsie said.

'Oh, yes, good point,' Janine said.

'Saturday's probably best anyway because we're heading out to lunch straight-ish after,' Elsie said. 'Well, when they've packed up or done whatever they need to.'

'Yes. We've allowed an hour before we're due to be at the cafe.' Howard said.

'Okay, Saturday it is,' Corinne said.

'Yep, sounds like a plan,' Janine said.

'So we'll get two extra tickets for the Saturday session?' Howard said.

'Yes, please,' Janine said.

'And me, thanks,' Corinne said.

'Perfect. Milly and Connor and Daniel will be thrilled. And you're going to love them. They're great.'

'Is it okay if we stay there with you?' Corinne asked.

'Yes, nothing's changed in that department?' Janine said.

'Oh, yes, that's fine. I mean, no, nothing has changed here – or there – oh, you know what I mean,' Howard said, looking at Elsie, who nodded her approval.

'Okay. Well, I need to go,' Corinne said.

'And me – I'm off to a work drinks get-together,' Janine said.

'Okay, then. Cheerio,' Howard said.

'Yes, bye for now,' Elsie said.

'Do you smell a rat, Howard?' Elsie asked once the call had ended.

'Yes and no.'

'Howard, you either can or you can't – I don't think it can be both, really, can it?'

'Well, they did say there are things they want to discuss – the rat is in the need for them to do so in person. And I reckon they might genuinely be visiting because they'd like to see us – being the part where, no, I don't smell a rat. See?'

'Okay. Yes. Fair enough. Strange they booked without checking with us first – they've never done that before, have they?' Elsie said.

'No. Us being invisible again?'

'Hmm.'

'I like that we were able to put them back in their box on that score – gently, and without needing to, really. Though perhaps I shouldn't say that,' Howard said.

'Well, I agree. And your secret's safe with me. I wonder what they're up to,' Elsie said.

'Maybe nothing?'

'No. I disagree.'

'Well, it's well established that you're the more perceptive of our partnership, so I won't argue. Oh well, we'll hear soon enough. Oh, speaking of which, I'd better get online and secure the extra tickets and change the booking for lunch,' Howard said, getting up.

'Good idea. Shall I make us a cuppa for when you're done?'

'Yes, please. Can I also have a couple of bikkies?'

'Good idea.'

'I wonder if Milly is going to pop in.'

'I shouldn't think so – I think they're rehearsing for the play, aren't they, today?'

'Oh, yes, you're quite right. Tea for two then, it is,' Elsie said, getting up.

Chapter Thirty-three

'Hi, Milly,' Howard said to the child standing beyond the door he'd just opened.

'Hi, Grandpa. You're never going to guess what.'

'Um.' Howard pretended to be deep in thought for a moment before saying, 'You've got another chicken and it's called Four?'

'Nope. I said you'll never guess.'

'Oh. Would you like to come in?'

'Yes, please.'

'Firstly, how's the play preparations coming along?'

'Okay. Our costumes are the best bit – they're awesome and are going to be the best of the lot. Connor agrees.'

'That's great to hear, Milly. So, are you going to tell me this other thing or should I keep guessing?' Howard said as he followed Milly into the house.

'Hello, Milly,' Elsie called from the kitchen bench.

'Hi, Granny.'

'I'm making a cup of tea. Would you like something?' Elsie said.

'Yes, please. Milo, please. Hot, if that's okay? I think we're going to need it.'

'Oh? What's happened?' Elsie said. She turned from the bench to scrutinise the child, but she didn't seem upset.

'Apparently something we will never guess,' Howard said.

'Ah, well that could cover a whole host of things. Are we to guess?' Elsie said.

'You can try, but you never will,' Milly said with a shrug. 'But I think you'd better be sitting down for this one.'

'This sounds serious. Just give me two secs,' Elsie said, popping Milly's Milo in the microwave.

'Table or lounge?' Howard asked.

'I don't mind,' Elsie said. 'Milly?'

Milly shrugged. 'Doesn't matter, I don't think.'

'Table it is, for want of making a decision and in the interests of not spilling our drinks,' Howard said, taking his mug from the bench and heading over to the table and sitting down. 'Is it good or bad news?' Howard asked as Elsie and Milly made their way over.

God, please don't tell me you're moving – leaving us. Howard was shocked at the stab of pain under his ribs the thought brought on. He'd never had heart problems, but he could see that ending, if this was the news he was about to hear.

'Um. Neither, really, I don't think,' Milly said. Though to Howard she didn't seem convinced.

'You're looking a bit grim, though, I must say,' Howard said, 'for someone who says the news isn't bad.'

'Yes,' Elsie said.

'Well, it's a bit weird. That's all.'

'We're all ears,' Howard said. He found himself holding his breath – priming his faculties for quickly finding the right words to respond to whatever was about to come out of Milly's mouth.

'You know how I've been talking about fostering some puppies?' Milly said.

'Yes. You said your dad was waiting to see how you got on with the chickens, right?' Elsie said.

'To see how responsible you are, wasn't that it?' Howard added.

Milly nodded. 'That's right. Well, it's happening!' she declared.

'That's great news. Isn't it?' Elsie said.

'I knew you'd pass your dad's test with flying colours. Well done.'

'And when is this exciting event occurring?' Elsie said.

'Yes, when are your first charges arriving?'

'Last night, actually. We got them last night. A mum dog and three puppies.'

'Oh, wow. And how are things? How are they settling in?' Elsie said.

'How are you going with them?' Howard said.

'Do they need much care?' Elsie said.

But there was something in Milly's quiet seriousness that pulled them both up. Clearly the fact she had her first foster dog was not the answer to the *you'll never guess what* topic. The child was downcast and thoughtful, though still didn't actually seem upset. So that was something.

'Milly, what is it?' Elsie asked.

'Is something wrong with them?' Howard asked. Though then he remembered earlier she'd said whatever it was was neither good nor bad. Howard scratched his head.

'Well ...' Milly took one of her deep breaths and dramatic pauses. 'The thing is ...'

'Yes ...?' Howard almost laughed at realising both he and Elsie were leaning forward, as good as literally hanging on her every syllable. The kid sure could work an audience.

'Um. You're really not going to believe it.'

'I think we've established this fact,' Elsie said, trying not to grin too broadly.

'Yes, come on, Milly, the suspense is killing me,' Howard said with a laugh.

'Me too,' Elsie said.

'Well, not only have we got a mum and three puppies – they're really little, so tiny they're still with their mum ...'

Howard's mind drifted as Milly stretched things out again. *Is this actually a pitch for pet ownership – for us to re-embark on pet ownership?* he wondered. That might explain things. Again he held his breath, this time in readiness for the awkwardness and difficulty in having to say no to the darling child. It wasn't something they'd had to do yet, really. He dreaded the inevitable crestfallen expression and possibly more so, the stoicism. Because that's what Milly would do. She'd say it was okay while, inside, her little heart was breaking. And there'd be tears, later, that they wouldn't see, which would be worse than seeing them and having the opportunity of attempting to hug them away. Oh, goodness, he was in deep. Shit.

Elsie must have sensed his inner goings-on because he felt her hand cover his resting on the table. She was most likely thinking the same things. *Oh, god.*

'The puppies don't have a name yet. But the mum dog is called Maisie,' Milly said.

Maisie? This word stopped Howard's brain with the speed and intensity of a gunshot.

'What did you say?' Elsie said.

'Yes, did you just say the dog you're fostering is called Maisie?'

Milly nodded. 'Yep. And, I promise you, I'm not making it up. It's mind-blowing, isn't it?'

'Yep, it sure is,' Howard said.

'Wow. Goodness. That's something,' Elsie said, her brain firing with hot pokers of intense thought and a variety of emotions. *Please don't say this is meant to be – that it means we have to adopt her, or any such thing.*

'So, anyway –' Milly continued.

Elsie held her breath, getting ready to be strong enough to upset the little girl who had come to mean so much to them.

'– I just wanted you to know for when you visited. I didn't want you to be too shocked,' she added with a shrug.

'And you really didn't name her?' Howard said, his astonishment spilling over. He hated that he was as good as saying he didn't believe Milly. But he was just too astounded. Though, really, he thought, pulling himself back together slightly, if their dog had been named Maisie, why couldn't or wouldn't someone else call theirs that too? Shelters must be grappling for names for all the animals that pass through. And everything does come back around into fashion, eventually, he supposed.

'I promise it had nothing to do with me or Dad,' Milly said, thankfully ignoring any hurt at not being believed.

'Thank you for coming and telling us first,' Howard said.

'Yes, that's very thoughtful of you,' Elsie said.

'Yes, we really appreciate it,' Howard said. He was damn sure that going in to meet the dog with puppies and learning this could have been the start of previously unknown heart problems. 'Okay, so that's that. Weird, a little unsettling, but it is what it is,' he muttered, working through it all.

'So, tell us about your Maisie and her puppies,' Elsie said. Howard was grateful for her taking over.

'Well, she's not *my* Maisie. We're just fostering until they're ready to find homes.'

'Sorry, yes, quite right. You did say that,' Elsie said. 'How are you going to be strong enough to say goodbye to them when the times comes? I don't think I could.'

'No, me neither,' Howard said, having regained enough composure.

'Well, I'll have to be – strong, that is – and remember that I can then help more. It's all about finding happy homes.'

'Yes, I suppose,' Elsie said.

'Anyway, we'll have to wait and see,' Milly said, sounding like someone much older, as she was wont to.

'So, what breed is she – are *they*?' Howard said.

'She's sad. No, *very* sad,' Milly corrected herself, ignoring Howard's question. 'She's come from a puppy farm. Do you know what that means?'

'Sadly, yes,' Elsie said.

'Unfortunately, we sure do – a horrible existence, from what I understand,' Howard said. 'It's, perhaps, best not to think too much about her past – Maisie's past – and focus on doing all you can for her and her puppies.'

Elsie nodded. She could feel herself being dragged back to when they'd first got their own Maisie – also the prisoner of a dreadful puppy farm. She shuddered.

'Yes, that would be best. That's what Dad says, but it is hard,' Milly said. 'She has a sad look in her eyes.'

'Oh, darling girl,' Howard said, putting his arm around the child whose eyes were now brimming with tears.

'Sweetheart,' Elsie said, leaning in from the other side to comfort Milly. The sight of Milly's bottom lip quivering and chin wobbling caused the emotion in Elsie to turn into a lump in her throat. Milly looked up. The sun streaming through the window caught the tears on her lashes, making them glisten. She wiped her eyes quickly, picked up her mug, and took several large gulps of her Milo.

Howard and Elsie moved away from her and focussed on their own mugs and drinks.

Several minutes had passed when Milly looked up and spoke again. 'Would you like to come and meet her?'

'Oh, yes, of course. I'd love to,' Elsie said, glad to see most of the earlier intense emotion had left Milly.

'Yes, please,' Howard said.

Milly pushed her now empty mug away, signalling she was finished.

'Now?' Elsie said, picking up on Milly's mood.

Milly nodded. 'Would you like to see them now? Could you?'

'Oh,' Howard said, just catching on. 'Sure can, can't we, Elsie?'

Elsie nodded. Though she was quite sure she wasn't ready. She firmly told herself to stop being silly. 'I don't see why not,' Elsie said. She couldn't let Milly down just because she had a dog that was called Maisie – a dog that someone else had called Maisie. It was just another dog with the same name. A completely different breed – had she said what breed it was? Oh no, surely not. No. It would be just too weird if it looked similar to their darling old recently departed treasured companion, the departure of which she still felt incredibly sad, guilty, and also a little bit relieved about. A rush of intense emotion nearly brought her undone again. She felt Howard squeeze her hand. It was the reassurance that they could and should do this. It would be okay.

'Are you sure it's all right to disturb her?' Elsie asked.

'Oh yes, if we're quiet, it should be fine.'

'Come on, then?' Howard looked intently at Elsie as he got up. She nodded in response as she rose from her chair.

'Yay! You're going to love her. She's really sweet.' Milly bounded from her chair and across the space and down the hall, chatting as she went, her words gradually getting lost in the ether.

'Dad, it's just me and Granny and Grandpa,' Milly called.

Daniel came out from the hall.

'Hi Daniel, we've come to meet Milly's new friends,' Howard said.

'Yes, we hope that's okay.'

'Great. Can I get you a cuppa?'

'No, thanks, we've just had one with Milly.'

'Hello, Maisie, aren't you lovely,' Elsie said to the chocolate labrador standing in front of her, tail waving back and forth slowly. Thank goodness it looked nothing like their Maisie, otherwise she would have lost her composure completely: those were the saddest eyes she'd ever looked into, perhaps even worse than their own dear old Maisie when they'd rescued her – or at least on a par. She longed to kneel before the dog and wrap her arms around her neck, bury her head in her fur and sob. *Shit. This was a really bad idea*, she thought, trying to swallow the emotion rising up again.

'Hello, there, aren't you lovely?' Howard said beside her. 'And where are your puppies, Maisie? Can we see them, do you think?'

The dog seemed to understand, because she turned and walked off slowly towards the laundry, pausing and looking at them over her shoulder several times, as if leading them or beckoning them to follow.

'Aren't you a clever girl? They're beauties,' Howard said.

Elsie stared at three snoozing puppies, all in a pile, all plain brown just like their mother, with big tummies rising up and down as they slept. Maisie stood leaning against Elsie, the warmth of her coming through Elsie's jeans. As Elsie looked down at the dog, the dog looked up at her. Elsie gulped and looked away before the dam forming inside her spilled over.

'Yes, you're very clever,' Howard said, leaning down to stroke the sleek head.

'Isn't she beautiful, and amazing? She's such a good mum,' Milly said. Elsie studied the tiles on the wall. She wanted to go home and have a big cry. No amount of scolding herself to pull herself together was helping.

Elsie felt a small hand push its way into hers. 'I didn't want to make you sad, Granny,' Milly said quietly.

'It's okay, Milly, I'm happy-sad — happy for Maisie to have found you,' she said, needing to take care with each word. She hated lying to Milly, but her insides were a maelstrom of emotion that she couldn't pick one bit of debris out of to offer — this was the best she had.

'It's why I wanted to warn you,' Milly said sagely. 'It must be quite a shock.'

'Yes, it is a bit, Milly,' Howard said.

But not nearly as much as if she had been a German shepherd, like our Maisie. That would have completely felled me. Howard, please get me out of here. 'She's lucky to have you, Milly,' Elsie said, now struggling to speak.

'Yes. We'll have to come back to get a good look at the puppies when they are awake,' Howard said beside her.

'Yes,' Elsie said.

'Now, sorry to rush off, Milly, but I've just remembered that the hose is running on the garden,' Howard said. 'So, we'd better get back.'

'Oh no,' Milly said.

'It's okay, it's a soaker hose,' Howard cut in, just in case they were about to be told off for wasting water. 'But, still, best to get back to it. Its time is up,' he said, making a point of checking his watch.

'Okay, then, thanks for coming over,' Milly said.

'Thanks for inviting us. Thank you for showing us your beautiful puppies, Maisie,' Howard said, rubbing the dog's head again, wishing he could rub away the sad expression from her face and the pain in her eyes.

'Yes, lovely to meet you, Maisie, and your gorgeous brood,' Elsie said, now on autopilot and feeling as if she was in a tunnel. She was grateful when Howard clasped her hand and helped turn her around and point her in the direction of home. Thankfully Milly was too caught up with Maisie and the puppies to leave the laundry.

'Bye, Daniel, sorry to rush, but we must be off,' Howard said as they got to the kitchen and kept going.

Elsie nodded beside him. She was becoming limp.

'We've forgotten a hose is running on the garden,' Howard added.

'Ah. Okay. See you again soon,' Daniel said.

They were silent as they made their way down the Wynters' driveway and then up their own and inside, where they slumped together onto the nearest lounge.

'Are you okay?' Howard asked, his first words since leaving Daniel and Milly's house.

'I think so. Thanks for engineering the swift exit. Though, I hope we haven't upset Milly too much.'

'No. I think she'll understand. She was aware enough to come and warn us about the situation. Isn't it something – the Maisie thing?' Howard said.

'Yes, that's one way to put it.'

'Mind-blowing really.'

'I miss our Maisie,' Elsie said.

'I do too,' Howard said.

'I thought I was doing okay, but that's just about damned near taken me right back to square one,' Elsie said.

'Hmm. The nature of grief, I'm afraid,' Howard said. 'Swirling bloody quagmire that it is.'

'I feel really quite wrung out, actually.'

'Let's run a bath, shall we?'

'Yes, that's a good idea.'

'Soak away our troubles.'

Ten minutes later, Howard had filled the bath, got it to the perfect temperature and they were luxuriating in it comfortably.

'Ah, that's much better,' Elsie said, taking deep breaths of the lavender scent rising up from drops of glistening oil floating on top.

'Yes, just the ticket,' Howard said, leaning back and closing his eyes. 'Hey,' he said a moment later, 'you don't think dragging us in there was a ploy to offload the dog onto us at some point, do you?'

'I wouldn't be surprised,' Elsie said. 'I don't like saying this, because I adore that child to bits, but I think we do have to keep our wits about our girl Milly,' she said. 'Perhaps she did just want to show off her new charges and we're being paranoid. I do miss having a dog,' Elsie said with a sigh.

'A dog, or just Maisie?' Howard asked.

Elsie searched for the answer.

'Brian is interesting and nice to have wandering around – well, when he's behaving – but it's the presence of another heartbeat,' Elsie said. 'I'm not saying we need to do anything about it, just saying what's in my heart. I do still agree it would be irresponsible at our age to get another dog who could quite likely outlive us.'

'Our girls haven't mentioned being interested in pet ownership for a long time, so it would quite possibly have to be put up for adoption with strangers.'

'Yes. That hurts my heart more than living without the companionship,' Elsie said.

'Well, at least you have me,' Howard said. 'And I'm pretty good at fetch too.'

'Yes, you are. Bit slow. But quite accurate,' Elsie said, playing along, enormously grateful for Howard and his ability to, if not remedy every situation, at least lighten this one.

'So, we're all good, dear?' he asked.

'Yes, we're all good, my love. When those puppies are running around causing havoc, and young Milly expresses her tiredness and exasperation at the work involved, we'll feel much better.'

'Yes, quite right. I don't miss the chewing up of things,' Howard said.

'Or, I imagine, the picking up of poo,' Elsie said.

'No, not that. But I do miss sitting outside and watching her pottering around and snuffling at the flowers. And the way she flopped down and then got up like an old person, groaning – even before she was old.'

'Yes, she did that from day one, didn't she? I think she had an old soul,' Elsie said.

'That dog, Maisie, next door nearly destroyed my soul with those eyes.'

'Yes, speaking of souls, I could practically see the miserable life she'd had – the tiny cage – through her eyes; windows to her soul.'

'We don't know she had a miserable life, dear, or was in a tiny cage,' Howard said.

'Milly said she came from a puppy farm, Howard, and she's with a shelter – a rescue organisation – and will be up for adoption when she's ready.'

'Yes, true. Doesn't bear thinking about, really.'

'I'm trying not to, but it's got lodged now,' Elsie said, sniffling, her chest aching.

'Just go with it dear. Be sad for a bit. Cry. Maybe a good cry is what we need,' Howard said, leaning forward and reaching for Elsie's hand. He gave it a squeeze before letting it go and leaning back again. He closed his eyes and let the tears leak out.

Chapter Thirty-four

'Oh my goodness, look at them,' Elsie, said, nudging Howard. She could barely sit still.

'Yes. Never before has a better head of broccoli or a finer mushroom graced a stage,' Howard said proudly.

'We did well, my love. Genius idea of yours to do their top parts different heights so they could still stand nice and close together.'

'Thank you. It worked quite well in the end, I thought – a big help that we could make both costumes together and therefore measure accurately.'

While they were thrilled with the costumes – both fashioned out of miles of coloured crepe paper – they were even more thrilled at being asked by Milly and Connor to be backstage to help them get ready. They'd only just come to their seats and exchanged grins with their neighbouring audience – complete strangers – keen to declare, *These are our grandkids; aren't they marvellous?* But everyone was in the same boat, weren't they?

There was a rabble of excited voices. And movement in chairs. No doubt everyone was saying the same thing. Elsie and Howard looked around, caught the eyes of several people around their age who they had met at the Grandparents' Appreciation Day and smiled and nodded to them. Howard's heart swelled. *Ridiculous to think just how much this means.*

'Isn't it exciting?' Elsie said beside him, reaching over and clasping his hand.

He nodded. 'I'm a bit nervous for them, though.'

'Yes, I hope they don't forget the words to their songs.'

'Oh well. I've given last minute strict instructions, that if they do, they're to just concentrate on moving their lips and pretend.'

'Judging by the number of vegetables milling about back there, I'd say they would get away with it, volume-wise,' Elsie said.

'Yes, true. Some great costumes. But ours are the best,' Howard added, lowering his voice.

'Oh, Howard, it's not a competition. But, yes, I agree,' Elsie whispered.

'Here we go,' Howard said as the lights went down and everyone fell silent.

'Don't forget to film it,' Elsie whispered, nudging him.

'Oh, god, yes. I nearly did forget,' Howard said, pulling his phone out. 'Can you take some stills with yours? In case my hands are too shaky.'

'Yes,' she said, diving into her handbag for her phone. 'Don't worry too much,' she said, sitting upright again, 'I'm sure there'll be plenty of videos kicking about afterwards.'

'True. I'm sure they'll be very good but, I must say, I'm glad it's not a full show – you know, one that goes on for well over an hour and has an interval.'

'Yes. I guess that's because they're little kids who can't be expected to follow directions and behave and concentrate for too long.'

'Shh. Shh. They're starting,' Howard said.

Just as predicted by Milly, the play – or skit or musical, or whatever you wanted to call it – could be best described as very silly.

Every second minute, Howard wanted to whisper to that effect to Elsie, but refrained. Much of the laughter going on was a little awkward. He wasn't sure if it was his lack of attention span, or what, but he couldn't follow what the story was about, beyond a few jingles comprising singing vegetables. And of course, if there was any actual story involved. Several minutes in, he gave up and just laughed along with everyone else, enjoying looking at the range of colourful costumes. They joined in on the chorus – the parts near the end of the tunes – as invited by the butternut pumpkin, who seemed to be considered the king of the vegetables, or emcee. Several times Howard wished he could have got his hands into producing *that* costume. While he didn't want to be rude, it really wasn't much chop. He only knew it was a butternut pumpkin because it said so in the program he held. He thought it looked more like a potato. And he'd be surprised if it held together right through being taken off and put back on again, let alone tomorrow's matinee as well.

'Oh, bravo! Bravo,' Howard and Elsie cried, getting to their feet when the curtain came down and the lights went up.

Thank god that's over, Howard thought as he clapped heartily, broad grin plastered across his face as they stood through four curtain calls.

Finally, the clapping stopped and the audience began leaving their seats. Howard and Elsie stayed put.

They watched on as the kids poured out through the closed curtain and from the edges and proceeded to leap off the stage or clatter down the steps at the sides, despite the teachers clearly trying to stop them. First it was with hissing voices from unseen adults, and then loud instructions for them to get backstage. Then a bunch of adults, all dressed in black — those in charge, Howard assumed — appeared and were giving a fine impression, with their arms outstretched, of a group of farmers trying to herd a mob of sheep back together and out of sight. Kids laughed, screamed and squealed, and dodged around.

'They've got their work cut out for them,' Howard said to Elsie, leaning over and grinning.

'Yes. They don't stand a chance — they're all so hyper.'

Despite the teachers' best efforts, most of the kids were now milling around greeting their loved ones or still racing amongst the gathered throng looking for them.

As Howard looked on, he chuckled to himself and thought this was infinitely better and funnier than the actual play they'd just sat through.

He looked for Milly and Connor in the sea of milling vegetables. He was keen to stay where he was.

Elsie, moving in her seat beside him, appeared to be of the same opinion.

Gradually the teachers seemed to give up. Howard noticed a few shoulder shrugs, raising of hands, palms up, and gradually fewer people dressed in all black. The kids ran riot.

'I'm staying put and out of the way. That lot's going to take a while to sort out,' Howard declared.

'Yes. Best to just wait until they've burnt off their excess energy.'

They settled back into their chairs again.

'Well, that was interesting,' Elsie said.

'Yes, hilarious. Those teachers will be exhausted after all that, if they weren't already,' he said.

'I was actually referring to the play.'

'Oh. Yes, that's one way of putting it,' he said, looking at her now, his eyebrows raised. 'I'm kind of regretting agreeing to do the whole season,' he added, leaning in close so no one else could hear.

'It won't hurt us. It's just a couple of hours,' Elsie said. 'It's good to support them and help with raising some money.'

'Not sure I agree with the propaganda they're pushing. Don't they know climate change and the environmental mess can't be solved just by giving up meat?' Howard said.

'Best not to start, dear.'

'I know, but is it wise to be pushing that particular line? Fine in a private setting maybe, but a school? It's a bit raging-greenie, isn't it?'

'I know what you mean, but I'm too tired to think beyond it being a bit of cheerful and colourful educational fun,' Elsie said. 'Though, I'm not sure what Corinne and Janine will make of it.'

'Yes. I'm regretting all but insisting they attend, now, too,' Howard said, cringing.

They waited while the seats around them emptied. Soon they were the last two sitting there.

'I think I'll let them off the hook,' Howard said, folding his arms.

'No, it's for less than an hour. They can sit through it. They might even enjoy it, and I do rather like the idea of providing more of a cheer squad for young Milly and Connor, since they don't have anyone else,' Elsie said.

'That's true. It's a good thing to do,' Howard said, uncrossing his arms.

'Exactly,' Elsie said. 'I think you're forgetting some of the horrific productions we sat through when the girls were at school. Remember the one with them dressed as animals in a circus?'

'Oh god. I do. That was a disaster. The two kids dressed as a donkey tripped over their own hooves and fell off the stage. Is that the one you're referring to?'

Elsie nodded. 'Yes. That was one of many mishaps that night.'

'I seem to remember them as being funny in mostly a cringe-worthy way,' Howard said.

'One of those kids broke his leg. Badly, I seem to recall.'

'Oh, yes, that's right. That was quite traumatic for everyone in attendance, but lucky for us, they cancelled the next three nights' performances as a result. You're right, probably good for the girls to sit through this tomorrow, since they've dodged the particular bullet – and many others – through not having had kids.'

'I love that we still get to be grandparents – well, sort of,' Elsie said.

'Yes, all care and no responsibility! And in our case, we could walk away completely if we wanted to, because they're not actually related.'

'Not that we would, because they're two pretty great kids,' Elsie said.

'Yes, they sure are. And they deserve two old gits who love and care for them,' Howard said.

'Did you see us?!' Milly cried, clambering onto the empty seat in front and leaning over. Connor copied her, though was silent.

'Here you are. Oh yes. You were both fabulous,' Howard said.

'Absolutely brilliant,' Elsie said. 'How was it for you?'

'Okay,' Connor said.

'Silly, as predicted,' Milly said, 'but also pretty fun, actually.'

'I'm glad to hear that,' Howard said.

'We didn't even forget our words,' Milly said.

'That's great,' Elsie said.

'Yes, well done,' Howard said.

'I did,' Connor said quietly and a little sheepishly. 'But I did what you said, Grandpa, and I don't think anyone knew it.'

'Good for you. I didn't notice,' Howard said.

'I didn't either, so well done,' Elsie said. 'Did you manage to get out of your costumes okay?'

'Yes, Mr Wynter helped us take them off,' Connor said.

'We got in quick while the other children were running around being naughty,' Milly said.

'Good kids, we're very proud of you,' Elsie said.

'Yes. Very. Do you need us to do anything before we go?'

'Thanks for saying, Granny. No, thank you, Grandpa. Dad carefully put our costumes up nice and high on the shelf so they'd be safe and ready for tomorrow. He said he'd meet us just outside. We'd probably actually better go. I'm sure he won't be long.'

'Yes. And Mr Wynter has our bags already. Plus I've just had a wee,' Connor announced.

'Great. Come on, then, lead the way,' Howard said, getting up and moving to the end of the row of chairs, followed by Elsie.

Chapter Thirty-five

'You've left your lights on,' Milly said as Daniel pulled up in Howard and Elsie's driveway to let them out. Connor was asleep, leaning on Milly.

'Milly, they need to be able to see,' Daniel said.

'Not the outside light. There's one on inside too,' she said, clearly miffed.

'That'll be our daughters, who will have arrived after we left,' Howard said. 'I can assure you we didn't leave any extra lights on.'

While Howard was concerned more with the cost of the electricity, Milly's focus was on the environmental impact. Same goal in the end, Elsie thought.

'I guess that's okay, then,' Milly said. 'It's just that you do really have to keep on top of these things,' she added, clearly keen to have the last word.

Howard nodded. 'Good thinking. I appreciate your diligence,' he said.

'I don't know what that means. Dad?'

'I'll explain in a minute,' Daniel said.

'Well, thanks for the ride,' Elsie said, opening her door. 'Again, great play, kids.'

'Yes, well done,' Howard said. 'Okay to leave that in your hands, Daniel?' Howard said.

'Oh yes, I'll take it from here.'

Elsie couldn't see from where she was, but just knew they'd be exchanging raised eyebrows and knowing grins. Bless Milly for keeping everyone honest. She loved the kid but, goodness, she wasn't sure how she'd go dealing with the questions, commentary, and judgement twenty-four seven. 'See you tomorrow,' she said, now standing outside the car.

'Yes, rest up ready for another big performance,' Howard said from beside Elsie.

'Don't remind us,' Connor said suddenly, clearly, having just woken up, and with a slight start by the looks.

Elsie thought he had fallen asleep as soon as the car door had closed in the school's car park and not stirred in the past twenty or so minutes. Milly had reached around and pulled his seatbelt across him and Elsie had taken the buckle and snapped it into place, sharing a smile with Milly as she did. No words had been needed for their tag team effort.

'Are you coming to watch again?' Connor asked, sitting up straight.

'Oh yes, we wouldn't miss a performance, Connor,' Elsie said.

'Sure are, champ,' Howard said.

'Cool,' Connor said.

'Thank you. We really appreciate the support,' Milly said in that voice she sometimes used that caused Elsie to wonder who had spoken. Did the kid have an adult residing inside her?

'You're very welcome,' she said.

'Well, cheerio. See you tomorrow,' Howard said.

'Yes. Sleep well,' Elsie said.

'Thanks – you too,' Daniel and Milly said at once.

'Ah, wasn't that fun?' Howard said as he put the key in the lock, watched on by Daniel, Connor and Milly from the car.

He pushed open the door and they both turned and raised a hand as they stepped into the lit hallway. Daniel waved before reversing out and proceeding onto his own driveway just a couple of metres away.

'That's nice of Daniel to wait until we're right inside,' Howard said.

'It was.'

'Though I can't help wondering if Daniel might have just got told off for running the car while they did,' Howard said.

Elsie chuckled. 'Yes, good point. She's going to whip the planet into line if it's the last thing she does.'

'More like the people in charge of things,' Howard pointed out.

'Yes, bless her.'

'Hello, we're home,' Howard called.

'In here,' came a reply that Elsie immediately detected was that of their elder daughter, but who sounded weary.

'Hello, you two,' Corinne said, coming across to hug them. 'How was the kids' play?'

'Silly, cute, ridiculous,' Howard said with a laugh. 'But we're glad we were there, right, dear?'

'Oh yes,' Elsie said. 'It was quite good fun.'

'Where's your sister?' Howard asked.

He beat Elsie to the same question. She was still busy looking about the space for Janine.

Corinne pointed, her face contorted into an expression somewhere between amusement and concern, Elsie thought.

'Where?' Howard said. He moved forward. Elsie followed him.

'Over there. On the floor,' Corinne added.

'What is she doing?' Elsie said.

'Oh, I say,' Howard said.

The three of them now stood with their hands on their hips, looking at Janine, who was lying on the floor behind the couches. She appeared to be making snow angels – her arms and legs moving back and forth beside her.

Corinne looked at each of her parents with raised eyebrows.

'Hello,' Janine called. 'I'm an angel. The snow is lovely, very soft, not too cold, just perfect.'

'Yes, I can see,' Howard said.

'What's going on?' Elsie said to Corinne quietly. 'Has she taken something? Drugs?'

'I have no idea. She was here before I arrived. I stopped to get something to eat in the Uber on the way. I'm not sure how long she'd been here before I got here. Before the snow angel, she was ranting about a butterfly. I'm not entirely sure if she thought she could see one or actually thought she was one. Lots of hand flapping. It's a little funny, but I am a bit worried … she's … um … been going through some … er … stuff … so it wouldn't surprise me if she's taken something,' Corinne said.

'What do you mean by taken something? Is she a regular drug user?' Howard asked. 'And like what?'

'Oh, I don't know. I don't know she is – she does – I'm just saying it wouldn't surprise me if she took something. I'm not talking illicit – something from the doctor, like Ambien or something.'

'So, what do you mean she's going through something?' Elsie said. 'What's going on?'

'Better wait until she can tell you herself. You know how she can get,' Corinne said.

'Right, but how long until that will be?' Howard said.

'How would I know? I don't know what's going on at all.'

'Do you think we should call an ambulance or something?' Howard said.

'No, definitely not. I think she seems safe enough. She actually looks pretty happy, which might be a good respite from …'

'Shall I put the kettle on?' Howard said, making his way to the kitchen.

'Sure. I could have a herbal tea to be sociable, thanks,' Corinne said. 'But I really need a shower. I just didn't want to leave Janine alone.'

'Oh,' Howard said, staring at the empty plastic container in the sink.

'What is it?' Elsie asked, catching his concerned tone and moving to where he stood, her hand coming over her mouth as she looked down and realised what they were both looking at.

'What? What is it?' Corinne said, moving to where her parents stood.

Howard had picked up the lid. *L&S's SM Risotto*. He tried not to smirk. 'Oops,' he said.

'Oh dear,' Elsie said. She looked up at Howard and bit her lip. 'Whoops indeed,' she added in a mutter.

'What?' Corinne said again. 'What is up with you two?' She peered at the plastic lid with black marker labelling, frowning, and then looked from one parent to the other. 'I don't get it – whatever *it* is – what's weird about, um, *L and S's SM Risotto*,' she said, reading out the black print. 'You two are behaving very strangely, I must say.'

'*L and S's SM Risotto* refers to Larry and Susan Coventry's special mushroom risotto – special mushrooms being, er, magic – ah, hallucinogenic,' Howard said.

Elsie nodded. Oh how she wanted to laugh, but she was also concerned about their youngest daughter tripping in the corner, now apparently trying to build a snowman, she thought, glancing over. She put her hand over her mouth to stop the rising laughter. Janine was on all fours, making scooping motions with their hands.

'Do you think she's traumatised because we didn't take you both to see snow for the first time until you were teenagers?' Howard asked. 'That's what she's up to now, isn't it? Making a snowman – snowperson, whatever,' he said.

'Oh god,' Corinne said, rubbing her hands over her face. 'I think the more pertinent question at this juncture is: Mum, Dad, what the hell are you doing with risotto containing magic mushrooms in the freezer?'

'It's a bit of a long story,' Elsie said, suddenly very weary after their evening out.

'Oh, I have all night to hear this,' Corinne said, standing with her arms folded across her chest, laughter twitching at the corners of her mouth. 'When I said you needed more on your bucket list, I didn't mean trying drugs,' she said.

'Actually, I'll have you know, this is not such a new experience,' Elsie said.

'Oh, really? Do tell,' Corinne said.

'You know those photos in the album of the architraves and decorative ceilings ...?'

'The ones you have always claimed to be *arty* shots – Dad apparently being *creative*? Which I could never see, by the way. Those? From the seventies or thereabouts? No idea why you kept them, let alone devoted album space to them.'

'Thanks a lot, I quite like them,' Howard said, pouting.

'Sorry. Anyway, you were saying?' Corinne said.

'Actually, it's not a long story at all,' Howard said. 'The long and the short of it is they're the result of an evening on magic mushrooms at Larry and Susan Coventry's New Year's Eve party.'

'Yes, I gathered that much — they're well labelled. And this?' Corinne said, waving her hand at the sink and then in the direction of Janine, who was now back to doing snow angels.

'We caught up with them, Larry and Susan, recently and they gave us some magic mushrooms. Quite good fun, if a little disconcerting,' Howard said.

'Yes,' Elsie said, 'quite the adventure.'

'Right. Good to know.' Corinne said.

'And apparently safe,' Elsie said.

'Yes. Well, it's a relief to know that Janine is, in all likelihood, going to be fine in around six hours from when she ate the risotto,' Howard said.

'Oh, well, that's okay, then,' Corinne said, oozing sarcasm.

'What's not fine is her eating our only supply,' Howard said, hands on hips again.

'Yes, that's really rather disappointing,' Elsie said.

'Are you two being serious right now? That's the important part in all this?' Corinne said. 'Not your daughter over there tripping in the corner? Do I even know you?' She shook her head.

'Well, they died — the mushroom people; Larry and Susan Coventry. So this is the end of it. And we rather liked the idea of a bit of an escape from the hideousness that is old age,' Howard said.

'Yes. Exactly,' Elsie said, nodding.

'Wow, you two. Just wow.'

'On second thoughts, I'm going to up the drinks stakes and have a Scotch, and perch myself down to watch and live vicariously through Janine,' Howard said, putting a mug back as the kettle bubbled.

'Make that two, dear,' Elsie called.

'I'll still have the tea, thanks. Just leave it to steep. I'm going to have a shower. Hopefully when I get back, I will have woken from this weird dream. Who are you?' Corinne muttered as she left the room.

Howard and Elsie looked at each other with raised eyebrows.

'Well,' Elsie said.

'Yes, that about covers it,' Howard said, going over to the drinks cabinet.

'Hi, Mum, hi, Dad, why are you so colourful – like rainbows,' Janine said, now on her feet, standing a little distance from her parents and twirling around, swinging her arms.

'It's like charades, though a weird iteration of it,' Howard said, sipping his drink.

'Yes, I think we're now being a ballerina,' Elsie said, standing beside Howard by the built-in shelves.

'Oh, yes, I think you're right. Well done. Could also be a butterfly catcher.'

'True.'

'Cheers, dear,' Howard said.

'Cheers, my love. Here's to … an unusual evening.'

'Yes.' *Clink.*

'Why are there labels on the shelves in the linen press?' Corinne asked, coming back out, her short hair wet from the shower.

'Oh, you know, just being organised. Nothing better to do,' Elsie said.

'Haven't you gone a bit overboard with the decluttering? It's all so *tidy*,' Corinne said.

'Don't sound so surprised,' Elsie said indignantly.

'Yes, we've never exactly been hoarders,' Howard said.

'No, but something's different. And you can't blame Covid, because the house wasn't like this last time I was here. Are you sick?' Corinne said, looking from one of her parents to the other, scrutinising them. 'Are you preparing to move into a home? Are you selling up?'

'God no,' Howard said.

'No, absolutely not,' Elsie reiterated.

'You're worrying me now,' Corinne said.

'Sorry. Don't be. All is well with us,' Elsie said.

'Yes, everything's fine. We're fine, I assure you,' Howard said. *It's a completely different tree to the one you're barking up*, he mused to himself.

'Okay, then. Thank goodness for that,' Corinne said, getting her mug of tea from the kitchen. 'So, I see the Janine show is still going on,' she said, sitting down on the couch.

'Yes, your father and I are playing charades with her – well, *about* her, more precisely.'

'Okay. Right, let me see.'

'Ooh, I'm not sure that's a good idea, dear,' Elsie said, noticing Howard now had his phone out and was holding it up.

'Just capturing a short video for prosperity. Or blackmailing purposes. We'll see,' Howard said with a grin.

'I'm not sure she's going to see the funny side for quite some time, though I did snap a few photos and a quick clip myself earlier – of the snow angel,' Corinne said.

'You've alluded to issues with Janine. Twice now. Are you sure it wouldn't be best to enlighten us on that?' Howard said.

'Quite sure. It's not my story to tell. I must say, the house is very different without dear old Maisie,' Corinne said, looking around.

'Yes, Brian doesn't have the same charm,' Elsie said.

'Who's Brian?' Corinne said, looking around again. 'Have you got another dog? Or a cat?'

'Oh, no. No, Brian is your father's robotic vacuum cleaner,' Elsie said.

'Yes, he's rather good company. Though somewhat useless with the actual cleaning,' Howard added.

'But we don't mention that, so as not to offend,' Elsie said, sipping from her glass.

'Oh my god, you two have completely lost the plot. It's a bloody machine. You are aware of this fact, right? Which means he can't be offended because he's a machine! He doesn't have feelings! Oh god, and now you've got me referring to it as *he*. Just shoot me now.' She shook her head and blinked.

'What's this then, do you think – tiptoe through the tulips?' Corinne said a moment later, nodding towards Janine.

'Could be,' Howard said.

'Or walking on the moon. Maybe,' Elsie said.

'I wonder how she's going to react to finding out her own parents have drugged her,' Corinne said with raised eyebrows, before sipping from her mug.

'I don't think we can be held entirely to blame,' Howard said.

'Or at all, really,' Elsie said. 'The risotto was clearly marked.'

'That's a poor defence, Mummy dearest. *L and S's SM risotto* does in no way indicate that this' – again she waved her hand in the general direction of her sister – 'would occur from consuming contents therein.'

'It's clear to us,' Elsie said.

'Yes, I really am quite miffed about our loss,' Howard said.

'Well, take consolation in the fact she seems to be making the most of it. And apparently enjoying her trip. As fun as all this is, I need to go to bed,' Corinne said, getting up.

'Yes, I think I'll turn in too,' Elsie said. 'Are you happy to stay up and keep an eye on things here, Howard?'

'Oh, yes, probably best someone does. Hopefully she'll be worn out from all the activity soon and will sit down and then fall asleep.'

'Will she come to with a fright, do you think?' Corinne said from the kitchen sink.

'I shouldn't think so. We didn't,' Howard said.

'No, we just gradually became normal again,' Elsie said. 'I'm not sure if I fell asleep or not, but I know I did wake up feeling quite refreshed.'

'Yes. Much better than drinking and ending up with a hangover,' Howard said.

'Honestly, can you hear yourselves? I feel like I'm in the twilight zone myself. All too much. Goodnight,' Corinne said, heading for the hall.

'Night,' Howard said.

'Yes, goodnight, darling,' Elsie said.

'It's wonderful to see you,' Howard said.

'Yes. Sorry about all this weirdness,' Elsie added.

'And you keep saying your lives are dull,' Corinne said from the doorway, shaking her head.

'Goodnight, dear,' Elsie, said, kissing Howard on the head. 'What a funny end to an already strange-ish evening,' she added.

'Yes, that play could be considered a bit trippy in itself,' Howard said, chuckling.

'Exactly. You might want to put a blanket over her, if she goes to sleep,' Elsie said, nodding towards Janine, who was now pirou-etting, arms raised above her head, in front of the glass doors.

'Righteo,' Howard said, raising his hand in acknowledgement.

Chapter Thirty-six

'Good morning,' Howard said from the kitchen table where he already had a mug of coffee and the newspaper laid out in front of him.

'Here they are,' Elsie said, looking up from the crossword. 'How did you sleep?'

Howard wondered if Elsie was pondering, as he was, how much, and if anything, one ought to say to Janine about last night's antics. Thank goodness she seemed none the worse for wear. He was a little bleary-eyed, on account of being up with her until two am, when she finally seemed to come out of her trance state and make her way to bed. They had exchanged quick greetings, but he'd left her be as she'd seemed a little bewildered to see him there; confused or mortified, he hadn't been able to tell. He got up to distract himself from his thoughts.

Howard held up the jar of coffee and wriggled it, to which both daughters nodded and said, 'Yes, thanks.'

'And it's okay,' Corinne said. 'Our friend here is well aware of last night's shenanigans, and she's fine, aren't you, Janine?'

'I can't believe you drugged me,' Janine said, slumping onto a chair.

I can't believe you ate most of our last fix, Howard thought to himself.

'It was a bloody good risotto. Very tasty, because of, or in spite of, the addition of the other,' she added. 'Which I remember actually quite enjoying too. I don't remember much else, but the muscles in my arms are sore, which makes sense now I've seen Corinne's video. Oh. Now I remember. I couldn't get the car started – I wanted to go and get some Maccas or KFC. What's wrong with the car?'

Uh-oh. Um ... Howard searched for something to say to deflect the line of questioning. He handed over a mug of coffee to Janine and then one to Corinne, keeping his eyes down as he did, before returning to the bench. Thankfully the distraction did the trick and after a beat, Janine carried on talking.

'Thanks, Dad. Oh, am I in need of coffee!' Janine said.

'I'm not surprised,' Corinne said, laughing. 'Me too, though – thanks, Dad.'

'Sorry it's just instant. I know how you Melbournians are about your coffee.'

'Ah, but the instant evokes wonderful memories of family and home, doesn't it, Janine?' Corinne said.

'Yes, because it's the only place I'll drink it,' Janine said. 'It's strange that I actually even like it.'

'That's the love that goes into it, dears,' Elsie chimed in.

'Exactly,' Howard said.

'Mmm. You must be right. It's going down a treat. Anyway, thanks, older sister – not – for the incriminating evidence,' Janine said.

'If there isn't a video clip, it didn't happen,' Corinne said, grinning.

'Well, don't you dare put it online!'

Corinne shrugged.

Howard wanted to tell her not to wind her sister up, but restrained himself; they weren't twelve anymore and did not, or rather should not, need parental intervention.

'It's okay, calm your farm. I promise I won't – just milking the situation.'

'Oh, you two,' Elsie said, shaking her head at them. 'What are you?'

'Us?' Janine said, staring at her mother. 'I can't believe you two partake in magic mushrooms. Mind. Blown,' she added.

'Anyone else want toast?' Howard asked, now at the open freezer to retrieve the bag of frozen bread.

'Yes, please,' Janine said.

'Got the munchies have we? Oh, this is priceless,' Corinne said, laughing.

'Yes, thank you. Glad you're enjoying yourself.'

Howard added cutlery to the tray of breakfast spreads and took it over to the table.

'But I am glad you're a little more cheerful this morning than you have been. Seriously, it's good to see,' Corinne said.

Elsie watched Janine shoot Corinne a stricken look.

'It's okay, she hasn't told us anything,' Howard said, returning to the bench.

'What's that supposed to mean? Clearly she has, if you're jumping to defend her like that,' Janine said.

'She only said something's going on in your life,' Howard said, retrieving the four pieces of toast that had just popped up, the metallic clank sounding extraordinarily loud in the silence.

'I'm worried about you, Janine,' Corinne said. 'Tell them.'

'Yes. Talk to us. What's up?' A twinge of fear pinged inside Elsie.

'I wouldn't mind some more of that risotto,' Janine said.

No, neither would we, Howard thought, delivering the plate of toast to the table where he sat down. He couldn't remember who else, if anyone, had requested toast and in the dwindling atmosphere it didn't feel right to press the subject.

'Because you're hungry or are wanting to run away and not tell us?' Elsie said, adding Vegemite to a piece of toast she'd just buttered, which she slid, on a small plate, across the table towards Janine.

'Whatever it is,' Howard said, eyebrows raised. When had they stopped sharing things? Not so long ago they used to joke amongst themselves that they were a family of oversharers. He noticed Janine staring down into the mug she had both hands wrapped around. Or perhaps it was the toast that had her attention – he couldn't tell. *Not really pertinent, Howard,* he told himself, and raised his gaze. He longed for a piece of toast, but it didn't seem right to just carry on.

'Sonia and I broke up. That's all,' Janine said with a shrug.

'Oh, Janine, I'm so sorry,' Elsie said. She put her hands on the edge of her seat, ready to get up to go and hug her youngest daughter. But the tightness in Janine's shoulders, that told her any physical affection would be shrugged off, stopped her going any further.

'Yes, darling, you poor thing,' Howard said, his insides deflating and leaving behind a heavy ache. 'We really liked Sonia and thought you guys would go the distance. Sorry, should I not have said that?' He looked at Elsie and Corinne as he realised one of them had sucked in their breath noisily.

Corinne was shaking her head and Elsie looked to be cringing.

Am I meant to denigrate her when she's been a part of the family for the past five or so years? he wondered. He liked Sonia very much and hoped she was okay. But, yes, his loyalties must lie with Janine. 'What happened?' he asked.

'She wouldn't come back to Adelaide with me. It's a backwater, apparently, with no decent jobs.'

'Oh. I see,' Elsie said.

What do you see? Howard wondered. *So what if she didn't want to come back here for the weekend?*

'Oh well, there'll be other –' he said.

'Don't you dare say there will be other fish in the sea, Dad. Just don't,' Janine said, her eyes flashing angrily at him.

I wasn't. He felt Elsie's hand on his leg and then her squeeze his knee. It was their agreed sign – with no malice – to shut up, for want of another term.

'I wasn't, actually,' he said carefully. 'I was *going* to say, there will be other weekends. Surely one won't matter in the scheme of things, will it? Pick one's battles and all that?'

'Permanently, Dad,' Janine said.

'Sorry, now you're losing me,' Howard said, frowning.

'I'm moving back – permanently.'

'Oh, that's brilliant to hear,' Howard said.

'Yes, that's wonderful news,' Elsie said.

Oops, not the right thing to say, Howard thought, as he caught the furious glare of Janine across the table.

'Sorry, not the point, I suppose,' he said.

'No,' Elsie said, looking at Howard. 'I'm sorry, too, Janine, go on,' she said.

'So, there must be more to it than that,' Howard said when silence had stretched on for too long and Janine didn't appear to be preparing to speak.

Her toast remained untouched and she was again staring down at her hands, which were still wrapped around her mug. He knew when she was being thoughtful, sorting out the words in her mind – she was a chip off his old block there. He watched a tear roll down her face and drop onto the tablecloth, leaving a dark patch.

'Oh, sweetheart,' he said, reaching across and putting his hand on her arm.

'I loved her. I really loved her,' Janine said, lips quivering.

'I know you did,' he said. 'Is there any way you can come back from this – patch things up?'

'No,' Janine said, shaking her head. 'And there's really not much more to it. She just didn't love me enough to leave Melbourne, or her job.'

Oh, sweetheart. Elsie felt a shard of her barely mended heart, after the loss of Maisie, break off and bump about painfully inside her like a sharp iceberg puncturing her soul.

'And Maisie's not here to cuddle,' Janine said, looking up at both Howard and Elsie, her bottom lip stuck out in a pout.

'No. It's not the same without the dear old thing,' Corinne said.

Tell us about it, Elsie thought, nodding. She didn't trust herself to speak – she might just cry herself. Was there anything more painful to a parent than seeing their child hurting and not being able to do anything to help erase that pain? She didn't think so.

Suddenly there was a loud plastic and electronic whirring and then a clatter as Brian trundled out from his docking station in the study. To Howard he looked like he was blinking in that sleepy state the girls did as littlies when coming out of their bedrooms into the light of the loungeroom or kitchen late at night, looking for a drink or the loo or a cuddle after a bad dream, or some noise, had woken them.

'Good morning, Brian,' Howard said. 'I trust you slept well.'

'Who's Brian?' Janine said, turning around to see what her father was looking at. 'What is that noise?'

'That's your father's new friend, Brian. The robotic vacuum,' Elsie said. 'You get used to the din after a while; I barely notice it these days.'

'Sorry. He's programmed for nine on weekends. I'll turn him off. Actually, we'd better think about getting ourselves ready for the play.'

'Hello, Brian. Good morning,' Elsie said as the machine came near her feet. She rather liked the little fellow's presence roaming about – he gave the place some life. 'He's actually rather cute,' Elsie said, 'though he's not much of a conversationalist – and completely useless with the crossword clues.'

'Poor Maisie would have had a fit,' Janine said, looking down.

'Well, of course we waited until she wasn't here. What do you take me for?' Howard said, his sadness over the reminder of Maisie coming out a little too sharply.

'Sorry,' Janine said.

'No, that's okay. He's just a bit of fun.'

'Some company – good for you, Dad,' Corinne said.

'Yes. We can't have any more pets. We're decided on that,' Elsie said. 'So ...' she added, waving a hand towards where Brian was now twirling around, apparently negotiating the legs of the occasional table sitting against the wall.

They lapsed into silence again as they all watched Brian making his way back and forth.

'I see what you mean. He's a very good distraction,' Janine finally said. 'I've actually been wondering about getting one for a while.'

'Well, I'm not sure he's doing much of a job cleaning. He's a little disappointing in that area. And he gets himself muddled and has to head back home a bit too frequently for my liking,' Howard said, now whispering.

'Dad, he can't hear you,' Janine said.

'Actually, he probably can. He has a camera,' Elsie pointed out.

'Oh, that's a little creepy,' Janine said.

'Yes. Nanny cam scandal, anyone?' Corinne said.

'It's so you can sort him out from afar via the app, if he gets stuck. In theory. Not sure that really works all that well, either,' Howard mused. He didn't like speaking ill of the little chap.

'I can't believe you talk to it like it's part of the family,' Corinne said.

'So do we tell everyone we have an adopted brother called Brian now?' Janine said, grinning.

Corinne laughed. 'Too funny,' she said.

'He's rather hypnotic. I could watch him for hours go back and forth. And I love the little pirouette he does to turn around,' Janine said.

'Yes, he's a right little drama queen. Quite unnecessary, I'm sure,' Elsie said.

'He's being a bit loud and intrusive. I'll send him back home to sleep,' Howard said, picking up his phone and tapping on the screen.

They all watched as Brian retreated into the study.

'There, that's better. Sorry, Brian,' Howard said, putting his phone down.

'I'm sorry you're sad, Janine,' Elsie said.

'Thanks, Mum.'

'Yes, me too. If there's anything we can do, just say,' Howard said.

'Thanks. It's not really a tub of ice cream breakup, this one,' Janine said and let out a heavy sigh.

'No,' Elsie said.

'And we're going to have to do financial and property settlement and everything. Fun times ahead.'

'Well, hopefully you can work things out quickly and amicably,' Howard said.

'We'll see.'

'Why didn't you tell us?' Elsie said.

'I don't know – embarrassment?' Janine said, looking up.

'But we're your parents. We love you,' Elsie said.

'Yes. And will always support you, whatever,' Howard said. 'And, embarrassed? Why on earth would you be embarrassed?'

'Yes,' Elsie said, nodding.

'Well, look at you two. You *three*, for that matter,' Janine said, looking at her parents and swivelling to look at her sister. 'You've all married your childhood best friends. I'm the odd one out. The failure? I fuck up relationship after relationship.'

'Just because they haven't worked out long term doesn't make you a fuck-up, Janine,' Corinne said.

'Don't patronise me. What would any of you know about it – the heartbreak over and over? You have to love me, find me lovable – you're family. But no one else seems to, for any great length of time.'

'You're a strong, independent woman with a heart of gold,' Howard said.

'Exactly,' Elsie said, floundering.

'Yes, so what's not to love? You tell me. Apparently strong and independent is appealing until you're living with it. And my heart of gold is apparently fool's gold, or just there to be taken advantage of and then trampled all over. Oh, whatever, I'm done. I don't want to talk about it. There's nothing much to say, anyway.'

'Okay, if you're sure,' Elsie said.

Janine nodded.

'So, what's this about you moving back permanently?' Howard asked.

'Nothing really to say there, either. I miss Adelaide and you guys,' she said with a shrug. 'Probably pathetic, at my age, but there you go.'

'Oh no, I think it's lovely,' Elsie said.

'Yes, it's wonderful news from where I'm sitting,' Howard said. He felt the scar tissue of his heart harden and shore up a little.

'I'm going out on my own, starting my own firm,' Janine added.

'Wow, that's fantastic news,' Elsie said.

'Yes. Thanks for not leading with the most interesting part,' Howard said, attempting joviality, but most likely failing.

'And I'm considering moving back too, actually,' Corinne said. 'Well, both Stephen and I – we're still together.'

'Thanks for the dig,' Janine said.

'Sorry, I didn't mean it to be – was providing clarification. You're just being prickly, which is perfectly understandable,' Corinne added, raising her hand when Janine opened her mouth, her eyes black hard marbles.

'Oh, wow, well, welcome home. What a great weekend,' Howard said.

'Don't get too excited. We've got some sorting out back in Melbourne to do yet,' Corinne said.

'Yes,' Janine said.

'But it's really happening?' Howard said, looking from Janine to Corinne.

'I think so,' Corinne said.

Janine nodded. 'Definitely.'

At that moment Howard's phone on the table began vibrating and ringing. He picked it up. 'Excuse me a minute,' he said, striding off and over to the far side of the room before answering.

Elsie watched Howard talking on the phone. He was pacing back and forth, and from his expression it looked like bad news. Which friend has died this time, she wondered.

'I can't believe you guys are into magic mushrooms,' Janine said, dragging Elsie's attention back to the table and her daughters.

'Well, it's not like we went looking for it,' Elsie said. 'The people who had it were at a lunch we were at and Howard mentioned the photos he'd taken at their New Year's Eve party ages ago – we'd lost touch with them since then. And Susan ... well, she slipped it into the pocket of my coat. I found it and some marijuana when we got home.'

'Oh, it gets even juicier,' Corinne said.

'Yes, dope too? God, you two are full of surprises. I could do with some of that, right about now – the dope that is, not the surprises,' Janine said, picking up a piece of toast and taking a bite.

'Well, we haven't been game to roll a joint – not that we have any of the accoutrements, anyway, because we've discovered we have – well, rather, had, until a few weeks ago – a policeman living across the road,' Elsie said, buttering her own piece of toast. 'We were contemplating making some brownies, but are pacing ourselves on account of the fact the mushroom people – sorry, Larry and Susan, I should say – are now dead. Sadly.'

'What, both of them?'

'Yes, hit by a car crossing the road in Norwood. Absolutely horrific. But at least they went together, I suppose,' she added. 'So there's no more to be had, I'm afraid.'

'Sorry to upset the applecart by hoeing into the risotto,' Janine said sheepishly. 'For what it's worth, it was delicious. As I said.'

'Oh yes. Your father and I have already had some and an ... um ... a bit of a trip. He saw flying little boys. That I do remember,' Elsie said, smiling at the memory.

'Huh?' Corinne said.

'You know, frankfurters. And I saw lots of pretty colours.'

'When was this?' Janine said.

'Oh, just the other week.'

'Mind. Blown,' Corinne said, shaking her head.

'Don't worry, you can easily get dope around Adelaide, so you can most likely find a supplier of magic mushrooms too, if you're so inclined,' Janine said.

'Though I'm not sure what yours and Dad's old cronies will think if you get banged up on a drugs charge. Oh my god, that's priceless,' Corinne said, laughing and holding her stomach.

'Well, I have good news and bad news,' Howard said, striding back across to the table, phone still in hand. 'The performance is off. The kids' play. No repeat show today after all. A bout of diarrhoea and upset stomachs has gone through half the cast. But Milly, Daniel and Connor are fine, so we can still go to lunch with them. I've just managed to bring forward the time for our booking, too, online, so we're not all starving.' He was pleased to see the toast was finally being eaten. He hadn't fancied tossing it – though he supposed he could have re-heated it or put it with the scraps for Milly's chooks. Though that was only marginally less wasteful.

'So, which bit is the bad news, exactly?' Corinne asked.

'You miss out on the play, of course,' Elsie said. 'It really was quite funny.'

'Au contraire,' Howard said, taking a piece of toast for himself from the large plate. 'You don't have to miss out – I found a video online late last night for us to watch. It's better than the one I took.'

'Oh, great,' Janine said.

'Now come on, don't be like that,' Elsie said.

'Just kidding, I'm keen to see it,' Corinne said. 'Especially the costumes you mentioned making. They sounded awesome.'

'I think it's wonderful, you being involved,' Janine said.

'We've had such great fun doing it. We told you about them making us their honorary grandparents, too, didn't we?' Howard said, proudly.

'You did,' Janine said.

'Yes, and the excellent afternoon tea you were treated to,' Corinne said.

'And we can't fail to notice the artwork adorning the fridge,' Janine said, nodding her head in the direction of the kitchen.

'You're all caught up with everything, then. So, who wants to watch the play?' Howard said, wiping his fingers on the paper serviette beside him to dislodge the crumbs from the toast he'd quickly devoured.

'Oh. Now?' Corinne said.

'Well, what else are we going to do before lunch? Unless either of you – or both of you – have plans?' Howard said.

'No,' Janine said.

'No, me neither,' Corinne said, getting up.

'Come on, gather round, then. I'll hook up the iPad to the TV for the whole experience.'

Elsie thought she enjoyed the play even more the second time round and found herself giggling ahead of the funny parts. Several times the girls doubled over in laughter and they all had tears streaming down their faces at what Elsie suspected wasn't meant to be nearly as funny as they found it.

'Oh my god – it's like tripping on mushrooms without the mushrooms,' Janine said, wiping her eyes as the credits that whoever had done the video had added began to roll.

'That was priceless. Oh, butternut pumpkins, the great leaders of the vegetable family! Who would have thought? Potatoes have always been my favourite,' Corinne said.

'Mine too,' Janine said.

'Anyway, your costumes were the best,' Corinne said.

'Thank you. See, told you, dear,' Howard said.

'Not that we're petty enough to be competitive about a bunch of eight-year-olds,' Elsie said, despite her pride.

'Oh, come on, who are you kidding here?' Janine said. 'I remember you looking very serious while sewing late into the night on plenty of outfits for us.'

'Yes, and unpicking. Lots of unpicking, when it wasn't quite perfect. You were very competitive, Mum, I seem to recall,' Corinne said.

'In my defence, if something is worth doing, it's worth doing properly,' Elsie said.

'You tell yourself whatever you need too, Mumsy,' Janine said, laughing.

'Well, I'm glad I saw that, so I can speak with authority to the kids over lunch later,' Corinne said.

'Speaking of which,' Howard said. 'We'd better get ourselves organised. Time is a-marching. I've got the taxi booked to come in ... oh! Less than three quarters of an hour.'

'I can't believe how quickly the time has gone,' Elsie said.

'It's our scintillating company,' Corinne said. 'Hang on. Why do you have a taxi booked? Can't we just call the RAA roadside assistance to get the car started?'

'We decided not to renew our licences,' Howard said.

'Okay, but one of us can drive,' Corinne said, looking at Janine.

'Actually, probably best I don't,' Janine added.

'We cancelled the RAA too – no point having it, with us not driving,' Elsie said.

'Lucky I couldn't get it started – you'd have cancelled the registration and insurance then, wouldn't you?' Janine said.

'Oh, no. We left those in place, in case one of you needed it,' Howard said.

Janine frowned at him before saying, 'So how come it wouldn't start? I didn't think it seemed like the battery – the interior light came on.'

'Sorry. There's no fuel in it,' Howard said.

'But how can you have …?' Janine started before stopping and waving a dismissive hand.

'Well, I'm just going to get changed,' Corinne said.

'And me,' Janine said. They got up.

Elsie looked at Howard with her eyebrows raised. Were they going to have to tell the girls about their now abandoned plan at some point? That could be a tricky conversation. Hopefully not. *Positive energy, Howard, old man.*

'Okay?' Howard said, putting his arm around her.

'I'm sad and worried about Janine,' Elsie said.

'Yes, I really liked Sonia.'

'Me too. Family get-togethers won't be the same now.'

'No, but we'd better keep our thoughts to ourselves,' Elsie said. She now knew what friends meant about the silent pain of a marriage or serious relationship of one of their children breaking up and the grief that must remain hidden in order to not heap more anguish upon the child going through the breakup. There were so many sources of pain and grief that no one gave any – or little – credence to in this world.

Howard thought about Sonia. He longed to phone her and make sure she was okay. She'd said so many times he and Elsie where the parents she'd never had, having ceased contact with her own dysfunctional and toxic family long before meeting Janine. And Howard and Elsie had often commented that they considered her another daughter, just as Corinne's Stephen was the son they hadn't birthed. But that wouldn't be the thing to do it. Or would it? Would it be inappropriate? Oh, it was a potential minefield. Best to just let the dust settle for a bit. *Won't someone think of the parents?* Howard mused sardonically.

He turned his attention to their impending outing. He would enjoy the exuberance of the little people over lunch. And Daniel was good company too.

Chapter Thirty-seven

'Right, all ready to go?' Howard said. 'The taxi should be here any minute. Let's wait out the front so the driver doesn't have to get out of the car – save them some trouble.' They all made their way out of the house and Howard locked up behind them.

'I still don't understand why we couldn't have gone with a container to get fuel and then driven ourselves,' Janine said.

'Yes, we had plenty of time,' Corinne said.

'Can you please stop harping on about it,' Howard said.

'It's much easier to just catch a cab,' Elsie said.

Too many questions were being asked and they couldn't have it all coming out, Howard thought.

Elsie noticed Corinne and Janine swap worried glances. God, she really hoped they wouldn't ask anything else, or connect any dots, particularly right before the lunch with friends who included sensitive young children. She and Howard didn't know how they would react if their plan, despite now being obsolete, came out. Hopefully, if it did come out – and she really hoped it wouldn't – Corinne and Janine would simply roll their eyes at their parents having weirdly practical ideas.

Howard noticed his daughters' expressions. No doubt they were wondering where their fiscally prudent father had got to. He found himself becoming defensive, and before he could rein it in, said as much. 'Look, I stuffed up. I'm sorry. It was a while ago and I'd completely forgotten. Please drop it for now. I'll tell you later. Can't we just concentrate on having a nice lunch out? And anyway, I'm wearing the cost of the taxi, with no impact on you, so I don't see the issue. Lunch is on me, too, in case I haven't made that clear.' Hopefully they'd just think he was being sensitive over no longer having a driver's licence.

'Okay. Well, that's us told,' Janine said, folding her arms. Elsie caught Corinne looking at her sister with knowing raised eyebrows.

The taxi arrived right on time, much to Howard's and Elsie's relief.

Howard confirmed they were the right people and the destination, got in, and off they set, the tension making the full car a little stuffy to Elsie's mind.

In the cloying, tense atmosphere, Elsie could only hope the mood improved in the next fifteen minutes or when the energy of Daniel and the kids was injected.

Damn all the questions. Damn getting defensive, Howard thought. He hadn't meant to, or wanted to do that. *But goodness me!* He forced himself to relax his shoulders and take a couple of slow breaths. Really, they were only doing exactly what he would have in the same situation. No doubt it was quite confronting to discover your usually sharp, well-organised parents had let something happen like running the car out of fuel. Oh well, at least lunch would be fun. If he could only get his mind back in the right gear.

They had just got out of the taxi and Elsie, Corinne and Janine were standing on the pavement out the front of the cafe while Howard paid and waited for the receipt, which caused the driver to mutter and sigh with annoyance.

'Sorry to be a bother,' Howard said. He didn't like being difficult, though why simple paperwork was considered so onerous as to warrant this carry-on, he didn't know. But he was keen to keep his accounts in order. Why should he have shoddy record keeping just because someone else couldn't be bothered to have their system up to scratch? Another of the many standards that seemed to have slipped in society. Once a proper receipt, showing all the details clearly, was the norm and you had to request not to have one, if so inclined.

Howard exited the taxi, now the one muttering with annoyance, and tucked the receipt into his wallet. *Move on, Howard*, he told himself, forcibly readjusting his facial features from a scowl into a welcoming smile before finishing his task and turning to face the others. He was glad he'd made the effort because Daniel, Milly and Connor were there now as well.

'Hello,' he said.

'Hello, Grandpa,' Milly said, beaming, and wrapping her arms around him.

'Hi, Grandpa,' Connor said, throwing himself into Howard's stomach once Milly had let go.

'Hi. This is very good of you,' Daniel said, beaming.

'It's our pleasure,' Howard said. 'Now, you've all met and been introduced?'

'Yes, Elsie has done the honours.'

'Great, great. Milly, Connor I'm sorry your second and last performance has been cancelled,' he said.

'We're not, actually,' Milly said boldly. 'The whole thing was rather exhausting.' She gave an exaggerated sigh, as if to drive home her point.

'I'm a *bit* disappointed. I actually quite enjoyed it,' Connor said quietly.

Howard patted his shoulder and said, 'Hopefully there'll be another play before too long. Come on. How about we head in, rather than standing out here?' He made shooing motions with his hands as he leant against the door to hold it open for everyone to enter.

And as he was about to close it, he noticed Connor still standing nearby with a very serious expression and his hands clasped in front of him.

'Good job, Connor,' Howard said, for no reason, really – it just seemed right to acknowledge the lad at that moment. He gave his hair a gentle ruffle and as he did felt the earlier tension slide away.

'Grandpa?'

The voice was so quiet Howard nearly missed it.

'Yes, son, what is it?' Howard bent down to listen, anticipating more quietness was to follow.

'Can I sit next to you?'

'Of course you can. I'd be honoured.'

Connor nodded and smiled, though it seemed a little forced. A bit like when he needed the loo that time – slightly constipated-looking, Howard thought. He looked expectantly at the child. 'Is something bothering you, Connor?'

Connor nodded. 'Can you tell me if I need to know something today?'

Howard blinked as he ran the phrase back through his mind, trying to gain clarity. *Nope. I've got nothing.* 'Sorry. I don't quite follow,' he said. 'What sort of something?'

'I've never been to a restaurant before. Can you please make sure I don't do the wrong thing? Like if there's special cutlery or something.'

'Ah, I see what you mean now. Yes, absolutely. Just follow my lead and give me a gentle nudge if there's anything you're not sure about. But it's not a very fancy restaurant, so I think you'll be fine. Just stick with me, kiddo,' he said, putting his arm around Connor's shoulders and giving him a gentle squeeze.

Connor nodded and smiled up at him, looking much more at ease now.

Their conversation delaying them meant that by the time Howard got fully inside, their group had been shown to their table and were standing beside it, clearly waiting for Howard and Conner to arrive before taking their seats.

Howard pulled out a chair. 'Here you go, Connor – this looks like a good spot for you, right here beside me.'

Gradually they were seated. Then there was a cluster of excited voices as they all discussed the menu and sought recommendations from each other. Howard overheard Corinne and Janine discussing when they'd last been there and what they'd eaten – several years ago, before Covid.

The cafe had been around for decades and was the type of establishment where great, relatively simple fare and liveliness reigned, rather than low lighting and ambience – pale butcher's paper over wooden tables rather than white linen.

The muscles in Howard's shoulders uncoiled even more.

Howard chose a simple chicken pasta dish, suspecting Connor might just copy him when ordering, which was confirmed moments later.

'So, kids, I'm glad you haven't become sick like your classmates,' Elsie said, buttering a piece of bread. The hubbub had died down a little since they'd ordered and she was keen to enliven the slightly dwindling mood. Though why this was the first subject that had come to mind was beyond her – hardly a cheerful topic of conversation!

'Yes, you seem to have dodged a bullet there,' Howard said. He was grateful to Elsie for getting the ball rolling.

'We don't pick our noses, that's why,' Connor said conspiringly, causing chuckles to spread around the table.

'I'm not sure that's appropriate table conversation, Connor,' Daniel said quietly. Howard was relieved to see he was smiling, though, and that Connor didn't look too rebuked. He was copying the way Howard was buttering his bread.

'It's actually true, Dad. Dane and Lily pick their noses. A lot. And eat their boogers. And don't wash their hands very often. Or correctly, in my opinion,' Milly said and then focussed on buttering her bread.

'Right. Well, okay, then,' Daniel said.

He seemed to Howard to be trying to think of what to say next and failing. Out of the corner of Howard's eye he noticed Elsie, Corinne and Janine shoving bread into their mouths quickly, as if trying to stop themselves from laughing.

'Honestly,' Milly continued, putting her knife down, 'you'd think with all the hand-washing signs stuck up around the school they would do better. But nope.' She finished with a nonchalant shrug of what-can-you-do before taking a bite from her bread.

Laughter rolled around the table. Howard snuck a look at Corinne and Janine. Both were grinning widely, their eyes shining. *Brilliant, kids, go on, work your magic*, he thought. *Bless you.*

'We watched your play this morning – well, a video of it,' Janine said. 'I thought you were very good, Milly and Connor.'

'Yes, you were awesome,' Corinne said.

'Thank you,' Milly said. 'Granny and Grandpa's costumes were *amazing* – the best of all of them.'

Connor nodded enthusiastically; his cheeks were full of the bread he was chewing.

'But I thought the play was rather silly. That's why I'm glad we didn't have to do it again today,' Milly said. 'Though I quite liked the singing bit, actually,' she added a beat later, looking thoughtful.

'Fair enough. Thank goodness, in that case, for the nose-pickers you have in your class,' Corinne said.

'It might have had something to do with the amount of lollies they ate while we were getting ready, and all the running about afterwards, too,' Milly said before taking another bite of bread.

'Well, whatever it was, cheers to them and Milly and Connor getting let off the hook so they could come out and entertain us,' Janine said, holding up her glass.

Everyone followed suit and glasses were clinked – wine glasses held by the adults and tumblers by the children. Milly and Connor beamed.

Elsie cringed slightly.

Howard wanted to cheer, but managed to restrain himself.

'Connor and Milly are writing their own play now, about waste, aren't you?' Daniel said.

'We are,' Milly said.

'How's it going?' Howard asked.

'Good, thanks. There are no talking or singing vegetables involved at this stage,' she said.

'Well, let us know if you need any more costumes,' Elsie said.

'Yes, or anything else,' Howard added.

'Careful what you offer,' Daniel said with a laugh, which all the other adults joined in with.

'Oh, oh,' Connor said, putting his hand up and squidging in his chair.

'What is it, Connor?' Daniel said.

'I've got a joke,' Connor said.

'Is it clean?' Daniel asked. 'And appropriate for the lunch table?'

'Um.' Connor frowned. 'I think so.'

'Okay. Go ahead,' Daniel said.

Connor made a show of preparing himself, taking a few breaths, clearing his throat, and sitting up tall. 'What's black and sticky?'

'Connor, it's what's *brown* and sticky,' Milly said gently.

'Oh. Yeah. Sorry. Start again.'

Everyone around the table nodded.

Connor went through his preparation routine again, causing Howard to chuckle to himself. 'What's *brown* and sticky?'

Howard looked around the room. Everyone was shaking their heads.

'I don't know,' he said. 'What's brown and sticky?'

'A stick!'

The table erupted into laughter and Connor clapped his hands with joy.

'Oh. What's black and sticky?' he asked a moment later.

Milly frowned.

'I don't know, what's black and sticky?' Corinne asked, the edges of her lips upturned.

'A burnt stick!'

Another round of laughter rumbled around the table.

Grinning, Connor said, 'What's –'

'Connor, I think that's enough jokes for now,' Daniel said, gently.

'Pleeease, just one more. Please,' Connor said, looking up at Daniel.

'Dad. This I want to hear,' Milly said and crossed her arms.

Elsie tried not to laugh. Clearly Connor had gone off script and Milly was waiting for him to stuff up. For his sake, she really hoped he knew what he was doing.

'Oh, go on, then, Connor,' Daniel said.

'What's black and brown and sticky?'

'I don't know, Connor, what's black and brown and sticky,' Janine said.

'A half-burnt stick. Ha!' Connor clapped his hands and then grabbed his bread and took a bite.

They all laughed, though with slightly less exuberance this time around.

'That's actually pretty funny, Connor,' Milly said.

'Yes, well done,' Howard said.

The others around the table nodded and murmured words of agreement and encouragement.

'Thanks. I made those last two up myself,' Connor said proudly. 'Thanks for the tip, Milly,' he added, holding up his hand for a high five, which the two kids performed.

'Guess what?' Connor said when the rabble had died down again.

'You've got another joke?' Corinne said.

'No. That's all I've got,' Connor said. He screwed up his face and pouted.

'We'll have to find you some more,' Janine said.

'What were you going to tell us, Connor?' Howard said.

'I'm reading much better now. Thanks to you, Granny and Grandpa.'

'Oh, that's fantastic news,' Howard said.

'Yes, very good,' Elsie said. 'Well done. But I think you deserve all the credit. We barely did anything.'

'Oh no,' Milly said, 'reading aloud and having patient people to help is very ... um ... helpful, isn't it, Dad?'

'It sure is, kiddo. And, Howard and Elsie, I for one appreciate you reading with Milly when I can't do it,' Daniel said.

'I think we get the better end of the deal,' Howard said. 'We love having them at the house.'

'Yes, we so do,' Elsie said.

Milly and Connor gazed up adoringly up at Howard and Elsie, who mirrored their expressions.

'My maths is better now too,' Connor said. 'Actually, all my subjects. I got a really good report this term. I like school a lot more now,' he said with decisive nod.

'That's wonderful to hear, Connor,' Elsie said.

A series of utterances of agreement and reinforcement roamed around the table.

'I hear you have a foster dog and three puppies, Milly,' Corinne said. 'How's it going?'

'Um ... Quite good, thank you. Maisie's still sad, but not quite so much as before. She's the mum dog and the puppies are growing like mushrooms and starting to cause mischief,' Milly explained.

'Did you say she's called Maisie?' Janine said, looking from Howard to Elsie with a shocked expression.

'Yes,' Milly said. 'I didn't name her. She came like that.'

'Milly was very thoughtful and came over specially to warn us before we met them,' Elsie said.

Milly nodded. 'It is a strange coincidence and I knew about your old dog Maisie.'

'That's ... Wow,' Corinne said. 'How odd.'

'Yes, we were so glad for Milly's warning. Otherwise it would have been a big shock,' Howard said.

'She doesn't look anything like the other Maisie, though,' Milly said. 'My Maisie – well, not mine, actually; foster dog Maisie, that is – is a chocolate labrador, not a German shepherd like yours was. Same sad eyes, though,' she added a beat later, looking thoughtful as she picked up her bread again. 'Can you come and see them when we get back?' She looked up at Corinne and Janine with big pleading eyes.

'Oh,' Corinne said.

'It would mean a lot,' Milly quickly urged.

'I don't see why not,' Corinne said.

'No. Unless that'll mean too many people for her,' Janine said.

'I don't think so. She has to get used to meeting lots of people, if she's going to find a forever home soon. If we're quiet, I reckon it'll be okay.'

'Okay,' Corinne said.

'Fair enough,' Janine said.

'So you'll come?' Milly said.

Janine nodded. 'I'd love to meet your foster dog Maisie and her puppies,' she said.

'Me too,' Corinne said.

'We can stay away if it's too much of a crowd and visit again another time,' Elsie said.

'Yes, good point,' Howard said.

'I think it'll be okay,' Milly said. 'But we can see how Maisie feels when we get home. You can tell, you know – well, I can.'

Again, Corinne and Janine nodded.

They worked their way through their meals, chatting sporadically, including a barrage of questions, in rapid succession by Milly, directed back and forth to Corinne and Janine about their lives in Melbourne and moving back to Adelaide and comparisons and what they did for jobs.

'Milly, enough,' Daniel gently said during dessert. Howard felt for the kid who now sat on her hands looking a little restless. Though his head was starting to throb from the exertion of trying to keep track of the questions and answers – the episode reminding him of a tennis match with a ball flying back and forth over a net rather than across a table.

In the lull, Howard was about to ask if they wanted tea and coffee or hot chocolate to finish the meal when Daniel got in first and suggested they wait and have hot drinks back at his place. His eyebrows and tone, directed at Howard, across the table, told Howard he was keen to head off without delay. The kids did seem to be starting to get a bit ratty, for want of a better word, now he thought about it. Probably all that sugar in the dessert catching up with them. He was going the opposite way – rather fancied a nap.

Howard nodded enthusiastically and said, 'Sounds good to me, Daniel.' Though as he finished, it occurred to him his assent might have been a little too hearty and misconstrued as tightwad-dedness rather than adhering to Daniel's wish. Oh well, hopefully it went unnoticed and, if not, there were worse things than that to be labelled.

They vacated the table and after everyone uttered their thanks for lunch, Howard headed over to the cashier, followed by Daniel, while the others headed towards the door, thanking staff and raving about how lovely their meal and time was as they went. Howard noticed Daniel getting out his wallet. 'No. Please. I said it was our treat,' he said, putting a hand on Daniel's arm.

'Thank you. If you're sure?'

'Completely. It has been Elsie's and my absolute pleasure.'

'I'd better head out and make sure Milly isn't firing more questions,' Daniel said. He looked a little awkward to Howard. Howard nodded.

'She's a cracker – in a good way,' Howard said, grinning.

'Oh yes,' Daniel said with a big sigh, and headed off. Howard chuckled to himself.

'I've just phoned for a taxi,' Elsie said to Howard when he joined the little group milling outside.

'Oh. Ah,' Daniel said, appearing a little stricken and thoughtful, as if trying to figure out how to fit everyone into the one car.

'It's all good,' Elsie said. 'They said it's quiet and they will be along very soon.'

'And look, here we are,' Howard said mere moments later. 'Gosh, that was quick.'

'I can see why you encourage them to visit lots,' Corinne said when she and Janine and Howard and Elsie were settled into the cab and heading for home.

'Yes. They are delightful,' Janine said.

'Makes me almost wish I had kids,' Corinne said.

'Not me,' Janine said. 'I do, however, like this surrogate grandparent thing you've got going on – being able to hand them back when you like or when you've had enough.'

'Yes, and call Daniel to get them into line, if necessary,' Howard said. 'I like it too.'

'He seems lovely as well.'

'We certainly lucked out with the new neighbours,' Howard said. 'Is that how you say it? Or is it …? Hmm. We got lucky, that'll do.'

'Yes. They're very special and have really brought some energy to our lives,' Elsie said.

'I love that they call you Granny and Grandpa,' Corinne said.

'You don't mind?' Howard said.

'Why would I mind?' Corinne said.

'Yes, and me – why would I mind?' Janine said.

'Oh, I don't know.'

'Because you might feel pushed out?' Elsie suggested.

'Not at all. I think if they brighten your days, great. We haven't exactly been much help in that department lately – in person,' Corinne said.

'Yes, bloody Covid. I really hope it is completely over now,' Janine said.

'Do you think they, well, Milly, I mean, is trying to suck us in – to ultimately sell us Maisie, or one or more of the puppies?' Corinne said.

'Probably,' Howard said.

'Oh yes, without a doubt, she's quite the covert salesperson,' Elsie said.

'Less of the covert and more of the overt, most of the time, I reckon,' Howard added. 'She might not have, if you hadn't mentioned you were moving back.'

'Oh no, I think in that case she'd organise interstate transport – put together a GoFundMe or something,' Elsie said with a laugh.

'Yes, she certainly seems resourceful and so grown-up at times,' Howard said.

'It returns a bit of faith in the younger generation, doesn't it?' Janine said.

'I'll say,' Howard said.

'Yes, I'm liking children a lot more, having met those two,' Corinne said. 'And didn't you say they're not related – that Daniel is a foster carer for Connor?'

'Yes. I think it's called respite fostering,' Howard said.

'They could be siblings,' Janine said. 'Same hair, eyes and skin tone …'

'Gorgeous inside and out,' Elsie said, 'we love them to bits, don't we, Howard?'

'We sure do. Well, here we are,' Howard said as they turned into their cul-de-sac.

'Oh, look,' Janine said, pointing to the right of the car. 'The Chans' old house – that's who lived there before, wasn't it? – there's a For Sale sign.'

'That's where the policeman and his partner the paramedic, Joseph and Philip, were living until recently,' Elsie said.

'I'm disappointed we didn't get to know them or at least say goodbye properly – the one time we met them they seemed lovely,' Howard said.

'I wonder when it's open for inspection,' Janine said.

'We'd love you right across the road, but would you like that?' Howard said.

'Fair go, Dad,' Janine said with a laugh. 'I've only just seen a sign and commented on it.

'It's actually not a bad house,' she continued. 'I looked through it when the Chans had just moved out, I think it was, when I was home one weekend. Remember, Mum, we were being nosey neighbours?'

'I do. It's actually a very nice home. Well, it certainly was back then,' Elsie said.

'I wouldn't mind having a look through now. It is a great spot to live,' Corinne said. 'I happen to know there are some pretty good neighbours hereabouts,' she added with a laugh.

'I'm glad you think so,' Howard said.

'You might not be saying that when we're popping over every second hour for a cup of sugar,' Elsie said.

'Exactly. Because we've forgotten we were just there,' Howard said.

Corinne and Janine looked at their parents with concerned expressions.

'Just messing with you,' Howard said.

'Yes, we're teasing,' Elsie said.

'On a more serious note,' Howard said, 'I hope you two are not going to be fighting over the same house to buy – wherever that might be.'

'I imagine we'll have different budgets,' Corinne said.

'Yes, especially now I'm a singleton again,' Janine said.

'And Janine is more definite – further along the moving-back path, that is – than we are.'

'Are you happy to go straight over to their place to see the dogs or do you need to go inside for anything first?' Elsie said, changing the subject.

'Oh, hello. That's lovely. Look. It seems we have a welcoming committee,' Corinne said.

'She's making sure you don't escape, no doubt,' Howard said.

'Yes, and she's roped Connor in as reinforcement, bless them,' Elsie said.

'Come on, I could do with a cuddle from a dog. I'm really missing our dear old Maisie,' Corinne said, getting out.

Chapter Thirty-eight

Elsie got out of the taxi and waited while Howard finished paying the driver, smiling to herself as she watched Milly take Janine by the hand and Connor take Corinne's hand and lead them up the driveway.

'I think we've been replaced,' she said to Howard, now standing beside her, and nodded in the direction of the driveway.

'Ah, yes. Oh, well, should we join them, or are you too weary?'

'No, I'm good. Thank you again for lunch. That was a lovely meal, a fabulous treat and a very good idea.'

'Thank you, dear, I thought so, and the kids seem to love it, which makes this old coot very happy.'

'And this one. Come on, then,' Elsie said slipping her arm under Howard's elbow. They set off up the driveway towards Daniel's house. When they arrived inside, they saw Corinne, Janine, Milly and Connor sitting on the floor trying to coax the three puppies, who were running madly around, over to them. Maisie was off to the side watching on, tail swaying slowly.

'Hello there, Maisie, are you keeping well out of the chaos?' Howard said. 'Good plan, I reckon.'

'Yes, you have some very energetic puppies there,' Elsie said. Maisie turned at hearing her name, and then slowly wandered over. She stood looking up at Howard and Elsie. Her tail began to make larger and quicker sweeps. They took turns patting her.

'You're a beautiful girl, yes, you are,' Howard cooed.

'And such a good mumma-dog,' Elsie said gently.

'Hello. Come in and sit,' Daniel said, appearing from the hall. 'Thanks so much again for lunch. You really made the kids' day and probably their year, actually, judging by the chatter in the car on our way back. Anyway, it really means a lot.'

'Oh, our pleasure entirely,' Howard said.

'Yes, it's wonderful to get out amongst such delightful and lively company,' Elsie said.

'Well, they are lively. Pretty good on the whole, though,' Daniel said, looking across at the kids with the pups and Janine and Corinne.

'I hope Milly isn't counting on Corinne or Janine taking one of the pups,' Howard said.

'She's quite the salesperson, by the looks,' Elsie said.

'Ah yes. Just between us ...' Daniel said, lowering his voice, '... we're going to be keeping one of the pups. She has well and truly proven she's ready and pets are so good for teaching responsibility. And they're great company.'

'Oh, I'm thrilled. That's great news. We won't say a word until she tells us,' Howard said quietly.

'Yes, my lips are sealed,' Elsie added.

'Thanks,' Daniel said. 'Now tea, coffee, Milo, hot chocolate? And feel free to sit.'

'Tea for me, please. And I will sit, actually,' Elsie said.

'I'll stay and help with the carrying,' Howard said.

'Come on, Maisie, us two old ducks can sit and watch from a safe distance,' Elsie said, giving the dog's head a stroke on her way past.

Maisie followed, and when Elsie was settled on the couch, put her head on her knee, just at the perfect distance for Elsie to keep scratching her head and ears.

'You really are a beautiful girl. And while you look a lot different, I think you might have a similar soul to our dear old Maisie. You would have liked her. Yes, you would.' Elsie sighed to herself. Gosh she'd missed the presence of a dog this last while. 'But you have the same sad eyes, my dear. Hopefully you're getting happier by the day.' She leant down and kissed the dog on the head and received a quick lick to her hand in return. 'Thank you, sweetheart.'

'Okay, drinks are here, everyone. Milly, Connor, please go and wash your hands, and then come and sit at the table. Corinne and Janine, there's hand sanitiser here if you want some. Or the bathroom is up the hall – like at your folks' place.'

They enjoyed their drinks but didn't stay long after Milly announced they had to be quiet now because Maisie was feeding the puppies and then they were all going to most likely need a nap. Those adults assembled chuckled.

'I think I'll take a nap, actually,' Howard said.

'Yes, sounds like a good idea to me,' Elsie agreed.

'We're tired too, aren't we, Connor? Because we couldn't get to sleep for ages last night,' Milly said.

Connor nodded.

'I'm not surprised,' Howard said.

'No, me neither,' Elsie agreed.

They said their goodbyes and Milly and Connor followed them down the driveway, Milly urging Corinne and Janine to come and visit Maisie and the puppies again before they left, if they had time.

'She's really quite persistent, isn't she?' Corinne said with a laugh, when they were out of hearing, safely back inside Howard and Elsie's house.

'I'm exhausted,' Janine said.

'Hardly surprising, after your night,' Howard said.

'No. You used quite a bit of energy with all that moving and twirling and swaying,' Corinne said, grinning.

'I'm never going to live it down, am I?' Janine said, rolling her eyes. 'Changing the subject, that dog, Maisie, really seems to have taken a shine to you two.'

'Yes, I noticed that,' Corinne said.

'Oh, she probably just smells our old Maisie on us, or something,' Elsie said.

'She is a sweet thing – the feeling's mutual,' Howard said.

'Why don't you think about adopting her?' Janine said.

'Oh, no. We said Maisie would be the last,' Elsie said.

'Yes, it seems irresponsible to take on a dog that might outlive us, probably will,' Howard said.

'That sounds a bit ominous,' Corinne said. 'Is there something you're not telling us?'

'No, but we are nearly seventy-nine,' Howard said.

'Exactly. But right at this point we're as fit as fiddles,' Elsie said.

'Yes, other than our cranky dispositions,' Howard added with a chuckle.

'That's true,' Elsie said with a laugh.

'Can I just say something?' Janine said.

'Go ahead,' Howard said.

'About Maisie – well, having a dog, generally. If you'd like one, I could have it if anything happens,' Janine said. 'Since I'm moving back. Don't deny yourself pet ownership because ...' She shrugged. 'Oh, I don't know. Anyway, the offer's there.'

'Oh. Well, thank you. That provides much food for thought,' Howard said, looking at Elsie.

'I can help too, when I'm back. If you ever want to go away,' Corinne said.

'Thanks, but our days of travelling are over,' Elsie said.

'Well, anyway, actually I'm feeling my no-to-a-puppy resolve slipping,' Janine said. 'Fresh start and all that,' she added, slumping onto a chair at the table. Everyone else sat around her.

'Wow,' Howard said. 'Good for you.'

'Yes, there's nothing like the unconditional love of a dog to help mend a broken heart,' Corinne said. 'Hmm. Actually, it might be a good way to meet people after relocating, too. I'm going to ask Stephen what he thinks,' she added, getting up.

'Oh, Milly would be so thrilled to have homes for them all. Daniel just said he's keeping one for her, but don't say anything – it's hush-hush at this stage,' Howard said.

'That's great news. She'll be thrilled. She really is good with them,' Corinne said.

'Will you mind which puppy you get?' Elsie said, looking from Janine to Corinne.

'No,' Corinne said, moving across the space, with her phone out.

'Me neither – they're all lovely,' Janine said.

'What a great day,' Howard said and let out a long, contented sigh. He looked around his small family and reached across to Elsie's hand on her lap under the table and gave it a squeeze. He knew she'd be thinking the same as he.

Elsie squeezed Howard's hand. Was he, too, thinking about how lucky they'd got with their own daughters and new neighbours?

'What do you think about taking on Maisie?' Howard said to Elsie.

'I think we have to. I struggled to say goodbye to her just now. That face.'

'Yes, but can you look into those eyes every day?'

'I can if I know she's in a wonderful home with us and not going to face anything awful again.'

'I agree. Shall I phone Daniel, do you think?' Howard said.

'Let's just take a breath and wait to see what Stephen says,' Elsie said.

Corinne disappeared into the hall. Howard could hear her talking on the phone. 'Say hi to Stephen from us,' he called.

'Yes,' Elsie said.

A few minutes later Corinne came back. They all looked up at her.

'Looks like we're going to be puppy parents too. When they're ready to leave Maisie, that is.'

'Oh, that's great news,' Howard said.

'I'm so happy for you,' Elsie said.

'He says hi, by the way. I just hope the organisation Milly's fostering with are going to be okay with us all wanting them,' Corinne said.

'I think Milly will sort it out. I can see she could be very convincing, when she puts her mind to it,' Janine said.

'Yes,' Howard said. 'And Daniel must have cleared it with them already. And if it doesn't pan out, I'm sure there are plenty of other dogs needing homes.'

'True. And if it doesn't, it wasn't meant to be,' Corinne said.

'Oh no. I'll be devastated if we can't have Maisie,' Elsie said. 'I've rather got my hopes up now.'

'Yes. I'm just going to text Daniel right away to at least see how the land lies,' Howard said, picking up his phone and typing. 'Do you want me to tell him you each want a pup?'

'Okay, but let him know not right away; when they're ready. I want to get moved and settled first. Eek, it's all happening a little too quickly,' Janine said.

'I guess, if necessary, Milly might agree to keeping them a bit longer until we get settled, or something,' Corinne said.

'We probably could, couldn't we?' Howard said, looking at Elsie.

She nodded. 'I suppose we could probably manage for a few weeks.'

'I bet we could pay Daniel and Milly to take care of them for us,' Corinne said.

Elsie nodded. That sounded to her like a much better idea than dealing with a boisterous puppy or two.

Seconds after sending his text, Howard received a response. He read it and then said, 'He's thrilled, but isn't going to tell Milly just yet and asked us not to until he double-checks with his contact at the rescue centre. What a great day.'

'You just said that before. But I agree,' Elsie said with a laugh.

'I know I did. And it's still a great day. In fact, it's just got even better, which I think warrants a repeated utterance. Though, I am a bit weary. I'm going to have that nap.'

'Good idea,' Elsie said, taking Howard's cue. 'Can you two amuse yourselves for an hour?'

'Oh. Okay,' Janine said.

'Can I use the printer?' Corinne asked. 'I want to print out some floorplans of houses for Stephen and me.'

'Ooh, that's a good idea,' Janine said.

'Go for it – it's all yours. There's more fresh paper in the box with the lid on it. In the other box, without a lid, by the desk – that lot is for printing on the back of. You'll figure it out,' Howard said with a wave as he left the room, followed by Elsie.

Chapter Thirty-nine

Howard and Elsie came out into the living room after their nap to find Corinne and Janine sitting at the table, poring over some printed papers and looking serious.

'How's the house hunting going?' Howard asked, strolling over, with Elsie close behind. They both sat down.

The girls looked up at their parents.

'Good nap?' Corinne asked.

'Yes, thanks,' Elsie said.

'Hmm, though I might have overslept. I'm a bit groggy now,' Howard said, rubbing his hands over his face.

'What's this?' Corinne said, holding up a piece of paper.

'Ah, it's a bit hard to tell from here,' Howard said, frowning. He peered over, as did Elsie, and then accepted the piece of paper.

'Oh, that's a to-do list,' Howard said nonchalantly.

Elsie nodded against her tightening chest, which was in response to the atmosphere and tone. This was clearly one of those information gathering exercises where the answers were already known and responding only caused you to dig yourself a deeper hole.

'We told you we'd been sorting through stuff,' Howard added. 'You know us – we don't do anything without a list.' He leant over and retrieved the newspaper from the occasional table, where he kept a week's worth before taking them out to the recycling bin. He'd already read today's, but was in need of a prop and source of distraction.

Taking Howard's cue, Elsie opened her puzzle book, picked up the pencil serving as a bookmark and stared at the next crossword.

'Right. So what does *find a suitable exit strategy* mean?' Corinne said, reading out the second-to-last item on the list. 'And this one: *Exit before September 12*? That's the date of your joint birthdays and wedding anniversary.'

'Perhaps this might jog your memories,' Janine said, waving a thin wad of printed blank pages, stapled together, in front of her.

Elsie could see she was now looking at the poem she and Howard had written. She sucked in her breath. *Uh-oh.*

Oh dear, Howard thought. 'Well ... um ...' *Shit.*

'And we found these,' Corinne said, pushing two USB drives – a purple one with *Corinne* marked on it and an orange one labelled *Janine* – a little way across the table with two fingers. 'We know what they are, because we've read the ... er ... suicide note poem.'

'We weren't snooping, I promise,' Janine said. 'I was looking for a pen. Cute pen holder,' she added.

Howard wanted to divert the conversation by extolling the virtues of Connor's art piece, but knew from Janine's syrupy tone it wouldn't work.

'And I was looking for a pad of paper to write on,' Corinne said.

You know there have always been pens and scraps of paper in the drawer by the pantry where the phones charge. Why did you need to go fossicking in the office? Howard thought.

'Care to explain, one of you? Mum, Dad?' Corinne said, her gaze switching from one parent to the next.

'We've already read the poem,' Janine added. 'And the fact it's actually signed – that both of your signatures are on it – means it isn't just some ditty you put together on a whim to pass the time one wet afternoon,' she said.

Corinne nodded. Both women had their arms folded tightly and were leaning back in their chairs, waiting.

'We decided not to go through with it,' Howard said quietly. God, he felt like a naughty schoolboy caught bunking off class.

Elsie nibbled on her lip. 'Yes,' she said, feeling the need to say *something*. *Why hadn't Howard put it through the shredder?* 'We changed our minds.'

'We can see that,' Corinne said.

'Yes, it might have something to do with the fact you're both sitting right there,' Janine said.

Howard searched inside himself for something to say. What was there to say?

'Oh. Oh!' Janine said, looking up with enormous eyes.

'What?' Corinne said, looking at her sister.

'The car.'

'What about it?' Corinne said.

'That's why there's no fuel in it – like, none at all. Why it won't start. You tried, didn't you?'

'Why? Tried what?' Corinne said. 'I'm not following.'

'Keep up, Corinne! What's one of the most common ways to die by suicide?'

'How would I know?'

'Well, it was in that movie we watched together, not so long ago.'

'Oh. Yes, that's right. That was absolutely heartbreaking – I wish I'd never seen it. But that's quite the leap, Janine, to think …

Cars run out of fuel all the time. It doesn't mean … No, don't be ridiculous, Janine. Mum, Dad?' Corinne turned and looked at her parents.

Both Howard and Elsie shifted in their seats under the scrutiny.

'Oh my god. She's right?' Corinne said, wide-eyed.

Howard nodded.

Elsie nodded. 'But it's okay. We failed. The fuel was one problem. And we didn't have the right pipe. Anyway, as I said, we changed our minds.'

'But why?' Corinne said.

'Well, Milly came along and wormed her way into our lives, and I suppose you could say, brightened things up,' Howard said.

'And she'd had so much loss already that we couldn't leave her too, and put her through that as well,' Elsie said.

'But what about us?' Janine said. 'Don't you think *we* brighten your lives?'

'Exactly. And that *we'd* be perfectly fine with your deaths?' Corinne said. 'Anyway, I meant: why did you want to kill yourselves? Because that's what you're saying, isn't it?'

'Yes,' Elsie said.

'That's right,' Howard said. 'Isn't it rather self-explanatory on the note – well, poem there?' he said, nodding towards the pages his daughter held. 'I don't expect you to understand, but trust us, being old in this day and age is not at all beer and skittles.'

'No,' Elsie said.

'I don't know what to say,' Janine said, raising her hands and dropping them again.

'Yes, it's hard not to be offended that you decided against this course of action for a child you barely know over your own daughters,' Corinne said.

'Oh, come on, we've raised you to be strong, independent and wise – everything you need to be. You don't need us. You're doing so well,' Howard said.

'But perhaps we'd *like* you to be around,' Janine said.

'Surely *we* don't make you feel invisible,' Corinne said.

'Well, no, not specifically. That's more a general observation,' Howard said.

'Yes, a reality of old age,' Elsie added. 'And, actually, of being a woman generally in this society, in many respects.'

'Yes, that's actually true,' Janine said. 'It's pretty much why I'm starting my own firm.'

'Exactly,' Howard said.

'Don't think this lets you off the hook,' Corinne said.

'Can't we just forget about it?' Howard said. 'Since we've decided against that course of action anyway.'

'But what about the next time you say you don't want to be apart or to deal with a serious illness if it arises? Because it's bound to happen,' Corinne said.

'Yes, the odds are against you,' Janine said.

'Gee, thanks, that's cheering me up no end,' Howard said.

'But that's exactly what you're alluding to here,' Corinne said.

'Well, I guess we'll have to deal with that then,' Howard said with a shrug.

'Yes,' Elsie said, nodding.

'Hopefully there will be easier, more accessible options when that time comes,' Howard said. 'Do you know how hard it is to find a way to die while not involving someone else?'

'And without leaving a mess, et cetera,' Elsie said.

'Is it, though?' Janine said. 'Carbon monoxide poisoning should have worked perfectly well, if you'd prepared adequately.'

'They didn't actually need to prepare anything. Why wouldn't you just suck on some gas?' Corinne said.

'Are you being serious right now?' Janine said. 'Don't encourage them!'

'We don't have the gas on, remember?' Howard said.

'Well, what's supplying the barbecue out the back – chopped liver?' Corinne said.

Oh no, Howard thought.

Oh dear. Whoops, Elsie thought.

Howard and Elsie looked at each other, rolled their eyes in unison, and began to giggle. Their laughter built until they were roaring loudly.

After a good few moments, they stopped and wiped their eyes between bouts of holding their painful sides.

'It's actually not that funny,' Corinne said.

'No, not funny at all, from where I'm sitting,' Janine said.

'Oh, you had to be there, I think, dears,' Elsie said, wiping her dripping nose and tears with a tissue she'd pulled from her sleeve.

'Yes. Exactly,' Howard said, chuckling and shaking his head.

'So, you promise you're over this … ah … phase?' Corinne said.

'Yes, definitely,' Howard said.

Elsie nodded.

'And you promise you won't be utilising the method your elder daughter has just pointed out? Good one, Corinne,' Janine said.

'You know, actually I get it,' Corinne said. 'I wouldn't want to live without Stephen, either.'

'Great. We all know how wonderful it is having a lifelong partner,' Janine said. 'There's no need to rub it in.'

Corinne ignored Janine and held her hand up. 'So, Mum, Dad, promise me that if it's needed in the future, you will tell me and we will make it happen, right, Janine?'

'No, I'm not having any part in' — she waved her hand — 'whatever this is.'

'Just at least promise me — both of us — that if you begin thinking along these lines again, you will tell us,' Corinne said.

Janine nodded.

'Okay. We promise, right, Elsie?' Howard said.

'Yes. I promise,' Elsie said.

'And while we're on the subject,' Corinne said. 'This line about resources dwindling,' she said, pointing at the poem. 'Are you having trouble financially?'

Howard and Elsie looked at each other and nodded.

'Of sorts,' Howard said, 'we didn't bank on being around for much longer — beyond September 12 — so we are rather running low now we've decided to stay. We might have to look at a reverse mortgage or something.'

'Perhaps start with applying for a pension and stop being so damned stubborn about your independence,' Corinne said. 'If it's about dealing with Centrelink ... and I get it, I really do ... but we can help. Lean on us. After all you've done for us over the years, I, for one, would like to help.'

'And me,' Janine said. 'Exactly. There could be all sorts of programs for your age group to access that you might not even know about.'

'I suppose,' Howard said.

'Yes, all right. I suppose we've been a little short-sighted,' Elsie said.

'You reckon?' Corinne said.

'And selfish,' Janine said.

'Okay. Well, no need to scold us further,' Elsie said.

'Yes. We've learnt our lesson,' Howard said.

'As long as you have?' Corinne said, staring at her parents.

Howard and Elsie nodded.

'But seriously, I get it. I really do,' Corinne continued. 'Not just the fear or unwillingness to be alone long term, but the invisibility and all the loss that goes along with ageing. I'm only in my fifties and I'm seeing and experiencing it already. It's okay, nothing serious,' she added, raising a hand when Howard and Elsie, in unison, looked at her with worried frowns.

The next moment Corinne and Janine were up and standing on either side of their parents and wrapping their arms around them.

'We love you guys, and more than you'll ever know,' Corinne said.

'Yes, exactly,' Janine said.

'Thank you, darlings, and we love you more than you'll ever know,' Elsie said.

'Yes. Which is a big part of why we wanted to spare you the hideous last part of our elderly lives,' Howard said.

'Well, how about you let us worry about that, thanks?' Corinne said.

Janine nodded.

'And, don't forget, you're both only children. We're not. We have each other for support,' Corinne said, looking at Janine, who nodded again.

'Exactly. That's added reinforcements, sharing the load,' Janine said.

'And you're not a burden now and you won't be in the future, whatever happens down the track,' Corinne said.

'And if you are, we'll just turn on the gas and shove your heads in the barbecue,' Janine said with a gentle, lopsided smile.

'Janine,' Corinne remonstrated.

'Good to know,' Howard said, beginning to smile.

'As you say, it's always good to have a plan,' Janine said cheerfully.

'Oh, we quite agree. Don't we, Elsie?'

'We sure do. It's held us in good stead all our lives,' Elsie said.

'And is anyone going to address the elephant in the room?' Corinne said when they were all sitting down again and silence had reigned for a few moments.

'Huh?' Janine said, looking at her sister.

'Yes, what's that?' Howard said, genuinely confused.

'The terrible poetry!' Corinne laughed.

'Oh, yes! Lucky you're retired, you two, otherwise we'd have to say: Don't give up your day jobs!' Janine said, also laughing.

'Gee, thanks,' Howard said, pouting with exaggeration. 'I'll have you know we spent ages on that.'

'Exactly. And while I do agree it's a little lengthy, I don't think we did too badly, considering we haven't attempted anything like that for at least sixty years,' Elsie said.

'Well, perhaps leave it for another sixty,' Corinne said, laughing again.

'Yes. Please,' Janine said. Both girls laughed so much they needed to wipe tears from their eyes.

'Oh no. Maybe we've found a new hobby to get our teeth into. Better yet, *performance* poetry. As in, in public. What do you say, Howard?'

'Yes, good idea, dear. You girls are going to be so glad you moved back!'

'Oh god. I hope you're joking,' Corinne said.

'Well, if they're not, it's your fault for bringing it up and planting the seed, Corinne,' Janine said.

'And there'll be no missing a gig – remember you were just saying how keen you are to be supportive?' Elsie said, trying hard to keep her grin and laughter at bay. *Oh, how fun is winding up the kids?*

'I'll be buying a spare bottle of gas to have on hand as soon I've got settled – in readiness,' Janine said.

'Good idea, sis,' Corinne said, grinning.

'Oh, ha ha. Very funny, you two,' Elsie said.

'Yes, you'll keep! Oh, that's me,' Howard said, peering at his phone as it began vibrating and then ringing. 'Should I answer it or let it go to voicemail?'

'It's okay, answer it,' Corinne said. 'We've finished picking on you.'

'Yes. All good,' Janine said.

Howard got up and answered his phone as he moved away from the table.

'Oh dear,' Elsie said, chuckling, for something to say while watching Howard on his phone over in the corner. 'Oh. Okay. Thank you,' she heard him say.

They all looked up as Howard returned, having finished the call.

'In the words of dear Milly, guess what? No, you'll never guess,' he added a beat later. 'Good news, people. That was the mushroom people's – sorry, Larry and Susan Coventry's – grandson enquiring if we'd like to be put on their mailing list. They found our names in Larry and Susan's effects – the Little Black Book of contacts, I presume,' he said, complete with making quote marks with his fingers beside his head.

'Oh, that's wonderful news,' Elsie said.

'You two are unbelievable,' Corinne said, rolling her eyes.

'You just don't know what you're missing, sis,' Janine said. 'The family that trips together stays together; don't you know?'

'Yes, quite,' Elsie said, and laughed.

'Ahh.' Howard slumped back onto his chair. 'All is right with the world again,' he said and let out a long sigh.

'Yep,' Elsie said, also sighing. 'Particularly now we are going to have another dog in the house again and our darling daughters close by.'

At that moment their attention was captured by a whirling sound. They all looked around to see Brian coming out of the study.

'Brian, you're not due out to clean until the morning, what are you doing?' Howard said to the machine, which was now stopped nearby. 'Oh dear.'

'What are you going to do when you get Maisie?' Corinne asked.

'What do you mean?' Howard said.

'Well, you always said you wouldn't get a robotic cleaner while our dear old Maisie was alive because it might be too scary.'

'Oh, yes, I see what you mean. Um ...' As Howard looked at Brian, an intense wave of sadness rushed in and settled as a heaviness in his chest.

'I've become rather fond of him,' Elsie said, jumping in, keen to rescue Howard, who was looking quite bereft and lost at that moment.

'As ridiculous as this sounds, I have too,' Janine said with a laugh. 'Poor Brian,' she added sadly and pouted.

'I think let's wait and see how Maisie feels when she arrives,' said Elsie. 'She might be perfectly okay. And if not, we can at least try carefully teaching her to accept him. Because haven't we learnt recently, Howard darling, that old dogs really can learn new tricks?' she added.

'We sure have! You are so right, as always. That's a good idea. Oh, I feel very relieved. Do you hear that, Brian? You're staying!'

Brian whizzed around on the spot several times before heading back the way he'd come. A moment later he'd disappeared into the office. They heard what sounded like a faint plastic clunk – him settling himself back onto his charging station – and then there was silence.

'I guess he's changed his mind, then. No cleaning today!' Janine said with another laugh. 'Good for you, Brian!'

'He's a law unto himself,' Howard muttered, shaking his head.

'Or that's his way of giving us all the middle finger!' Corinne said, laughing. 'I see what you mean – I'm warming to the little guy too. He really does seem to understand things. And his obstinance is particularly cute.'

'Oh yes, he has quite the attitude!' Howard said, grinning and feeling lighter again.

Corinne's phone pinged and she turned it over. 'Ah, we might be closer than you think,' she said with a laugh. 'Stephen's keen to put in an offer on the Chans' house across the way. I'm just going to call him,' she said, getting up and heading across the room.

Another phone pinged. 'That's me,' Janine said. 'Oh.' She stared at it.

'What is it?' Howard said.

'Is everything okay?' Elsie said, noticing the concerned expression on her younger daughter's face.

'Hmm. It's a text from Sonia. She says she's thinking about coming over.'

'Oh, that's fabulous,' Howard said.

'Yes. I'm so pleased for you,' Elsie said.

'It's just for a visit at this stage, so don't get too excited,' Janine said.

'But you're communicating, and that's the main thing,' Howard said.

'Yes,' Janine said, nodding. 'She wants me to call. Do you mind?'

'Go. And say hi from us, if it's appropriate,' Elsie said.

Janine got up and moved away, carrying her phone, prodding it as she went.

As she looked over at their daughters, both talking on their phones at opposite ends of the space, Elsie felt Howard's arm around her.

'What did we do to get so lucky?' he said, nodding at Corinne and Janine.

'I love you, Howard,' Elsie said.

'And I love you, my love,' Howard said.

'Oh, look, it's Milly via Daniel,' Howard said, picking up his phone again. 'He must have just told her about our plans and his for her. Aww, isn't that a gorgeous photo of Maisie and her puppies?' He turned the phone towards Elsie.

'Beautiful. I can't wait to get her and pamper the darling thing,' she said.

'Phew, what a rollercoaster of a day,' Howard said wearily.

'Yep, that about sums it up, dear,' Elsie said, grinning at him.

Acknowledgements

Many thanks to:

Nicola Robinson and Suzanne O'Sullivan for their editorial expertise and guidance to bring out the best in my writing and this story.

Jo Mackay, Sue Brockhoff, Jo Munroe, Johanna Baker and everyone at Harlequin and HarperCollins Australia for turning my manuscripts into beautiful books and for continuing to make my dreams come true.

The media outlets, bloggers, reviewers, librarians, booksellers and readers for all the amazing support. It really does mean so much to me to hear of people enjoying my stories and connecting with my characters.

And, finally, to my dear friends who provide so much love, support and encouragement – especially Mel Sabeeney, Bernadette Foley, WTC and LMR. I am truly blessed to have you in my life.

Turn over for a sneak peek.

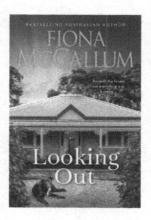

Looking
Out

by

FIONA
MCCALLUM

Available April 2024

Chapter One

'Something smells good,' Mitchell heard his wife Natasha call as she came down the long hallway, daughters Willow, nearly thirteen, and Lara, twelve, thumping along noisily behind her. Mitchell smiled at having his family come in, a sudden and rather loud disruption to the home and his workspace. It was a welcome addition to the stone house on the outskirts of the rural Adelaide Hills town of Balhannah. The rabble reached the door into the kitchen where he was putting the finishing touches on dinner – a lamb roast, being as it was Tuesday and the girls had just been to netball. It was a tradition of theirs, but he wasn't sure it would last much longer with rising financial pressures. He shoved that aside – his family was here and that was all that mattered right now.

'Hello, darlings, how was it?' he asked, turning from the sink to smile at his daughters.

Willow and Lara threw themselves onto kitchen stools with a weight more akin to sacks of potatoes rather than the lithe teenagers they were.

'Okay,' Willow said, returning a tired smile. 'We didn't win – got slammed.'

'Oh dear, that doesn't sound good.'

'_We_ had a great game – winners, winners, chicken dinners!' Lara said.

'And you both played well, regardless of the outcome,' Natasha said. 'You should have seen them, Mitchell.'

'Who else was there?' Mitchell asked, keen to divert the attention away from him. Yes, he should have been there.

'Everyone – Monica, Anastasia, Vanessa, Miriam – the whole contingent tonight. None of the men, though.'

'It's pretty awesome of Monica to come when she doesn't have her own kids to watch,' Lara said.

'Well, she _is_ our official photographer, so she has to,' Willow said, swivelling on her stool.

'But only because she was coming along anyway – to support us, which _I_ happen to think is pretty awesome,' Lara said.

'That's true. She is pretty awesome. We're lucky to have her as our sort-of auntie.'

'Maybe she's hoping to meet one of the single dads,' Mitchell suggested.

'I think she's sworn off men, full stop, after trying online dating,' Natasha said, hoisting the several bags of groceries she'd carried in onto the benchtop.

'I know. But I still think that's a pity,' Mitchell said.

'I do know what you mean, though. She has a lot to offer, particularly as she's such a nurturer.'

'Exactly. And she's very wise,' Mitchell said. 'A decent man would be very lucky to have her.' He'd always had a soft spot for Natasha's oldest and dearest friend – as well as being warm and friendly, she was smart, funny, sensible, easy to be around and good looking.

'But, as she says, it'll happen when and if it's meant to, without any effort on her part,' Natasha said with a shrug. 'I tell you, the supermarket was bloody bedlam, wasn't it, girls?' she continued, opening the fridge to put things away.

'Yep. Do you want a hand, Mum? Except I'm not sure I can get up again now,' Willow said.

'Hmm, me too,' Lara said, slumping forward onto the island's stone bench and resting her head on her folded arms.

'It's okay, I'll let you off this time – you two rest for a bit.'

'Well, thanks for doing it. I appreciate not having to head out,' Mitchell said. He sighed to himself. He was finding it harder to leave the house these days, even worse than five years ago when he'd started fully working from home. He used to go to all their netball games, but had stopped recently, citing too much work. No one had seemed to mind. He felt a little guilty about it, but not enough to go. Anyway, what was the point in him doing the groceries if they were already out and going right past?

'Hmm,' Natasha said absently. She was standing with her head in the fridge. 'Where's the bottle of white wine?' she asked, half-turning back, hand still on the door.

'Over here. I've already poured you a glass – did it when I heard the door,' Mitchell said, holding out the glass. 'And it's the last of the bottle. I'll bring some more up from the cellar later. I'm having a glass of red.' He tried not to think about the dwindling stash of wine downstairs.

'Oh,' Natasha said. 'Okay.' She shut the fridge door.

'Cheers,' Mitchell said, handing her the glass, condensation already sliding down the outside.

'Thanks.' They clinked glasses and leant on the bench near the sink underneath the large window facing the once carefully manicured garden outside, which was now cloaked in dusky yellow light. 'Dinner really does smell amazing.'

Mitchell smiled. He loved hearing her appreciation, complete with a satisfied sigh. 'It'll be ready in a couple of minutes, so maybe go through and take a seat?' He put his glass down and returned to the saucepan on the hotplate.

He'd almost forgotten about the peas, damn it. *Close call*, he thought, giving them a quick stir. He hated it when they became overcooked and floury instead of plump and sweet.

'You're the best, Dad,' Willow said, standing beside him to fill a glass of water from the tap.

'Yeah. Absolutely. Can you get me a glass of water too, Willow?' Lara said.

'And me too, thanks, sweetheart,' Mitchell said.

'Righto.'

Mitchell draped his arm around his elder daughter as she went about her task.

'Daaad,' she said with a giggle as water spilled. But instead of shrugging him off – it was only a matter of time at this stage, wasn't it? – she leant into him for a moment.

He released her and returned his focus to dinner – this time stirring the gravy. 'Lara, darling, could you please get the plates? They're warming in the bottom drawer under the oven here.' Mitchell pointed with his foot.

Lara slid off the stool.

'Hopefully they're not too hot, but use the oven mitts, just in case,' he added, handing them to her. 'On the table, thanks, it's a help-yourself-night tonight.'

After everything had been carted in, plates were laid out on the table around platters of meat and roast vegetables and bowls of steamed greens and a jug of gravy. Having done a quick survey of the table and checking the oven one last time, Mitchell took his place at the end of the dining table.

'How was work for you today?' he asked Natasha. The girls' cutlery scaped and clinked as they devoured their meals with more gusto than other nights, on account of their earlier sporty endeavours.

'Okay. Same.'

He winced at seeing the tension and frustration clouding her features. 'It'll pick up. I have faith,' he said. He resisted running his hand over his face in response to his own fears about their financial situation. Things *really* needed to pick up – and soon – for all of their sakes.

'Thanks. Thank goodness for candles, diffusers and clocks,' she said, smiling faintly and rolling her eyes.

'Clocks? What's with that?' he asked.

'Yes, wall clocks, of all things – there's been a run on them.'

'We've all got the time on our phones and most of us are wearing smart watches. Why would wall clocks suddenly be popular again?'

'No idea. But I'm glad I decided to stock them.'

'Yes. I remember you debating over them. Maybe it's the clean lines everyone's craving – you know, after the pandemic; the general mental chaos of it all.'

'Maybe.' She shrugged. 'Though I've sold a few of those colourful abstract paintings, too. So, bang goes that theory.'

'Oh. I know you wanted to be doing better, but you'll get there,' Mitchell said. They were in too deep to just close Natasha's shop down now, and, anyway, the small business was pretty much all hers. He assisted with advice and behind the scenes, so he couldn't make that call, even if he wanted to. He just hoped he wouldn't have to ask her to. While it was tough going and far too often she'd bemoan, 'What was I thinking, starting a retail store?', she did still mostly enjoy it, he thought. They didn't tend to discuss things in as much depth these days.

He shifted his attention to the girls. 'Tell me about your day, girls. Willow, you first.'

'Not much to report, Dad. Some bits were okay, some bits were dull,' she said.

'Same,' Lara said.

'Oh, I got a good mark for my painting I did in art,' Willow added. 'I'll show you later.'

'I can't believe you forgot!' Lara said. 'It's great. It's really good, Dad, Mum.' She looked from one parent to the other. 'Hey, maybe Mum can commission some pieces for the shop.'

Natasha, busy chewing a mouthful of food, raised her eyebrows in an expression he couldn't quite read.

'I'm not sure she could afford me,' Willow said, pretending to flick her hair before smiling sweetly.

'Ha! Good for you,' Mitchell said.

'I think we're doing ceramics next week. Great dinner, Dad,' Lara said.

'Yes, it totally is,' Willow said.

'Any homework tonight?' Natasha asked. Mitchell was a little disappointed to not have longer basking under his family's glow of appreciation.

'Yes,' the girls said in unison, complete with groans.

'I'll tidy up if you two want to head off and have showers and then get your homework done,' Mitchell said, when they'd finished their meals.

'Thanks.' Willow and Lara got up, tucked their chairs in and practically bolted from the table.

Mitchell smiled at the clatter of feet and dog paws as Angel, their black kelpie cross, leapt up from her nearby bed and followed to provide her assistance.

Chapter Two

Natasha drained her glass and sat for a moment, savouring the peace and satisfaction of the lovely meal and the resulting lethargy from the wine and food.

'Do you have more work to do?' Mitchell asked as he got up and moved around the table, gathering the empty plates.

'Yes, I need to update the website and probably should post something on social media. And you?' Natasha said, reluctantly getting up to help.

'Yup.'

It was a waste of breath, really. Mitchell was like a teenage boy these days – spent all his time holed up in his bedroom/home office, only coming out for meals and brief trips to the supermarket if necessary. Granted, he did make most of the meals and of course he was working still, trading on the US stock exchange at odd times. She tried not to feel piqued, but a slight wave of resentment wound its way through her. She sometimes missed his body nearby now he slept in another room so he didn't wake her with his unusual working hours and insomnia, but had to admit she did sleep better with him gone. Sleep seemed harder to come by these days and the heat fluctuations and her needing to alternate between throwing off and then retrieving the covers all through the night would no doubt drive him mad.

When had they last had sex? Natasha paused, one hand on the gravy jug and the other on the bowl of broccoli and beans. For the first year or so of sleeping in separate rooms, they'd both quietly padded down the hall for 'visiting rights' – the novelty giving them a rush and more powerful orgasms. But the ship seemed to have sailed on all that ages ago.

Natasha wasn't sure what time worked for him now – if any time did – and she suspected that might be the case for Mitchell, too. Anyway, she was usually too tired to get up again once she'd turned in and not really inclined. Her libido seemed to have all but disappeared – no doubt another of the downsides of perimenopause. Or perhaps just life and being a business owner and mum were to blame; energy was always in short supply. She should probably make more of an effort, initiate occasionally.

She frowned as they stood shoulder to shoulder stacking the dishwasher and tidying up the kitchen.

'What's with the frown?' he asked, holding a hand out for the plate she'd just scraped off into the compost bin.

'Oh, nothing, just trying to remember something I have to do tomorrow,' she lied. She smiled at him, having to force her expression slightly.

'You'll remember, you always do,' he said, smiling back and touching her gently on the tip of the nose.

'Okay, that's that,' he said a few moments later while surveying the space.

Natasha wrapped her arms around him. 'Thanks again for dinner.'

'You're welcome,' he said, leaning into her and ruffling her hair. 'Lasagne tomorrow, if that suits you?'

'Sure does. If you can be bothered.'

'Of course. Better than twiddling my thumbs, waiting for the market to open,' Mitchell said, releasing her before closing the dishwasher and setting it going.

Natasha nodded distractedly.

'Can I get you more wine before I get back to it?'

'I'll get it. You go.'

He kissed her on the forehead and filled his own glass. 'Well, I'll go and make us all some money, fingers crossed,' he said, raising both his eyebrows and his wine glass.

'Good luck,' Natasha called to his retreating back.

She slumped onto the plush, feather-filled couch, turned on the TV and got out her tablet. Her thoughts went back to Mitchell. He was okay, wasn't he? He hadn't seemed stressed? No. He might work odd, unsociable hours, but at least he loved what he did. And he was much happier now than when he'd been an accountant working in the city. Perhaps not quite as buoyant now as then, but still … It was nice having him home to cook and not having to worry about him driving back and forth on the winding road that had claimed so many lives.

She took another long swig of wine and pushed back her meandering concerns as she picked up the remote and looked for something to put on in the background while she worked. She answered a couple of quick emails, using form responses she'd put together along the way that could simply be copied and pasted. She didn't mind too much that they were the same topics covered by her website's frequently asked questions page already. At the moment the volume was manageable – which was a bit problematic in itself; she'd been hoping the shop and her interior design services business would be thriving by now. She really wanted to be doing more consultations and projects and to be able to afford a staff member. She sighed. What more could she do, other than perhaps move somewhere more populated? Say, the east coast of Australia? Trouble was, she liked this town, which was close to Adelaide yet reasonably rural – though becoming more crowded and citified by the day.

She knew Mitchell would move back to Sydney in a heartbeat if she asked. They'd met there – though both were South Australian born and bred. He wouldn't want to leave the Adelaide Hills, but he'd do anything for her. She knew that. She was determined to become a success here. And anyway, wasn't Sydney and surrounds saturated by interior designers and homewares?

The problem was getting people to pay for her services. The current cost of living and increasing interest rates were killing her business. She was a luxury people couldn't afford or simply didn't want to pay for. Everyone thought they could do it themselves by trawling Instagram and watching shows like *The Block*.

Though she seemed to have enough pieces in her shop that were still selling well. People were always after a bit of luxury in the form of throw cushions and rugs and scented soap and candles. Particularly as many still didn't seem to be going on holidays so much since the pandemic. That was the theme of her marketing at the moment: stay put, add a bit of luxury and enjoy your own home. They'd all had far too much of home during the recent Covid years, but things were starting to look a little more like they had before their lives had been rudely interrupted. While those who had most craved escaping overseas for a long-put-off holiday had done so, it appeared many only seemed to have one trip in them. People just didn't have the patience or necessary resilience to stand in lines or wait for their luggage or whatever anymore. The world was tired, full stop. She certainly was. And frustrated and distracted.

Maybe what she and Mitchell needed was to get away for a bit. Europe for Christmas? Snow, beautiful old buildings adorned for the festive season, gorgeous markets to wander … The girls would love it too. And it would be good research for her. She might even be able to meet some new suppliers … Oh, yes …

But, no. Mitchell was too much of a homebody, and seemed to be only becoming more so by the week. She doubted she'd get him on a plane anywhere now, including a short hop interstate. So, there was no way he'd be keen on getting on a long-haul flight. Hell, she probably wouldn't be able to even get him to agree to a weekend in a B&B just over an hour drive away on the Fleurieu Peninsula.

Anyway, she couldn't really justify the expense of an overseas trip for her business when it wasn't yet pulling its weight, could she? Even if they could afford it, and she wasn't sure about that either: Mitchell took care of the family finances.

talk about it

Let's talk about books.

Join the conversation:

@harlequinaustralia

@hqanz

@harlequinaus

harpercollins.com.au/hq

If you love reading and want to know about our authors and titles, then let's talk about it.